P9-BZX-551

ST. MARTIN'S

MINOTAUR

MYSTERIES

PRAISE FOR THE NOVELS OF SARAH ANDREWS

FAULT LINE

"Em Hansen's seventh well-paced outing. . . . Em Hansen is rapidly carving out a niche for herself as a forensic geologist . . . and may eventually make her field as popular as that of forensic anthropology or medicine."

—*Publishers Weekly*

"The resourceful and intelligent Hansen makes a terrific series heroine . . . what has made the series shine has been the amount of 'hard science' that Andrews, a professional geologist herself, was able to work into the stories."

—*Booklist*

"An entertaining story. . . . [Andrews] has a winning detective in Em Hansen."

—*Dallas Morning News*

"A fine series."

—*Library Journal*

AN EYE FOR GOLD

"Em Hansen is plucky and smart . . . [and] the mystery is complicated and absorbing."

—*Booklist*

"Suspense every step of the way . . . twists and turns that [will] keep you turning the pages."

—*The Press Democrat*

"A fine series."

—*Library Journal*

MORE . . .

BONE HUNTER

"[Em Hansen is] a clear-thinking, straight-talking heroine whose unabashed naivete is endearing."
—*The New York Times Book Review*

"Andrews . . . has become a leading light. The fifth entry in her series rivets both as a crime story and as a discussion of the relationship between science and religion. . . . Her novel is a suspenseful mystery spiked with dinosaurs, science, and religion: what more could readers ask for?"
—*Publishers Weekly* (starred review)

"The latest Em Hansen mystery is by far the best yet. . . . Andrews makes the most of her paleontological background. She clearly knows her subject and, unlike many crime writers, she does not use the surroundings merely as window dressing. The novel is, in addition to a fine mystery, a lively exploration of the high-stakes world of dinosaur research and perceptive rumination on the debate between science and creationism."
—*Booklist*

"Geologist Em Hansen's adventures become more and more intriguing with each new book. . . . A most fascinating tale."
—*Romantic Times*

"Appealing characters and fluent prose." —*Library Journal*

LOOK FOR THESE BOOKS IN
THE EM HANSEN MYSTERY SERIES

An Eye For Gold

Bone Hunter

Only Flesh and Bones

Mother Nature

Fault Line

AVAILABLE FROM
ST. MARTIN'S/MINOTAUR PAPERBACKS

KILLER DUST

SARAH ANDREWS

St. Martin's Paperbacks

NOTE: If you purchased this book without a cover you should be aware that this book is stolen property. It was reported as "unsold and destroyed" to the publisher, and neither the author nor the publisher has received any payment for this "stripped book."

KILLER DUST

Copyright © 2003 by Sarah Andrews Brown.
Excerpt from *Earth Colors* © 2004 by Sarah Andrews Brown.

All rights reserved. No part of this book may be used or reproduced in any manner whatsoever without written permission except in the case of brief quotations embodied in critical articles or reviews. For information address St. Martin's Press, 175 Fifth Avenue, New York, NY 10010.

Library of Congress Catalog Card Number: 2002031889

ISBN: 0-312-99548-2

Printed in the United States of America

St. Martin's Press hardcover edition / February 2003
St. Martin's Paperbacks edition / March 2004

St. Martin's Paperbacks are published by St. Martin's Press, 175 Fifth Avenue, New York, NY 10010.

10 9 8 7 6 5 4 3 2

In honor of
M. Lee Allison
Jonathan G. Price
Thomas M. Scott
and all the other brilliant rascals who comprise the
Association of American State Geologists.

Who's next?

ACKNOWLEDGMENTS

A disclaimer: Those who know the folks at the United States Geological Survey at St. Petersburg, Florida, might have a field day trying to identify real people from the fictional ones here portrayed. However, while the scientific investigations described herein are based on factual efforts underway at that location, each character is entirely my own invention, as are their personalities, motivations, and quirks. If any similarities occur, it is merely because humans vary only so much, and scientists vary from each other even less than do the extremes of the population at large. I did allow myself a few inside jokes, but please don't sue me.

Having said all that, I wish to acknowledge the groundbreaking work of Eugene A. Shinn, Dale Griffin, and Christina Kellogg, the nonfiction persons who discovered that microbes do in fact survive transoceanic trips inside clouds of dust. The author wishes therefore to thank and acknowledge the inspiration, assistance, badgering, and outright extortion wreaked upon her by that same Gene Shinn, geologist, U.S. Geological Survey Coastal Marine Branch, also coral-reef cognoscente, Key West conch, drummer, champion spear fisherman, and mixer of strong drink, whose singular and persistent idea it was that she drag her unwitting heroine out of her precious, arid Western landscape into the swamps of Florida in order to publicize and thereby advance his scientific agenda regarding the impact of African dust on coral reefs and human health. In concert, I wish to thank the sainted Pat Shinn for her gracious hospitality on so many occasions while her husband worked his mischief. I am grateful also to the rest of the staff of U.S. Geological Survey Center for Marine and Coastal Geology, principally Lisa Robbins, chief scientist; Ginger Garrison, ecologist; Dale Griffin and Christina Kellogg, microbiologists; and Robert Halley, geologist, for sharing their expertise and astonishingly durable humor. Thanks also to Walt Swain and Ann Tihansky, hydrologists, USGS Water Resources Discipline. May Congress bless you all with abundant funding.

My deep and abiding thanks to Susan H. "She Who Understands Gardens" Oliver, ace cousin, and research pal, for assistance above and beyond the call and right out into the swamps in gathering materials and understandings for this book. Your instincts were, as always, impeccable.

My sincere thanks also to Florida Assistant State Geologist Thomas M. Scott, for his memorable three-day crash field course in Florida geology and hydrology, and to Shirley Scott for fueling, housing, and counseling the troops.

My geoscience thanks go also to Cinzia Cervato, Iowa State University, for her support in my understanding of the prehistory and geology of the Mediterranean region.

Lifelong thanks go to Walt Whippo, kenetic engineer, lyricist, solver of the O-ring problem, designer of the IBM Selectric typewriter, kite maker, and painter of flying fruit, for illuminating certain engineering feats, and the inner workings and motivations of NASA, and for showing me a view of the box outside of which we all need to think (and which, he suggests, is in fact shaped like a doughnut).

Munificent thanks go to Nancy Maynard of NASA Goddard Space Flight Center for helping me attend plenary sessions on African dust and the launch of STS-100 (space-shuttle orbiter *Endeavor*), and to Dr. Kathryn Sullivan, former astronaut and currently CEO, COSI. I am awed.

My thanks on a great many levels go to John and Brad for helping me to understand the training, experiences, and philosophies of Special Operations personnel, in particular Navy SEALs. My thanks also that you and your brethren are out there doing what you do.

Gastronomic and linguistic thanks go to Eileen Rodriguez for bugging me about my rotten Spanish, vetting all such that appears herein, and taking me to some great Hispanic restaurants.

Thanks for the wild delights of souped-up, hard-bottom inflatables go to Lewis Tanenbaum.

Special thanks go to Gus Batista of the Billie Swamp Safari, the Seminole tribe, the National Audubon Society, and the U.S. National Park Service for their assistance in teaching me about the Everglades and its creatures.

In preparing this book, I drew heavily upon published sources. They include: *The Garden of Their Desires: Desertification and Culture in World History* by Brian Griffith; *The Voyage of the Beagle* by Charles Darwin; *Desert Dust: Origin, Characteristics, and Effect on Man, Geol. Soc. America Special Paper 186*, edited by Troy L. Péwé; *Desertification: Its Causes and Consequences*, compiled and edited by the Secretariat of the United Nations Conference on Desertification, Nairobi; *Bank Margin Environment* by Robert B. Halley *in AAPG Memoir 33, Carbonate Depositional Environment; Dust in the Wind* by Dale W. Griffith, Christina Kellogg, and Eugene A. Shinn; *The Orchid Thief* by Susan Orlean; *Germs: Biological Weapons and America's Secret War* by Judith Miller, Stephen Engelberg, and William Broad; *The Secret Life of Dust* by Hannah Holmes; *Hormone Deception* by D. Lindsey Berkson; *Geologic Map of the State of Florida* by Thomas M. Scott, Kenneth M. Campbell, Frank R. Rupert, Jonathan D. Arthur, Thomas M. Missimer, Jaqueline M. Lloyd, J. William Yon, and Joel G. Duncan; *Florida Atlas & Gazetteer* (DeLorme); *Florida's Geological History and Geological Resources*, Florida Geological Survey Spec. Pub. No. 35, edited by Ed Lane; and *Terraces and Shorelines of Florida* by Henry G. Healy.

The Golden Machete Critique Group (Mary Hallock, Thea Castleman, Ken Dalton, and Jon Howe) again did yeoman's duty. Kelley Ragland was again a dream editor.

And, as always, my steadfastly patient husband, Damon Brown, and our bouyant and infinitely curious son, Duncan, came through with substantive comments, encouragement, and the love that makes it possible for me to create these books. Glad I could at least repay your kindnesses this time with warm surf and a space shuttle launch.

Generally the atmosphere is hazy; and this is caused by the falling of impalpably fine dust . . . The morning before we anchored at Porto Praya [Canary Islands], I collected a little packet of this brown-colored dust, which appears to have been filtered from the wind by the gauze of the vane at the masthead . . . I have found no less than fifteen different accounts of dust having fallen on vessels when far out in the Atlantic. From the direction of the wind whenever it has fallen, and from its always having fallen during those months when the harmattan is known to raise clouds of dust high into the atmosphere, we feel certain that it all comes from Africa. The dust falls in such quantities as to dirty everything on board, and to hurt people's eyes; vessels even have run on shore owing to the obscurity of the atmosphere. It has often fallen on ships when several hundreds, and even more than a thousand miles from the coast of Africa . . . I was much surprised to find particles of stone above the thousandth of an inch, mixed with finer matter. After this fact one need not be surprised at the diffusion of the far lighter and smaller sporules of cryptogrammic plants.

 —*Charles Darwin, January 16, 1832,* The Voyage of the *Beagle*

One popular estimate says the Sahara hurls about 600 million tons of dust into the sky every year. Another estimate puts the annual cloud at a *billion* tons. At the lower rate a boxcar of Sahara dust would leave Africa about every four seconds. Every minute, sixteen cars. Every hour, a thousand. Day after day, year after year.

 —*Hannah Holmes,* The Secret Life of Dust

Florida is an organism, and it is a poem. Both living organisms and poems are complexly evolved to fill a specific niche. They create a condensed system to efficiently transmit energy or a message. With time, they thoroughly organize themselves and slowly, they build a beautiful structure, like a crystal. Florida is a poem, from a scientific description, a technical haiku.

> Sand, clay, carbonate
> Transmit the liquid treasure
> We all drink it in

         —*Ann Tihansky*

– 1 –

Jack came alive in my senses. He rolled toward me, all warm and naked, a cresting wave of perfect masculinity. He took me in his hands, all rough but gentle, and I reached out and touched the place where golden wires of hair curled all moist with sweat above his heart. I inhaled the perfume of his maleness, the separate scents of sweet clean skin and acrid sexuality entwining in my nostrils, more intoxicating than the exhalations of fresh hay, more riveting than the arrow of first light across the prairie on a clear, crisp morning. Now I tasted his kiss, a mixing of vital juices served up in the glass of life. I listened to his breath, a long, shuddering exhalation that bore my name like a leaf on a river that flows out of the mountains: "Em."

He came to me with the force and surrender of the ocean meeting the shore. He was smiling, and yet his hands trembled, as if with fear. Again he whispered my name, and again. "Em. Em . . ." It became a hum, a rumbling from his deep interiors, a cat purr, an earthquake. He was in love, now kissing my neck, my throat, the place between my breasts. In the clarity of those moments, I was real only where he touched me, a taut line of existence that ran from my head clear through to my crotch as one burning wire. I squirmed on the sheets, unable to process the chaos of sensation.

Our promise thus offered to the changing winds of the

Fates, we fell asleep, long months of courtship settled at last. He had loved me that night so long and so intensely that although I at last lay quietly, I still felt the rolling of his hips in the muscles of my own, much as (I would soon come to know) a sailor still feels the sea hours after walking onto land. Even the arrival of sleep came in waves, by turns submerging me in dreams and lifting me to the waking clarity of peace and happiness in the roll of dust motes all golden in the first light of a perfect summer's dawn.

The damned telephone woke us not two hours later. How I wish he had not answered it.

"Hello?" he said groggily, one hand clutching the instrument to his ear, the other sliding down my belly in proprietary exploration.

It was my turn to roll toward him. I nuzzled up under his chin, worked one thigh between his, licked his neck. I heard a tiny voice coming out of the phone, squeaky, all quick and agitated. He said, "Yeah, you woke me but— okay—no, give me a moment, will you?" And then he got out of bed. As I watched him walk away, I thought playfully, *He'll come right back if he knows what's good for him!*

But he didn't. I suppose I fell back to sleep, because the next thing I remember was the shower running, and then the scent of bacon frying, and the breakfast tray landing gently on the bed. He was already dressed, and not in his customary Saturday sweatshirt and jeans but in chinos and a pressed shirt, ready for work.

"You're kidding," I said. "Tell me this is some kind of joke."

Jack blushed, which was rare. He's blond enough that after it rose past his receding hairline, I could see the redness transit his scalp. "I'm sorry. I'm afraid I do have to go. You can stay here, of course, as long as you like. Make yourself to home." Then, slipping into his most Southern of Southern drawls, he popped me on the nose and said, "I got to go fer a while, cupcake. Bum timing. I'll be back. Don' chew fret."

"*When* will you be back?"

He cleared his throat. "I'm, really, truly sorry to tell you, my succulent little treat,"—here he took my chin in his hand and bent to kiss me—"but it could be days. I'll be in touch as often as possible. Come on, eat up, this is getting cold."

I thought, *Getting cold? No shit!* But I put a lid on my temper and ate. There's no excuse for wasting good eggs and bacon.

So that was it. We had just one night together before he left on his unspecified assignment.

He called the first night. "Hi there, love."

"Jack! Where are you?"

A sigh. "Sorry, but I can't tell you. I'd like to set up a time each day when I can phone you."

"Does this mean you might be gone more than a couple of days?" I tried to keep the edge out of my voice. I told myself, *This is how it might always be, Em. The man's a security specialist. A spook. He goes to places he can't admit to being and does things he can't talk about. You knew this going into the relationship.*

Yeah, but before last night, the phone calls weren't calling him out of my bed, I countered, *arguing with myself.*

It wasn't your bed, it was his.

Don't get technical!

(I lose a lot of arguments with myself.)

So we set up a time when he'd call. And then he didn't.

One night. Just long enough to catch me like a thorn, just short enough to make me doubt my heart, and my sanity. Either way, enough to send me looking for him. To Florida, of all places.

You say, Florida? Em Hansen, renegade Wyoming cowgirl, itinerant geologist, in *Florida*? The Em Hansen who regards open water with something akin to morbid fear? Em Hansen in a state almost completely *surrounded* by water? No, it's even worse than that. Florida is not only surrounded by water, it's *saturated* with it. The parts that aren't chin-deep swamp are undercut by limestone solution cavities that are *full* of water, and at any moment the ground might collapse and drop you and your Buick into a brand-new lake. But yes, I went to Florida and I'm here to tell the tale.

I went to Florida with the standard measures of ignorance—that Florida doesn't even have any geology, for starts, and that instead of cattle ranches they farm alligators, when in fact they have all three. Geology, I mean, *and* cattle ranches, *and* alligator farms. Reptiles, for heaven's sake. We have reptiles in Wyoming—snakes and lizards, to be precise—but you can whack them with a shovel if you have to, and like as not you'll never even see them, the both of you going your own way and having a nice life, just as things were meant to be. You don't have to worry that they're going to walk up across your lawn and eat your pet dog. Not that we have many lawns in Wyoming, or keep dogs just as pets, but bottom line, we have no reptiles in Wyoming bigger than you can stuff in your hat.

In summary, therefore, you might ask if I had taken leave of my senses. On the contrary, going to Florida was *entirely* a thing of the senses. Each time I thought of Jack, and each time the wind brushed my cheek, and each time my nostrils caught the scent of a flower, he came to me all over again, and the day-to-day sanity of the ordinary world would dissolve into a thing sight and sound and touch and taste and scent all over again; a thing more real and riveting than the moment, so intoxicating that wherever I was, I'd stop, and grab a railing, or touch a wall so I wouldn't fall over. Eyes closed, I'd be right back in that place where all things came together in a moment that belonged to him.

It would come over me like a wave. Overpowering. Compelling. Debilitating. Enough to make me, who feared water, long for it as the nearest substitute for the completeness of the experience. Eyes closed, hand groping for some solid object, I was gone in memory again, both loving it and terrified.

It was a haunting, pure and simple: Having caught my

heart, Jack vanished like a ghost, and I was left with all the agony of being fully corporeal, stuck in a body that longed for his. You just don't do that to a woman. Or at least, not this woman. I had waited too long for him. The middle of my thirties had come and was quickly leaving. That made me old enough to value life and too young to be philosophical about it.

I told myself to relax, that he'd call when he could. Bereft of contact, I ran my sensory movie, or should I say it ran me, until remembering worked its way deep enough to drive me into foolish action.

That action was a visit to Tom Latimer, the man who had introduced us. As I drove to Tom's house, I promised myself that I'd just ask a few questions. Drop by and say hello. Maybe ask if he had heard from Jack. Real casual-like. But as I stared at the carpet in Tom's living room, fighting back the latest wave of longing, I couldn't hide the fact that I was worried.

Out of the corner of one eye I saw Tom's wife, Faye Carter (who was lounging back on the couch in an attempt to get comfortable) move her legs to a new position, then try another. She looked down at her belly as if having a conversation with it. The baby was getting big in there. Her lips curved in a private smile. Was the baby kicking her?

Tom and Faye had been married and formally cohabiting only a handful of months, and the living room still had a look of impermanence and all-too-recent attempts to weave two lifestyles into one. Pictures leaned against the wall waiting to be hung, and books were stacked randomly. Isolating himself within this chaos, Tom observed me as abstractly as if watching a dog sniffing something on the sidewalk across the street. In his usual austere fashion, he sat sideways in a straight-backed chair, supporting his grizzled chin in one hand. Since marrying Faye and taking early retirement from the FBI, he seemed to have gone slightly out of focus. On this occasion, he had forgotten to shave, or perhaps had decided consciously that such matters of outward concern could wait. The salt-and-pepper stubble made him look older, old enough to be Faye's father (which was very nearly the case), even though he still kept his long, lean body rock hard. I almost wished he would return to work. Then, I would have a clue what was going on in the remote vastness of his mind. Clearing his throat, he said, "Jack won't be gone all that long, Em."

"He said maybe just a few days."

"Right, and it's only been, what? Four?"

"Six. And I haven't heard from him in five, even though he said he'd call every evening."

"Not even a week. That's nothing. It's like this in the Bureau."

Faye grunted derisively.

He considered the stink-eyed stare she fixed on him, then said, "That's one reason in so many that I was willing to quit, Faye. It's not much of a life when you get sent out of state. Adventure, maybe . . ." He sighed, then turned his words toward me. "Em, you're forgetting that Jack was sent *here* from out of state to begin with. It was just as long as we were working on that project together that he got to stay here. Now he's off on some other ops. Or something." His gaze suddenly turned inward, like a sea creature retracting a tentacle when poked. What had he just said to himself that had triggered that reaction?

I said, "Where out of state, Tom? What state, for instance?"

Tom did not answer.

I said, "Have you heard from him?"

Without looking at me, he shook his head.

I glanced over at Faye for support. She gave me doe eyes and pursed her lips sympathetically. She knew my little fact, that Jack Sampler and I had slept together . . . made love . . . for the first time the night before he had taken off.

From the close examination Tom was now making of his fingernails, I knew that he knew this fact of my personal history, too. Faye would not have exactly *told* Tom, but he had, after all, been an FBI agent, one of the best, and was damned good at reading between the lines.

I began interpreting ambient data a little bit myself, such as the fact that Tom was choosing his words carefully and avoiding making eye contact with me. I wondered for a moment if this was an unspoken judgment of the predicament in which I found myself, and thought: *Tom, you social dinosaur*, but then told myself, *Don't project this on Tom, Em. He is for once just trying to stay out of your business. And your business is legitimate. Jack's a good man and he loves you. And he'll be back. People walking out of your life, and you walking out of theirs, is a thing of the past.*

I stared at my own fingernails for a while, reassuring myself that there had been nothing casual in what Jack and I had done. Jack and I had met on a job. After the case was wrapped up, we had kept seeing each other. Jack came along as witness when Tom got married, and I was there for Faye. After that, everything seemed to glide along smoothly. It was all very natural.

Jack wore well, as my mother used to say. He was a big man, nicely framed and pleasantly muscled, the kind of guy who's fun to show off. He was a Southerner by upbringing, or at least, that was what I had come to presume about him. He was not much on offering up details about himself and he gave short answers to leading questions. Asking, "Where did you go to high school?" got me, "Down South." I tried a few times to pump Tom Latimer for information about him, but he said little beyond, "Jack? I don't know. But I'd trust him with my life." So Jack was a friend for the long haul, but also a creature of the moment, and that suited me well enough that I had quit asking questions after a while.

Then one day we went hiking in the mountains east of Salt Lake, and he sat me down on a rock next to a beautiful stream and went down on one knee. "Em, sweet thang," he murmured, nuzzling my hand, "will you be my lady?"

I watched the mountain breezes play though his hair. A fish broke the surface of the nearest pool, and a woodpecker jumped from one tree to the next. "I thought I kind of was," I replied.

"I mean, would you please accompany me to the clinic for a little blood work?"

How times have changed, I thought, *we now prove our love by our willingness to visit professionals in white coats to check for viruses before we jump in the sack. About as sensual and spontaneous as filling out a form 1040 for the IRS.*

Remembering this, sitting in Tom and Faye's living room, the wave of longing hit me again, so strong this time that I gasped for air. The room seemed to dissolve, and Tom and Faye seemed like people outside a fish bowl staring in at me.

I snapped, "How long will he be gone, Tom?"

"As I said, another week. Maybe two. Three, tops."

"Where'd he go?"

Tom stared out the window. "I don't know."

"Don't know or can't say?"

Tom's face darkened. "I'm out of the loop, Em. I'm retired from the Bureau, remember?"

"Yeah, but he's your pal."

He fixed an unreadable gaze on me and said concisely, "I think that now you are closer to him than I am."

He was twisting words. I could feel it in the little muscles that were tensing up all over my body. But I said nothing more. I didn't want to tell him about the craving I felt to be near Jack, or the boredom I felt sitting around waiting for him to return.

Faye shifted slightly on the couch. It was a subtle movement; just an odd rotation of her hip, but something in it seemed like a signal. And the expression on her face was suddenly a little too innocent. "Tom," she said, "I've been thinking. It's about time for a last trip before baby comes. How about Em and I go down to Florida and visit my aunt? Get a little sunshine, and—"

Tom's eyes snapped toward her. His voice hardening

into a tone of warning, he said, "It's perfectly sunny *here,* darling."

I pounced. "Florida?"

Faye went into a cat stretch, pointing her long legs toward Tom. It arched her round, smooth belly outward, emphasizing the voluptuousness of her pregnancy. She fixed a smile on him that would melt butter in January. "Florida is lovely this time of year, no matter what anyone says. The humidity is good for the skin, and it rains almost every afternoon, breaking the heat. We could just hang out . . ."

Tom closed his eyes and pinched thumb and forefinger to the bridge of his nose.

She purred, "Tell her, Tom. Come on."

Tom slammed his fist against the back of the chair. "Faye! Have you been listening in on my private conversations?"

I jumped in quickly lest the point of my conversation be lost in another of a long string of domestic squabbles. "Where in Florida?"

Tom's entire person was focused on Faye, his head down like a stalking animal. Faye shrank back into the couch, no doubt wondering how her do-gooding had gone wrong for her this time. Tom spoke from between clenched teeth, his voice a hiss. "Yes, Faye, I'd like to know that myself. And I'd like to know exactly how you know it!"

"It was nothing, Tom! The word 'Florida' was all I heard. Honest. You raised your voice for a moment while you had your head in the refrigerator to get him a beer, that was all." Faye's tone waxed sarcastic. "I admit I had to strain a little to hear, but aren't you proud of me? Doesn't that make me a good detective?"

Tom cackled viciously. "No, you are *not*. Your friend *Em* here is the detective."

"Forensic geologist," I interjected, still trying to knock him off his track.

Tom said, "Forensic geo-detective, Junior Woodchuck, whatever; Em, you just stay out of this. Faye, I demand to know! Have you or have you not been listening in on my private discussions?"

Faye managed to look affronted. "No. You guys were just talking—you know, having your beer before Jack took off—and I was lying down in the bedroom there minding my own business, thank you very much!" Quickly she added, "I suppose you didn't know I was in the house."

"We damned well did not!"

I hollered, "Is there some good reason I can't know where Jack is?"

Tom's posture stiffened, which told me that until then, he hadn't been as worked up as he'd been trying to appear. He had jumped on Faye to try to shut her up, and had continued his attack as a crude subterfuge to evade my questions. Faye seemed to have read that in him, too. She smiled brightly, a kind of girl-scout-cookie-salesperson grin meant to sell him on something he didn't want. On Faye's aristocratic face it looked downright goony. "That's all I heard you say. Honest." She wiggled her eyebrows at him.

He wiggled his graying eyebrows back.

Afraid now that I might at any moment lose them into the bedroom, I roared, "Come on, Faye! If that's all you heard Tom say, then what did *Jack* say?"

Faye looked from her husband to me doubtfully, then shrugged her shoulders. "Well, he said he was going to Florida."

Tom groaned.

I said, "And?"

"And something about 'code-name dust,' and 'don't tell Em, she'll get the wrong idea.'"

I glanced at Tom. His lips twisted wildly for a moment, then he turned and stormed out of the room. I heard the back door open and slam shut. Heard a car engine start up. Heard the sound of tires squealing on blacktop as the vehicle left the curb abruptly.

I looked at Faye. We both knew that *this* was no act.

She stared at her belly and began to cry.

I thought of going to her and trying to comfort her, but

found that I could not move. I now knew where Jack was, geographically—two thousand miles east and south—but without more information, that was just a compass direction along which to direct my longing. And, jammed right up against that longing, I now suffered a new, infinitely worse emotion: the first shards of fear.

– 2 –

A woman stood alone on the beach, clinging to her aloneness. The wind played games with the soft tendrils of hair that grew in random curls around her face. She took off her sandals, threaded the straps through one belt loop of her rolled-up jeans, and buckled them together so that she could run with her hands free. She stepped forward and looked down, examining her footprints.

Her name was Lucy, and she had almost majored in anthropology in sympathy for the prehuman namesake who had long ago left tiny footprints in Africa, but she had abandoned such romances of the past. Hers was a life of the future, and she would walk where few could follow her. She stood now with her own bare feet on the sands of Cape Canaveral, deep in the vastness of the Kennedy Space Center. And when the space shuttle next rose into the skies, she would rise with it, and take her first steps in space.

But that moment had not yet come, and she had first to deal with the agony of waiting through each hour and each day that hung between her and her goal. Lately that agony had darkened. She felt eyes on her back; the eyes of the world, yes, but also other eyes, and escaping that gaze had become as important as rising into space.

She marked this rare moment of relative privacy by closing her eyes, so she could concentrate on the sensation of sand rubbing against her skin. It was almost like a message.

But as she opened herself to this pleasure, she could for an instant also perceive emotional pain, and a bolt of it shot through her heart and mind.

Unable to stop herself now from searching for a source for her anxiety, she glanced nervously over her shoulder, even though she knew he could not be there. *He might track me home to Florida, but he can't follow me this deep into the cape. I am safe here. Even safer in space. He can't follow me there....*

Anxious that any of her colleagues should witness her anxiety, she forced her gaze forward again and squared her shoulders. She must look normal, casual, in charge of her destiny, just out for a jog on the beach. Physical training. Dedication. Her lips stiffened as she thought, *I am in charge, damn it!*

She closed her eyes and drew the thought inward, inhaled the salt air, opened them again. She examined the world, once again the observer, and not the observed.

The beach stretched long and smooth down the cape, fading into the mists. She regarded the wave-sculpted quartz sand, just one section of the apron of sand that edged the pancake-flat complex of ancient sea deposits that geographers called Florida. Waves washed the beach, grinding the cast-off shells of a hundred zillion sea creatures, working and rolling them along an endless conveyor belt that transported them slowly along the shore, perhaps one day to be the cement in a new generation of stone.

Lucy turned her face fully into the wind. The waves were big, and thirsty. They marched in from the broad Atlantic and heaved themselves up steeper and steeper as they approached the shore. She thought for a moment that they looked like prides of lions pacing across the veldt from Mother Africa and opening their mouths to roar as they drew near.

Lions! That's absurd, she told herself firmly. *The stuff of childhood.* She scanned her body for tension. Arms. Fingers still clutching, as if on the ready to grasp a weapon. Anxiety must still be lurking within her brain. She reminded herself that she had made it to her destination. That she was in charge.

So why can't I let go of this foolish anxiety?

Focusing her mind on abstraction as she had so doggedly trained herself to do, Lucy studied one single wave as it approached, forced herself to think rationally of the series of circles each molecule of water described as it came, her mind's eye now replicating the diagram on wave motion that had been in her freshman geology text. The long fetch of the Atlantic wind was a comforting surety. Just physics. Sanity. All in control. *There is no mystery to the wind*, she assured herself.

But the wind had drawn its hand across the water's surface, dragging it first into cat's paws and then into swells, forming long, sensuous troughs of water that marched across the open water, and the lions again emerged.

Better African lions than a Florida panther. Lucy forced both images out of her mind. *It's just water. H-two-O. With salt. In motion. It's all just physics.*

But as she watched, the waves again became stalking lions. *Lionesses,* she insisted, still fighting for some shred of control of her thoughts. Bewilderment turning to anger, she thought, *The females do the work while the males sleep, then the sons of bitches climb on board and have themselves a good fuck!*

She drew in a ragged breath, let it out, the sound of it lost in the wind. *Focus harder.* The wave she had been watching began to rise, the lioness heaving her body into a self-sacrificing pounce. Lucy gritted her teeth, forced her mind to imagine the oscillatory circle of its individual molecules stretching into ellipses as they intersected the slope of the beach and tripped bottom. *Now the axis of that ellipse flattens with the drag of the undertow, now the wave oversteepens and collapses.* . . . The chaos of tumbling water churned up the beach. More powerful than most, this wave kept coming, swept clear up to where she stood, snatched at her feet, wiping out her footprints with one jealous swipe of its paw. Lucy felt its sucking caress pull at her ankles and shuddered, her mind suddenly free of words. Tears burst from her eyes as she finally released herself into the tide of her emotions.

Springing into a run, Lucy dashed along the swash line, pounding a string of footprints into the sands. She ran hard, filling her lungs with salt air, raising her face to the north, drinking in the privileged privacy of this farthest reach of the space center. She felt her well-trained muscles respond with grace, raising her above the bonds of earth with every stride, carrying her northward with the long-shore wind. The mists clung to the waves and sand and beach ridge, almost obscuring the magnificent machinery that towered ahead of her. *Yes!* This was her destiny, to rise above the Florida peninsula once and for all! As her breathing deepened rhythmically into her belly, she regarded the rocket that would carry her skyward: four and a half million pounds of rockets and fuel, and mounted on its side, space shuttle *Endeavor*, 122 feet of technologically marvelous craft. It hugged its boosters like an emerging butterfly clinging to its cocoon, as if hanging there in wait for its stubby wings to pump themselves to a fuller potential. Lucy shook her head ruefully, again defying such imaginings. *A butterfly's gossamer wings would snap under the stresses of launch,* she told herself. *Or fry to a crisp in the heat of reentry. Better these laughable little tile-encrusted planes that protrude from* Endeavor*'s chubby tail!*

Once again assured of her rationality, Lucy fairly flew up the beach, her hands describing the same circles as the waves, her feet making a dance with the sands, here sinking in a little deeper, there barely digging in a toe. Her mind opened outward, observing variations in the packing of the grains of sand—*Is it the waves that determine the softness and hardness, or is it also grain size, roundness, and sorting?*—no matter, years of fierce training had brought her to this moment, to this opportunity.

But *Endeavor* was leaving the launch pad. Some little quirk in the vast, ultrasophisticated assemblage of machinery had nudged the schedule past its safe launch window.

Her crew had stood like stone, each looking at the other as they heard, "Sorry. With this weather coming in we'll have to start off-loading fuel, and . . ." NASA was rolling back the shuttle—she watched it go, sliding dumbly along on its crawler, a butterfly not yet ready to emerge from its cocoon, creeping meekly back toward the safety of the assembly building. She had been all suited up—so close!—and the countdown had stopped and . . . but with luck, it would be a short delay. Get the flaw in the machinery fixed, get these storms past, roll the shuttle back out. . . .

Surely she could endure that much more to gain the fulfillment of her lifelong dream. She, Lucy of all Lucys, would snap loose her tether to this earth, ride that rocket to the sky, the thundering pressure of five gravities pressing at her slender back like the fist of God.

In ecstasy, she arched her neck and threw her face open to the heavens. *Yes, yes, yes,* her feet chanted to the sands, her angry dash transformed into a swell of victory. *Yes, I have made it. Yes, I have prevailed. Yes, I can do this, I can make it at last, I can rise above this ground—*

A seagull glided into her field of vision. It was mottled with dark feathers. It swooped closer, eyed her coldly. An untamed corner of Lucy's mind found something all too familiar its primitive gaze, and issued a fearful thought. *He sent this bird—no, worse yet, he has climbed inside the creatures of the sky!* Her adrenal glands jolted their chemical stimulant into her unwitting bloodstream, ramming her heart against her ribs like a trapped animal trying to escape its cage.

She wanted to scream, "No! Not here! Not now! Someone might be watching, someone might see, and even now shake his head, say Lucy is weak, and scratch me from the duty roster. Oh, God . . ."

The worst part of waiting is going back to Houston to wait, where he can find me. . . .

Her gait fumbled. She slowed for a moment to correct it, bring it back under control. Forcing herself not to look over her shoulder, turning her vision instead to the far horizon, away from the evilness of gulls and those who would inspire rage, Lucy transformed the shot of adrenaline into an even faster gallop. *Yes, that's good; anyone watching will think I'm simply forwarding my training, and never know what's truly chasing me up the beach. In fact, yes, I can now already slow my pace, move it back into an easy lope. Easy now, remember where I am, remember that I am the predator here, not the prey. No matter that the space program puts its scientist astronauts at the bottom of the food chain, and treats those women among them even worse; money is the bottom line here, and they have invested plenty in my training. I am part of a team. An essential part of a team, a team that has prepared rigorously to do a job.*

Lucy pounded on up the beach, building her future one footprint at a time. NASA would not fail to use her now, she assured herself, and when she rode that thrumming monster into the sky, no adolescent gull, or any of the searing memories it unearthed, could possibly reach high enough to find her.

– 3 –

Calvin Wheat bent over his apparatus, cussing at the cone-shaped filter that was once again acting up. How in hell was he supposed to get a valid dust sample if the filter kept slipping? He had committed himself to all these days on board in order to get it, and now this. Damned budgetary constraints, how was he supposed to do science with no data? This experiment had just better work, because in order to collect these data, he had begged and fussed his way onto this Caribbean cruise, selling his soul to the tune of giving three dumbed-down lectures to the paying passengers so he could inhabit the so-called free scientist's berth on this ship—*This over-decorated party tub on steroids,* he mentally grumbled to himself, *this techno-idiot's equivalent of snake oil; this gold-plated floating spa; this sheltered workshop where Joe and Betty eco-tourist loll about in their carpeted staterooms, gorge on fish that ought to be on the endangered species list, cultivate their tans, never quite make it to the squash courts, swill their rum punches with the little parasols, and feel noble about paying twenty-five dollars for three-dollar "I 'heart' sea turtles" T-shirts. I wish they'd all just go on home to New Jersey and get it over with, tell their neighbors what a deep and meaningful time they had learning about the natural splendors of the Caribbean, and leave me to my frigging work!*

Calvin bared his teeth at his sampling equipment. *All*

this I suffer in the faint hope of catching a midocean dust sample, and now I can't get the damned filter paper straight. What crap!

He stepped over the bright yellow "CAUTION, KEEP OUT!" tape he had strung from rail to rail across the bow of the ship and began jimmying the apparatus from another direction, his head bent close to the intake valve. The caution tape had become an essential bit of equipment, as it seemed that each female aboard—*Each wishful drum of hair spray abuse that's roaming this ship*—seemed to find it necessary, when they thought he wasn't looking, to rush into the bow and attempt a Kate-Winslet-aboard-the-*Titanic* pose. More than one of these cows had gotten upwind of the intake valve while the apparatus was collecting—*Offering up her own unique mix of talcum powder, psoriasis, deodorant, dandruff, eyelash mites, and who knows what other bodily flora and effluvia*—to a sample he had been hoping to keep pristine. It had been necessary to run those samples over again, a loss of precious time and opportunity.

The ship would be putting in at its easternmost port tomorrow, and thereafter would be steaming back westward toward its proprietary island in the Bahamas and thence back to Port Canaveral, snaking its way downwind of one island or another the whole way. What a sap he'd been to think that grabbing a sample of dust blown off Africa would be a simple matter of setting up the equipment, keying the timer, and then wandering off to dinner while the little gizmo swilled the easterly breeze. He'd even bought the tuxedo required for dining at the captain's table—*I did okay there, found a tail tux auctioned for forty dollars on eBay*, he reminded himself—*but I've yet to make it to a single dinner, it being easiest to keep the stampede of fantasy artists off the bow when they're all off chowing down their grits.*

The filter cone finally slid securely into place. With satisfaction, Calvin decided that this sampling run would be good, and had every chance of staying good, as everyone else on the ship was at dinner or hanging over the stern toasting the setting sun with a glass of rum. *And*—this he barely dared acknowledge even to himself—*I am a lucky man. The latest storm off Africa is just now arriving, and here's a nice haze of red smut dusting the whole ship just to prove it. Hell, I could get this sample with a catcher's mitt!* But four years of undergraduate training in biology, two years to get a Master's in public health, three more for a Ph.D. in microbiology and two more for post-doctorate fellowships had taught him that it was just plain essential to get his sample onto the sterile filter paper that waited deep inside the little mechanical lung he now set into action. *And with these data, there's no way in hell Chip Hiller and his band of idiots can claim that my results aren't valid!*

The machine hissed, its metal lips offering the evening breeze a hungry kiss. Calvin hovered downwind, inhaling the wind as if it were perfume, regardless of the fungi, bacteria, and viruses he knew to be riding it. The ship was now completely upwind of the Windward Islands. The air his canister was sucking had not passed over any land mass—no dalliances over islands, no sojourns over South America—since leaving mother Africa. Life was sweet.

He allowed himself a smug grin. *If this sample doesn't win funding for the rest of the research, I'll eat my tuxedo. . . . No, it looks too good on me. Okay, I'll kiss the next would-be Winslet who comes near me. Fuck Chip Hiller and his attempts to block this project, because with adequate funding I, Calvin Wheat, will be the man of the hour in microbiological circles, the smart little cracker who will prove beyond the last foolish shreds of malingering doubt that the dust blowing off Africa is carrying live pathogens that threaten every organism on which it lands. Germs. Bacteria and fungi, not to mention the odd virus, all tucked tenderly into the crevices of the mineral dust that spall off that godforsaken continent like rats off a sinking environmental ship!*

Finding live germs in the samples collected in Africa itself had been a slam dunk; those little nasties had barely left the dung heaps they'd blown from. Testing the air over the Caribbean islands and Florida had turned up plenty as well, but the naysayers and critics argued that the "bugs" had originated as the wind swept the islands, and could not have survived three to six days of transit. It was necessary to prove that the little critters could and did survive exposure to ultraviolet light, and survived it for up to 5,000 miles.

Calvin leaned down over his machinery one more time to retest the offending clips, leaning hard onto the port rail. As he did so, he saw, out of the corner of one eye, the sudden appearance of yet one more idiot rushing at the bow, bearing down on him. Calvin had only enough time to put out one arm to protect his apparatus, and no time at all to choose an epithet before he felt himself being lifted over the side. As shock and fear exploded though his body, he flailed his arms and legs, trying desperately to connect with the outside of the rail. He missed. That hope dashed, he tried instead to propel himself outward, away from the curling bow wake that waited, three stories below, ready to suck him under the length of the ship before spitting him one limb at a time through its immense propellers.

- 4 -

When Tom Latimer returned (his head bowed with some abstract form of repentance), it was too late for him to regain control of his immediate future. Faye and I had already decided to go to Florida.

In the first minutes of the hour that he was gone, Faye dissolved to tears, but that was nothing new. Tears had been flowing down her face with fair regularity ever since she had become pregnant, and she had long since asked me to quit noticing them. The hormonal shifts brought on by her little hitchhiker had wreaked havoc with her usual cool stoicism, and the difficulty of adjusting to the consequent marriage to her very cerebral lover had filled in where the hormones left off. This time she made it additionally clear that she didn't want my help by locking herself in the bathroom and running water to cover her sobs.

I jumped onto the computer that Tom had left running in the living room and got to work, stopping only to shout over the water when I couldn't figure out how to get through the security system he had rigged to keep prying eyes out of the business he did through that portal. Security systems of all types were now his stock-in-trade. Since the terrorist attacks on the World Trade Center and the Pentagon, antiterrorist security had been his FBI assignment, and since his so-called retirement, he had become a consultant, again making it his professional pursuit. The retirement was part of the deal he and Faye had cut to form sufficient common ground on which to build a marriage: His work for the FBI had been dangerous, and she didn't want to raise a kid with a father who might at any moment get shot. Consulting seemed suitably remote from chasing bad guys down dark alleys, allowing Faye the pleasant fantasy that Tom had settled down.

Faye gave me instructions that would get me into her section of the computer's hard drive and onto the Internet. Once there, I logged on to a search engine and typed in FLORIDA DUST. I wasn't trying to kid myself that such a casual action would help me figure out where Jack was in Florida or what he was doing there, but at times like this, I liked to keep my mind busy.

My hands shook slightly as I worked. Jack had originally come to Salt Lake City to work with Tom on antiterrorist security. Did his current assignment mean that there was another wave of terrorism on the horizon? Certainly Florida had been in the news since the September 11 attacks . . . the first anthrax death had occurred there, and anthrax came in the form of dust. I had pushed specific notions about Jack's assignment far to the back of my mind since his sudden departure, but now they crowded to the front. Terrorism made my blood run cold; not only did I not want that happening to my country, or in my world, but I didn't want the man I loved right smack in the middle of it. Call me selfish, but the very thought turned my innards to soup.

So I tried to concentrate on the computer. It, at least, was holding still, just a dumb box. Not a potential source of trouble. Even there, I was wrong.

In the brief moment between hitting the ENTER key and watching the results appear on the screen, I wondered if I should have narrowed the search to U.S. government activities by typing FLORIDA DUST + FBI, but the first entry on the list that came up referenced the feds anyway. It concerned work being done by the U.S. Geological Survey, the federal agency charged with the study of the Earth. It was a news story from a major television network. The headline read, "Long Distance Dust: African Dust Clouds Bring Fungi, Bacteria to United States," and the story began like this:

> Scientists have long known that upper-level winds carry particles great distances. But now they've found that hazardous bacteria and fungi hitchhike across the Atlantic on North African dust plumes.
>
> "It shows we're all connected in one way or the other, much more than I would ever have dreamed," says Miles Guffey, one of the researchers of dust plumes at the U.S. Geological Survey.

The next two stories also referenced investigations of microbes riding dust clouds blowing off North Africa. Both took me to NASA's Web site and its prodigious publicity machinery. I wondered at first why America's space agency was involved with a geology story, but then realized that the first *A* in *NASA* stood for *atmospheric,* and the *S* for *space.* So NASA's interests were not as much in observing geology as in the act of looking down from above.

The headlines read, "Desert Dust Kills Florida Fish: New Research Links Huge African Dust Clouds with 'Red Tides,' " and "Dust from Africa Leads to Large Toxic Algae Blooms in Gulf of Mexico, Study Finds." And sure enough, both articles were illustrated by images beamed down from NASA equipment that was riding through the heavens mounted on satellite steeds, proudly demonstrating what NASA had done for us lately.

I did not for a moment think that dust blowing off African deserts onto Florida and surrounding waters might account for Jack's sudden departure, especially because it was clear from the articles that the process had been going on for quite some time. In fact, dust had been blowing off Africa for as long as there had been deserts there and wind blowing over them, hardly something that would suddenly rouse the FBI.

The satellite images showed dust blowing far out over

the ocean. Peering into those images got me thinking about water, and water got me thinking about waves, and by now you know where the concept of waves took me. With all that rolling around I relaxed just enough to get an idea: Armed with the smidgeon of information that Faye had divulged, I could call Jack's office and ask how things were going for him in Florida, sound casual, and hopefully kid someone into telling me what Jack was up to and when he might return. As I punched in the numbers, I decided that my sweet love would be pleased with the elegant simplicity of this ruse: If I presumed to call and sounded like I knew a little, then whoever I talked to would counterpresume that I knew a lot and would speak openly. Or as Tom had taught me, the best way to lie is to attach it to the truth, and in this case all I had to do was artfully leave off the critical detail that I had not heard about Jack's whereabouts from Jack himself.

As luck would have it, an office manager named Tanya, with whom I had a chatty sort of relationship, received my call. "Hi, Em," she cooed. "Hear anything from Jack?"

"No. But, um, I was hoping you could help me with that. I've . . . been off fishing for the last several days." Warming to my fabrication, I blustered on, getting girl-to-girl confidential. "You know . . . I miss him and all, so I thought it easier to pretend that *I* was the one who left."

Tanya laughed like she knew this sport.

"Anyway," I continued, really rolling now, "I got back and there was a message from him on my phone, and I'm supposed to call him, but he didn't leave the number again, and um, well, I can't find the piece of paper where he wrote it down, you know, and . . ." I let it trail off, making room for her to jump in there and give me what I wanted. I was amazed at myself, and in fact wondered why it had taken me so long to think of this.

Tanya laughed. "Em, dear, ol' Jack-o isn't in the habit of telling me where he spends his vacation time, much less does he leave a number where he can be reached."

Vacation? "Oh. Well, I . . ."

"So you're telling me he isn't back yet?"

This wasn't going my way at all. "Ah, no . . ."

"And he didn't take you?"

"Well, I . . ."

"Listen, I know how you're feeling, but calm down, that boy really has it for you. Maybe the fishing was just extra good where *he* is!"

Now I was completely confused. Jack hadn't told me he was going fishing, and if he had gone without me, it was over between us! *Wham!* So where was he? And what was he doing?

"The other line is ringing," Tanya said. "Gotta go."

"Right."

I sat listening to a dial tone for longer than I care to admit.

Finally, Faye came out of the bathroom. "Get anything out of Tanya?" she inquired, as she dabbed a cold washcloth at her tear-swollen eyes.

My bafflement dissolved into pettishness. I said, "Your ears *are* good! No wonder Tom gets pissed."

"Now *you're* not answering my question."

I couldn't work up much volume as I said, "She says he's on vacation."

Faye's eyebrows joined into one straight line. "Oooh, that sounds bad. Something's up. No wonder Tom's been wired." She put her hands on her widening hips and stared out the window toward the high sweep of the Wasatch Range. "So what's Jack up to, then?"

"You tell me. I looked up 'Florida dust' on the search engine, and all I got was a bunch of NASA images and some jive about research some geologists are doing there."

Faye asked, "Where in Florida?"

"Oh, come on, Faye, I was just keeping myself busy. I—"

"Where?"

I clicked back to that story. "It's the USGS. Looks like its Florida office is in . . . let's see. . . . St. Petersburg."

Faye put a hand on my shoulder and peered into the

monitor. "I have an aunt there. Nice town, if you like retired white people. Has a Salvador Dali museum."

"Great," I mumbled. "A little added surrealism with your monoculturalism. Tell me more about what Jack told Tom, Faye."

"Just that he was going to Florida, and that Tom would understand about 'killer dust.' "

"I thought you said *project* dust!"

Faye twisted her face into a concerned wince. "Yeah. Okay. Thought you might not like the 'killer' part."

I put my head down on the desk. I said, "And Tom would understand *what* about this killer dust thing?"

"Tom said, 'If you go there and do that, I can't help you,' or something like that."

I began to moan.

Faye patted my back. Then she reached forward, grasped the computer's mouse, and started scrolling down through the article. "We can go see my aunt, and you can visit Jack."

"Are you losing your grip? This is a geology project. The chances are slim to nil that it has anything to do with Jack's whereabouts."

"Well, at least according to this article, it's the fish that are being killed, not wandering FBI agents who've gone AWOL from their jobs."

I lifted my head and glared at her. "Way to calm my nerves, Faye."

"Just trying for a little levity."

"Right. Very little. Try this: Jack told me only that he had a job to do. 'Job' does not usually mean 'vacation time.' And Jack likes to fish, but not so much that he'd run off and do it five minutes after we . . ."

"Right."

I closed my eyes. "It was getting so nice."

"Don't put it in the past tense, Em. Have a little faith."

I was on the edge of tears. "Where *is* he? And what's he *doing* there?"

"I'll get it out of Tom."

"For once in my life I meet a man who's smart, good-looking, employed, *sane*, kind, funny . . . faithful. . . ."

"Yes." She had a hand on my shoulder.

"He is sane, isn't he, Faye?"

Faye let her breath out heavily. "Strikes me that way."

"And faithful?"

She patted my hair. "Follows you around like a dog. He'll come back."

"Sure. The man's an FBI agent. Carries a loaded weapon. Heads out somewhere on his own to do something he doesn't want even his 'lady' to know about. How long do you think I should wait before I panic?"

"So let's fly to St. Pete. Didn't he say his mother lives in Orlando? Two hours' drive from the airport. We could call her, and—"

"Orlando? I didn't even know *that*. And with what money? I can't afford the book-two-weeks-ahead, super-discount kind of plane ticket to Florida, let alone the last-minute, pay-through-the-nose variety!"

"I seem to remember I have a perfectly good airplane parked out at the airport."

That was true. Faye was a professional pilot; or at least, she was a commercially rated pilot who had, on occasion, charged money to carry people and small freight. I'd been all over the western states with her. But that was in the before times. Before losing her trust fund. Before marrying Tom. Before growing so pregnant that she did little else but lounge around and sleep. I wasn't sure she could concentrate long enough to fly us to Florida, or even reach past her belly to the control wheel. I said, "Florida's a long way from here. And you don't have a bottomless wallet anymore. And you're more than a little bit pregnant."

She turned a shoulder to indicate that she felt affronted. "I can fly just fine, thank you very much. The cabin's fully pressurized, and you can always take the controls for a while if I need to stretch or barf. And I thought it all through while I was in the bathroom: Tom's being a pain in the butt. I can use the break from him. And once this baby comes, I won't have time for any such adventures. My aunt would love to have us, so much so that she'd probably pay for the gas, and she'd loan us one of her spare Mercedeses. Even if we can't find Jack, we can run down to the Everglades. I'll bet you've never seen a live alligator, now have you? I mean, have you ever *been* to Florida?"

"No. But I don't want to be a party to your running away from Tom."

Ignoring my second statement, she said, "Well, then, no better time than the present. Now, quit hanging around here moping and get going. You've got twenty-four hours to plan your dream vacation. Go down to the bookstore and read some travel guides. If Jack comes back before then, you can make small talk about where he's been, and if he doesn't, then you'll at least be occupying your mind with something other than ultimate downside scenarios. It's gorgeous down there. Now, quit arguing with me and go pack your bikini."

I stared up at her. I've never worn a bikini in my life— high-plains ranch women aren't much inclined to exposing that much skin to the risk of sunburn—and the thought of Faye's burgeoning belly hanging out over a little slip of fabric made me gape. But if she wanted to take a little field trip, I was game. But I had to play it just right. If I went to Florida with Faye without first talking to Jack, I could come off looking meddlesome, or worse yet, clingy. But if I went there to do some work, I could play a game of rationalization: *I became interested in the place because you were there, Jack, but went there because of this really cool geological project.* But it had to be something I could back out of if he came back before we headed out. I needed a target to train my brain on, and I knew just what kind of a bull's-eye would do nicely.

– 5 –

I headed up the hill to the University of Utah to see Molly
Chang, a professor in the geology department. I'd gotten to
know her during the winter semester, when I took some
classes there in preparation for starting a Master's program—or, at least, that had been my plan at the time. When
I began to get tight with Jack, I started to wonder if some
nice university closer to where he was more typically sta-
tioned might be even nicer. Call me fickle, but that's how
my mind works: life first, and career . . . in there somewhere.

I found Molly sitting at her desk in her office, leaning
back so far in her swivel chair that her hiking-boot-clad
feet dangled above the floor. Her desk and surrounding
bookshelves were populated by the usual array of rock samples and obscure images that seem to bloom wherever a
geologist is planted. She looked up from a clutter of books
and papers and gave me an expectant look.

Molly is a sedimentologist, which means she studies
how fragments of rock, animal shells, twigs, and what have
you get transported and deposited as things like riverbeds,
beaches, and so forth. If left deposited for a while, the fragments get cemented into sedimentary rock. I went to Molly
because she is an expert on desert sediments, and so far
"African" was the only word I could put with "Florida
dust." Leaning against her doorjamb, I said, "Dust storms

from North Africa would come off the Sahara desert. Is that right?"

"Usually. Back before Homo sapiens," Molly said. "Mineral dust deflates off the Sahara, sure, and always has. But the topsoil blew off the Sahara a while ago."

"Say what?" That's the thing about talking to a geologist. You never know what time frame you're going to land in. We are the historical science, and our minds jump straight to the time scale and epoch that seems most significant.

"Well, the Sahara wasn't always a desert, you knew that," she said.

"In fact I did not. What epoch are we discussing?"

"Post-Pleistocene. In human terms, the Stone Age."

We were discussing a time considered recent to a geologist, but to a historian of human events, the dim, distant past. "I savvy the warming of the western U.S., the climate change from wet and cool to hot and dry, but I've never chased it overseas."

"Ten or twelve thousand years ago, the Sahara was green, a savannah. It had some nice forests, even. The climate was cooler and wetter. Paleolithic man chipped pictures of giraffes into the rock outcroppings that surrounded the water holes where the animals came to feed. The women dug up wild onions and raised a couple kids and maybe an orphaned fawn or two. Life was easy. Then as the ice age retreated, the Sahara warmed and grew increasingly arid. Life got tougher. Game and grass grew scarce, so the men took over the care of the domesticated animals and started herding them to far pastures, stripping the vegetative cover there as well. The topsoil started to get up and go."

"How long ago?"

"Call that seven, eight thousand years ago. But the advance of the desert is still happening, expanding south into the semi-arid zone called the Sahel. The loss of topsoil has accelerated over the past thirty years, through the current drought cycle, which has been going on unusually long.

Lake Chad is all but dried up, between lack of rain and people pulling water out of the watershed to stay alive. And then there's the fact that there are even more people there than there used to be, what with all the improvement in medical care and so forth, for both the people and their animals. More people and animals leads to more overgrazing, gathering of every twig of wood for cook fires, and the cycle intensifies."

"Are you taking a shot at me because I'm an old ranch girl?"

"No. You come from a so-called advanced culture. You brought your fuels in by tank truck, right? And I imagine your family culled the herd rather than let it overgraze your land."

"That's right. We had dry years, but Wyoming is probably a lot less arid than North Africa anyway. Even the driest part of Wyoming is considered only semidesert."

"Exactly. But in North Africa, we're talking full-on desert. And the people are nomadic. They move the herds with the grass, and they don't own any pickup truck to run into town for fuel. Instead, they push the herd until it strips the vegetation, as I said. That sooner or later degrades the biological capacity of the land. For instance, where you used to have grass and trees creating a baffle that kept the air quiet next to the ground—a microclimatic effect—you now have wind right at ground level, and sediment is plucked up into the air with each little breeze."

"You mean like our 'dust bowl' years here in the United States during the 1930s, when farmers left the ground naked to the wind after harvest."

"Right. The next dust devil sucks up all the fine sediments and off it goes."

I said, "Doesn't a certain amount of it happen anyway?"

"Right, and there are biological systems downwind that depend on the nutrients that come packaged in the dust. But when we disrupt the vegetation, the system accelerates." Molly cocked her head to one side. "So what's going on? Are you getting interested in this stuff?"

This was where I intended to set up my target and do a little archery. So I said, "Sure. I was thinking that with your specialty in desert sedimentology, you might be interested in my doing a report on this African dust thing."

"You mean for your Master's thesis?"

Whoops! "No, I was thinking of more like a term paper. Or a special studies project."

Molly narrowed her eyes. "Are you planning a trip to Africa?"

"No, Florida. That's where the research is being done, you see, and—"

"Florida? What's the sudden interest in Florida?"

If I'd been prone to blushing, I would have been beet red about then. "I have a chance to go there is all, and—"

"Does this involve that big, good-looking FBI guy you've been hanging around with?"

"Okay, well, yes, Jack's in Florida for a little while. But I was thinking I could sort of kill two birds with one stone: See him, visit the USGS there, and come back with research for a paper. Get course credit." The idea suddenly sounded stupid, really stupid.

Molly rocked her head back and laughed heartily. *"Cherchez le homme."*

"This isn't a joke, Molly."

Molly held up a hand. "Far be it from me to judge a woman who adjusts her career to her private life. I passed up a chance for the astronaut corps because I wanted to be there each evening to read my kids to sleep."

I hadn't taken her for the adventuresome type, but then, Molly kept a lot of herself where no one saw it. All I could think to say was, "Wow."

"Right. So what you're really saying is that you want an introduction to the people at the USGS in St. Petersburg, right?"

"Guilty as charged."

"Fine. I could put you in touch with Miles Guffey, the guy who sort of started all that African dust business. It's a breaking-news kind of project, very high profile in the media, but they're doing some interesting science."

"Great!"

"Now, hold your horses. If you want to nose around in all that, fine, but I'm not going to risk a perfectly good professional connection on less than a thesis project."

I realized a little too late that I was losing control of the conversation. "Well, I know a thesis is required for the Master's degree in geology here, but I thought that came later, like after I formally enroll in the program."

"Show some spine," Molly chided. "Quit waffling. I pulled some strings to get you into the classes you've already taken, so you owe me. As your advisor, whether you've asked me to be that or not, I advise you to look a little more dedicated, like you live and breathe only to study geology. I know that's bullshit, but hey, it's how the game is played."

"Hmm."

Molly's dark eyes clouded with annoyance. "Come on, Hansen, get it together. What are you, thirty-five? You're not a kid anymore; you don't need to be spoon-fed. You're a seasoned professional. Get that lovesick look out of your eyes and start pretending that nothing else matters to you, just like the rest of us idiots."

I tried to smile. "Okay. Right. Let me at it. Ride 'em cowgirl."

"Yeah. Ride *Em*. That's my job. But seriously, you want to prepare yourself for more of your forensic work, right? Well then, a dust thesis might be just the thing. Documenting source terrain, analyzing sediments and geochemistry and so forth. I'll bet that's just what the FBI guys are looking for."

"I could treat it like a crime scene," I said, trying to sound enthusiastic. But oddly, as soon as I spoke the words, my brain began to tilt its machinery in that direction, and little connections began to bloom. . . .

Molly's eyes narrowed down to slits as she broke into fresh laughter. She turned her swivel chair to face one of her bookshelves. "Let's see. . . . I have it somewhere here. . . .

Ah." She pulled a book off a shelf. "The United Nations report on desertification."

"What's 'desertification'?"

"I believe it is defined as 'the reduction of the biological capacity of arid lands,' as in, if you strip off the topsoil things don't grow as well. Just what we've been talking about. Note the publication date."

I opened the book. "1982. Is there anything more recent?"

"Ah, good, your mind is functioning. There was a big push back in the 1970s, when the drought started, but when they ran out of money, *pfft*. There's still a lot being done, but not much is seeing print. Try the UN Web site."

My stomach sank. This was beginning to sound like work. "Maybe I should start with the recent work the guys at the USGS are doing."

"Okay. Hit the Internet, and the library. But the USGS doesn't have any money either, so I'm not sure what you're going to find past the news stories, which are hardly a scientific source."

"Wait just a moment here! You think I should take on a thesis project that won't get funded?"

Molly leaned back in her chair again and studied me for several moments. Her smooth Asiatic face had gone as hard as porcelain, her eyes to flint. "I would in fact *prefer* you work on something that has no funding."

"Why? What am I supposed to live on? What—?"

"You're an independent type. I should think you'd want to work on an unfunded project precisely so you can maintain your independence."

I took a breath and gave myself time to think. "You mean, so I don't have to dance with the boys what brung me."

"Em, these days most science is bought and paid for by the wrong interests."

"You mean the corporations?"

"Sure. The corporations fund what they fund and don't what they don't, and that's how we're supposed to decide what we should study? That in itself is an important part of your education. When you're on one of your detective cases, do you study only the evidence that someone tells you to look at? And do you only come to conclusions that someone with money thinks you should arrive at?"

"What about government grants? The National Science Foundation, or the—"

"The corporations bought Congress years ago. Even the NSF is not without its political overtones and its cronyism. Oh, we should try to get you some money, Em, but we should try first for the kind that comes with no strings attached, and no presumed results. But we're getting ahead of ourselves. First, you go read around in that book and decide if you're really interested in that stuff. If you are, I'll make you some introductions. And here, take this book, too." She pulled a volume out from between a stack of test papers waiting to be graded and a box of thin sections waiting for petrographic analysis. With a wry flourish, she dusted off the book.

I took the book from her. It was entitled *The Secret Life of Dust* by Hannah Holmes. "Looks like a novel," I said.

"No, but it reads like one. Science writing for the lay public." She chuckled. "It takes the dryness out of the dust. And one more thing: Watch out for Miles Guffey."

"Oh, now you tell me."

"No, don't get me wrong, he's highly regarded. He's one of the big thinkers, puts together the big picture like few people can. But people like him ride the edges of things, and you'll find that part of what he does is connect with all kinds of strange people and see which ones have something he can use. He uses his high profile like a knife, to cut through red tape. The downside is that there are all sorts of hangers-on that kind of catch on the smart man's fur like so many burrs just traveling along for the ride. I hear he's got a microbiologist working for him now who's real bright, but he came out of a lab where people are messing with some bad microbes."

"What are you talking about?"

"I mean anthrax. Biological warfare. Here, you ought to read this, too." She added a book entitled *Germs: Biological Weapons and America's Secret War* by Judith Miller, Stephen Engelberg, and William Broad to my weighty stack. "I don't trust these guys who make a bad germ worse and call it security. If Guffey tries to connect you with that crap in any way, you tell him you'll find your own way home."

I stared at the books in my hands, wondering what I'd gotten myself into this time.

– 6 –

In the twenty-four hours that followed, I threw together a travel kit—that didn't take long, as all I did was stuff a change of jeans, some shorts, my swimsuit, and all the clean T-shirts and underwear I could find into a bag—then sat down and read Hannah Holmes's book about dust: desert dust, space dust, household dust, smoke, chemical aerosols, pollen, pocket lint, you name it, because *dust* was one of the only three words I had that connected me to Jack's current whereabouts and his reason for being there. The first—*Florida*—I would soon experience firsthand, and the second—*killer*—I did not yet wish to consider.

I made a list of everything and anything that can be considered dust or that is ever referred to as dust, everything Holmes had put in her book and a few ideas and associations of my own. I developed quite an affection for the topic. *The Secret Life of Dust* read like greased lightning and even had a section on the USGS's African dust project in St. Petersburg. Even as slow a reader as I am, I had gobbled up about two-thirds of it by bedtime. Having still not heard from Jack, I was wired and could not sleep, so I turned the light back on and read further. I was amazed at how much threaded in and out of the topic, doubled back, and headed right through it again.

For instance, did you know that the entire universe is made of dust? Space dust is the basic interstellar particle, the building block between raw atoms and the stars and planets they gang up to become. Since the launching of the Hubble Space Telescope, the shroud of obscurity has been lifted from the star-birth business, revealing clouds of swirling dust that act as giant wombs.

Or here's a little tidbit: The human lung breathes in dust, but anything smaller than ten microns (about half a hair's width) gets stuck, and that means that anything really little, like the finest desert dust that is blown across oceans, or the dried residue of the fine spray from the pesticide trucks that squirt the local fruit orchards, stays in your lungs. Imagine the health effects of that.

Killer dust. The thought did not help me sleep. Could dust's threat to human health in fact have something to do with Jack's presence in Florida? If so, what? I lay on my back, staring at the ceiling, and conjured scenarios that matched the various types of dust with death and Florida. Pesticides were one thing, but of course drugs were another. What of the traffic in cocaine that visited Florida's shores? Wasn't dust another nickname for cocaine? Or was that snow?

It was late when I finally fell asleep.

Faye phoned bright and early the next morning and told me to come to dinner that evening to discuss our plans. I said yes, made myself some breakfast, and settled in to read *Germs: Biological Weapons and America's Secret War*. I quickly lost my appetite.

It was a work of investigative journalism. I quickly garnered some important points: First and foremost, the United States was not prepared to deal with attack by biological weapons. No country was. Worse yet, the symptoms of an attack would be hard to distinguish from a natural epidemic, so the germs could be spread far and wide before anyone became the wiser. A stunning, yet little known, example was the 1984 attack by insiders at the Rajneesh religious commune in Oregon on residents of the surrounding community. Starter germs of *Salmonella typhimurium* (a form of food poisoning) had been purchased parcel post from the

American Type Culture Collection, a private sector germ bank located on the East Coast, and nurtured into multiplication by a bizarre team of megalomaniacs who wanted to sway the outcome of a local election by limiting the number of opposing citizens that could leave their bathrooms long enough to struggle into the voting booth. Nearly 1,000 people were sickened when Rajneeshee operatives disbursed their nasty dose on public salad bars, and an Oregonian record of 751 cases of *Salmonella typhimurium* were confirmed.

Second, I learned that anthrax—a deadly bacillus originally found in soils but cultivated by United States government research into extraordinary virulent, easily transportable spores with the shelf life of bricks—had been produced in unbelievable quantities both here and abroad, and whole tank-car-sized loads of it were missing and unaccounted for.

Third, I read that the fate and popularity of such projects varied with the whims and opinions of whatever presidential administration was in office. As with most weapons, they were developed whether the unknowing public wanted them or not.

Needless to say, such reading matter did nothing to calm my concerns about where Jack had gone and what he was doing.

By the time I showed up for dinner at Faye and Tom's, it was clear that Tom was now worried about Jack, too. When he saw me coming up the walk, he got out of his chair and started pacing. Faye stood where he couldn't see her and made a gesture like she was talking on a telephone and pointed at Tom, mouthing the words, "I think he heard from Jack."

So I said, "Tom, have you heard from Jack?"

"No," he said, and left the room until dinner was served.

Over some truly delicious pork chops sautéed with rosemary, sage, and caramelized onions and topped with sour cream, Faye dropped her bomb. "Tom, Em and I are planning to run down to St. Petersburg, and visit my aunt."

Tom froze with his fork halfway to his face. "St. Petersburg, Florida?"

"Yes. The one in Russia doesn't have as nice a pilot's lounge."

Tom closed his eyes and put the fork back down. When he spoke, his voice was rough with feeling. "Any way I can talk you out of this?"

I said, "No."

He lifted one hand and ran it back through his salt-and-pepper crew cut. The breath hissed out of him like a deflating tire.

I looked at Faye, knowing she wasn't going to like my next move. I said, "Tom, I'd like it if you came along. You know where Jack is and what he's doing and—"

"No, in fact I do not," he interjected.

"You know he's in Florida."

"No. I know he *went* to Florida. I have no idea where he went next, or even if he got there."

"Bull. You heard from him today."

"I heard from his mother." From the look on his face, this was not a good thing.

My voice rose half an octave. "But you know what he's doing?"

Tom stared at his pork chops. He said, "Em, I think it's best if we both stay out of this."

"Why?"

"Because . . . oh hell, Em! Jack went to Florida on personal business."

"He's not on assignment?"

"No."

"Vacation?"

"No."

Mark it up to lack of sleep or malingering insecurity, but I lost control and started shouting. "Quit being so coy! I give you ten seconds to start dishing up information, or I'm going to head on down there without you and find Jack on my own. And you can damn well live with it if I get myself in trouble out of ignorance you could easily dispel, you hopeless shithead!"

Tom looked up, startled. "Christ, you really do love this guy."

"Tom, you are moving me to thoughts of—"

Very softly he said, "Em, all he told me was that he was going down there to find someone. He didn't give me a name, or his exact destination. I really know precious little."

"What kind of person? A man? A . . . a woman?"

"I am not going to tell you any more, precisely because it is not your business, and because for your own safety Jack would not want you involved."

"But his mother phoned you. What does that mean?"

"Leah is . . . hell, I ought to put you on the phone to her. She'd set you straight. There's a woman who knows how to stay out of trouble!"

"What do you mean?"

Tom let out a deep growl. "I should not have said that. The fact that she intimidates *me* does not mean *you* have the brains to back off. Listen, Em, you've got to stay out of this and let Jack do his job. Besides, he's a smart man, and when he wants to keep something under his hat, he's very good at doing exactly that." Under his breath, he added, "His mother taught him well."

"Maybe I *should* talk to his mother. What's her number?"

Tom shook his head. "Stop! Jack told me nothing of any substance that would help you find him, and if you value your relationship with him, I—as your friend—urge you to stay out of this."

My mouth flapped open and shut a few times. "Well, what about this 'killer dust' business? Doesn't that tell you something? I mean, what kind of dust? Drugs? Anthrax?"

Tom threw down his fork and grabbed my wrist. "Anthrax? Where'd you get that idea?"

I froze. Tom was gripping my arm hard. I had hit a nerve. Jarred and confused, I threw out the few connections that had occurred to me during the night. "Florida. Dust. Killing. That's anthrax. It's a spore, or a bacillus or something, but it's deadly. And you FBI guys have been trying to find the guy who put it in the letters and killed that guy down there in Florida. And the letters that came through the post office up in New Jersey, and the Senate building. So I figured Jack must be assigned to something so deep that even Tanya at the office wouldn't know about it. You keep me guessing, Tom, and I'm going to do just that: guess."

Tom opened his hand and let go of me. I could see that it was taking conscious intent on his part to calm down. All he said in reply was, "Jack's been vaccinated. So have I, and so have you, Faye. But not you, Em."

Faye threw her hands up. "So *that* was the inoculation you insisted I have. Thanks for telling me!"

"I didn't want to worry you."

Quick, before they got into another tiff, I said, "Tom, can we go see Jack's mother?"

"He didn't go to his mother's. She hadn't—no, Em, let's stay on the straight and narrow here. There are plenty of airports in Florida: Orlando, Tampa, Fort Lauderdale, Miami. . . ." He looked back and forth between Faye and me. "You fur balls are really going to go there, aren't you!"

Faye nodded. "I just need a break, Tom. I called my aunt. She'll foot the bill for the fuel, so it really won't hurt our budget. Promise. This business with Jack is nothing, right? He'll surface again any day now, and when he does, Em will be right there to greet him."

Tom looked from her to me and shook his head. "That's nuts."

I turned my palms upward. "Probably. But in the meantime, I've kind of gotten into this dust thing, and my professor has made a contact for me at the USGS there in St. Pete. She's thinking I might get a thesis project out of this."

Tom put a hand on Faye's. Almost tenderly, he said, "Is it really okay if I come along?"

Faye's face sagged. She had wanted a girl's road trip,

not another round of dealing with Tom. But she squeezed his hand and said, "Of course, dear; I would in fact prefer you come."

"Okay then, lay in your flight plan."

"I've done that already. We lift off at four A.M."

Tom gaped. "Four A.M.? *Tomorrow?*"

"It's hurricane season down there. There's one cooking along the southern Caribbean, and even if it's no influence yet, the clouds build all morning and by afternoon, it's the land of the thunderstorm. I want to get down there before the storm gets close to Florida and kicks up winds and rain. And Em has an appointment tomorrow afternoon with some science geek."

I said, "Hurricane? You didn't tell me about no hurricane!"

"Weenie. I'll have you there well ahead of it."

Tom said, "Have you forgotten what Hurricane Andrew did to light aircraft, Faye? As in, even the ones that were *chained down*?"

Faye glared at him, but said, "Em, are you packed?"

"Gear's in the truck, right outside."

Tom groaned. "I suppose you have a kit ready for me, too."

Faye nodded. "I packed your usual field gear: laptop, extra batteries, .45 automatic, extra clips, change of skivvies. I found a pair of swim trunks in your bottom drawer—*très* antique, Dude, get with modern fashion—and check this out!" She got up from the table, opened the coat closet, pulled out a suitcase, and flipped it open. A brilliant red fabric glared from the top, all crazy with parrots and tropical leaves.

Tom's eyes went round with horror. "What," he said, gasping between each few words, "in God's name—is *that?*"

Faye gave him a grin that would have lit Los Angeles. "It's a luau shirt! If you want to blend in with the natives you've got to dress the part. There's a swell golf shirt in here, too. And honey, don't you even worry about the cost. I got them at the Salvation Army!"

– 7 –

The Floridian night was as warm and close as a lover's kiss, but the man at the Holiday Inn at Cocoa Beach was oblivious to outward signals of reality. All that mattered was the chaos inside, and that mattered, mattered, mattered. *She* was the cause of that chaos. He was ready to burst again, big and turbulent as a thundercloud, and it was all her fault. *Her* fault. It didn't matter what anyone said, she was the cause, and she had to pay. It was payback time, and she was going to pay big. BIG. Yes, Lucy had to pay.

Waiting, waiting, waiting . . . why did he have to wait! Damn the delay! He'd been *so close*! .

Dinner at the Denny's on the strip had been the usual shit. The waitress had stuffed the plate in front of him as if he had worms crawling on him. Another one of those bitches. They all knew each other and whispered about him. The greasy hamburger sat like a brick in his stomach. Sleeping was not an option, he knew. He knew. To fix the hell of sleeplessness, it was necessary to fix its cause.

He looked up and down the row of motel rooms, counting lights. Only two people awake. Probably men married to bitches that slammed doors when they saw them coming. He'd show them how to deal with bitches who slammed doors.

Time to go.

He strolled along the walkway in front of the rooms and

across the parking lot, hands in pockets, real casual. He chuckled to himself. Just another tourist out for a stroll. He stretched, for the moment feeling the strength of his long, muscular arms, enjoying the sense of power he felt even thinking about what he was going to do. At the far side of the parking lot, he crossed through a narrow wooden walkway that led to the beach. Once on the beach itself, he shambled slightly as his large frame adjusted to the loose sand. Just another tourist out for a midnight walk.

Except that it was two A.M. No sleep. Fucking Lucy. Time for her to pay. Big-time.

The surf rolled up to a clutter of shells. He strolled onward. North. Toward Cape Canaveral. Toward Kennedy Space Center. He knew he could not walk all the way to it. It was twenty miles along the sand to the shuttle launch pads—fifteen miles as the crow flies—but even if he could get across the inlet of the Banana River, the ground up there on the Cape was rotten with runways and lesser launch pads and crazy hero boys with rifles. But no matter, his little firecracker would jump those miles in a blink. And no one would be looking for his kind of trouble as far south as Cocoa Beach. Fuck the flyboys in their helicopters, making their puny sweeps!

A crooked grin spread across his face as he played the movie in his head: Fire boiling out from under space shuttle *Endeavor* as tons of fuel were ignited to take fucking Lucy skyward. The bitch thought she could get away from him, but she would not, because the next fire would be his as he triggered his little love message. He would trigger it and watch it go. It would blaze through the sky, accelerating to Mach 2 much faster than the shit Lucy was riding, and then, in another glorious moment of fire, his little firecracker would find hers and the big, dumb boosters would explode and that would be that for little Lucy's tour of the heavens. Fuck her. Fuck her. *Fuck* her!

And then she would flutter down like a little moth. . . .

And he would be there to catch her. . . .

Only he would understand what she needed. Only he

would understand what it meant to lose so much. Only he could console her.

And she would turn to him then, and throw herself at his feet in anguish.

She would marry him. Bear his children. It would all be as it was supposed to be.

He checked his digital wristwatch, poking the button that made the date flash green, just as he had done every ten minutes for the past week. He would get the new schedule somehow. Just a few more days to endure until the launch. . . .

Just a few more days to hide in plain sight.

Lucy sat at her desk at Johnson Space Center in Houston trying to look like she was working. That was difficult, because of late she had had trouble sitting with her back to the door, and she didn't dare rearrange the furniture for fear someone might ask her why she had done it. She knew intellectually that there was no way *he* could get this far into the building without someone stopping him and asking for his identification, but rational knowledge did little to calm her limbic system. Security had risen astronomically since the terrorist attacks on New York and Washington, so surely *he* couldn't get through, even with his connections, but still every atom of her skin scanned the air for danger.

She tried to focus her attention on the page in front of her, a briefing sheet for a proposed project she hoped to support during her upcoming space flight. She had done her doctoral dissertation on desert sediments, and had hoped to connect that work with observations from space. In the abstract, the idea had great merit. Her dissertation had taken her out into the dry lands, where she had observed at close range the migration of desert sediments. There she had collected samples of these sands and silts and clays and had made detailed analyses using first her unaided eye, observing millions of grains at a glance. Next, she had moved the

samples closer to her eye and had used her hand lens, which
narrowed the field of view to a few hundred grains mag-
nified by a power of ten. Back at the university, she had
gone even closer, using a petrographic microscope, and finally, she had climbed right down to the world of the single
particle, claiming the fantastic imaging powers of scanning
electron microscopy, where one single grain filled the
screen with astonishing detail, enlarged thousands of diameters. Each step tighter in observation had given her a
factor of ten or one hundred or even a thousand times
greater resolution. Now, she wanted to move the other direction, and take her observation to the level of the gods.

The paper in front of her proposed that she do exactly
that. It was perfect for her, a project already supported by
NASA, tracking the migration of desert dust over the surrounding oceans. Lucy turned back to the first page of the
proposal. The author's name was Miles Guffey. The project
seemed quite interesting, dealing with sediments blown off
Africa into the Caribbean. It suggested, among other things,
that the storm winds carried pathogen-laced dust clear over
the Caribbean reefs, and that the reefs were dying.

Dying. Death. The word took her mind straight back to
the thoughts she was trying to force from her mind. *He
can't possibly make good his threat, can he? No,* she told
herself firmly. *He cannot.* She pressed her fingertips to her
forehead. For perhaps the thousandth time, she reminded
herself, *He's a little boy in the body of a man. Boys say
'kill' all the time. It means nothing. He's crazy. He only
wants to play mind games. He can't really stop me. And
I've taken care of all that.*

But still, the whirl of worry spiraled inward, making her
almost dizzy.

A sudden sound behind her made her jump, but she managed to restrict the motion to her forearms and hands. She
turned quickly in her chair.

Len Schwartz stood in the doorway. "You okay?" he
asked.

"Yes, of course. Fine. What's up?" She gave him her

best smile, her warm, "meet the public" smile, even though he was another scientist like herself, a member of her crew, after all their training almost an extension of her own brain and body.

He raised his eyebrows in further question, but he said, "I just came by to see if you wanted to join me for lunch. Got to keep the calories up, with all that extra training you've been doing."

"I already ate," she lied. Lately the idea of food had begun to make her nauseated.

Len stepped inside her office and lowered his voice. "Everything okay, Lucy?"

"Yes," she said again, too quickly this time. "Sure. Why?"

Len folded his arms across his chest.

Lucy read his body posture. A show of shoulders and biceps, chest shielded. *Meant to appear strong but subtly defensive,* she decided.

He said, "Come on, you can tell me."

"Tell you what?" Lucy fought an urge to run her hands over her face. *Oh God, does it show? Have I lost weight? Do I look thin, or worn? Has the lost sleep etched my face?*

He said, "You just seem kind of tense. The launch delay has been tough on all of us, but it seems like it's gotten to you the worst. Please excuse me if I'm being too blunt."

You're not being blunt, you're being self-preserving, Lucy thought, with brutality aimed as sharply at herself as at him. *You're going up into space, where your ass is on the line every second, and you don't want to go with someone who can't hold up her end of the job.* Even as she made this analysis, Lucy's mind went into high-speed forward gear, searching for the appropriate response to Len's question. She knew that, as a scientist, he was as highly observant and analytical as she was, so she couldn't just bullshit him as she would the fighter jocks on the crew. *Who would have been too insensitive to ask me the question in the first place,* she thought acerbically. She rubbed at the bridge of her nose, buying herself time. In the next three seconds, she considered denial, misdirection, and outright deceit, and then ran a quick risk analysis to compare these options. That done, she realized that none of these solutions appealed to her, as none would work on Len. Instead, she cobbled up option number four, simply agreeing with him. She smiled. "Well, Len, I guess no one is as observant as you are. I suppose you're right, I'm so gung-ho that if the weather keeps us waiting much longer, I'm going to blast into space without a ship." She quit rubbing her nose and watched his reaction. He was still just observing her. "Sweet of you to notice," she added, hoping to engage his masculinity and thereby befuddle his intellect.

Len just stood there. Didn't blink.

Lucy said, "What do you need, Len?"

Len shifted his weight to one foot.

Typical male, she noted. *Bowels turn to mush the instant you mention anything as touchy-feely as needs. Well, best not to play that card too strongly, or I breach the team's sense of trust. Can't risk that. But why is he just standing there? Is he hoping to see me crack? Wait, that's paranoid! Len's a good guy. He's only trying to help! But he doesn't know I need help, does he?* And she quickly reminded herself, *I don't need help!*

Lucy stood up from her desk in an attempt to focus her mind on present circumstances: her office, deep inside stringent security perimeters; a crew member, her colleague of many years and a proven team player; the comfort of a casual pair of slacks and good shoes. Once up, she had to act. "What the hell," she said, managing to sound almost bored. "A little dessert can't hurt. Lead on. We'll get some chow and then it'll be time for more drills."

She took one last glance at her desk, checking to make certain that she had left nothing in sight that would betray her trouble. Her eyes swept the phone to make certain that she had left no messages on it, even though *he* had (unfortunately or not?) never been so stupid as to leave one there (but still she worried: *Is my phone being monitored? Might someone from security listen in one day and hear the veiled threats, the edge of madness in his voice?*) She checked her desktop to make certain that she had left no evidence of the work she was doing to document his movements. *No, that list is at home, well hidden,* she assured herself. She opened a desk drawer and pulled out her purse, automatically weighing it to make certain that nothing had been put into it since she had seen and lifted it last.

Len led the way out through the maze of corridors, past security, and into the parking lot. Here Lucy's eyes began their scan, checking each place—each tree, each minivan— behind which *he* might be hiding. Managing to make it sound casual, she said, "Oops! Forgot my keys. Can we take your car?"

"Sure. Right over here."

The knots in Lucy's shoulders relaxed just a little. She had seen no sign of him. She hadn't expected to, because if he had been telling her the truth during last night's fuck- with-Lucy's-head-so-she-can't-go-to-sleep call, he was in Florida. Waiting for her big debut, he had told her—or told her answering machine, because she never answered the phone anymore without first screening the call—but still, it was best to ride in someone else's car, just in case he had slipped in on an early flight and done something that would show, like the slashed tires that had greeted her ten morn- ings prior when she left her house. How had he gotten inside her garage without being noticed?

Lucy blinked, trying to escape this negative fantasy that kept cropping up in her brain. She had analyzed the data a thousand times, and each time had arrived back at the same explanation for the telephone calls, the slashed tires, the little clues he left around her house so she'd know he was watching while she tried to sleep: He would not hurt her, not physically, because more than anything he wanted her alive and suffering. Domination, that was the game. Extor- tion. Extortion of control. *He just wants to scare me, put me on edge. Steal my sleep. Get me kicked out of the as- tronaut corps so I'll need him, of all things. Need him, of all people.* Forgetting where she was, and who she was with, Lucy snorted.

Len glanced sideways at her. "Something funny?" he inquired.

Lucy felt the blood drain from her face. "Just a joke."

"Let me in on it."

"Ah—" Her mind raced, searching for some tidbit to fill her lapse. "A friend told me about all those pervert priests."

Len nodded. "Give it here."

"Abstinence makes the church grow fondlers."

He laughed in a pro-forma fashion, a quick *ha-ha.* "Good one. So what's got sweet Lucy telling dirty jokes all of a sudden?"

Lucy fought an urge to whirl around at Len and start shouting at him. Give him a good dose of her pent-up rage, really hand it to him. But then she'd have to make a new excuse. She could blame her nerves on PMS, a total laugh, as before these recent "events" she'd never had it. Or at least, not like she was having it now. But blaming her behavior on female hormones was about the last thing she could do. That, too, would make her seem weak. Instead, she raised a hand, mechanically balled it into a fist, and punched Len on the arm. "Just raising our level of intimacy, crewmate. Gonna be tight quarters up there, remember?"

They reached Len's classic Corvette. After they had gotten in and left the compound for the nearest highway, he said, "All right, now that we're for sure and certain alone, Lucy, I'm going to give it to you straight. You look tense to me, and I can't help but think there's something seriously wrong." As she stiffened, he held up a hand. "No, don't try to stop me. I know you're a very private person, but I'm going uphill with you in just a few days, and space is not a place for secrets. We've trained as a team and if you have a problem, I have a problem, and we address it as a team. So please—give! Because if you won't talk to me, I'll figure you've got the heebie-jeebies about the flight."

At Len's words, Lucy felt the weight of five gravities.

For a moment she suffered near vertigo, as if she were going through the windshield of the car. If her secret came out—if NASA knew that there was a man out there stalking her—they'd scrub her from the roster, and it would be permanent. Her judgment would be drawn into question. *Even I doubt my own mind these days,* she thought bitterly. *After all, I was stupid enough to accept a date with that monster!*

But instead she groaned, and stretched idly, letting her head fall backward and her arms flop at her sides. "No. Len, trust me, I want to be on that flight so badly I'd go without a pressure suit. Nervousness about the mission is about the farthest thing from my mind. I have been wanting to take that ride uphill every moment of every day since I was eight years old and watched Neil Armstrong step down onto the moon. Jesus, Len, I am type-rated in jet aircraft. I'm the best in the crew at spin training and—"

"No one doubts you, Lucy."

I do! I doubt my sanity every night as I think up ways to get away from that son of a bitch! Images of the fortresses she had dreamed up clamped down on her mind. The underground tunnel with trip wires and motion detectors describing a thousand-yard perimeter around its opening. And even that fantasy had not felt safe enough, because she knew she would need air to breath and water to drink, and there was no way to ensure that he could not suffocate her or poison the water.

Why is this upsetting me so much? she had asked herself for the thousandth time. *He's never gotten closer than shitty little pranks like slashing my tires and cutting the power to the house. He's never laid a hand on me . . . but I managed to slam the door that time he was hiding outside. I've grown radar on each square inch of my skin, and could feel him waiting there. What did he have in mind?* But to Len, Lucy said, "You're so sweet to worry, but it's just a little thing about . . ." Inspiration struck, deeply entwined with irony and the heat of fantasy. "About an old boyfriend. He died. I guess it's really hit me hard." Then, to give her story the ballast of verisimilitude, she said, "I chose career over marriage, Len. But some days, I have my regrets."

Len let the situation lapse, but Lucy found her last words cutting deep into her heart.

– 8 –

Faye piloted us eastward from Utah and over the Rocky Mountains, down across the open plains of Colorado and Oklahoma into Arkansas, where she stopped to refuel at a place called Arkadelphia because she liked the name. As we skimmed at 20,000 feet over the murky green states where magnolias and something slightly ominous called kudzu are fabled to grow, the horizon evolved from a sharp line to a bleary smudge even though the sky was still cloudless. I was in the catbird's seat, namely the copilot's position to the right of Faye. Tom was, as usual, using the flight to catch a rare nap in one of the backseats. Life was good.

For a long time I watched the marks of human civilization snake and jig through the surface effects of geology, but by-and-by I looked up ahead and noticed a wide, ragged arc where the darkness of the ground turned to a shiny steel blue.

Faye's voice came through the headphones. "What's up?" she asked. "You've gone rigid."

I pointed sheepishly through the windshield. "What's that up ahead?"

Faye took a look, trying to divine what feature had caught my attention.

"Well, just to our right is Lake Pontchartrain. That's New Orleans to the south, and beyond that, your Mississippi delta."

"Then, um, may I discern from this that we are about to fly out over a, er, body of water?"

"Why, yes, Em, and that body of water would be called the Gulf of Mexico."

"But why?"

"Why would it be called the Gulf of Mexico?"

"No, why are we going to fly over it?"

"Uh, because it's between us and where we're going?"

"Uh, very nice, but isn't there a better route?"

"Uh, such as?"

"Such as, why not follow the coastline?"

Faye cocked her head to one side and evaluated me. "No. We're headed southeast on a nice, normal, great-circle route between Salt Lake City and St. Petersburg. And as you can see, St. Petersburg happens to be halfway down a peninsula that is called Florida." She unfolded her chart, which showed that great arm of land cranking south at almost a right angle to the east-west trend of the coast that clips across east of Louisiana through Mississippi, Alabama, and the Florida panhandle. "Do I, on my part, discern that you perhaps have a problem with that?"

"Well, the horizon just goes to a blur. Isn't it safer to keep terra firma underneath us?"

Faye blinked. "No. See those funny white clouds over there to the east? They sit over the land. As you can see, the air over the water is clear. Much, much more stable air. I was quite sure you would prefer a smooth ride to a bumpy one. I know I do. End of subject, or is there something else you need to tell me?"

"Um, yes, I would prefer the bumpy ride."

"Why?"

"Well, because that's water out there."

"And you have a problem with water?"

A whiff of panic made me begin to babble. "Yes. Back home in Wyoming, water is a rare thing. If one learns to swim, it is in a stock tank, because a river is something barely deep enough to wet one's ankles, except during the spring runoff, when one is better advised to stay out of it due to such matters as the hydraulic might of a river in full flood. Mountain creeks are likewise decidedly hazardous, although a great thing to stand beside with a fly rod. And most important of all, ranch children such as I was are warned at pain of excommunication from the tribe to stay the hell out of irrigation ditches; case very sadly in point, my brother drowned in one when we were kids."

"Oh. Sorry. I forgot. But Em, you swim beautifully. I've seen you do it."

"Yes. In swimming pools. I learned to swim in prep school, because great woe betides any adolescent who fails to accomplish certain assigned tasks in front of her peers. I managed to sufficiently compartmentalize my paranoia to construct a special case in my aquatic pantheon for water that is contained within four concrete walls and rimmed with tiling and nice little numbers that do not exceed the height of my chin. The deep end of the pool is decidedly not for me. So need I say, oceans are not my thing. I am a child of the land, and the more arid, the better. Which was why I had agreed to even *think* about doing a Master's thesis on African dust. May I at least close my eyes?"

Faye took both her hands off the control wheel to make a *who, me?* gesture. "Em, I'm sorry. I didn't know you had a problem with this kind of thing."

"Well, I do. I've tried to get over this, but it hasn't worked."

"It would cost a couple hundred dollars extra just in fuel to take this thing the long way around, and you'd still have water on one side of the plane. We'd also have to land again to refuel to accomplish the extra distance, and that would take us low over the water twice instead of just once."

"Forget I ever spoke." I squeezed my eyes shut.

"I'd offer you a Valium, but you're my emergency backup."

I popped my eyes open at her. "You're carrying drugs on this thing? Aren't you afraid the *federales* might confiscate your airplane when we pass customs in Florida?"

Faye laughed. "Florida is not a foreign country, dear heart."

"They have kudzu there. That's foreign enough for me."

"Em, have you ever been out of the United States?"

"I saw a bit of Canada once from a mountain peak in Montana."

"But you have been east of the Mississippi before, haven't you?"

"I spent two miserable years in a Massachusetts prep school. My maternal grandmother lived in Boston."

Faye slapped the control wheel. "Man! I've been on all continents except Antarctica! This is amazing! You're— you're like some kind of living fossil or something!"

"I prefer the term 'autochthonous.' "

"What the hell does that mean?"

"Formed in place. It is a perfectly good adjective used to describe rocks 'that have been moved comparatively little from their original site of formation, although they may have been intensely folded or faulted,' if I accurately recall the wording."

"In whose dictionary?"

"*The Dictionary of Geological Terms.* Don't you have one, my dear?"

"No good library is complete without one, I am sure."

"Just so. You, by contrast to me, are allochthonous, meaning moved from your original place."

"What a relief."

"Pleased to be of service."

"I was so afraid I might be as bent as you are."

"Oh, no, much worse. Allochthons show the wear and tear of transit. They're full of overthrusting, recumbent folding, and sometimes even . . . drum roll here . . . *gravity sliding.*"

"Well, I knew life was a downhill ride, but . . ."

"Just fly the plane. But what about those clouds to the south of us? Are we going to run into weather or something?"

Faye shrugged. "Yeah, there's some weather building.

It's hurricane season, and there are several storms bowling across from Africa. One of them is hanging right on the edge of becoming a full-blown hurricane. That's part of why I wanted to get down here so quickly, get in between the blows. I'm instrument rated, but I prefer to fly when I can see where I'm going."

"Well, I'll take comfort in that, anyway. It looks like a squall line to me."

"You nervous Nellie. Yeah, well, you're right actually; NASA delayed this month's shuttle launch because of all this mess. But see? I'm threading us in right between the fronts, pretty as you please."

"Oh, that really gives me confidence. NASA won't fly but you will."

Faye laughed. "Flying a turbo jet twin at 20,000 feet is a lot different from heaving a rocket into space, Em. They require almost placid skies, *and* they have to have clear weather at their emergency landing strip over in Spain in case they have to abort before they get into orbit. This is an airplane, built for dodging other aircraft. The shuttle is an overblown kite made of bricks. An entirely different picture, I promise you."

"Yeah. Promise me," I said. "Promise me all the way back onto dry ground, okay?"

She grinned. "Done."

And so we proceeded. I stared up at the sky and hummed an old cowboy lullaby until the clouds near the land soaked us up like a giant cotton wad. We swam blind through the murk for a while, then fell out the bottom of it and skimmed in over a ragged, marshy coastline dotted with little swampy islands ("They call them 'keys,' " Faye told me) and lined up on St. Petersburg–Clearwater International Airport. Assured that we were over land, I looked down as we descended, and spotted increasing numbers of golf courses and larger and larger houses, their red tile roofs baking in the patches of sun that cooked down between the tall, wooly clouds. The impacts of human life came into focus and revealed finer and finer detail as we swept down to the pavement and landed. Faye taxied the plane over to the general aviation building and gave the guy with the paddles the wink. He gave her a grin, because she is one dishy babe. You can imagine how he dropped his jaw when she popped the door and stood up on the wing and proudly swung her pregnancy into his face. It was a gag she had begun exploiting to the max.

My enjoyment of her little joke was lost in my experience of the first hit of Floridian air, which descended through Faye's open door like a hot, humid fist. It must have been close to a hundred degrees outside that plane, and the amount of water in the air teetered at the ragged edge between raining and not. It all but pushed me back into my seat. I glanced at Tom. It was hitting him, too. His eyelids fluttered, and he tugged at his collar.

Faye arched her back in delight. "Doesn't this feel great?" she crowed. "It's like a 10-million-passenger steam bath!"

Faye stepped down from the wing and gave the ground-crew fellow a friendly pat on the back, just close enough to his buns to give him the idea she'd noticed and just high enough to keep her out of jail if he didn't like it.

Tom rolled his eyes, and he and I schlepped the bags onto the baking tarmac and tried to straighten up in the heat. We were just beginning to stooge around and try to figure out what we were supposed to do next when a really strange elder woman trotted out of the building and hailed us.

"Whoo-hoo! You must be *Tom*," she crooned, throwing a well-muscled arm around his neck. She wore dark glasses like something out of the 1950s and a sundress that showed off her leathery tan, and the contrast between her bright red lipstick and brilliant white teeth was dazzling. Maintaining the half Nelson she had thrown on Tom, she dragged him over to Faye, patted her belly with the other hand, and leaned forward for a puckery smooch. "Faye, sweetie, it is so extraordinarily *good* to see you!"

Faye gave her a very affectionate hug. "Tom Latimer,

Em Hansen, I present my aunt, Nancy Wallace! Ain't she
the coolest?"

Tom sagged even further. "Charmed," he said.

I'm afraid I said nothing at all.

Nancy shucked Tom and headed off toward the terminal
with Faye. "The car's right here. General aviation is *so*
civilized. This young man will get the bags, and we'll be
off. Don't want to dally in the heat, do we? You might pop
that baby out right here in front of God and everyone. So
how was your flight? You must tell me *all* about it!"

Faye said, "Em here needs to pay a call on some dude
at the USGS. It's down near the Dali museum or something. Can we drop her off there and then get settled? We
can catch up and get a swim in, and then . . ." About there
their voices faded into the distance.

I turned to Tom.

He shrugged and mopped his brow, all in one wilting
motion. "Welcome to Florida," he said.

We drove south into St. Petersburg. My impression-
gathering equipment was on full alert, taking in the towering, layered cloudscapes, the sultry older houses built
wide and open to breathe with the breezes, the astonishing
arrays and varieties of rich green foliage that hung out brash
and tropical at every turn. Pedestrians strolled the sidewalks
in shorts and tank tops; comely girls and some older women
who should have known better wore tight, skimpy blouses
and dresses that maximized all curves. I gawked in amazement. There was something subtly or not-so-subtly more
sexual about this display than I was used to seeing in Utah.
I rode in a state of refrigerated automotive separation, both
stimulated and lulled by the display.

The USGS occupied a two-story, Art Deco, brick building that had once been a Studebaker salesroom and was
now externally ossified and internally renovated by dint of
having been placed on some sort of historical register. I
thought, *Just perfect: Don't know what to do with a bunch*

of rock heads? Think they're sort of miscellaneous, unimportant, or otherwise underfoot? Jam them into a space built to sell cars. All in one, you stack 'em in a warehouse and resolve the problem of what to do with that building the society ma'ams wouldn't let you tear down.

In fact, it was a very nice building, a lot snazzier than most places geologists get stacked. When I dodged from Nancy's air-conditioned car through twenty feet of heat and humidity to the air-conditioned building, I found myself in a two-story foyer with hallways leading out in two directions and a modern steel staircase rising up to a balcony. The walls were covered with maps and full-color displays of technical research projects.

There were a lot of people standing about in the foyer, which was unusual. Geologists do not like to stand around in groups. It offends their sense of individuality and makes them nervous. They are, however, inveterate observers, so many of them turned and looked at me.

I, in turn, looked at them. Flummoxed to find myself the center of attention, I quickly turned to look at the receptionist, who sat facing me at a desk with her eyebrows raised in qualified greeting. "Are you with the press or the police?" she inquired.

Without thinking, I said, "FBI." I was making a joke. Sort of.

The woman rose from her desk, gestured for me to follow, and headed down the hallway to my right. "Your meeting is right this way," she said, leading me into a large room full of chairs arrayed in rows. "The press conference will be in here also, as soon as you all are done."

Being an adventuresome soul, I trotted right into that room. The good girl inside me—you know, the one who's usually locked up in a cage with a rag stuffed in her mouth—wanted to explain to the receptionist that I had been kidding, but it was obvious that something was up, and I figured that as long as they didn't mind giving me a leg up on finding out exactly what that was, I wasn't going to make things difficult for them by getting particular about who I was and why I was there. Besides, my schedule with Miles Guffey, the geologist Molly Chang knew, was casual at best, a sort of "give me a holler when you arrive" kind of arrangement, so I reasoned that I could check out this action and then go talk about dust. Okay, so I'm an old fire horse and someone rang the bell; my game plan was business first and ask forgiveness later.

So I wandered into the room. Inside I found chairs for about one hundred people, but nobody sitting in them. There were four men standing over to one side of the room, communing by a coffee urn. Only one was in uniform, and he looked as clueless as I felt. He was young and had bad skin. One of the other men had the look of a plainclothes cop. He was conservatively dressed, impatient, and imbued with a certain aura of crafty intelligence. The third man was short and cheaply dressed and looked like he was only along for the ride. The fourth was the oldest among them by probably twenty years, judging by his great swath of silver hair and his sun-battered skin. He was wiry in build and made a lot of quick, foxlike movements. He was dressed in white linen slacks and a dark blue silk shirt. He was the first to notice my arrival, his lively eyes riveting on me with a look of interest and welcome. "And who do we have here?" he asked with a Southern twang.

I looked over my shoulder to see if someone was behind me. Finding no one, I said my name.

"Emily! Fantastic timing! Say, fellows, this is just the person you need to help you with this. Emily here is known all over the place for the work she's done with police and FBI. She's what you call a forensic geologist, deals with murders and things. A real sleuth. She can sniff the jack of spades out of a deck of cards with a blindfold on. Hey, welcome, Emily. Come right on in. Can I get you some coffee?"

I stuck out my hand and shook his. "I'm sorry," I said. "I didn't get your name."

"Miles Guffey at your service. My, but you couldn't have come at a better time. Did y'all hear what happened?"

Several possible replies zapped through my brain, such as *You can't be a geologist; you look like a nightclub performer!* but I said, "Why don't you give me an update?"

Guffey's eyes darted back and forth between me and the other men. "First let me introduce you to these fellers. This here is Detective James and this one's Officer Petry, both with the local constabulary. This other guy works here. Well, I was explaining to these fellers when you walked up that our microbiologist has gone missing. It's a terrible thing. Terrible." His face grew grave. "Last seen on a cruise ship where he was trying to get some samples for our dust project." To the detective he said, "Now you tell me how's a feller just go and disappear off a 500-foot ocean liner a hundred miles from the nearest shore? You don't just fall off'n those things. There's got to be foul play, fellers, I feel it in my bones!"

Detective James cleared his throat. "Now, Dr. Guffey, I know this is upsetting, but I'm sure there's some other explanation to cover the facts. You're saying no one that was on board knows exactly when he was last seen; in fact, no one was even certain he was gone until the ship pulled into port in Barbados the next day. He could have gotten off without telling anyone, or—"

Guffey jumped on that. "I'm telling you, this is murder! I should have heard from him that evening before they reached port, so he was gone by then. He was collecting samples for a very sensitive project. It's a matter of homeland security. It's . . ."

Just then, several more people came into the room led by a petite, middle-aged woman in a fuchsia blazer. She moved with the force and precision of a drill sergeant.

The detective took advantage of the moment to cut Dr. Guffey off. "Here's your press corps. Listen, I'm sure this is upsetting for you, and I understand your concern, but there's two things you need in order to make that a crime scene, and one of them is a body." I never got to hear what the other thing was, because he went on quickly with, "And no matter what the case, I'm not your man. If your biologist is dead, he died in a foreign country, or on the high seas, neither of which are my jurisdiction. If he's alive, all you have is a missing person, and that likewise would be managed by the jurisdiction in which he went missing. I suggest you pursue things with the authorities in Barbados. Now, I'm going to get myself out of here before I have to talk to the press about a matter I know nothing about." With that, he left, Officer Petry bobbing along in his wake.

His eyes as bright as an addict trying to spot his source, Guffey scanned the assembling press, the police detective already forgotten. "Thank you for coming," he cried, waving them in as if setting up for a revival meeting. "We got coffee for y'all right here. We'll get started in just a minute."

The woman in the fuchsia blazer was closing now on the lectern at the head of the room. When she reached it, she clicked on the microphone, whipped her hand spasmodically through her glossy black hair, and said, "Okay, I think we can get started. Now, you all know me, I'm Olivia Rodríguez Garcia, the chief scientist here at the St. Petersburg office of the Coastal and Marine Geology Program of the U.S. Geological Survey. As most of you know, one of our colleagues has disappeared while in the line of duty. His name is Calvin Wheat, and he is a microbiologist in the employ of the USGS as contract personnel. He is working on the identification of microbes that we hypothesize to be traveling in the atmospheric dust that is derived from Africa. Dr. Wheat was last seen on board the cruise ship *Caribbean Queen* about ten hours before the ship put into Barbados, where he was scheduled to present a talk at a technical conference that begins in a few days. That is all the information we have on him at this time. Are there any questions?"

A young woman with close-cropped hair raised her pen and started speaking. "Dr. Wheat came to you from the National Institute for Health, is that correct?"

"No. Dr. Wheat holds certification in public health, but

prior to working with us, he was on postdoctoral fellowships in Puerto Rico and here in the U.S."

Another reporter asked, "He was gathering sensitive information. Has this office received any threats that might
be connected with his disappearance?"

"No, none whatsoever. I believe you are referring to Dr.
Guffey's assertions of a possible correlation between intercontinental dust clouds with outbreaks of diseases such as
foot-and-mouth or citrus canker." Here she shot Miles Guffey a look over her half-glasses. "But I assure you, our
mandate is as a government organization that does science.
We are charged with reporting findings but do not create
policy or present unsubstantiated ideas. Next?"

The questioning continued for several more rounds, during which Olivia Rodríguez Garcia volleyed differing arrangements of the same bits of information but added none
that were new. Finally, one of the reporters turned to Miles
Guffey and said, "Miles, you called this press conference.
For all we know, Calvin Wheat is alive and well and sipping rum in Barbados. What makes you think this is murder?"

Guffey's posture went through some interesting adjust-
ments as he strolled up to the podium. His head slid back,
and his spine grew sinuous with the motion of his walk.
When he reached the front, he leaned sideways against the
podium and rested an elbow next to the microphone. In one
smooth gesture that was half charismatic preacher and half
lounge lizard, he had completely upstaged his boss. When
he spoke, his voice was sonorous and almost confidential
in tone. "Friends, what we have here is a situation that
requires attention but isn't getting any. I refer both to the
disappearance of a dear friend and a highly valued colleague, and to the problems of dust-borne particles dam-
aging the health of humans and our coral reefs. We got
folks getting sinus headaches and going to the emergency
rooms with asthma when the wind gets to blowing off Africa. They know all about it down in the islands; that's
where they've been scrubbing that red silt out of their cis-

terns and off their boats for years. Everyone knows that we've seen a die-off of staghorn corals and sea fans throughout the Caribbean, and in one season, about ninety-five percent of *Diadema* sea urchins died, and they're the fellers that keep the algae off what's left of the reef so's it can grow."

A reporter interjected a question. "Don't other researchers theorize that the reef die-off is from sewage outfall from the islands?"

"Folks have all sorts of ideas, but now we got hard data. Garriett Smith up at University of South Carolina has documented that it's a nonmarine fungus killing the sea fans. That means one thing only, that the source of that infection is from the land, and is constantly replenished from the land. Just look at this satellite image."

Here he turned, herding their attention to the screen behind him. He pressed a button and an image appeared, a view from space of the west coast of northern Africa, the broad band of the Sahara Desert a parched brown against the deep blues of surrounding seas. But to the west of it, curling out into the white clouds that bedecked the Atlantic, lay a swirling mass of brown smut that stretched thousands of miles.

"This," he said, "is airborne dust. Our data indicate that it is carrying live pathogens. This is groundbreaking data. Critical to our national welfare. So now, you tell me: Why's a guy who was about to prove beyond any doubt that these diseases are being transported from Africa suddenly find himself missing off the ship from which he was catching his samples?"

Another reporter spoke. "But hasn't dust always blown off Africa?"

Guffey nodded. "Sure. And we need that dust, or some of it. It provides important nutrients to seawater, and it's all we got for soil on some of the islands. But the thing is, there's a whole lot more dust getting launched into the skies than there used to be. There's been a drought going on thirty years now in Africa, and they've drained Lake Chad down to one-tenth its original size. Now it's just a big dust-pan. And that same wind crosses Mali before it gets to the west coast of Africa, and do you know how folks get rid of their garbage there? They burn it. Piles of plastic bags and rubber tires just burning, no scrubbers, nothing. And heaps of camel dung just drying in the sun. That's what we're breathing, folks: burned plastics, camel dung, and way too much mineral dust. And that dust is down below ten microns in size—that's half a human hair in width—and that means you can breath it in, but you can't breathe it out. The human lung's not built to expel such tiny particles. Nasty little cocktail, huh?"

I glanced around the room. The reporters looked respectfully bored. I began to gather the impression that they had heard from Dr. Guffey once or twice before. So I asked a question of my own. "Dr. Guffey, why was Dr. Wheat traveling on a commercial cruise liner to gather his samples?"

Guffey gave me a look that was pure appreciation. "That's a very good question, young lady. And the answer is this: Because we can't get these samples any other way. We simply lack the funding. We're having to scrounge for opportunities to do meaningful science. Calvin's berth on that ship was paid for by the cruise line in exchange for him giving lectures. The USGS gives us no funding to cover this important work, and we can't get it from the Center for Disease Control or the Department of Agriculture. So far, in fact, the only funding we've received is from NASA, and that was barely covering Dr. Wheat's salary."

Slam dunk, I decided. *He's worried about his colleague maybe, but he's a whole lot more worried about where his funding for the next piece of corroboration of his theory is coming from.*

Miles Guffey was happy enough with my little assist that he offered to buy me lunch before driving me over to Aunt Nancy's house. "It's right on my way," he said. "I got to get home now anyway. The pool guy's coming to fix a leak, and my wife is out selling real estate or something. And that way we can have our little chat away from prying ears."

I was only too happy to comply with the idea of eating, having been up flying since I couldn't remember when. We swam through the hot, humid air beyond the building to Guffey's car, which was what I'd have to call unbearably hot, even though the windshield had been armed with a set of telescoping covers. The seats were searingly hot. The car's air-conditioning unit did its best, but was just getting the interior temperature down from scald to broil as we pulled in at our destination.

Chattaway's is an outdoor lunch joint set off from the road and the parking lot by a bulwark of pink claw-foot bathtubs planted with the most enormous philodendrons and trailing plants I'd ever seen. We sat down at a wooden picnic table under a big canvas umbrella and were handed menus by a young thing wearing short shorts and an incredibly tight tank top. I might have thought she was being provocative in interest of grubbing for tips except that she was no less clothed than half of her customers. I flapped the placket of my shirt, quickly realizing that Florida was a place where clothing seemed almost optional.

I turned my attention to my stomach. The menu featured something called grouper, which could be had fried and in a sandwich or batter fried and served with french fries, aka a 'Tony Blair Special.' "Does everything here come fried?" I asked.

"Darlin', you are south of the deep-fry line."

"Oh. What's grouper?"

"It's a kind of fish," my host replied, "but if you haven't never had it, you should come to the house and let me barbecue some for you first."

Okay . . . So I ordered the bacon-cheese Chattaburger, and Guffey had one without the bacon, saying he had to look after his boyish figure. After dispatching the waitress with our orders, Guffey waved at several colleagues who were just wandering out of the open-air bar that surrounded the grill, then turned back to me and opened with, "Molly Chang says you're looking for a thesis project. That right?"

"Possibly. My background is in oil and gas, but I've been around blowing dust before, growing up in Wyoming."

"Oh yeah, you got illite clays that blow clear to the Chesapeake. But I hear you got another trick or two up your sleeve."

"Excuse me?"

"Beyond your oil and gas experience."

The waitress brought us each a giant glass of lemonade, and I used the distraction to collect my thoughts. I considered pouring the lemonade over my head, but instead drained it rather quickly down my throat. Thus more fully hydrated, I began to mind the heat a little less. I said, "You mean the work I've done on crime scenes. Yeah, I was thinking my angle might be to treat the project as just that: a crime scene. The forensic geology of African dust." Having made my pitch, I watched him carefully.

Guffey took a healthy draw on his own lemonade. "I like that. It's got panache. But it looks like we got us two crimes to solve, now don't it?"

I took another swill of lemonade and pondered this. "You got me there. I just rode into town as it were, and you say there's been a fight. What's your evidence? I mean, the part you didn't tell the police or the press."

Guffey nodded. "We been having all kinds of problems with this funding picture," he began. "First off, there's the point-source guys who don't want us to be right, because then they lose *their* funding. Then we got the agribiz guys who don't want people even thinking about what's getting into the food supply. And that crosses right over into the medical field. We got docs saying if you blow the whistle on certain things that's flying around in that dust, you're likely to find yourself in a one-car accident way out in the boonies."

"You mean a Karen Silkwood kind of story."

"Essackly."

"You said at the press conference that the Center for Disease Control isn't interested."

"The CDC won't ante up 'cause they want proof it's a health hazard before they'll add it to their list of woes. And even if we do, they got their rigid parameters about how they go about things, like maybe if we find a big enough red cape to wave at them they'll find a spare bull to give it a charge."

"Got their own funding problems, no doubt."

"Essackly."

"And let me guess: Congress doesn't like it because the source is out of our control. As in, even if we identify the problem, they can't make the Africans quit stacking their camel dung where the wind's going to pick at it."

"Essackly. My, I do see why Molly likes you."

I considered feeling puffed up by the compliment but remembered that I was being worked over by a pro. Molly Chang might or might not have said anything nice about me, but this Miles Guffey was in the business of recruiting free labor. So I did my best to ignore his bait. "I'm looking for something that would give me some good training in forensic work," I said noncommittally.

Guffey cleared his throat. "Oh sure, I can set ch'all up with a project. We got arsenic showing up in cisterns in the Caribbean, and we got to show where that's coming from. That could be a good way in for you. Prove the source terrain for that, maybe. See if you can fingerprint some of the minerals, maybe attach them to mining being done in North Africa. What d'you think?"

I bit into the hamburger that had just arrived. It was succulent. I could see why the USGS gave Chattaway's its business. It offered the perfect fuel for the discerning geologist: cheap, unpretentious, al fresco, yummy, and plenty of it.

I used the time it took me to chew and swallow to decide how I was going to play things now that I knew a little more. I had read up on Miles Guffey's reputation during my brief sortie through the university library, and he was highly respected. He had umpteen-jillion publications and had served at a number of prominent posts within the profession and had taught highly regarded short courses. Judging by his white hair and heavily sun-blasted skin, he was somewhere between sixty-five and seventy, definitely nearing the sunset of his career, at least as a federal employee. But he also had the bearing and crowd-handling technique of a carnival barker. And that, for me, was a red flag. He was skating right to the edge of sensationalism. Did I want my career associated with that?

The answer was no, and yet I was intrigued. So I said, "Tell me more."

Guffey's lips curved almost clownlike around the job of chewing another bite. "Here's a little book y'all oughtta read," he said. He prized a slender trade paperback out of the satchel he'd brought with him from the car and handed it to me ever so casually, facedown and bottom for top. "It might appeal to the feminist in you or something, give you a place to dig in historically."

I didn't like being played as a feminist by a male of the species, but I turned the book over. It was entitled, *The Garden of Their Desires: Desertification and Culture in World History* by Brian Griffith. "Okay," I mumbled. "I'll give it a read. Funny, I didn't find this one in the university library when I was doing my literature search the other day."

"You wouldn't. This is pretty obscure. Most of the literature and data we deal with is pretty far off the beaten path."

"Okay," I said, half delighted to be invited into a small club and half ready to bolt for the tall timber.

"Great," he said. "And for your part, you can tell me more about your work with the FBI."

I decided not to mention Jack, and certainly not his present assignment. "Mostly I've worked with a guy named Tom Latimer, but he's retired from the Bureau now. He married my friend Faye and went into security work."

Guffey chewed assiduously. "Faye. That's Nancy Wallace's niece, who got you down here."

I stopped with my burger half an inch from my lips. "How'd you know that?"

"This be a small town, my friend." Guffey gave me a ha-ha smile. "Okay, my wife was at the veterinarian with our schnauzer this morning and ran into Nancy. She said her niece was coming down from Salt Lake and bringing a friend who was coming to see me. Doesn't take a genius to patch that one together. You know the theorem: There are six and a half billion people in this world, but only 10,000 of them get around, and sooner or later they all know each other. So, did you ladies bring this Tom Latimer feller to Florida with you, too?"

I allowed myself a deep sigh. It didn't take a genius to see where he was going with this one, either.

Accurately reading my hesitation as a guarded yes, Guffey said, "That's neat. So here's what we'll do. Y'all bring him along to the house tonight, and anyone else in your retinue that don't mind a good party. I'll barbecue some grouper, and we can all get acquainted."

My mind chunked up a tiny little squeak of a question that was something like, *What if the person Miles Guffey really wants to get at is Tom Latimer?* I sat there with my mouth hanging open and my hamburger dripping juice down one wrist.

Miles Guffey stared back with a grin so big and sloppy and seemingly innocent that it scared me silly.

The afternoon sky was building from a mixture of soft-edged cumulus clouds to towering black cumulonimbus when Miles Guffey dropped me off at Nancy Wallace's residence. I term her dwelling "a residence" because you don't call something that big a house. She lived in a sprawling mansion, about 4,000 square feet of Spanish Colonial splendor laid out in a lush patch of tropical paradise, all palm trees and philodendrons and other things with enormous leaves that seemed to have been designed by an angel in heat. Her housekeeper answered the door and showed me in, through the house, and out the back into a vast jungle completely enclosed in screening. The structure was two stories high and even the roof was made of screening. Deep in the shade of this jungle I found a kidney-shaped swimming pool, and on the pool deck I found Nancy and Faye, who had donned bathing gear and arranged themselves on chaise lounges, and were sipping iced tea from tall, expensive-looking glasses. "Hello, Em!" Nancy hollered. "How'd it go with your science friends?"

"We might see it on the evening news," I said. "I think there was a TV camera there. Or certainly it will be in the newspaper."

Faye's eyebrows shot up from behind her Ray Bans.

I described the press conference.

"I've seen your Miles Guffey in the news many a time,"

Nancy drawled. "Interesting character. Highly respected around here. He has a decent boat, and his wife plays bridge very well when she's not out running up the price of real estate." She paused ruminantly. "But I've often wondered whether the cheese might have slid a little ways off his cracker."

Faye snorted.

I was about to ask Nancy to enlarge on that metaphor when I realized that Faye was smiling at me a little more broadly than the joke warranted. Something was up. "What?" I asked.

Her smile went to full toothiness. About then I began to notice voices coming from the guesthouse that joined the far end of the screened enclosure. The front door to it lay some distance away, past the far edge of the pool. Closed windows and the drone of an air conditioner muffled the voices. One voice was Tom's. He was shouting at someone, but I couldn't make out his words. He went quiet for a moment, during which time I heard snatches of a second voice, from which I deduced that Tom was not alone in there expressing rage into a telephone. I had about time enough to start wondering who in St. Petersburg (apart from me and Faye) Tom would shout at when he began bellowing. This time I heard each word quite distinctly. He roared, "Jack, you are one stupid son of a bitch!"

My jaw dropped.

"Yup," Faye announced. "He's here!"

I charged off toward the guesthouse, barely skirting the edge of the pool in my haste. My mind bounced like a puppy. *Jack's here? Oh, this is wonderful! We can go to the beach together, or the Everglades, or—*About there, I realized that Jack was now yelling, too.

"I *can't*!" he shouted.

"You *have* to report this!" Tom hollered back. "You *have* to!"

"Then I'd have nothing!" Jack roared. As I got close enough to the door to put an ear to it, I heard him say, his voice tightly drawn back down to a normal level, "I make a grab for it and the whole deal comes apart."

Tom said, "Whole deal? What do you mean, 'whole deal?' You got some romantic notion about all this, but let me tell you, this thing's a whole lot bigger than your little fantasies can handle."

There was silence for a while, then Jack said, "I was *this close*! We call in the posse and you *know* what's going to happen. They'll jump all over this and we've got nothing. The guy takes off and we don't know where he got it or if there's another, or ten, or a hundred of the damned things. That's *it*. *No* second chances."

Tom bellowed, "You're way off the mark! You come down off your high horse and do the right thing!" Then, more pleadingly, he added, "What about the rest of the program?"

There was silence for a while, or if Jack said anything, I couldn't hear it. Then I heard Tom speak again. "I know you've got to protect your family. But you've got a fine woman waiting for you, Jack. You're worrying her, and I'd say she has good reason this time. If she catches wind of this . . . well, I wouldn't blame her a bit if she took a walk. You want that? You got to set your priorities, Jack. Let the other one go."

My breath caught in my throat. *The other one?*

Jack said, "Em doesn't need to know about this. I can handle it."

"Oh, bull*shit*. Come on, you're throwing your career in the toilet, too, if you go on with this. I called the office before I came down here, and they said you had one week to come back, or it's off with your head this time and that's final. No more of your little leaves of absence. No more, Jack."

I heard Jack say, "This is more important than last time. This is the whole bag of doughnuts."

"No shit."

"You going to help me or not?"

There was a longer silence, and then Tom spoke again. "No. Absolutely not. You've got to stop this kind of shit,

Jack." Then, with almost frantic exasperation, he added, "Be real, Jack. I got a baby coming. I got a wonderful wife. You're the guy throwing your chances in the shitter, not me. And I'm not even giving you a week. You've got forty-eight hours, then I'm blowing the whistle."

I heard a low mumble.

Tom said, so low I could barely hear him, "And you leave a copy of that goddamned map here. Give it to me. I'll stuff it through my copier right now."

I heard the sounds of movement and hurried back toward the pool, hoping that the foliage and narrow blinds on the windows had obscured my presence. I was just settling into a chair and kicking my feet up onto an ottoman when the door opened and Tom came out, carrying a piece of paper that he quickly folded up and shoved into his shirt pocket. "Em!" he growled, when he saw me. "Good. You're here. Get over here! I got a little surprise for you."

I think I managed to conceal my excitement, but my heart was hammering wildly, both with the anticipation of seeing Jack again and with confusion over having heard him raise his voice. Until that moment, I had thought Jack constitutionally incapable of getting flapped, so in the mix of my feelings there was a bit of trepidation. "What's up, Tom?"

Tom pointed in through the doorway. "Get in there and see if you can nail both his feet to the floor," he told me. "You'd be doing him a kindness, trust me on that."

I trotted down the path again and stepped into the refrigerated air of the cottage, all ready to throw myself into my lover's arms, but as I caught the scene inside that room, I stopped cold.

Jack sat with his head hanging. He wasn't looking at me, even though he must have known I was coming, and that in itself scared me. He looked bedraggled and diminished. His wonderfully muscular shoulders were bowed down as if under a tremendous load of failure. His clothes were so soiled and rumpled that he looked like he'd slept in them for several days. And even at a distance of ten feet, my nose told me that in fact he probably had, and without bathing.

Jack is a master of the subtle disguise, a man who can look like someone else just by shifting his posture—forty points higher or lower IQ, for instance, or notches higher or lower on the scale of who's in charge and who's a putz—but this took the cake. This time, the effect was no act. I whispered, "Jack?"

He took a moment to raise his head and look at me, and then only made a flickering of eye contact. There were dark circles under his eyes, and his face was blurred with several days' growth of stubble. He tried to smile. It seemed forced. "Hi, sweetie," he said. His voice came out tired, almost ghostly.

I moved toward him. Raised a hand. Laid it on his head. His hair felt greasy.

"Want to take a shower together?" I inquired, immediately seeing the foolishness of offering sex to a man in his condition.

Jack took my hand and pulled it down to his lips, but seemed to forget to kiss it. "Not now, hon. Sorry."

"Oh. Can I get you anything? A beer? Glass of water?" I felt stupid, like a flight attendant trying to figure out what to serve to a stray yeti that has somehow gotten onto the plane. I cringed. Nowhere in our relationship had I felt moved to servility before.

"Water would be nice," he said hoarsely.

Growing numb, I found my way into the kitchenette at the far end of the L-shaped room, got some water, and brought it back. Jack had not gotten up. Had not hugged me. Had not kissed my lips. I felt that I must have done something wrong, and at the same time knew that I had done nothing at all. Except come to Florida . . .

Jack sipped at the water for a moment and then set the glass down on the terrazzo floor next to him. Without looking at me, he said, "I think I do need a shower, but I think I need to take it alone."

"Okay. I'll . . . just be outside if you need me."

"Right."

I waited a moment longer, hoping he'd stand up and at least kiss me, but he didn't, so I left, closing the door behind me.

I sat back down by the pool and pretended to listen to Faye and Nancy's conversation, which, with my sudden return, became notably stilted. They watched me out of the corners of their eyes. I waited.

About ten minutes later, Jack came out of the cottage wearing the same clothes, but his face was freshly scrubbed and his stubble shaven. His shirt stuck to him in patches where he had put it back on without having fully toweled himself off. He came up to me, took me by the hand, and led me through the main house to the driveway, where he stopped by a forgettable-looking beige car. He leaned on it, and then took my hand and squeezed it. Hard. He still did not look at me. When he began to speak, he stuttered slightly, almost as if he were cold and shivering. "I—I . . . g-got to go again. Sorry. I'm . . . I'm sorry."

"Jack, what in the hell's name is going on?"

"Can't tell you."

"You're scaring me."

He bowed his head. His lower lip stuck forward. "Yeah. Well, I got to go."

About then I began to lose it. "I don't even get a kiss? I mean cripes, fellah, I flew all the way down here to . . ." I trailed off, struggled to pull my thoughts and words together. I took a deep breath. Said, "Sorry. That's not fair. You didn't know I was coming." I squeezed his hand back. "I know you didn't expect me to show up here, and I hope I haven't gone and done something you don't like. But I . . ." *I what? Love you but am so immature I can't put your obvious distress before my own?* "You sure there's nothing I can do to help?"

Jack shook his head. He let go of my hand, opened the trunk of the car, and rummaged around in an open duffel bag for a clean shirt. He peeled off his dirty shirt in preparation for putting it on.

At the sight of his bare chest, the wave of desire swept over me again, almost making me sick with its force. The humid air pressed in around me, adding to the intensity of this instantaneous meltdown.

Perhaps Jack felt me begin to swoon, because as he came back around the car toward the driver's door, he grabbed me into a fierce hug, and kissed me almost violently. Then, just as abruptly, he got into the car, fired the ignition, and drove away. As the car disappeared from sight around a curve between tall rows of palm trees, my heart gave a sickening lurch, as if someone was tugging at it.

His moist scent lingered against my skin.

The wind was picking up, all cool and wet, presaging rain.

A chaos of emotions pulled me in every direction at once, and one panicked edge of my mind asked, *What am I going to do?*

Totally at a loss, I did what any self-respecting woman would have done: I threw back my head to the bleary Floridian sky and screamed bloody murder.

– 10 –

By the time I had pulled myself together and returned to the pool deck, Tom had disappeared. Faye's eyes were round with alertness. Nancy was just stabbing the OFF button on a cordless phone. "That was Miles Guffey," she caroled, overriding the deadly mood that had settled on her pool deck in the time-honored manner of the efficient hostess. "Sweet man; he apologized for not coming in when he dropped you off, but he said he wanted to check with his lovely wife, and she said yes, so he has invited us all over to dinner. He gives terrific parties. My, but I knew it would be fun to have you two down here, but I hadn't counted on this!" Giving me a good looking-over, she added, "We have about two hours to relax first, so maybe you'd like to take a nap."

"Tom go back into the guesthouse?" I inquired.

Faye nodded. She had shifted into another position, and the roundness of her pregnancy bulged over her blue bikini bottom like the full moon rising over a lake. She had gained very little weight with the pregnancy, and her long, smooth legs caught the filtered sun like spun sugar. At that moment, I envied her position—her marriage, the commitment and stability that a coming family represented—like I cannot describe.

I returned to the guesthouse and knocked on the door. "Tom, it's me."

"If you must," he growled.

Inside, I found him pacing back and forth in the small living room.

I said, "I suppose this is one of those times when you're going to keep things from me."

"That is correct."

"That is stupid."

Tom balled his hands into fists. "Shit!"

"That sums things up nicely," I hissed.

Tom's pacing accelerated. He made two more tight passes and then charged straight at me, catching me by the shoulders. "Listen," he said. "Listen good. If I thought it would do any good, I'd tell you everything. Right now, it will just do harm. A *lot* of harm." Anxiety shone from his eyes.

I realized that Tom was scared. My mind went numb.

I must have been hanging there between his hands like a wooden doll, because he shook me slightly. "Jack loves you," he said. "Remember that. And he's going to be okay." His tone suggested that he needed to convince me of this so that he could believe it himself.

I began to tremble. The mixture of fatigue from having gotten up so early to fly down there, the long hours in the airplane, the long days of worrying when I might see Jack again, and the shock of finally seeing him, but finding him smack in the middle of some kind of hornet's nest, was taking its toll. I hung my head. I began to whimper.

That got Tom mad again. For an instant, he squeezed my arms a little too hard, but then he abruptly pulled me to him and hugged me. That was another shock. It was the first time he had ever touched me beyond a handshake. As I was busy trying to deal with this new closeness, he put his lips to my ear and whispered, "Okay, I'll admit it. I'm worried about him, too. Given his background, I have to wonder."

I managed to say, "Wonder what? And what background?"

Tom seemed not to have heard my questions. "But we're

just going to have to get through the next two days and give him a chance."

"What *background*, Tom?"

Tom hurried right along. "Then we'll go beat the crap out of him, okay? You and me. I'll throw the first punch and then hold him for you while you throw the second."

"Give him a chance to *what*?" I whispered back. I had the eerie sensation that I had jumped back thirty years in time, and was hiding behind the hay bales in the barn with my brother, hatching plans.

Tom stroked my back. He held my head to his chest and patted my hair like I was a little girl. He said nothing.

"Tom, you lied to me again," I whispered. "You knew how to reach Jack the whole time."

"No. Well, yes, I had a phone number to reach him, but he didn't answer for days. I caught him this morning, just as we were getting ready to take off from Salt Lake."

"And he drove over? What's that mean, he was six, eight hours away by road?"

Tom squeezed me again. "Don't do the math, Em. It won't help you."

"So where is he *now*, Tom? Where's he going? What's he doing that's so scary?"

Tom nuzzled his face against the top of my head. "I'll tell you just as soon as I can. That's a promise."

"But what's all this about his background?" I was fighting back tears now.

"I'm sorry. Forget what I said. It doesn't matter anyway. He's a great guy, always remember that. And he's got two days."

So there it was. Tom had made a promise, and while he's a man who knows how to lie, he's also a man who keeps his commitments. "Okay," I said. "Two days. But I'm going to hold you to it."

"Done."

The rain started half an hour before we went to dinner, and was coming down so hard as we drove that the wipers could not keep the windshield clear. It came down with a passionate vengeance, in drops that seemed the size of dinner plates, splashing on a pavement overwhelmed with runoff, pouring off awnings and palm fronds like cascading fountains. Then, as we approached our destination at the shore, it moderated, quickly tapered off, and then stopped entirely, leaving behind a shameless wetness and the fresh perfumes of lawn, unseen jasmine, and concrete.

Miles Guffey and his wife, Pamela, also had a fancy place, though only half the size of Nancy Wallace's. Like Nancy's, it had a screened enclosure—I was beginning to get the idea that biting insects might be a bit of a problem in Florida—but beyond it lay a dock with a big cruising boat instead of a guesthouse. There were boats and yachts all over the place, in fact; they lived on an inlet lined with dripping foliage and stuccoed party homes.

"Welcome, y'all!" Miles called, as Pamela showed us onto the pool deck. "I got the coals going real good, but first we gots to prime the pumps! So whatcha drinkin'?"

"A beer would do nicely," I replied. "A dark ale. Something I can sort of chew on."

"Not none of your Coors you cowgirls drink?"

"My tastes have evolved," I informed him.

"We got. Next?" Guffey pointed at Nancy.

"I hear you mix a noble Salty Dog," Nancy crooned. "I'd like you to meet my niece, Faye."

"Nancy, you're my kind of gal," Guffey chortled. "Faye, what can I get you?"

Faye patted her belly. "Mineral water for me. So nice of you to have us over, Miles. This is my husband, Tom Latimer."

Guffey pumped Tom's hand. "Tom Latimer. The great Tom Latimer. I am truly pleased to meet you. My, my, my. Yes. Well, surely you aren't holding off on the little lady's account?"

Tom smiled as a wolf might when it smells prey. "I'm a single-malt man, if you've got anything in that category."

Guffey's eyes went as wide as his smile, making him look kind of loopy. "Do I? Why, Mr. Latimer, sir, what'll it be, Talisker, Tamdhu, or some of dis?" He whipped a small, globular bottle out from behind the wet bar that stood by the pool. The label appeared to have been handwritten. "Special stock. They only bottle a couple casks a year."

Tom smacked his lips. "Cracked ice, and not too much of it, if you please."

Guffey pulled a drawer out of the bar and fished around in it. When he couldn't find what he was looking for, he hollered, "Pammy, where'd my ice pick get to?"

"You took it out to the boat, hon."

Guffey blinked. "Excuse me a mo," he said, and dashed out to the dock and onto the boat. He was back in a flash with an ice pick big enough to do some real damage. He kicked open the refrigerator below the bar and went at his craft with gusto, lining up glasses and chipping at a block of ice like a mad sculptor. When he was done, and, through some miracle of subtle communication or prescripted agreement, Pamela had taken Faye and Nancy into the house to see some new acquisition in home décor, and Tom and he and I were settled into wicker chairs with hors d'oeuvres within easy reach, he jumped right into what was on his mind.

"Em here's got a nice reputation for figgerin' out geological riddles," he began. "And you, Tom, are legendary in the trade. So I got me a puzzle for you."

Tom shot a sideways look at me, then took a miserly sip of his Scotch and watched his host carefully. "Mm?"

I settled in with my beer, hunkering down so the two men would speak freely and I could listen. I thought, *What a flatterer this man is. Tom is in fact legendary, but only within the FBI; he's worked hard to maintain a low profile in the outside world. Now Tom's going to think I talked him up to Guffey and blew his cover!* I said, "Tell Tom about the problem with the reefs, Miles."

Guffey said, "Yes, well, we got this dust thing. We think

dust is carrying pathogens that are killing the coral reefs here in the Caribbean. But we got to prove our theory. Now, our problem is this: In geology, as in any science, the game doesn't end with your initial observation of a phenomenon; in fact, that's just where it begins. Say it's reefs that's dying, and you don't know why. So you get an idea about what might be causing your phenomenon. So you start gathering data, try to figger out what makes your phenomenon tick. Your idea begins to grow into a hypothesis. A hypothesis should explain your data, and if you're a good, law-abiding scientist, you in fact look for alternate explanations. Multiple working hypotheses, we call it. Then you got to test each one of 'em. Identify all your variables and test 'em one at a time, or as best you can. Or test 'em in concert, if that's what seems appropriate. Or both. You follow me so far?"

"Smooth sailing."

"Good. I like that. On the basis of whatever testing and data gathering you can perform, you move from a hypothesis to a theory. A theory should explain all the data and be predictive, meaning it should explain all new data you find later. Otherwise, you have to modify or discard your theory. Okay?"

Tom nodded. He had settled back in his chair and looked quite comfortable. His eyes had closed halfway. He was concentrating on what Guffey was saying, one oddly packaged intellectual communing with another.

Guffey continued. "So here's the deal. We got us a big project. We need all the fresh ideas and smart thinking we can get. Em here tells me she'd like to look at this dust thing like a crime scene. Now, that's great. So tell me, how's the way a detective works similar to what I just described, and how's it different?"

Tom shifted around in his seat. "It's mostly the same. You start with a phenomenon. Evidence of a crime. Like a corpse or a theft. Extortion. Someone squealing, or making an accusation of something that falls within the purview of your jurisdiction. Then we go through a loop you haven't yet described, and that's where you look to make certain you're not getting snookered by some game your informant or your supposed victim is playing."

Guffey laughed. "Oh, yeah. We get that in the earth sciences, too. Say the boys and girls upstairs tell me to look at cross-contamination of the aquifers here in Florida, like when the brain trusts that dug the canals to drain the Everglades punched through from one aquifer to the next, mixing good water with bad; well, then first I got to decide whether the crime's actually happened. What was water quality *A* and *B* like before they got started? Did both aquifers really get tapped? Do we really have a corpse, or are the Everglades alive and well?"

"Make me a metaphor that involves your African dust," Tom said.

"Okay, in the case of my dead corals, I got to make sure first this isn't something Mother Nature does periodically on her own just to clean house. And I can't always prove things like that. So somewhere in there, I consult my guts. I say, in the case of the corals, it happened way too fast, and too many other creatures are obviously in distress, like the *Diadema* sea urchins. The reefs are dying. So I say, yes, we got a crime here, all right. As in, I think something's upset the balance, and gone and mucked things up for the corals. And we even have that little jurisdiction thing you mentioned. We're the USGS, not the CDC; we're supposed to look at rocks, not disease. But the CDC won't worry itself about corals, but they might some day get interested in all the asthmatic humans who live hear those reefs. We wind up fighting over something no one else wants to worry about in the first place."

Tom cleared his throat to indicate that he was listening.

Guffey said, "But then here's the next bit, and this really crosses lines of jurisdiction: I think there's a few humans 'at's gone and gotten personal with what's riding on the winds."

Tom tented his fingers. His eyes closed down to dark slits. He purred, "What do you have in mind, Miles?"

"Bioterrorism."

I almost choked on the cracker I was eating. The first thought that shot through my head was, *There goes my Master's thesis!*

The muscles along Tom's jaws tightened. Dryly, he said, "That would be upsetting."

Guffey's eyes flared. "Yes. I see you understand."

I broke my silence. "What's your evidence? You got an observer in West Africa who's seen someone kicking a drum of anthrax into a dust storm? And how's that going to affect us this many miles downwind? It wouldn't all get this far, and there'd be dispersion, and . . ."

Guffey leaned back in his chair and stared up through the overhead screen into the sky, which was full of puffy clouds turning rose-pink with the sunset. Chameleons ran across the screening, hanging upside down by their tiny toes. Guffey's eyes panned with one of them, an observer doing what he did incessantly, and did best. When he spoke, all trace of humor had left him. "Right. That's what any intelligent person would ask first. And I got to admit, the idea only tumbled out of my mind as a subparagraph of the working hypotheses, a sort of 'if-then.' An abstraction. An intellectual pursuit, just letting the mind follow where it might go. And the first time I waved that flag in front of anyone else, I was trying to get funding from the military. Trying to get someone worked up enough to notice the project."

He took a swig of his drink and continued. "I like reefs. Been diving all my life. Want to do something for them. But as I got into it with these guys, looking for funding— with the CDC, the Department of Agriculture, the military—I started getting asked to speak at different kinds of conferences, outside my specialty, outside geology even. I began working with the biologists, the medical people, the chemists, the meteorologists. The picture began to change." He trailed off, continuing to watch the progress of the lizard across the screen. "All this on a shoestring. Couldn't have done it without the power of the Internet."

Tom waited. I waited.

"September 11 happened," Guffey said. "Terrorism on our own turf. Then what came next, remember? Anthrax. The first death was right here in Florida. Then more in New Jersey, and the scare at the Senate Office Building."

I said, "But that was done through the mail. Those spores were in letters. It's a lethal bacillus, and it doesn't take much to cause illness, but it takes more than one spore. You throw it into the wind over North Africa, it's going to be so diffused by the time it gets here, no one's going to even notice, let alone get sick."

Guffey said, "That's what everyone thinks. But everyone has been wrong more than once in this man's universe. Hey, all those people went to work in the World Trade Center towers that morning, and I'll betcha not too many of them thought they'd be lying under tons of rubble by noon."

I said, "In *The Secret Life of Dust*, the author quotes scientists as saying that the UV light kills the microbes when they fly up into the air."

Miles said, "That was the prevailing wisdom, but it wasn't exactly true. The author of that book had to go to press before we got our early data. We have plenty of germs arriving hale and hearty. I have to suppose that the dust is so thick that whatever's toward the center of the cloud is sheltered from the UV. But that's just another scientific wild-assed guess. We get so hung up on guesses that we come to think they're facts, and they aren't facts until we put 'em to the test."

Tom's face had gone hard with concentration. He said, "But like Em said, show me the evidence that single spores can do what a jet aircraft hitting the Trade Center can do."

Guffey sat up, frustration making his movements abrupt. "Who says they can't? Did you know the last person to die of anthrax in that series was a frail old lady in Connecticut? In her nineties. No one could figure that one out. She hadn't gotten any mail, hadn't left home in days, but *bam*, there she was in the morgue with lungs as black and festering as anything you'd see in your worst nightmare. Even I thought: Oh, it's just a fluke. They missed something in their analysis.

"Well, then I got an e-mail from a feller in England who's a meteorologist. Like I say, I been traveling in some different circles, and I've become part of a grass-roots network of people 'at's interested in all this medical stuff. So this guy says he analyzed the winds and air conditions recorded for metropolitan New York the evening when that old lady's exposure would have occurred. What did he find? Moist, cold air flowing straight from the postal building where the letters were handled right over toward the town in Connecticut where this old lady lived. The air would have stayed low to the ground, and there was almost no turbulence. No diffusion. That lady was old and frail, her immune system pretty well shot. Maybe she went out to call the cat, took a deep breath of the night air so she could holler, 'Here puss-puss.' You tell me how she got that dose. Thing is, in her case it didn't take much.

"But here's the thing: The point of bioterrorism is not to kill everyone. All you got to do to be effective is make enough people sick that the nation's resources get sucked up into nursing a bunch of invalids. And we are a graying society. We got all these boomers and their elderly mothers living in tight clusters we call cities. Hell, down here in Florida we got all your snowbirds. Medical wizardry has kept them alive long past their three score and ten, and if they don't get their meds, they'd drop like flies. We're a hothouse society, used to our little supports. Imagine what a disease like anthrax could do if you moved beyond a half teaspoon in a letter to a whole drum of it dumped purposefully into the wind."

"We have vaccines," said Tom. "And antibiotics."

Guffey laughed humorlessly. "Tests show the vaccines don't do the whole job." As Tom's eyebrows shot up in alarm, Guffey pressed onward. "A combination of vaccination and antibiotics worked the best in clinical trials. Hell, we don't even know for sure what those tests mean, because we ran them on monkeys! Do you know any human that would have volunteered for that? Nobody in their right mind would even think of it. Not even prisoners. We're talking about a lethal disease, not the common cold. Even with both vaccination and drugs, you have to start administering the drugs within twenty-four hours of exposure, and the first symptoms take at least forty-eight to emerge, and even then, it comes on like a case of the flu, and no one even goes to the doctor until they're five inches from gone.

"What's more, these bugs used by terrorists have teeth as long as your arm. Hell, that's no normal anthrax floating out of those envelopes. Our own smart guys worked hard to make them as potent as possible, and as you no doubt know, our strains are the source of most of the terrorist supplies in the Middle East. Saddam Hussein's boys bought their starter supply from the American Type Culture Collection, a private germ bank in Maryland."

Tom was starting to squirm in his seat. He'd long since forgotten his Scotch. "All right," he said. "You've got my attention. But take a number on the big list of things to worry about. English Muslims wearing explosive tennis shoes climbing on airliners. Suitcase-sized A-bombs. Pregnant women wearing plastique. The list is endless. We simply have too many things to fear these days."

I said, "And if you really want to make people sick, rent a crop duster and buzz Miami."

Guffey took a gulp of his drink. "Sure enough, Emily. Go to the head of the class."

Tom set down his drink. "Then you're not talking about Africa."

Guffey said, "Oh, hell no. I'm talking much closer to home. All's anyone's got to do to nail us and hide it under the cover of nature is this: wait for a nice dust storm to work its way across the ocean, then run a drone trawler past us just outside the international limit with a nice smudging device running. Our own military researchers developed the technique. A small canister of the stuff would be enough to kill every man, woman, and child in this state several times over. Hell, the Russians made whole tank cars of that bacillus that are unaccounted for. Where'd it all go? You tell me, Tom. You tell me."

Tom sat up straight and leaned toward Guffey. "But you're not really talking about Russian anthrax left over from the Cold War. You're talking about new germs being cultured right now."

Guffey stared off toward the sunset. The golden orb had disappeared below the horizon, and great billowy clouds had darkened to a moldering gray. "You are correct. Now we're getting back to our missing microbiologist."

– 11 –

Lucy fumbled with the buttons on the front of her best be-seen-in-public dress, wishing that, when the publicist had called and asked her to sub for a colleague, who had developed laryngitis, at this evening's public appearance she had had the intelligence to say no. She would have been within her rights to do so, citing an interest in staying free of germ exposure before a flight. But as usual, she had said yes, unwilling to risk anyone thinking she was not tough enough to do whatever needed to be done. Deep inside the closely kept privacy of her mind, Lucy grumbled, *Can't the PR department do its job without making me trot in front of the public?* As her fear and frustration mounted, she thought, *Damn NASA for using its astronaut corps like freaks in a sideshow!*

The force of her emotions made her feel like she was losing her balance. She caught herself and leaned on the edge of the sink, eyes closed, remembering to breathe. *This is not me,* she told herself. *I am a team player. I have not forgotten that it's the public that is paying for this flight. And all my training. And all the years I spent at university. The least I can do is help them celebrate American's highest achievement.*

She opened her eyes and stared at the floor. Her gaze came into focus with her eyes aimed at infinity, focusing on the centers of two tiles in the pattern instead of one.

The wider parallax made the tiles jump and float with an illusion of greater depth, as if she were staring at a stereo pair of air photographs. Her mind slipped into a tight observation of the phenomenon, careening away from the stress of the evening's coming event. But she was unable to maintain the abstraction, and her mind soon crashed back to her ongoing awareness of the danger she must face by being seen in public. Her ears rushed with a sound like the crowd of people who would fill the hall, earthbound enthusiasts and their semi-interested spouses hoping to be inspired or at least entertained by what she had to say. Like a drowning woman clutching a floating piece of wreckage, she clamped onto the thought of the task itself, and ran the assignment through her head, rehearsing. She was to speak to them about the various projects in which a geologist would be involved in space. She would go for the usual laughs—What's a rock hound doing going into space, where there are no rocks?—and when they were warmed up, she would speak to them of observation. Of the beauty of patterns and what they told her, seen close up through a microscope, or as the naked-eye observer standing in the landscape, or from a distant platform in space or beyond, a never-ending expansion of fractals.

And she would speak to them of one objective of her voyage: the whirls of dust that blew off the Earth's deserts. She would tell them of the diseases carried on that mineral dust, and tell them about the synthetic chemicals riding along as aerosols, and help them to perceive the importance of doing primary research on these phenomena. She would describe the various observation platforms NASA was using to study them, what and how much was riding on the wind, and how and where it originated, and when the problem had reached lethal proportions. She would tell them about the satellite image slices used—TOMs, SeaWiFS—and about observations made from the International Space Station and from the shuttle itself.

And she would try, desperately, to convey to them her passion for the beautiful orb over which she would soon float, a lover levitated by her force of feeling. But she wouldn't use such words. Such words were too revealing, too intimate. Instead, she would keep her voice level and forceful and pump out scientific terms that aimed more abstractly at her truths.

She had learned public speaking in graduate school. Years working as a teaching assistant to earn her funding had long since ironed out the wrinkles of terror that used to fall like heavy drapery around her as she walked to the front of the room, turned, and faced the assembled listeners. She had learned to be poised, confident, dynamic . . . at times even charming. More usually, people perceived her as aloof. The PR coach at NASA had taken pains to tell her this, trying to get her to drop some of her multisyllabic, Latinate terms for simpler words with more emotional punch. And to smile, and make better eye contact. Lucy had fought this badgering every inch of the way and would tonight of all nights perform her task any way she damned well could, interpersonal warmth be damned.

Tonight, she would not be looking into her audience's eyes except to scan each face to make certain that *he* was not there. After confirming this, she would be staring over their heads, keenly watching the entrances to the room. But what would she do if *he* appeared?

Her mind shot backward to the evening she had met him. How ironic that it was at a speaking event like this. He had come up after her talk to compliment her. She had been tired, lonely, hungry for approval, and . . . he had been quite attractive, all big and brawny and blond, just the way she liked her men. How she wished she could take back that night, rewind, and live forward again without the fateful accident of that meeting. Her mind went blank with dissociation as the intensity of that upset once again overwhelmed her.

Shaking herself back to the present moment, Lucy straightened up, picked up her hairbrush, and began, mechanically, to pull it through her hair. Three strokes on the left, three on the right, one front-to-back to lift it off her forehead. She stared at her reflection in the mirror, assessing the weight of the years. She was a month shy of forty and had never married. Marriage and raising children had just never seemed an option, not with everything she aimed to accomplish . . . or were her former boyfriends right when they said that she had armored her heart to protect her precious mind and ambitions? *To hell with them all*, she thought bitterly. *In just days, or at worst weeks, I will achieve my goal. We'll climb into the T-38's and fly to the Cape. The next day, final prep, begin to suit up. The day after that, we climb aboard* Endeavor *for the final countdown. At T minus O, we have ignition, we lift off, and I . . .* She stared into the mirror at the dark areas under each eye, and thought, *How strange to be looking forward to the risk of space travel to feel safe.*

The timer she had set in the kitchen buzzed distantly. She dropped the brush into the sink. Time to go. She moved out of the bathroom, headed down the hall toward the hat stand that filled the space next to the door into the garage. There she had ritually placed her pocketbook, her keys, and the light jacket that protected her from the ubiquitous air-conditioning of house, car, office, and meeting rooms. She surely did not need it for the sultry Houstonian night air.

She paused with her hand on the knob of the door into the garage. This was the moment that scared her most, ever since the morning she had opened this very door and found *him* standing on the other side.

In one terrible moment, she had frozen.

He had lunged, hands flying toward her.

Thawing, she had slammed the door and shot the bolt, saved by decades of physical training and the lightning-fast reflexes it took to make the astronaut corps in the first place.

Had he held a knife, or had she just imagined that?

And—this question tormented her—how had he gotten into the garage? How had he gotten past the security system?

She still did not know.

Her mind plummeted back to that day. How long ago

had it been? Two months? Three? Was it really that long ago? That recent? Time seemed to dilate either way, the effect of stress.

The knob felt cold in her hand. Too cold. Did that mean that he was there now, on the other side of her door again, waiting for her to unlock it?

For the thousandth time, her mind whispered its question: *What would he have done to me if I had not stopped him?*

She knew, and did not want to know. A spurned lover, insane, willing to do anything to get her under his control. He'd have her chained to his bedstead if he could.

Her mind reeled out of control, spinning back through the events that had led to her present moment of terror, of torture. He had at first seemed so charming, almost impish in his capacity to shift from one apparent personality to another, like dating an actor who was always in rehearsal. But there had always been little signals, even from their first meeting, telling her that something was wrong, each clue too small or inconsequential in itself to make her turn and say, "Sorry, but I don't want to see you again." One moment he'd seem infinitely suave and pulled together and then, suddenly, she'd note a moment of disarray, the man flickering instantaneously toward the inchoate rage and panic of an abandoned child; then, not a word or a gesture having quite skidded over the line past which she could be sure of what was happening, he would resume the appearance of normalcy, a sly deception giving him the image of an adult male.

She had dated him erratically, when he was in town on business that was never quite described. She had gone to bed with him three, no, four times, and wondered still how he had talked her into it. Why had she let him? Was it his intensity, or his obvious need of her? She had let herself imagine that it could work, his house of mirrors encouraging her to select whichever fantasy suited her own fragile needs. But always something about him seemed off, discolored. Yet each meeting seemed innocuous enough, and he even handed her the rationalizations. *We're not kids*, he'd tell her. *Be my lady just this night.* And one more night. And one more. Inching ever closer to the darkness that seethed within him. Just one more. As if, having hugged this tar baby and become slightly soiled, she could tell herself that she might as well hug again and wash later. His sexual demands had been by turns exciting, overwhelming, unnerving, and finally . . . frightening.

She had decided—for the fifth or sixth time—to see him maybe one more time before breaking off the relationship when a mutual acquaintance phoned. An old classmate, a member of the association that had invited her to that first fateful meeting. He invited her now to join him for a cup of coffee at a public café. His tone was casual, but she knew something was up. Over the smell of beans, he had revealed the awful truth. This man she had been dating—this creature that she had let near her—had held another woman at knifepoint, naked, squirming, begging for her life.

"What do you mean?" Lucy had asked.

"I mean he very nearly killed her," he had replied.

"But he didn't."

The friend had looked at her. Blinked. "No. She said he was interrupted. The bastard heard the mailman coming up the walk. He made her promise she would not tell." When Lucy said nothing in response, he continued. "She said it was as if he suddenly became a small boy. He let her up and told her to put her clothes on. Said it was their secret. Imagine."

"Did she go to the police?"

"No. She was too frightened. She left town instead. I only know about this through a mutual friend."

"Then there's no record of the event."

"Correct."

Lucy had sat there, her coffee untouched and going cold, stray bits of observation finally clicking together.

"Sorry," the friend had said. "It must be tough; I mean, you've given up so much of your social life to get this far, making the astronaut corps and all. You're my age, right? Almost forty? Is there anything I can do?"

Leaping past his pity, Lucy had said, "No," the word flying from her lips, the old pattern of denial closing all access to her heart. She had managed a wry smile to indicate a lack of importance. She had said, "I'll take care of this. I appreciate your telling me. I was just breaking it off anyway. Only went out a couple of times. He's not my type." So casual. Let everyone think it was barely a scratch.

But the scratch had proved a vicious gash as talons sank deep into her flesh, a predator who would not let go.

That night he had called just as she was turning out the light to go to sleep. Even from their first meeting, he had thus moved to throw her off her rhythms, keeping her awake past her schedule. This night she would not let him steal her sleep. This night, she decided, she would not answer. Not answer to the creature who had lied so deeply about himself.

When the phone clicked over to the machine, he had left a message. His words had been innocuous enough, but his tone told her that, by the very fact that she had not picked up the phone, he knew she knew. She lay back on her bed and waited. Fifteen minutes later, she had heard a car drive up and slow down, its driver scanning her house.

Her hand moving faster than conscious thought, she had clicked off the bedside light.

The car had stopped, its engine idling.

Seconds later, the phone rang.

She did not answer. No message was left.

The next day, he had phoned her at work, asking her to lunch. She had declined, citing EVA practice drills in the pool. *You can't do this,* he had said. *Can't.* And had repeated the word twice, like a chant, then told her, *You haven't asked my permission.*

The morning after that she first found footprints pressed into the dew in her backyard. Large, like him.

No night after that had borne the rest she needed.

A cycle quickly emerged. Always the phone call at bedtime, and an ebb and swelling of signs appeared, telling her that he had often been there, watching her, while she tried to sleep. Each clue cut like a knife through her gossamer illusion of safety.

And then came the morning that he was right there outside her door. In the garage. In the brief instant before she slammed the door, his hands had swung toward her. He had held something shiny.

She had begun to live in the dark, only leaving lights on in rooms other than the one she was in. She used only the downstairs bathroom, because it had no windows. She installed security alarms on all the doors and windows including the garage, but still she languished in uncertainty.

One evening, she had come home late to find the house pitch dark and a note from the security company taped to the door to demonstrate that they had done their bit and checked on her when the interruption of power at her house had set off an alarm at their monitoring station. *How long did it take them to get here?* she asked herself. *Ten minutes? Twenty? When the stroke of a knife takes no time at all?*

The electrician she called found duct tape between the meter and the house current, breaking supply. A sophisticated job, he had told her. Do this wrong, and you electrocute yourself.

That night she did not sleep at all.

She knew instinctively that reporting this vandalism, this harassment, this *stalking* to anyone, least of all the law, was not an option. One thought always stopped her: *Involvement in such a mess will bump me from the flight. And, most likely, from all future flights.*

I just have to outlast this. . . .

In the hours before dawn, she had decided to hire a lawyer to advise her. A lawyer was held to stringent codes of client-lawyer privilege. She would pay cash, give a false name.

She had made the appointment. Waited, hardly breathing, hanging from the slim thread of hope that this man would be able to tell her how to deal with *him*.

The day of her appointment had arrived. The lawyer drew lazy circles with one finger on his desktop and listened, his eyes glazed, the meter running. She spoke with a constricted throat, her voice tight with rage and the humiliation of telling this agony to a stranger.

When she was done with her recitation, he leaned back, studied her a moment longer, and then told her the awful truth: That in the eyes of the law, *he* hadn't really done anything yet. That her fear did not motivate a warrant for his arrest. She had to have evidence of a crime. A crime? "You mean theft of my peace of mind is no crime?" she had said. "How about breaking and entering? How about skulking around my personal space, unwelcome, unbidden?"

"No witnesses," he had said. "Your word against his. Do you want to play this in court? Your insistence on paying in cash says that you do not."

"But he's breaking the law."

"Yes, but you are not the law. You have no right to prosecute. You are not sleeping, but nothing has really happened to you. The law would consider him merely a nuisance." Here the lawyer had laughed humorlessly and stared out the window. Then he had told her, his voice tight with anger, that the slogan painted on police cruisers in some cities—*To Serve and Protect*—should in fact be *To Clean Up the Mess*.

Sorry, lady, he was telling her. Your life is screwed.

She changed tacks. Asked, "Do you think I really have anything to worry about?"

"Oh, yes. The graveyards are full of women who did not take action."

Moments had passed, then she asked, "What action can I take?"

"None. Are you authorized to carry a concealed weapon? You might consider it. You could get a restraining order. A simple thing. I take you into court, and you tell the judge that you fear for your life, that gets you a temporary restraining order. To make it permanent, he gets his day in court to contest the fact that you are in effect relieving him of some small part of his liberty. It becomes a matter of public record."

Here he had sat back and observed her for a moment, knowing that the last thing this Miss Jones or Smith or whatever she called herself would do was to let anything show up in the public record.

"Moreover," he had said, "the restraining order is no kind of armor. It is a piece of paper. It is a civil order, not criminally enforceable. He will not be arrested on the basis that you are scared, or even should he cross the lines set by the order. If he does, you must tell the police, and they will go to a judge—when next court is in session—and ask the judge to issue a bench warrant for his arrest. The judge might not do it. After all, you have done a good job of preventing injury so far. Further, if you call the police, they will classify your complaint as domestic violence because you know this man, and then you are caught on another hook. You are in essence blamed as part of the problem, as if it's just your bad relationship that is at fault and not the state of his mind or the wrongfulness of his actions."

Her voice was almost gone, as thin and colorless as a ghost, as she said: "But all I want is to be left alone."

He had picked at his cuticles, said, "Not much to ask, I agree, but even if you have gotten a restraining order and a permit to carry and he breaks down your door, you will be asked why you did not leave the state to escape him. Do you understand? If you use lethal force to stop him from hurting you, you will be held accountable. The statistics are that you will go to jail—ninety-eight percent chance—because you knew him. The police call this a dirty crime. The first thing they ask is: Did you sleep with him?"

Lucy's face had gone tight.

He had his answer. "They'll search your house. Take your sheets. Even if you've washed them, chances are there will be public hairs still in them. Or in your bed. Or in the carpet underneath it."

"But if it's self-defense?"

"If you shoot him coming over the threshold, drag him inside. At least then your sentence will be shorter."

The exchange had continued, relentless in its loss of hope: "So what do you recommend I do?"

"How old is he?"

"About my age."

"About forty. These guys usually burn out by then. If he's still active at this age, he's outside the FBI profile. Less predictable. And don't just hope he finds someone else to bother. They don't do that. They just add another victim to the list."

Silence had settled on the room like snow falling without wind, covering the desk, the chairs, and Lucy with its ice.

Then Lucy asked her question again: "What do you recommend I do?"

"Leave town. Your life as you know it here is ended. Leave no forwarding address. Start over somewhere else. Keep a low profile. Consider changing your name; there's no real privacy anymore."

Lucy forced the memory of that conversation out of her mind. She snapped her attention back to the present moment, her hand growing cold on the doorknob that would twist and open out into the garage. Even as the lawyer had spoken, she had known that his plan was in no way compatible with her own. Even now, she laughed bitterly, a quick *huh*. A low profile? That she would love, but NASA and the space-hungry American public had other ideas.

She looked down at her hand, and at the door that stood like fragile armor between her and the world. At least this was the last talk she must give before the launch. Even with the weather delay, it was just a matter of a few days or a week before she'd be back at the Cape, tucked carefully into the safe house, guarded around the clock by the nation's finest. How she hungered for that moment. How she cursed the fact that this filthy concern for safety in the mundane reaches of her daily life had, at this time of all times, asserted itself as a greater preoccupation than her lifelong hunger to hurtle into space.

Hissing with rage, she tapped the security system control box to make sure it was armed. She set the program to allow her to pass through, get into her car, open the roll-up door, and drive away before it automatically armed itself again. Then she turned the knob and walked out into the dark night of human frailty.

– 12 –

The pounding of the fast boat across the waves hammered at his spine, but it suited him. Sixty miles per hour across the darkening sea, the damp wind whipping around him like jealous snakes. He knew he should have waited for the cover of total darkness before leaving the coast, but he had felt the pressure to leave, leave, leave. He had felt eyes watching him, like insects crawling over his body.

The Coast Guard probably had him on radar by now, but he was the cat and they were his mice when it came down to cases. The thugs he ran with had them under greater surveillance than they had on him. That was what was so sweet about the whole deal.

Another half hour and he'd be at the island. A ration of their strange food and then some sleep. Sleep. Sleep, God damn it, if he could get the worms of Lucy's deceit out of his intestines he would sleep! She had used him. Used *him*! Cast him off like a dirty sock, like a used fucking *condom*. Women. You shoot your life force into them, and they bite off your cock! The fucking Arabs were right, they should be kept in cages, and only let out to be fucked, and even then only when tied down and gagged. Fucking *shoot* them when you're done.

The boat jumped an especially large wave, and slammed down hard, almost toppling his hulking form over the steering wheel. A chunk of trim snapped free and pinwheeled off into the night. He laughed. His "employers" knew so little of who he truly was. It had been so easy to delude them. Make them think he sympathized with their bullshit. And through them, he had access to such excellent equipment, this boat the least of it. In this boat, he looked like an ordinary drug runner. No one would guess what he had buried in the beach! No one would know until it was too late!

He tapped the control panel quickly to check his course. Made a minor correction in the automatic pilot. Damned thing was always off just a hair, pulled to starboard. His hand itched to switch on the radar to see if it yet painted the island where he was headed, but his instructions had been to run quiet as much as possible. Quiet, hell; this can roared like an F-14. His employers were a crazy bunch, but very useful. What idiots, they thought they had recruited him, but it was he who was using them. All their fundamentalist shit about the Satan America stepping on the throats of the true believers. They were rough sons of bitches, running around with their high-powered rifles and night-vision goggles, practicing their little raids, but he knew how to avoid them, just do his little errands for them, and slip a hand into their supplies for whatever little goodies he needed. Fucking shitheads couldn't count. And they needed a white boy like him to run their errands, any one of them would stand out like a sore thumb, even on the island, if any of the tourists saw them. Hah! They ran for cover like so many cockroaches when the boats showed up. As long as he sang their little songs and ran their loads back and forth, they foolishly took him for granted.

But there were two other Americans on the island, and one seemed to have him under a watchful eye. The professor, they called him, crackling over his little laboratory projects, patting him on the back and saying yes, you're on the right path, the righteous path. Everybody stroking everybody else, a fucking circle jerk. They all watched him. He did his "stupid" act. He had them fooled.

Eyes on him. His mind bounced randomly from their

dark-lashed eyes to Lucy's to the eyes of the clerk at the motel. He had felt the eyes of the clerk boring into him. He'd deal with him another time, get even, perhaps wire his car with a little device the boys on the island had. That would please them probably. Treachery was their name, disruption their game. Best to leave for now anyway. The launch was delayed. Why pay their rates when he had a bunk with his employers for free, damn their feral eyes. He'd wait there on the island and zip back in plenty of time to dig up his prize and ready it for the launch. With luck the new launch window would come at night, when he could move under cover of darkness and *she* would make a nice, bright target.

Too bad he'd missed her little talk this evening, a perfect chance to show her how far her precious superiority could really take her. He'd had the flight to Houston all scheduled, but his fucking employers had told him to come back and run a load of the white stuff to shore for them. Missing tonight's opportunity to show Lucy who was in charge couldn't be helped. How ironic to use drugs as a cover! He grinned into the flying salt and night air. It was enough that she'd be watching for him, afraid.

– 13 –

After the tension of the cocktail hour, Guffey prepared the fish for the barbecue. "I speared this myself," he said. "Guess an old fart can still hunt somethin' to go with what the wife gathers."

Dinner was delicious, the fish grilled to tender, moist perfection. I discovered that I had a taste for grouper, and the salad was fine as well. But the conversation didn't help my digestion.

Miles managed to stretch a teasing preamble to his dissertation on the relevance of his missing microbiologist to threats to homeland security clear through barbecuing the fish, tossing the salad, and calling everyone to the table. Thus Faye and Nancy were there to hear what he had to say.

Which was not much. Basically, he thought something was up. He had a hunch, but no hard evidence. But his hunches had borne fruit in the past, he asserted, so this one was probably good, too.

The whole performance had me on edge. I didn't like being strung along, particularly where it came to a discussion of a project that might in some way connect to the horrifying condition in which I had just seen my lover that afternoon. But I held back and let Tom work over our host.

"I tell you, the threat is real," said Guffey.

Tom arranged his features to indicate waning interest.

Guffey offered to top up his glass of wine.

Tom declined. "I'm good for now."

Guffey shrugged his shoulders. To his wife, he said, "What's for dessert, hon?"

"Peaches. And I hope they aren't mealy."

Fuck the peaches, I thought. *Stick with the dust.*

Tom said, "A hunch is all very well, but . . ." and let his words trail off.

I draped a hand over my mouth to cover my amusement. They were really getting into it now, playing a game of liar's poker, each one tried to engage the other to spill his information first. I expected that at any moment, Tom would have to pull on the brass knuckles and really go to work, because this time, he was up against world-class talent charading as a Southern good old boy.

Guffey swirled the wine in his own glass. "You know what I been talking about," he said suggestively, trying in turn to get Tom to say the word first.

Tom slipped an artistically furtive glance at his watch.

"Well, this anthrax threat is a real problem," said Guffey.

Tom folded his hands on the table edge, indicating polite interest. "Mm?"

"Well, you know our missing man, Calvin Wheat?"

"I've not met him, no."

Ignoring that bit of polite insolence, Guffey said, "He did his doctorate at a place where some folks were interested in all that, see."

"Ah. Then he has experience in handling and refining *Bacillus anthracis?*"

"Oh, no. Not Cal, not directly. But he knew people there, see, and one of them was, well . . ." He twirled one index finger around an ear. "These guys get competitive sometimes, and other times they think they've done a great service to humankind and ought to be rewarded with fat research contracts. They get bitter, y'know? Kinda makes them slide off their moorings a bit, lose their ethical center."

Faye said, "And other times they think the government isn't taking proper precautions, and decide to show us all just how scary biological weapons can be." She shot a look at Tom, who studiously avoided making eye contact with her.

Guffey said, "Yeah, well, Cal said this one guy, name of Ben Farnsworth, got real bent out of shape, and was last seen taking his football and heading out to play health clinic manager for some outfit offshore. I don't like that. My personal opinion? He's got a lab going out there. He's got to be stopped. That shit's bad enough in our hands. I don't want it in anyone else's."

Bacillus anthracis. Was this the killer dust that Jack had gone looking for? I didn't like this, not one bit. It didn't matter how well-trained or how well-vaccinated Jack was, the stuff was lethal, particularly if they were talking about a new strain.

Tom tented his fingers. It took someone who knew him as well as I did to know that he was now as tense as a bird dog that has a pheasant in sight. "Where offshore?"

Guffey said, "The Bahamas. Damned islands start only fifty-five miles east of the Atlantic coast here." He shook his head. "I used to like going out there. Thought it was a piece of paradise. Now I wonder."

Tom said, "Which island, precisely?"

"Don't I wish I knew. But any one of 'em is too close for my comfort, let me tell you. And Cal, he predicts—" Here he paused for dramatic effect. "*Predicted* that he'd be finding something pretty damning when he compared dust samples collected at open sea with those collected onshore in certain islands in the Bahamas, *and* in Florida."

Tom shifted in his chair. "But he had yet to collect those data?"

"Correct. Or at least, he did not yet have the bit that would clinch his theory. He needed samples from open ocean and from downwind of various islands. Unless I miss my guess, he was about to get the pristine upwind sample he needed. He had all the others sitting right there in his stateroom."

I asked, "Has anyone looked through his stateroom to see if anything's missing?"

Miles smiled his approval at me. "No. The cruise line's official position is that he must have gotten off the ship in Barbados. And it's not back to Port Canaveral yet, so we haven't been able to check."

Tom looked blank. He had withdrawn inside his head to cogitate.

Guffey eyed Tom with apparent satisfaction. He knew he'd hit his mark.

Faye shifted the conversation from the specific to the general. "This terrorism really screws with our lives, doesn't it? It's a whole ugly new world. When I first got my pilot's license, it was considered a basic freedom that I could fly my plane anywhere I wanted. Now we've had crazies flying jets into tall buildings, and the White House can close the skies at a blink."

"You got a better way of handling this?" Tom inquired.

"Yes. I say we start thinking straight about things. There's the whole discussion now about whether the pilots on commercial airlines should carry guns. Some Congress people argue that we shouldn't allow that, because they might shoot a passenger by mistake. So instead, we have an executive order that permits a guy in an F-16 to shoot down the whole plane. That's crazy. I say arm the pilots."

Tom said, "And if the terrorists shoot the pilots?"

"*Then* bring out the F-16," she muttered. "The politicians want to ground all the private pilots, as if we're the threat. I didn't see them grounding all the Ryder trucks after Oklahoma City or that first attempt on the World Trade Center."

Miles said, "The rental-truck lobby must be stronger than you pilots."

"There are no perfect answers in the security business," Tom said soothingly. "It's a complex world, so there are no simple solutions."

Faye was not in a mood to be mollified. "If women ran this world, things would be different. Back in the Stone Age, we had it right. God was female. Women had high status. They raised the babies and gathered eighty percent of the food. The men just lolled around, and once in a while went and hunted for a little meat."

Tom said, "I guess you women raised too many babies, because now we've got runaway overpopulation."

Faye's face stiffened. "You're blaming this on women? Statistics show, Tom, that in countries where women have control over their reproductive capacities, there is no runaway population boom. It goes quickly toward zero population growth."

Tom caressed her arm. "So you're in control, are you?"

Faye's jaw muscles bunched with rage.

Miles Guffey stuck his oar back into the conversation. "I've been reading a book that agrees with your sentiments, Faye. It's called *The Garden of Their Desires*. It advances the theory that back at the end of the last Ice Age, when the climate was wetter and cooler, the big desert belt that runs from the Sahara through the Middle East and up into China was much more hospitable."

I said, "Molly Chang was calling it the 'green Sahara.' "

Miles leaned back in his chair. "It was probably never Eden, but it was a lot friendlier place than it is now. And God was feminine, because the earth was perceived as generous and hospitable; you know, fecund. Women raised babies and a few crops, and maybe a couple baby goats that the men brought home alive from the hunt. Then along comes the warming trend, and the land got to be a bit more forbidding. The pasture dries up, so the men start taking the goats up the hill for the summer, and that's one job status the women lose. It gets drier and drier, the goats eat everything that's holding the soil down, and you get desertification. Before long, life's so tough the men start raiding each others' camps, and we start selecting for just that: raiders. The biggest interloper gets the most status. And the women are reduced to camp followers, with no status expect as breeders."

Nancy said, "Nowadays we have corporate raiders. I guess we're still living in a cultural desert."

Miles grinned.

Tom said, "We're living in a time of enormous change, fraught with rage and uncertainty, and that leaves us open to the worst kinds of opportunism. We have corporate greed buying everything up to and including the White House. The common citizen no longer has a true voice in government. The damned White House is run by opportunists."

Pamela Guffey narrowed her eyes. "What do you mean, Tom?"

"Hell, those jets crashed into those buildings, and the administration lost no time sending our boys into Afghanistan."

"You call that opportunism? I call that sacrifice."

Tom said, "Oh, there's a sacrifice being made there, alright. All those servicemen giving up being home with their families, that is a sacrifice. And I believe in what they're doing there, just as they do. But I don't for a minute believe that the administration gives a shit whether we get the terrorists, except as is expedient for their ultimate goals."

Pamela said, "Which are?"

"Getting an oil pipeline from the Caspian Sea down to the ocean. Look who's in office: a bunch of oil barons."

By this point, I was ready to puke up my grouper.

Faye's eyes were brimful of tears. She said, "Here we are sitting around enjoying the good life while people are dying of malnutrition and leftover land mines in war-torn third-world countries. How in hell are we supposed to bring babies into a world like this?"

Tom put a comforting hand over hers. "Sorry to go off like that on politics, Faye. Bringing babies into this world is precisely what we need to do," he said. "We need to birth them kindly, and love them, and educate them to the best of our capacity, and help them grow up into citizens who can lead this world out of the mess it's in. But that will take many generations. In the meantime, we need to deal with things as we find them. We need to strengthen our security, toughen our nerves, and, every once in a while, we need to go out there and get proactive."

Faye's lips tightened. "You mean fight."

Tom nodded. "Yes, let the world know we don't lie down for the schoolyard bully. I mean go out there and stop the killing where it starts. And I know what you're going to say next: We're a bunch of self-satisfied, imperialist, hypocritical assholes who ought to be shot ourselves. You're right, we have to clean house right here at home and get over this greed shit. You think I'm the sourest old pessimist that ever lived but let me tell you, I believe in this country and the principles it runs on. We've got a Constitution that works provided we pay attention and keep the right people defending it. Our Founding Fathers were some smart sons of bitches."

Faye said, "When our Founding Fathers said 'all men were created equal' they meant white males. They kept slaves and didn't even consider sharing the vote with women."

"Yeah, and we've evolved as a culture, haven't we? Because we educate people. Those Founding Fathers were smart and educated, and they left the door wide open for positive change. Which comes with education. Education is the thing, Faye. We have to educate everyone. I hope our child is a girl, and if she is, I'm going to do everything in my power to raise her as well educated, free, and independent as you are, because fully empowered women raise sane sons. And if we have a boy, I'm going to make sure he knows what a lucky son of a bitch he is to have a mother like you."

Faye yanked her hand free and swatted Tom across the chops, but she was smiling now through her tears. She muttered, "Watch who you call a bitch."

The conversation drifted to other topics, such as the theft of native orchids from south Florida, and coral reefs in general. What the world was coming to. The Gaia theory.

Climate change. The Mediterranean as a vast, dry basin before the seas broke through Gibraltar and flooded it, long before human time. Noah's flood. The price of eggs in China.

When we took our leave after ice cream and cognac, it was agreed that I would present myself at the USGS the following morning to map out a strategy for a proposed research project. But the evening's topics had pushed me far from worrying about the long-range luxuries of Masters theses. I thanked Miles kindly for the dinner, but thought, *I'll make sure Jack's safe first, and then worry about your goddamned research, asshole.*

Back at Nancy Wallace's house, Faye showed me to the room where I was to sleep. I was billeted on the second floor of the main house in a wing that angled off beyond the far side of the living room, the house thus marking two sides of the two-story pool enclosure. My room was large and comfortable and featured plush, rose-pink carpeting and twin beds with ornate wicker headboards. The bedspreads were puffy quilts decorated with tropical birds and flowers, a turquoise blue rendition of the luau shirt I expected Tom would never wear. I wondered at the policy of moving to a hot climate and then refrigerating the house to the point where bed quilts were needed, but my mother and grandmother had ground it into me that polite guests smiled and said thank you a lot, so I kept my silence on that topic. Instead, I switched off the room's localized temperature control, opened the window to the warm, humid night air, and folded back the quilt on the bed closest to it. Underneath I found a cotton thermal blanket in pink to match the carpeting. I sat on it and stared out into the screened pool deck, wondering if I might just be more comfortable sleeping out there.

A moment later, Faye quietly let herself into the room. She lowered herself into a turquoise-blue overstuffed chair with a ruffled skirt and stretched her legs up onto the foot of the bed. "I'm tired," she said.

"You did just fly us here from Utah seven months pregnant."

"Sure, maybe this pregnancy thing is beginning to get to me more than I like to admit. But you're something worse than tired."

"What?"

"Scared. Mixed with ambivalent. You want to be out finding out what's going on with Jack, not setting up some intellectual jigsaw puzzle."

At the sound of Jack's name, the wave of longing swept over me, this time followed by that odd tug at my heart I had first felt as he had driven away that afternoon. I shrugged my shoulders. They felt like lead. "I'm a geologist. I might as well do geology. Doing work is known to be useful when a person hopes to make a living."

"Come on, let it out. You're thinking that maybe Jack is some kind of hopeless flake, and here you've gone and slept with him. Makes you wonder about your IQ."

"Makes me wonder about my sanity."

"Give it two days, like Tom said."

I rubbed my face with the heels of my hands. "Faye, I don't know what to think. Jack and I have had a fine time with each other, truly. Things got really nice, so yeah, we became lovers."

"That sounds a little clinical."

I couldn't keep the bitterness out of my voice. "I am merely respecting the facts. We spent *one* night together. Next morning, he's gone. He phoned once. Next time I see him, he's a total wreck and won't say a word about what's going on. What am I supposed to think? Or feel? I'm numb, damn it. No; worse, I am pissed."

"So come gallivanting with me. We came down here to have a good time. Tell that Miles guy to take a hike. He sounded pretty full of shit, anyway."

"Well, he *is* a bit flamboyant, but his reputation is good. There's the old rub between broad-brush thinkers like him and those that get off on things as narrow as a gnat's eye-lash. The narrow guys want to debunk the big thinkers, say their science is weak, and the broad-brush guys think the narrow guys are a cartoon. I—"

Tom had suddenly filled the doorway.

"Come in," I said.

He moved slowly into the room, sloping along with his hands in his pockets until he was within reaching distance of where I was sitting, then put a hand on my shoulder. "Hi, friend. How's it going?"

I leaned my head against his hip and closed my eyes. All I could think of to say was, "Lousy."

He patted my hair. "I imagine."

Tom's sudden affection was confusing, especially considering that Faye and I were both in our thirties, and he was in his fifties, and he was married to her, and he had until then treated me like a cross between a slave and an errant niece. And this new side of Tom, this sympathetic hugs-and-squeezes Tom, flew right in under my emotional radar. It hit me right in the heart. Tears welled in my eyes, and I began to sniffle.

"That's my girl," he whispered. "That's it."

I fought the tears. "Can you tell me one thing?" I asked.

"I hope so."

"Why did Jack call his project 'Killer Dust'? I mean, is it in any way connected to what Miles Guffey's working on?"

Tom sighed and sat down with his arm around me. "I think so, Em."

"So, I mean, is it a wild coincidence that I'm being asked to work on it, too?"

"No."

"You going to tell me what that connection is?"

Tom heaved a sigh. "I can tell you this: It involves NASA. That's where Guffey's getting what funding he has, right?"

"Yeah. He told me at lunch that NASA likes to 'push the product on the populace.' Hell, Tom, I'm beginning to get the idea that it's all a game of self-justification these days in the sciences. You've got to continually let the public know what you've done for them lately, which is reasonable, but if you're doing it just to get a slice of the funding pie, it puts a weird spin on things. Guffey went to NASA for money because they understand publicity. They've got all those satellites up there, not to mention observation planes, and oh, yes, this thing called a space shuttle that goes up to a big tin can called a space station, and they've got to keep the taxpayer giddy about the whole works."

Tom said, "I guess we've gotten over being impressed that that space program brought us Tang and Velcro."

"Right. They have their gadgets up there looking down on the Earth from hundreds of miles up, but now they have to prove they're doing something important with them. They find they can observe dust clouds blowing off the desert regions. So that's all well and good, but you've got to prove that it's important to observe dust clouds. Guffey thinks that there are pathogens in those dust clouds, so he makes his project look like a NASA showpiece. So they tossed some chump change at Guffey so he could hire a microbiologist or two and set up a lab, move from idea to theory to fact. Oo-ee, big news story. That's what I found on the web at first glance. But what's that got to do with Jack? How's he connected to Miles Guffey's project?"

Tom gave me another little squeeze and then took his arm away, apparently done displaying affection for the day. "He's not connected, not directly, but think about it: Miles's project, NASA, your work as a geologist, and the FBI's work of detection all have one important thing in common: observation. You've got to think about who else is making those observations, or watching, and why, and ask yourself what gets seen."

My mind began to spin through the immense scope of what Tom had just suggested. Guffey's project, and NASA's work, and geology in general all embraced a vast span of observations, running the gamut from the tiniest specs of matter viewed through powerful microscopes, and the tight reckoning of laboratory tests, to the broad ruminative realm of field work, clear up to the widest view of the Earth we geologists had yet encompassed: the view from space. My mind conjured the satellite image of a dust cloud that Guffey had shown at the press conference. As I dove into that picture, watching the flowering of those connections and steps downward from the overwhelmingly immense swirling cloud down to the unimaginably tiny motes of dust, I felt that wave of sensuosity sweep through me again, felt my body reach for Jack's, felt that weird thump at my heart, all in rapid succession.

"Observing dust," I said. I turned to Tom, my mind skidding like a stone skipping across a pool of water. "But what's observation got to do with Jack?"

Tom looked at me with sympathy. "Poor Em, it's not mine to tell you, but it's got everything to do with Jack."

– 14 –

I lay down on the bed exhausted, turned out the light, and did try to sleep without the air-conditioning, honest. A last rainstorm had cooled the air nicely, and I thought I could sleep, but the relentless, variable singing of a mockingbird somewhere out beyond the pool deck quickly poked a hole right through the barrier I tried assiduously to build between me and my anxiety. The horrors of bioterrorism, or any kind of terrorism for that matter, bloomed in my head, and the song of the bird became torture.

I clicked on the bedside light and reached for something to read. The first thing that came to hand was *Germs: Biological Weapons and America's Secret War*, which I had brought with me from Utah. "Great," I said aloud. "Just the thing to lull me to sleep." But I opened it and began to read. I read for hours, and when my eyes, aching and feeling like the lids were made of sandpaper, finally refused to focus, I turned off the light and eventually caught two or three hours of sleep.

The next morning I went back to the USGS and was about to find my way down the hall to Miles Guffey's office when the director beckoned to me from her office doorway.

"I thought I should introduce myself," she said. "I'm

Olivia Rodríguez Garcia, the center chief here. I was wondering if you could join me for lunch."

Well, you could have knocked me over with a feather. I didn't know the lady knew I existed, and what was this "go to lunch" business? But I said yes. Of course I did. If nothing else, I wanted to know what was up. As in, what's the chief scientist of an office with maybe a hundred Ph.D.s doing taking the wandering maybe-sorta graduate student to lunch?

So I arranged to meet her by the front door at noon. Meanwhile, I went upstairs to Miles Guffey's office and was immediately sucked into what was important to him.

He took me first on a whirlwind tour of the laboratory the missing Calvin Wheat had put together. It was full of industrious-looking equipment that I was soon informed were things such as incubating boxes and RNA replicators, all spotlessly clean and nestled in among the usual clusters of gas and water jets that jutted out of high black counters.

As Miles began to show me through the setup, a young woman bustled into the room. She had chocolate-brown skin and was curvy and stunningly attractive, and wore a short, low-cut dress that looked like it had been put on with spray paint. Her eyes were calm and confident. She stuck out her hand to shake mine. "Hi, I'm Waltrine Sweet. You must be Em Hansen."

"Delighted," I said, and shook her hand. I immediately felt foolish, as my response had been more appropriate to a social meeting than a professional one, but in fact it did delight me to meet her. What I did not mention was that I also felt slightly intimidated. One tends to leave that detail out of a greeting.

Perhaps she read me more clearly than I wished, because she gave me a flicker of a smile, little more than a quick crimp at one corner of her mouth, and an undecipherable signal zapped through her eyes.

Guffey said, "Waltrine here's doing her doctoral dissertation on some of our data."

"So," she said, "I hear you're looking for a thesis project out of this dust we're collecting."

"That is correct."

"Well, cool. Why don't you come with me tomorrow? I'm going to talk to some engineering geeks about doing some sampling for us."

"Where are you going?"

"To Kennedy. Where the NASA goonies hang out. It's a big whoop. Rockets and stuff. You might like it."

I wasn't quite sure where to go with her dry humor, if that is what this was. I looked at Miles.

"Sure," he said. "That would be just super. You-all could do your girl-bonding exercises, keep the project rolling along."

"Okay," I said, not sure I meant it.

Waltrine said, "They have the eye in the sky, and we have the little sniffers. You'll be in charge of connecting some dots, if you can. Don't worry, you'll get the hang of it."

"Great," I answered, thinking, *Whatever you say, lady*.

"Right. Well, let me show you around. Okay, this is what the dust samples look like when we get them," she said, as she pulled a disk of white filter paper about two inches across out of a special cartridge. "We handle the real ones with gloves and all, natch."

"Natch."

"But this one's a dud. Someone dropped it. Shit happens. Okay, we culture them out. Then we do our count and then extract DNA from each individual bug and run it through PCR—polymerase chain reaction—to amplify the DNA for identification. It works kind of like a Xerox machine for biological sequences. With me so far?"

"Big ten-four," I lied.

She gave me a very dry look with her very big brown eyes. Proceeding to the next machine and the next, she whizzed me through about six or eight years of college and postgraduate biology, chemistry, and public health, all macerated and cross-riffled through a haze of cutting-edge technology.

"So," I said, "I take it you're a biologist, too, like Calvin Wheat?"

She let her heavy eyelids down and up, a somnolent display of just how impressed she was by my not very brilliant deduction of her curriculum vitae. "Yeah. You got it, Wheat and Sweet, microbiologists extraordinaire." As in, *You got a problem with any of this, honey?*

"Oh." I glanced sideways at Miles Guffey.

Guffey's face had settled into a mild smirk. He fiddled with a spare bit of filter paper, held it up to the light, generally did his best to look casual while he kept himself from guffawing at the deep hole I'd just found myself in. I could see that he was quite proud of his microbiologist lady.

I looked back and forth between Miles and Waltrine. Something was niggling at me, a steady signal that there was something I should be figuring out, as if there were a joker somewhere in the deck having a good laugh at Em. Such as, why weren't they more worried about their missing colleague? "Have you heard anything more about Calvin Wheat?" I asked.

Waltrine blinked, one quick bat of her enormously thick, curly eyelashes.

Miles Guffey cleared his throat. "Well, funny you should ask," he said, his expression turning somber. "We've heard from a lady on the cruise ship who says she saw him thrown overboard."

"*Thrown* overboard?" I gasped.

Miles gave me a probing look. "I *told* you."

"But—"

"Right, well, we have certain friends in port there in Barbados, and we got a report back that there's an eyewitness says she was watching him from her stateroom because she thought what he was doing was kinda interesting, and she didn't want to be at dinner. He was out there in his tuxedo fiddling with the sampling gear, and some big guy came and picked him up and tossed him clean over the rail."

"Shit!"

"As I said."

"Well, who would want to do that?"

Miles gave me a sardonic look. "I been tryin' to figger that out myself."

"What about the cruise line that owns the ship? Don't they want to know if they have someone on board that's ejecting their passengers before the boat gets to dock?"

"Well, essackly. You do ask the right questions."

"All flattery aside, Miles, what is the cruise line doing about this? And why did you have to hear this from a contact in Barbados?"

"*All* the right questions."

Something in Guffey's tone stopped me short. He was an odd one, simultaneously laser sharp and just a wee bit paranoid. Little red flags were popping up all over the place in my brain, telling me to back off before I got myself sucked into something I did not understand and did not need to be involved in. "Well, great," I said, backpedaling like mad. "So I'm on the right track. Meanwhile, let's get back to the tour here."

Waltrine nodded and took me through the rest of her setup.

When she was done, I asked. "How many critters have you ID'd so far?"

"Over 130," Waltrine replied. "Fungi, bacteria. The viruses are there but we can't culture them, because they won't grow outside specific hosts. But just the bacteria and fungi are enough to make me want to pee in my britches. We've got *Aspergillus, Cladosporium, Alternaria,* sixteen species of *Bacillus* already, and dozens of other genera are represented. About twenty-five percent are agricultural diseases and ten percent are opportunistic diseases in humans."

"Nasty." I reached for the little notebook I usually put in my pocket for such occasions, but found that I had forgotten it.

"Whatcha need?" Miles asked.

"I wanted to make some notes."

He grabbed a notepad off the counter. It was nicely printed with the logo and motto USGS: SCIENCE FOR A CHANGING WORLD. "Thanks," I said. I started to tear a page off of it.

"No, keep the whole pad," Miles said. "We call that 'outreach.' "

Waltrine said, "Yeah, they got money for fancy scratch pads, but not for doing science."

Their bitterness was beginning to snag at me like gum under my shoes. I looked away.

My eyes came to rest on a large ledger notebook, the kind with permanently bound pages. It lay open at the end of the lab bench. It was full of carefully handwritten notes. "Oh, isn't this great," I said, admiring it. "A woman after my own heart, you still take your primary notes by hand."

Waltrine lowered her lids halfway and raised her eyebrows. "That's lab protocol. Original notes *have* to be hard copy, and in ink." She flipped some pages. "That's how we document things. Otherwise, it would be too easy for folks to kind of edit things, know what I mean?"

Guffey gave me a satisfied wink, as if to say, *We be doin' the work that answers the questions.* He steered me back out into the hallway. We passed several large posters that depicted work being done for various projects underway at the center. There were plenty of air views of sand spits and coastal plains, some marked "before" and "after" relative to hurricane Andrew, the big killer of the 1990s. "So this is the Coastal Marine Branch of the USGS," I commented. "Is most of what's done here coastal geology? I see a lot of views of shoreline processes, hurricane damage and such."

Miles said, "It's not a branch, it's a program. Things got renamed a while back. 'Division' became 'discipline.' That makes everything more relavant, get it? That all came in with the downsizing and the outreach. Less science, more touchy-feely. But to answer your question, there are three centers to the program. This one, one in Menlo Park, California, and one in Woods Hole, Massachusetts. We all fight over one little pot of money."

I cocked an eyebrow at him. "Funding is the big thing."

"Essackly. I tell you, trying to get people to take science seriously is a durn close to impossible if it doesn't have an immediate and obvious dollar payoff for someone upstairs from you. I been trying to get this project adequately funded from the git-go, but I've run up against one stone wall after another. I can't get a nickel out of the USGS here."

"Why? Doesn't dust raining down on your coast count as coastal geology?"

"Not really. They want something that affects real estate straight up, so's the developers and taxpayers can line it up next to their property values. To hell with their health, or the health of the environment all around them. The USGS has a special fund for wild-ass cutting-edge ideas, but they say the project's too far out there one day and too well-established the next. What they do do is pay my salary and give me the freedom to think my thoughts."

"That's a lot."

"That's a great lot. Yes, that is a great lot."

"What exactly happened when you pitched it to the Center for Disease Control?"

"They're set up to deal with crises. So if I prove there's a problem, and hold it up to them like a red cape, they might see if they have a spare bull to charge at it. The military seems interested, but they prefer to do things in-house. The Department of Agriculture has its head in the sand and agribusiness doesn't want us thinking our food is tainted. The EPA is so focused on smokestack emissions that they don't want to know that half the particulates we inhale here in Florida come from Africa. The list goes on and on."

I looked more carefully at one of the displays on the wall. "Do the hurricanes get funding?"

"Oh yeah. Plenty bucks for when and where's it going

to hit and such like. There you got developers gonna lose money and people gonna die right this minute if you don't do something, much easier to grasp than the slow collapse of a whole ecosystem in the Caribbean. So we got lots of folks running around looking at what a good blow does to the shoreline sediments."

"I mean currently. I hear that a storm delayed a space shuttle launch."

"Yeah, that happens." He gestured at a large satellite image of the Caribbean and put a finger down by the Yucatan peninsula. "The current hurricane is right about here now, kicking up some winds along the east coast, not much happening here on this side. But it could easily turn ninety degrees and head on up here."

"The hurricanes are a problem for you, right? I noticed that boat you had at dockside beyond your house."

He snorted. "Not much you can do once a storm gets going. Them things can turn any which-away, you never know where they's gonna make landfall until it's too late to move a boat. You can't outrun it. Florida is a big place, but it's flat as a pancake, and anywhere the wind blows, it just blows and blows. So I just lash everything down and hope." He gave the satellite image a little tap right on St. Petersburg.

My eye riveted on the image, taking in all the blue water that surrounded the big, flat peninsula on which I had somehow found myself. Not for the first time, I wondered just what had really brought me here.

My lunch with Olivia Rodríguez Garcia brought a series of odd surprises. First, she did not take me to Chattaway's, or, for that matter, to any other place in St. Petersburg. Instead, she drove across the vast expanse of Tampa Bay— the elevated causeway must have been almost ten miles long, with water and nothing else on either side—to Tampa itself (St. Petersburg is on a neck of land that forms the western side of the bay, and Tampa forms the east). She drove like a seared bat and made idle chitchat as we rocketed along. I went with the flow as best I could, all the time wondering what her agenda was in inviting me to lunch.

Once off the causeway into Tampa, she turned north and maneuvered us around until we pulled up in front of a place called Mambo's Café. It was a small place with one row of booths and tables. At the sight of the owners, a husband and wife team, Olivia broke into rapid, elegantly enunciated Spanish that was full of idioms and contractions I could not follow. After quick hugs and what sounded like rounds of "Hi there" and "How's the family," she turned and introduced me. Then she said, "You are wondering why I brought you so far for a simple little meal, no?"

"I am wondering, yes."

She smiled. "Food is important. We women must stick together, celebrate over food. We have much to reclaim from the way our grandmothers, and our grandmothers' grandmothers, did business. We do our work differently from men: We understand working *together*." She gave me an expansive smile and opened her hands upward, presenting the restaurant to me. "So I bring you here. This is the food of my grandmother's grandmothers."

I thought of what I had heard the evening before, that the women in hunter-gatherer societies provided the grand majority of the nutrition, and I smiled in spite of my wariness.

She said, "Please, have anything you want. I remember too well being a graduate student and worrying about money. This is on me."

I said, "Thank you, Dr. Garcia."

She smiled a motherly smile, odd considering that she could not have been more than a decade my senior. "Please don't be so formal. We do not call each other 'doctor' at the USGS, or we'd be at it all day. Besides, in Latin culture the paternal surname—what you would call me in America—is the first of my last names, Rodríguez. Garcia is the maternal surname, and is not usually used here. My middle name is Carmen. So, Olivia Carmen Rodríguez Garcia. My family calls me 'Puru,' but you may call me Olivia until we know each other much better." She gave me a wink.

I'm afraid I gaped at her, wondering, *Why is this woman sucking up to me?* But I played along with it, partly because on the money side of things she was right, I was an inch from penniless. "Well, okay, uh—Olivia, what do you recommend?" Trying to meet her halfway with the cultural thing, I tried it again in Spanish. *"¿Que es bueno aqui?"*

"Ah, *que bien, señorita.* I recommend *la pechuga de pollo a la parilla.* And here, you must have *los tostones, y para beber, un jugo de mango."* She pronounced *mango* idiosyncratically, with the emphasis on the *o.*

"Is this a Cuban restaurant?" I asked.

She drew herself up with mock affrontedness. *"¿Cubano? No! Es Puertorriqueño!"*

She helped me choose from the cafeteria line and we sat down at a table. She gestured at each item on my tray. *"Mira:* Grilled chicken breast, seasoned with *adobo,* the best you'll ever eat this side of my mother's. White rice *(arroz blanco),* red beans *(habichuelas coloras)* seasoned with *sofrito, y* plaintains *(tostones),* very crispy." She made a sweeping gesture with both hands. *"Todo es Puertorriqueño."*

The way she was cutting from English to Spanish and back was beginning to make me feel a little swimmy. I smiled weakly at my hostess–Center Chief and found her observing me frankly, with no attempt to cover her intent. Tentatively, I said, "Your idioms are quite different from what I hear back in the Rockies."

She laughed easily. "I imagine so. It is as if you were comparing an American English speaker with one raised in Britain. Or South Africa. Or Australia. Very different sound to it. And here in Florida we have more than the one Spanish. We have the Cuban, as you supposed, as well as the Puerto Rican."

"How do they differ? Give me a for instance."

"Oh! You can always tell a Puerto Rican, because we say *'mira.'* A Cuban would say, *'oye.'* " She smiled, like it was a saucy little joke between just us two.

I tucked this away, thankful for something small and concise to think about in the middle of the growing miasma of feelings and impressions that had begun to ball up since I had gotten in the car with Olivia Rodríguez Garcia . . . or since I had arrived in Florida . . . hell, since I had gone to bed with Jack Sampler. A nice, intellectual examination of a difference in word usage was about my speed right then. *Mira* meant "look;" *oye* meant "listen," one small but significant difference in the way the two peoples caught each others' attention. "And I suppose the cuisines are different as well?" I took a bite of my red beans. They were delicious.

"*Sí.* Red beans. *Habichuelas coloras.* In Cuba, they would be *frijoles negros. En tu parte del paiz, tu dices, 'frijoles,' ¿verdad? Lo mismo en Cuba. Tu arroz es blanco. En Cuba, amarillo.* Come on, eat!" She tapped the edge of my plate with her fork and gestured that I use mine to shovel some food into my mouth.

I put my elbows on the edge of the table and put my face in my hands. I was feeling almost faint.

"Something the matter?" she inquired, not sounding convincingly concerned.

I shook my head. "Probably the heat getting to me. Or the humidity. It gets hot back in Utah, but it's a dry heat." I was beginning to feel like I was pouring through the tiles in the floor, all liquid and flowing, totally lacking in spine. What the hell was I doing talking about the weather?

"You're sure it's nothing else?"

I looked up. She was examining me again. I decided that I did not enjoy being examined. "Sure. There's plenty going on," I said, images of Jack all disheveled flashing through my head, chased quickly by Miles Guffey's rubbery smile. Both were shot full of holes by Olivia Rodríguez Garcia's gratuitous kindnesses. "But maybe we could get there faster if you tell me what I can do for you. I don't mean to be rude, but surely you have something on your mind."

Olivia nodded decisively. "Yes, yes. Business. Certainly.

Eat, and I will tell you." She gave my dish another whack with her fork. When she saw me pick up mine and take a stab at my chicken, she said, "You are thinking of working with Miles Guffey on his dust project. I am the Center Chief. It is my job to keep things running smoothly." She turned her attention to her dish and began to pick around among the beans.

I chewed and swallowed some delicious meat, then said, "Okay, let me guess: Dr. Guffey has his ways of making things go *un*smoothly."

Olivia nodded. "I see you understand. This makes things easier. And by the way, it is not Dr. Guffey. He has only a bachelor's degree."

I blinked in amazement.

"Yes," Olivia continued. "It is surprising. But this is how the Survey used to be. Bright people would come on straight out of college, and the Survey would train them, bring them along, almost an apprentice system. Heaven knows it hardly pays any better than that!" She laughed at her own joke.

"Well, he sure is highly regarded."

She nodded and stabbed into her rice. "Yes, yes. Miles has a way of involving people in his work, and that's good, but . . ."

"But he's trying to shake things up with the public to get some funding."

"*Sí*. . . . I thought I should explain a few things about the way work is done at the Survey. Help you fit in better." She glanced up at me.

So this was all about going along to get along, and bringing me all the way onto her ethnic turf was symbolic. I did the emotional math: Miles Guffey had pissed her off. He was bringing needed publicity to the USGS, but at the same time ignoring rules in order to get funding for his project. This made him a management nightmare. She had to answer to the chain of command over her head. He had to get funding, or his idea would stay an idea and never make it to fully fledged theory status, let alone proven fact.

I was from outside the system and therefore a resource each
of them could try to co-opt. "I'm all ears," I said, trying to
sound like I meant it. More than anything, I wanted to slap
my hands over my ears and hide under the table. I hated
politics with a passion. "So tell me, just what is the funding
picture at the USGS?"

Olivia glanced skyward. "We have been on hard times
since the self-imposed RIF—reduction in force—of the
1990s. There was bloodshed there. I came on board after
that, so I am not part of that fight. But it had to be done.
Congress was looking for an agency to cut, and we were
vulnerable, because the public did not know what we did
for them. And we were top-heavy: Over ninety percent of
the budget went to salaries; there was no money to fund
projects whatsoever. So something had to go. Now, we are
more stable, but we still have a very limited funding picture
unless we take in project money from other federal agencies, or even from private-sector grants. We are increasingly like a university department, or a consulting
company, where people fight for the small pieces of pie."

"But I am outside that picture," I said cautiously. "I am
a graduate student. I cost little or nothing. So why are you
concerned about me?"

Olivia lowered her eyelids halfway and cleared her
throat, her meal forgotten. "It is because of the nature of
the specific project." She ticked items off on her fingers as
she went. "First, African dust does not fall—pardon the
pun—within our mandate. Second, even if it did, we have
many projects far more critical in nature, and perhaps you
would find many of them more interesting as well. Third,
while Miles has managed to get quite a lot of publicity for
his dust, he has very few facts at his disposal, which means
that his dust may in fact be—and now I make the ironic
play on words—all wet. Again you might be better served
to consider another project, if only to be taken seriously as
a scientist."

I shot my eyebrows up. I was quite certain that what I

was hearing lay far outside the usual welcome-aboard pep talk.

Olivia put out a hand to shush me, then pointed a finger and waggled it at me. "I can see your surprise. I am speaking very candidly, no? I see in you a lot of myself, and I am concerned. As Center Chief, my responsibilities are many and varied. I have a lot of people to serve and hundreds of issues to juggle, and *I must not show preferential treatment.* But, as a woman working in a man's profession, I will *damned* well look out for other women if I please. It was not easy for me to get where I am, as you can imagine."

I blinked. It was the first time I had heard one woman scientist say anything like this to another. Embarrassed, moved, and unprepared to receive such a kindness or discern it from manipulation, if that was what this was, I changed the subject. "And then there is the matter of Calvin Wheat."

Olivia gave a quick nod. "Yes. Where is he? And what does this mean? And I am concerned that Miles is using this disappearance of one of his workers to promote his project. Really, this is the limit! Controversy, as I said. Not good in a budding career. *Ahora,* fifthly," she went back to counting on her fingers, then threw her hands up in a gesture of frustration. "*¡Ayi! Mira,* has Miles mentioned Chip Hiller's work?"

"Uh, no. . . ."

"Of course not. Miles will lead you to believe that he is the inventor of the African dust idea, but in fact it was Chip Hiller who first looked at this dust. And of course, the phenomenon is nothing new. We have iron-rich dust forming the bulk of the soil horizon on coral islands throughout the Atlantic, and the Pacific, for that matter. It is part of the history of our planet. It is where our planet came from! Ashes to ashes, dust to . . ." She trailed off dramatically, as if suddenly aware that she was raving, but I caught a glint in her eyes, as if she was watching to see what impact her words were having on me.

I cleared my throat and said nothing. We stared at each other a while. I let my thoughts drift to Jack, and to the longings and curiosity that had brought me to Florida in the first place. I felt that odd tug at my heart, and was, somehow, reminded by it that I had not come here as much to earn a degree as to find out how and why my lover had flown off into a cloud of dust. Finally I said, with the full irony of utter sincerity, "I thank you for your concern. I have never known a fellow scientist to go to bat for me to quite this extent. I am floored."

Olivia kept her gaze on me. "It is nothing," she murmured.

I watched her attack her grilled chicken with force and precision, wondering if she thought of me any differently from the meat on her plate. In that moment, I decided that I would indeed work on Miles Guffey's project, but not as a groveling graduate student massaging the dry dust of data under the tutelage of a master. No, I would attack the project solely and precisely as a crime scene, because it was now clear to me that, in one way or another, it was exactly that.

– 15 –

Back at the USGS, I got to work. I spoke with Miles Guffey and made a list of all scientists who were in any way connected to the project, and then interviewed a few of them so I could make thumbnails summarizing each investigator's involvement, both by specialty and by degree of professional commitment. If someone's career was hanging on the line, I wanted to know it. If someone was trying to discredit someone else, I wanted to make a mark by that name. If someone was feeding me a ration of shit, I most certainly wanted to know it and document it and understand what that meant, especially if that someone was Miles Guffey. Or Olivia Carmen "Puru" Rodríguez Garcia, God bless her many names.

A ration of shit. *Shit* was the word. Don't ever ask a girl raised on a ranch in Wyoming to confuse a cow flop with a cherry pie. And this was not your lone meadow muffin lying all by itself out there on the range; no, this was the whole pile of manure stacked up in the feedlot with steers stomping around in it snorting and mooing. I had not asked to go there, not really, but as long as I was now up past my belt buckle in it, I was going to take control of it or go down trying.

And somewhere out there, doing something that neither he nor Tom in their infinite wisdom had deigned to tell me about, Jack was languishing in the same pile of shit. To stretch the metaphor just a little farther, he may have climbed into this shit thinking he could transform it into something useful like compost, but by the time he had turned up at Nancy Wallace's, he'd gotten it all over him, and it did not look or sound or smell good. *No mira, oye, o huele.*

So I sat on a stool at the big drafting table in Miles Guffey's office as he ran around the building harassing his underlings, and I contemplated shit. I reminded myself that I had to use my brains as much as my sensory organs. I could not wade into the pile of shit past my eye sockets, or I'd be no good to Jack and no good to myself.

I was reasonably sure that some of the shit belonged to the fabled not-doctor Guffey himself, regardless of his reputation as a top scientist, and I was not convinced for a minute that things were "essackly" as they were being represented.

I was running on raw intuition, which by my lights is something that pops up where experience meets information. Geology is a highly intuitive science, because geologic information—the data we collect, or phenomena we observe—are fragmental, incomplete, discontinuous, and often downright ambiguous. Slavish adherence to the scientific method alone does not get the job done. We must constantly run our data through a fey part of our mental machinery, matching it to previously observed patterns, moving back and forth with it in time and space until the themes and variations emerge. We compare what's happening now with evidence of past events and project these patterns into the future. Geology is thus an historical science, and as with any study of history, the context of events is everything, and as context evolves, so does our understanding of it.

There was obviously some history involved in this crime, both geological and personal. Usually, the span of time considered in historical analysis and prediction amounts to eons—hundreds of millions, even billions, of years—and the subject of observation is something inspiring and uplifting, a grand synthesis that dwarfs the petty scurry of human events. But here I was dealing with something that was occurring within a very short time scale, geologically speaking—a drought in Africa spanning only a few decades, narrowing down to present-time occurrences, topped with the raw stink of something critical that was going to occur within a matter of days. And I was analyzing something that looked and smelled as base and familiar as . . . well, shit, to stay with the metaphor. Or simile, or whatever it was.

Miles had gone on walkabout somewhere else in the building. I sat at the drafting table in his office staring at my page of notes, my mind clicking along in a groove. I was thinking on the fly, moving fast, sucking up information like a dry/wet vacuum. In the back of my mind, I could see that Tom had, as usual, teased and manipulated me into—to throw out just one more metaphor—putting my shoulder to this wheel, or, at least, putting my brain on the project. His penchant for messing with my head had, in the past, always put me into a fair snit of indignation and insubordination, but this time I chose not to waste the energy a snit would consume. It struck me that I must have come to trust Tom, because I felt content to do what I did best and let him feed me what I could handle when I could handle it. And just so long as what *he* fed me wasn't a shit sandwich, I felt confident that we would, somehow, get the job done.

But what was the job?

I started over again, approaching through the lens of my specialty, forensic geology. I define that term to encompass two activities: 1) analysis of geologic materials collected at a crime scene, and 2) application of knowledge of the business of geology to understand the *context* of the crime. In the past, I had focused on the second activity. This time, Tom seemed to be steering me into the first. So I would do both.

The stench that was rising off the controversy over Miles Guffey's project belonged with 2) business, a perfect ex-

ample of why it took a geoscience insider to figure out what
was going on in a situation like this. For instance, the outside observer might not understand that it was abundantly
unusual for a Center Chief like Olivia Rodríguez to speak
to me the way she had at lunch. Her maneuvers had been
entirely political and not in the least bit motivated by science. Likewise, Miles Guffey's grandstanding attempts to
gain publicity for his project while trying to answer the
question of what had become of Calvin Wheat went far
outside the typical avenues of scientific research. Something was rotten in the state of the science, and I wanted
to know what it was, if only to know how to dodge around
it and save my own professional skin. Because Olivia Rodríguez had a point: There were rules of decorum within the
scientific community, and it was important to avoid coming
off looking like a pawn on someone else's chessboard.

About as I thought that thought, Miles Guffey swaggered back into the room, hands in pockets, eyes wide with
some kind of mischief. "Hoo-ee!" he expostulated. "Ol'
Waltrine's got her undies in a bundle now! You shoulda
seen her! She's going off like Mount Vesuvius!"

I swung around, ready to listen.

Guffey said, "You heard of Chip Hiller's work?"

Hadn't Dr. Rodríguez mentioned his name at lunch? "Uh
. . . He's another dust expert?"

Guffey's eyes popped with suppressed laughter. "Ah,
yeah, I suppose you'd have to call him that. Well, okay,
he's a dust guy all right, but I mean . . . he's like a little
old lady, fussin' and fumin' over how he's the only one
who knows how to work with the stuff. Hell, his sampling
protocol is like hitting a piano with a sledgehammer and
expecting to get music, but to go and criticize ours—"

Just then Waltrine Sweet marched into the room, her
brows down like a visor, neck stiff with rage, fists balled.
"I want that man's testicles on a *platter*!" she roared.

Guffey told me, "Here's where you ask, 'What man's
testicles, Waltrine?' "

I said, "What man's testicles, Waltrine?"

Waltrine threw back her head and roared. "Chip fucking Hiller's balls, that's whose! I want them in a vice! I want to slam them in a car door! I want to serve them to him for dinner with greens and some of the bull*shit* he is trying to feed *me*! That sumbitch thinks he can rip me off like this he's got—" She drew in a breath. "Another—think—COMING!"

Now I had another reason not to throw any snits: Waltrine's made mine look amateurish. "He get into your data or something, Waltrine?"

Waltrine leaned toward me, bending almost ninety degrees at the hip. "Data? Did you say raw data? Chip Hiller? Oh, no, you don't get the picture. This fucker stole whole *paragraphs* of my PAPER!"

I turned to Miles Guffey to get this translated. He said, "Waltrine submitted a paper to a prestigious microbiology journal. The Chipper is trying to scoop her by putting one in first. Only trouble is that it's a small poof of specialists in this field, so her paper was sent to him for review. So the stupid fucker's lifted her introductory paragraph just about verbatim, even swiped some of her finer idioms, *and* he thinks his data refute her findings. Only problem is he's a congenital half-wit who can't spot a correlation if it ran up and kicked him in the ass."

"*Only* problem," Waltrine seethed. "Only *problem*! This is *theft*! Theft of intellectual *property*! You think I'm going to sit around and *take* this? That motherfucker's got another thing coming, let me tell you! Where I come from, we stick pins into funny little dollies look like sumbitches like *him*!"

Miles chuckled appreciatively. "And he told Waltrine's thesis advisor that if she went to work for me, she'd be 'falling under a bad influence.' Huh! What's he call *his* action? Goody Two-shoes goes to church?"

I made my hands into a *T* to call time. "Hey, bring me up to speed on something here. What's this guy Hiller's overall position on the dust? Is he calling it sterile?"

Waltrine flung her arms out in wild arcs. "He's got to be snorting some kind of dust up his *nose* the way he goes on! He claims there are no live pathogens on the dust! But of course he ain't finding none! He goes out there and sucks the little fuckers so hard he blows them right out the back of the filter paper! He—"

Miles cut in. "Waltrine's a little upset. You see, the Chipper's figgered out some way of getting funding. We haven't. He's really only interested in the dust as an abstraction, an intellectual exercise. He's a linear thinker, can't see the correlations or the possibilities. He's been out there in the islands hanging out with his rum buddies, publishing his little papers in some forgotten scientific journal on what little minerals he's finding on a Monday or a Tuesday, and now *we* come along and make it into front-page news. Messed up his whole day."

"He's not with the Survey?" I asked.

"Oh, hell no. He *used* to be with a university. Little tenure, little grants, little mind." Miles wiped a tear of mirth of his cheek. "They forced him into early retirement. Now he's with what we politely call an independent institution."

"What's his agenda?" I asked.

"His agenda? Oh, hell, I guess his agenda would be to blow me and my little ideas out of the water at any cost. Twenty years he's been catching dust, and it never occurred to him to look for germs in it. Ol' Johnny-come-lately Guffey come in and turn his whole world upside down."

"So who exactly is he working for?" I asked.

Miles stopped laughing.

I asked again. "Where's he getting his funding?"

Again Miles did not answer. I made a mental note to check Chip Hiller out on my own.

Miles said, "I'm sorry, Em, I shouldn't go on like this about a colleague. Chip and I go way back. We get along. We—"

Waltrine drew in a big breath, preparatory to venting further rage. "*You* may go back, but *I* do not go back. Cal *Wheat* does not get a *chance* to go 'way back.' Cal *Wheat* got thrown off a fucking ship before he got to shove that bastard's face into his rotten data! And I am not going to take this sitting still! I am going to go over to NASA tomorrow and blow the *lid* off his petty little sampling protocol! I am going to publish my paper, and the next conference, I'm going to stand up there in front of all our au*gust* colleagues and personally trim his male appendages down to a *nub,* if in fact they are large enough to locate without a microscope!"

Miles broke into another fit of giggles. "Okay, Waltrine, okay!" He winked at me. "Gives the term 'microbiologist' a whole new meaning, huh?"

I said, "So Calvin Wheat had a personal gripe with this guy?"

Miles glanced out the window. Waltrine stared at the floor and tapped her foot. Miles said, "It's still hard to hear him spoken of in the past tense. . . ."

Trying to be consoling, I said, "Maybe he's still alive."

Waltrine kept her gaze aimed on the floor. Her foot tapping continued.

I asked, "Did Calvin ever work with Chip Hiller?"

Miles said, "Oh, hey, Waltrine! Remember to take Em with you tomorrow." He grinned. "We got this little buzz going with NASA. We're using their space imagery to track the dust, and here they've got some jockeys going to fly high-altitude missions. We want to put some sampling devices in those aircraft, prove once and for all that the microbes we're finding aren't coming from the wet hanky some tourist threw off a passing ship."

Waltrine clenched her teeth and said, "The wonderful Chip Hiller has the gall to suggest that our data come from foliage surrounding our sampling site. He says that because his is on the upwind end of the island, and ours is on the downwind—"

"Wait," I said. "You're sampling on the *down*wind end of an island? Why not the upwind? Why not avoid controversy?"

Waltrine made a gesture like she was plucking a recalcitrant chicken. "Another one! I will not drive clear across Florida with a skeptic!"

Miles said, "Our sampling station is on the downwind end of the island because that is where our sampling station *attendant* lives. We are doing this with volunteers. It's pretty hairy trying to do this with no funding, let me tell you! Now, if we could kiss butt like Chip Hiller . . ."

Waltrine screamed, "We would all have oral *herpes!*"

I glanced out the open office door. A few colleagues had gathered in the hallway, smiling, as if enjoying having ringside seats to an especially good fight. Evidently Waltrine's outburst was not counted as a surprise.

Miles said, "Spoken like a true microbiologist, Waltrine. But give Em a chance. Take her along tomorrow. Y'all'll get along like a couple hogs in the mud."

Waltrine shrugged a shoulder. "Sure, if you say so." She looked at me, her face suddenly back in control. "Can you be ready to go by eight? It's a two and a half hour drive, and our meeting is at eleven."

Miles sniggered. "Em, be sure to bring your crash helmet. Most people allow an hour or so longer than that."

I was somewhat frazzled by the extremity of Waltrine's outburst. I had heard plenty of foul language in my day, but hers had surprised me. I felt like something had just gotten past me here, just as the pathogens on the dust had gotten past Chip Hiller. No matter, I'd have a long car drive with Waltrine during which I could get to know her better and try to figure out what she was hiding in plain sight. "Okay," I said, folding my list and putting it in my pocket where no one could stumble upon it accidentally and know what I was really up to. "I'll be here."

Back at Nancy's, I took a quick swim to try to build up my tolerance to the idea of water, then went and found Tom.

He was back in the guesthouse, studying something on the screen of his notebook computer. He looked up at me over his half glasses as I came in and quickly folded the screen down flat so I couldn't see it. Faye, who was lolling naked on the couch doing her impression of a streamlined Venus of Willendorf, batted her eyelashes and said, "You try being pregnant in summer sometime." She looked tired.

I turned to Tom. "Lots to report."

"Spill."

"First I want to use your computer to look something up on the Internet."

"It's all yours," he said, moving out of his chair.

I sat down and brought up a search engine, and tapped in CHIP HILLER. It took me a while to crack a location for him, because of course Chip was a nickname, but I kept at it and eventually dug him up through HILLER + DUST. His full name was Wilbert Higby Hiller (if it were me, I'd go for a nickname, too), and he had previously published from a small university, as Miles had said. Currently, he held the lofty title of Director and Chief Scientist, Royal Caribbean Institute of Atmospheric Science, and it gave an address in the Bahamas. The Web page for the institute seemed so puffed up and nonspecific that I wondered if it really amounted to much. "How do you figure out who's funding an institute?" I asked, now typing in BENJAMIN FARNSWORTH, the anthrax researcher Calvin Wheat had known, figuring to round out my list of names.

Tom grew impatient. He said, "Drat. This guy I can't find."

"His name is Ben Farnsworth, and he's a microbiologist. I'm not finding anything on him in here."

Tom said testily, "It would help to know what you're looking for."

"Okay, I'll report. Well, there's trouble in paradise. Miles Guffey is pissing off half the profession, and the other half are standing outside his door laying bets on who wins which rounds. He's got a second microbiologist working for him, a woman named Waltrine Sweet who could cuss the bolts out of a battleship, and reading between the lines, she's under some pressure to come up with positive results for her doctoral dissertation. There's an antagonist named Chip Hiller in some other shop who's kicking up a major turf war; he says Guffey's ideas are hogwash. This Farnsworth guy knew Calvin Wheat at school. And I had lunch with the Center Chief, a woman who's playing the feminist card as a way to get me off the project. And I'm tagging along with Waltrine tomorrow to see the NASA guys at Kennedy."

Tom gave me a lips-only smile. "My, but you have been busy."

"Better'n sitting around."

Faye mumbled, "You're going clear over to Kennedy? We should go to the Dali museum. It has better air-conditioning."

Ignoring that, I asked, "You hear anything more from Jack?"

Tom shook his head. "Tell me more about your time with Miles Guffey."

"Oh, we tossed around some ideas about what part of the pie I might work on. I was appalled by how much there is to do. I wandered around there, talking to all the different experts that have a piece of the game, each one of them giving a little time to Guffey off the meter, because their time's really paid for by other projects. The scope of the dust project is huge—trying to document what-all's coming over here in those dust clouds, and exactly where some of it's coming from and going to. They have high arsenic levels in the cisterns out on the islands, for instance, and that can't be explained unless it's coming from the dust. So where's that at? Are the winds carrying away the spoils piles from mining operations? And we're talking the cradle of humanity here: Africa has mines that go back several millennia, piles of crud all over the place, and even today's mines aren't operated by the standards of environmental safety we have here in the U.S. And then there's the fact that most peoples who live there are living hand-to-mouth. One person I spoke to said that their idea of solid waste management is to pile up the camel dung and human feces right where the wind will pick it up and carry it off toward us, and do you know what they do with plastic bags and spent tires? They pile them up and burn them. She said the air quality in Mali, for instance, where ninety percent of the population lives on two percent of the land, right along the banks of the Niger River, is so bad, so full of petrochemicals and their daughter products, that she got a ripping sinus infection when she went over there to set up a sampling station."

Tom smiled sweetly. "This is what I love about you, Em. You're a regular sponge for pertinent information."

I couldn't help but preen slightly over that compliment. When it came down to cases, I really did want Tom's approval. "Thanks. So that's what I did, I tried to find out where the political bodies were buried, but I also learned what I could that would apply to that idea of approaching the project like a crime scene. Clearly one of the crimes is against nature: We've gone and put too many people in a very dry place, and they're having a hard go of it. So they drain the lakes and rivers for irrigation, leaving a big pan of silt that's charged with whatever mine drainage and so forth might have fed into it. Then they drive some goats out into the remaining vegetative cover and tear it up, and more soil—with its load of raw sewage and any other germs and spores that might be hanging around—gets sucked up by the wind."

Tom said, "So we humans are again despoiling our own nest."

I pondered that. "Yeah . . . but it's not that simple, Tom. We're not separate from nature. So the crime is against ourselves, *and* nature has a hand in it, by the bare facts of climate change over the past ten or fifteen millennia. I don't know . . . it just seems that there are a few more terms in the equation than just 'we screwed up.' " I sighed, frustrated by the sense that there was a thread hanging in the middle of the logic picture. "And then there's this whole anthrax bit."

Tom spoke softly. "About which Miles Guffey has been screaming for years."

I looked sharply at him. "You mean you've know about him right along?"

Tom's eyes had grown dark with something akin to sympathy, an unusually candid look coming from him. "Yes. You'll recall that while I still worked for the FBI, I made it my business to know as much as I could about threats to homeland security. Everything from simple tricks like loading a bunch of fertilizer and fuel oil into a rental truck and blowing up a government center in Oklahoma to the more sophisticated stunts, like the threat posed by weapons-grade anthrax. Talk about pissing in our own nest: It was our guys who developed the supervirulent strains. Then we were stupid enough to sell some of them to our so-called friends. But it takes sophistication to know how to handle it without getting hoisted by your own petard. So yes, I made it a point to keep track of smart people who take an interest in anthrax."

I let the knowledge that Tom had known all about Miles

Guffey trickle down through my mental sponge and see what it grabbed hold of.

Tom spoke again. "I want to go to Kennedy with you tomorrow."

That surprised me. "You taking time to be a tourist?"

He avoided my question by asking another one. "What's this Waltrine character driving?"

"A government vehicle, no doubt."

Tom winced at the memory of driving such stripped-down models. "Tell her I'll drive her there in regal comfort. Faye, will Nancy loan us a car?"

"Anything as long as it's a Mercedes," she sighed. "And *if* the air-conditioning is working, if you want me to come."

I said, "I'll have to check this all out with Waltrine. Rumor has it she drives like she's shot from a gun, so I'll give her a call and suggest we get an earlier start than she's planned on. We have to be there at eleven."

Faye gasped, "Eleven?" Then she looked at her husband through her eyelashes and sang, "To-om, it's a hundred and fifty *miles* to Kennedy. Three hours minimum, and that's if you go ballistic and manage to catapult yourself over all the traffic in Orlando."

"Orlando?" I said. "Isn't that where Jack's mother lives? Maybe we should stop and see her."

Tom shook his head. "Not a good idea, Em. Don't you think Jack would want to be the one to introduce you?"

Faye continued whining about the early hour. "You don't really want to get up that *early,* do you?"

I said, "What's going on, Faye? You didn't seem to mind getting up early yesterday."

"That was for flying." Suddenly she sat up. "Hey! Do you want to *fly* over there?"

Tom shook his head. "I need a car when I get there."

Faye pursed her lips coquettishly. "We could rent one at the airport over there. . . . Come on, I came down here to party, and you two are being a couple of workaholics."

Tom said, "No, flying's no good. I want to talk to this

Waltrine Sweet, then take a little dogleg and look at another location."

"Oh, bother," said Faye. "Chasing other women already, and I'm not even tacked down with a squalling infant yet. What kind of bomb are you going to save for my postpartum depression?" She arched her back and stretched, rolling her growing breasts and full-moon belly with sensuous grace. It was quite a show: She'd been out sunbathing, so her body was nicely browned and liberally oiled, and her pregnancy had turned her nipples big and brown, and there was a lovely brown stripe running right down the center of her roundness. Clearly pregnancy agreed with her, and I hoped that the griping was a gratuitous bid for extra attention while she kicked back and enjoyed herself liberally. But I wasn't sure. She seemed to be rocking between long naps and spates of pushing herself too hard, by turns giving into the pregnancy and then defying her growing dependency on Tom.

Tom smiled, eyeing his bride with lascivious pride. "I keep trying to tell you, Faye, that you look better to me with every new ounce of baby fat."

I stood up. "I think I'll go phone Waltrine," I said, and hustled out the door before things could get to where they were quickly going.

– 17 –

I phoned Waltrine. She was happy enough to accept Tom's offer to drive when I told her she'd be riding in a Mercedes Benz, but she did first inquire about the quality of the sound system, chasing her question with a simple statement: "I like good boogie." She also informed me that a geologist from Florida's state geological survey—not to be confused with the U.S. Geological Survey, which was federal—would be coming with us. He had busted a spring in his state vehicle while rocketing out of a quarry carrying too heavy a load of high-quality calcite crystals that had "accidentally" fallen into the back of his vehicle. He thought he'd come along to look after the state's interests in the space program while he waited for the spring to be repaired.

When she discovered that there would be that many people in the car, Faye opted out, saying she had an appointment with a chaise lounge and a bottle of suntan oil.

That night, when the insomnia set in, I turned to Miles Guffey's contribution to my reading stash, a slim trade paperback entitled, *The Garden of Their Desires: Desertification and Culture in World History*. It echoed Tom's words regarding the importance of the equality of women to the health of a culture, drawing a correlation between the drying climate, the subjugation of women, and the growth of patriarchal societies that thrived on raiding and wars as a means of acquiring resources. I finally drifted off to sleep, my mind a jumble of thoughts that whirled at the edge of connecting the steaming Floridian night, desert dust, terrorism, and my missing lover.

Eight-thirty the next morning found us cruising along on Interstate 4 east of Tampa in a light green, late-model Mercedes 500L listening to some excellent blues on the CD player. Waltrine sat up front with Tom playing disc jockey, and I sat in back with a terribly blond gentleman in blue jeans named Scott Thomas, who was entertaining us with a running travelogue of the scenery we were passing, geologist-style. "We're rising over a series of terraces," he was saying, referring to a geological term for stairsteps in the terrain.

"What terraces?" I inquired, glancing about for any break in the topography and seeing none. The ground was monotonously flat. "Am I looking in the right place?"

Scott made a smooth swipe with his hand. "I'm talking about old wave-cut terraces, paleoshorelines. They're subtle, just a few feet rise over many miles, but they're there. It takes a special eye."

I laughed. "I guess so."

Scott said, "Sea level hasn't always been where it is now. Back in Miocene or Pliocene time, it was up 300 feet, and all but a few square miles of Florida was underwater. Imagine just a couple little islands between us and the east coast, and another one way up north, almost into Georgia?" he said, falling into the Southerner's habit of making statements sound like questions. "That was all there was of peninsular Florida sticking out of the ocean. But there were still-stands in sea level as the sea came in and went out, so the waves worked a little harder at some of the elevations' cutting terraces."

I laughed. "This is indeed subtle. The only breaks in topography I can see are the freeway ramps leading up to bridges."

Scott said, "Yeah, we get a lot of flat jokes poked at us."

Waltrine turned in her seat and looked at us. "When my daddy heard I was moving to St. Petersburg, he said, 'Honey, on a clear day you can stand on the hood of your car and see Jacksonville.' "

"Ha, ha, ha," Scott enunciated, deadpan. "Oh, quick, Waltrine, looky up ahead by Orlando there: Can you see Mickey Mouse's ears? Oh, wait, I forgot we've got a hundred miles to go yet. We've got to allow for the curvature of the Earth."

Waltrine said, "Hasn't anyone explained to you that the Earth is flat? Of course, nothing is as flat as Florida." She swung around and pantomimed panning the horizon with a sailor's spyglass. "Oh, isn't that cute! I can see Mickey's little bitty asshole, too."

"Why, Waltrine, I hadn't taken you for a Flat Earther."

"I take my membership in the Flat Earth Society very seriously. Tomorrow I intend to testify in front of Congress against evolution. So beam me up, will you, Scottie?"

Scott said, "With pleasure will I put a beam in you, O goddess of my heart,'cause there's nothing flat about *you*!"

Waltrine stuck out her chest and pouted. "Discrimination! Sexual harassment! I'm a-gonna sue you, big fellah!"

"*Rowf!*"

"*Meow!*"

Tom glanced at me out of the corner of his eye.

I said, "Rock-head humor meets the biologist's avid interest in sex and feces, Tom. You'll get used to us."

"You rock jockeys are so *earthy*," Waltrine drawled.

"Bite me," Scott countered, then fell back into his travelogue as if no diversion from purely intellectual pursuit had occurred. "So now we're getting into the sand dunes," he said.

"Sand dunes?" I inquired. "Where?"

He pointed to the barely undulating topography that now stretched away from both sides of the road beneath a ragged forest of scrubby pine trees. "All through there," he said.

"I don't see any sand dunes. I can see that it's not quite as billiard-table flat as everything else I've seen so far, but you call those *dunes*?"

"Well, they're very *old* sand dunes. Pleistocene. Completely grown over."

"Oh, so you mean the soil is very sandy, because at one point there were dunes, but now it's all worn down and covered with trees."

"Yeah. But not just any trees. Those are scrub pines and turkey oaks, and other plants that thrive on relatively sterile sands from the old dunes."

"Subtle, like you say."

"Yeah, Florida is all about subtlety."

I asked, "What's beneath the fossil sort-of dunes?"

Scott answered, "Right here? Phosphatic sands and clays of the Hawthorne Group, say about a hundred feet, and below that, thousands of feet of limestones and dolostones."

"And what about the rest of the state?"

"Mostly limestone. We do a lot of limestone h'yar. Some limey sandstones. Some sandy limestones. It's really cool."

"But flat," I said.

Waltrine said, "You've got to *love* flat."

Scott raised one eyebrow one millimeter and said, "Opposites attract."

I said, "I hear that all that limestone is riddled with holes. Like a huge concrete sponge."

Scott chuckled. "Never thought of it like that. But yeah, that rock's full of water, all right. Some wonderful aquifers. The springs are fantastic. Excellent diving."

Tom broke into the conversation. "So you're into scuba?"

My ears pricked up, wondering where he was trying to steer the conversation.

Scott said, "Sure. I love to dive. I like diving the sinkholes best."

"Sinkholes?" Waltrine snorted. "You talking sweet nothings again?"

Scott said, "No, Waltrine, the limestone dissolves in the waters that percolate through the ground. Sometimes it makes a large cavity near the surface, and its roof collapses. One morning you get a little hole opening up on the surface, and then *wham*, it's a hundred feet across by lunchtime. One up in Winter Park was 300 feet across and ninety feet deep. Now, *that* was a sinkhole. Ate an auto shop and four Porsches."

Waltrine said, "No, *that* is sinful."

Tom glanced at me in the rearview mirror as if asking for help guiding the conversation.

Making a guess at what he was driving at, I said, "I think Tom's wondering about the impact of all the traffic we hear about in the news. Small-plane crashes and such."

Scott snorted. "Oh, you're talking about fishing for square grouper. When those drug planes go down in the ocean, or the go-fast boats have a little altercation with some sort of solid object out there, like maybe the Coast Guard, the bales of marijuana come floating ashore. Some beachcombers make a good living picking it up."

Tom said, "I thought smuggling had slowed down a bit."

Scott said, "No, if anything, it's up. Ever since 9/11, the homeland security guys have had their hands full watching for terrorists, and they don't have as much time and budget to spend on the dope smugglers."

Tom asked, "Where is this mostly? Off the Gulf Coast?"

Scott shrugged. "Both coasts. Off the Gulf side it's mostly planes going down, but off the Atlantic shore, it's the go-fast boats from the Bahamas. They can make it in from one of the out islands in just over an hour. It's nothing. Sometimes they put the load on a boat, set it on autopilot at high speed, and then jump overboard as the thing takes off. They swim back to their island, and the boat runs itself ashore on the barrier islands along the Atlantic coast. I suppose they have tracking devices on them and schedules so they can tell their pals on the mainland where to find them, but the idea is that with the value of the payload, the boat is expendable, and if it's intercepted, they're off scot-free."

"What if the boat hits someone's house?" I asked.

"Most of the way up and down, there are no houses immediately on the waterfront," Scott replied. "Y'all wouldn't want to build there. Y'all'd get taken out by the first hurricane."

I glanced at Tom. He was steering the car with his left hand and had his right arm draped across the back of the seat, the fingers relaxed, all just ho-hum casual. He had to already know the answers to these questions. So then, why was he asking them?

Scott's attention was once again on the scenery outside the car. "Okay, now we're getting into another whole to-pography." He pulled out another map, this one delineating the geomorphic provinces of Florida, the whole state broken up into chunks marked "Gulf coastal plain," "Ocala karst district," and so forth. He tapped a finger on it. "We're coming off the Lake Wales Ridge now."

"A ridge?" I asked. "Where?"

Waltrine said, "You missed it, with that nosebleed you got from the high altitude."

I peered out the window, trying to connect what he had showed me on the map to what I saw. I saw no ridge. The pine trees and turkey oaks had given over abruptly to a dense stand of lanky trees—cypresses, I think—growing out of standing water. The trees were covered—no, the word is *encrusted*—with other vegetation. It was a vast expanse of green on green on green, the variety of shapes and sizes of foliage absolutely bewildering; the ground, or should I say water, a forbidding obstacle course of roots and fallen logs. Shrugging off a chill of revulsion, I asked, "What's with those trees? They look like they've grown green fur."

"Epiphytes. Y'all never seen a swamp before, lady? But now, this is only one *type* of swamp. We have dozens of different kinds."

The complex, looping swags of greenery whizzed past

at seventy miles per hour, or should I say, we whizzed past them. But as we cruised onward, and Scott chattered on and on about what lay underneath the scenery, I slowly developed an appreciation—or at least a glimmering—of what he was trying to show me. Florida was indeed flat by my standards—500 miles long and 150 miles wide, and precious little of it rising more than a hundred feet above sea level—but that did not mean that the land did not vary. Swamp gave way to pine forest, and pine forest to pasture, and each vegetation type followed the geology. Scott had learned to observe it all just as clearly as I could see the big outcrops that were the rule rather than the exception in my part of the country. I began to appreciate his way of observing, and was impressed by the depth of experience that must have made it possible for him to see what he saw. But that's the game in geology: repeated observations adding up to the experience necessary to sort out what at first seems hopelessly jumbled, or in this case, cryptically flat.

"So you do geology by what's growing on it."

"Uh-huh. And we go by cores and drill cuttings from wells when we get 'em. We seldom get to know what's underneath by direct experience, like quarries or canal-digging."

I stared out into the landscape, trying to see it as he did. I had to admit that there was something weirdly alluring about Florida. With its shifting clouds and subtle topography, it seemed to be playing the dance of the seven veils with me, drawing me inward, into its depths. Again the question arose in my mind: *What did Florida have to do with African dust and the disappearance of the man that made my knees weak?* I asked, "What's at depth? I mean really *deep*. What's beneath the limestone?"

Scott made a dismissive gesture. "Part of Africa."

Bells went off. "Africa? *Really?*"

"Yeah, during the rifting that created the Atlantic Ocean when Pangaea broke up."

Waltrine said, "Come again?"

Scott said, "Pangaea, the supercontinent. Everything was

one big land mass two hundred million years ago. You know, plate tectonics? The unifying theory of geology? Or don't you biologists have to know that shit to understand the patterns of evolution?"

Waltrine rolled her eloquent eyes. "Yes, dear heart, but please to speak the English, not the geo-nerd-ese."

Scott raised his hands, forming them into great curving plates, and used them to describe a sphere in midair. I stared intently at his hands, willing the understanding I craved to spring from them. He slid them together into the top third of a sphere. "My hands are the land masses. Triassic Period, two hundred million years ago, everything one big lump. First rifting split North America and Eurasia from South America, Africa, and the rest. The Atlantic Ocean began to form as seafloor spread both east and west from the rift that runs down the middle." He shifted his hands around to demonstrate, great landmasses sliding on his invisible sphere.

I said, "And you're saying that a slice of western Africa sheared off and stayed on our side of the Atlantic."

"Yes."

Mimicking Scott, Waltrine drawled, "Y'all shitting me?"

Scott crooned, "Waltrine, Waltrine, Waltrine . . . honeybun . . . would I pass you through my intestines?"

The two kept up their banter for a while, but my mind had caught hold of a far land I had never visited. *A piece of Africa is right here underneath this place that's now being plagued by African dust? What is this, the wind trying to reunite the mother with the daughter?*

There was something unnervingly ethereal about the topic of dust. The ground seemed to be getting up and losing itself into the sky. The thought left me feeling lost and floating, as if the Earth had lost its gravity. That sensation in turn seemed disconcertingly aligned with Jack's disappearance and rude reappearance, and the way I felt each time I thought of him.

I forced myself to remember that gravity exerted its attraction even to objects as fine as dust, and that eventually those fine particles came down again, slowly, inexorably settling toward land and leaf and human alike, ready to fuel the ground with minerals, deliver its payload of disease and fertilizer, and clog human lungs.

"Oh, shit," Waltrine announced, jerking me from my reverie. "Tom, you passed the turnoff for 417."

He said, "This looked shorter on the map. I'm taking I-4 to the Beeline Highway."

"No, no, no, no. Oh, shit! You'll see."

Oh, shit was right. As we passed through Orlando, we waded eyeball-deep into a different type of swamp, namely the traffic around a clot of theme parks—"the attractions," Scott sneeringly called them. Traffic on the Interstate highway and all visible tributaries crawled even though it was the middle of the morning, nowhere near rush hour.

"All this traffic is for Disney World?" Tom asked.

"No, sadly not," Scott said. "It's also the home of Sea World, Magic Kingdom, Universal Studios Florida, and miscellaneous others. And you can see we got our hypnotic video billboards that form hazards to navigation, and we got every strip-mall-outlet extravaganza, five incarnations of each kind of burger chain, three of each taco stand, and about five hundred souvenir shops. And our rental cars full of seekers of prepackaged fun chugging ponderously by on their way from one dose of T-shirt shop poisoning and wallet fleecing to another."

Waltrine snarled, "You're waxing poetic in your old age, Scottie."

Tom set his jaw in his own brooding version of road rage. "Serving up pleasure in place of happiness, isn't that what Faye would say, Em? Hmm?"

Scott slouched down in his seat. "It was a nice place to grow up, before all this," he muttered.

I asked no questions. I didn't want to know more. I grew up in a place where I could not see the next ranch, let alone stare in the neighbor's living room window. If this was Jack's hometown, I could understand why he'd left.

We turned at last onto Route 528, the Beeline Highway,

which passed abruptly into fifty miles of land equally as unpopulated as Orlando had been overpopulated. I noticed that, once again, water stood about the bases of the trees beyond the edge of the road. I saw egrets rowing gracefully through the air. The paucity of human development was almost spooky after the crush of Orlando. The swamps ended again as abruptly as they had begun, and we found ourselves at a dense fringe of human development along the coast. Our journey ended as we came across a causeway bridge over a long narrow body of water full of wading birds. Ahead, I could see hummocky dune topography covered with yet another vegetative group.

"That's palmettos, live oaks, and sea grape there," Scott informed me, ignoring the human overprint. "Beach assemblage. You can see the prevailing wind direction by the way the trees have twisted. We're on Merritt Island now. It's part of a barrier island complex composed of fossil beach ridges. The longshore current and wave action carry the sand to us from the north. The ultimate source is the Appalachians. Just seaward of us, it forms a huge cusp called Cape Canaveral."

Cape Canaveral? We were at Cape Canaveral? Somehow, in all the stress and hurry and stimulation of the past twenty-four hours, this fact had failed to register in my overheated brain: Kennedy meant Kennedy Space Center, and that was at Cape Canaveral. Now I saw a cluster of rockets—real, honest-to-gosh rockets—tethered to the ground on display. This was the place from which Alan Shepard had ridden the first Redstone rocket into space. This was where the *Eagle* had lifted on its trip to the moon. Now we hurtled past a space shuttle and solid booster array that were mounted quite close to the road. I was glued to the windshield like a squashed gnat, gawking, twisting, trying to get a look at the fabulous chunk of history that was sliding past, this chunk of my childhood, this treasure trove of heroism and a huge part of what I, as an American, could feel indelibly proud.

"That was the visitor center," Scott drawled. "Y'all want the office center, down here a bit farther."

"I'd like to see those rockets," I said faintly.

Tom said, "You and I may be back another day, Em."

I unglued my face from the window and exchanged glances with him. His tone told me that something was definitely up, and my guts told me it had to do with whatever had brought him across Florida today. Something to do with Jack.

Scott said, "I've been here to see launches. It's the coolest thing you can imagine, much better than watching it on TV. And landings, those are cool, too. Here comes this big bird, and right next to it, a little T-38, flying observation." A soft smile had spread across his face. "I wanted to be an astronaut," he said, speaking to himself as much as to me. "I wanted to be the first geologist on Mars."

"What happened?"

He shrugged his shoulders. "Marriage. Kids. It doesn't work if your spouse is not behind it."

We passed through a security check. Tom informed the guard that he was dropping the three of us off and then intended to visit a friend for cocoa, or something like that, and needed clearance to get back in to pick us up at two. That arranged, Tom dropped us off, and we were met by a couple of men who weren't wearing pocket protectors but looked like they felt naked without them.

After looking pointedly at their digital wristwatches, the men showed us in through a rabbit warren of hallways and offices to a meeting room. Waltrine compensated for being late by digging into them fast and hard, pushing her program, and they spent their time sulking back all cavechested in their seats like they had forgotten to get in line when the spines were handed out. Waltrine explained the need for specific evidence that could only be gotten by gathering dust high above ground level. Number One kept pushing his glasses up his nose and clearing his throat. He harped on the special talents of a certain satellite that was good at reading dust and threw around a bunch of acronyms, but was evasive about the possibility of collecting actual samples. Number Two seemed to have precious little to say to us. Waltrine stated that having data from their flights would ground their satellite data in reality. She kept asking to speak directly to the pilots who flew the missions. Number One kept saying that requests like that had to go through channels.

Promptly at noon, the daring duo glanced at their watches and excused themselves, saying they'd be back after lunch, but pointedly did not ask us to join them. Waltrine, Scott, and I found the cafeteria and munched in silence, Waltrine chewing more and more forcefully as the hour ground on.

As we returned to the conference room, Scott said, "This dog ain't gonna hunt. I wonder what went wrong."

"It's always something," said Waltrine, quickening her pace. "I tell you, this place is just another government shrine to the triumph of bureaucracy over stated goals. They're so busy hanging onto their precious balls that they can't get a hand loose to open the purse strings, let alone do meaningful science. Bunch of technofreaks."

The gang of two arrived back ten minutes late and informed us that they would have to end our meeting early. Fifteen minutes before two, after trying every last angle she could to persuade these two men that they should be turning handsprings of joy over the dust project, Waltrine looked like she was going to explode. "Well, if *you* can't get any action, then why don't we talk to Lucy?" she said finally, infusing her voice with casual familiarity, as if talking about a personal friend.

Number One said, "Who?"

Waltrine said, "Didn't anyone tell you that one of your astronauts on the current launch is a geologist with an interest in desert sediments? She's very interested in this project."

Number Two suddenly smirked and found his voice. "We've heard nothing from any of our astronauts about your project. Besides, the current flight has been delayed.

Didn't anyone tell you? The shuttle was rolled back due to the hurricane. It's not rescheduled until . . ." He tapped at his computer. "Ah. Five days from now. I'm sure she's quite busy with other mission requirements."

Scott winced on Waltrine's behalf. Our meeting was over.

Scott and I got to spend fifteen minutes watching Waltrine fume about "Fucking Miles" not keeping her informed. "He said he'd gotten through to her. He said she had our proposal. Said she was on it."

Tom finally pulled up in the Mercedes. "Sorry to be late," he grumbled. Apparently, his meeting had not gone well, either.

Waltrine addressed Tom with a syrupy sweet voice. "I hope *your* day was good, Tom who is late, because *mine* certainly was a waste of time. These pinheads have no stroke upstairs. They don't have the imagination to do anything that doesn't come out of some damned memo, or perhaps the NASA book of games for boys with no fucking brains. But did they tell me that? No, they didn't have the balls to tell me that over the fucking *phone*, they had to let me drag my ass all the way across this swamp-infested *peninsula* so I could *see for myself* how tiny their pathetic little testicles are! Shit, I'd need my fucking *microscope* to see something that small!"

Tom gave Waltrine a look of deep respect.

We all got into the car and headed west, back the way we had come. I again glimpsed the alluring rocket garden and space-shuttle display, the beach ridges, the backridge waterway, and the various forms of swamps, pinewoods, sand dunes, billboards, and entrances to theme parks. The afternoon downpour caught us at Disney Junction, which is a highway exit built solely for the use of Disney World. As we crawled along nearly blinded by the torrent, I numbly witnessed the apparition of Mickey Mouse's ears, which indeed could be seen over the curvature of the Earth:

They formed one unmistakable, wildly curved head-and-ears-shaped power pole in a string of high-tension power lines that crossed the terrain. The best news about the return trip was that we caught the Highway 417 cutoff, so even with the rain slowdown, the trip took under three hours door-to-door. We were all silent for most of the trip.

I was tired and preoccupied, wondering if Jack had looked out upon the scenery I was now seeing. Had he brought girlfriends out to the beach at Cape Canaveral? Had he avoided the trackless regions of the swamps, or explored them? As the miles and hours rolled past and the silence sank deeper within the car, I found myself alone in my thoughts, and my longing for Jack came back on me with such intensity that I found myself fighting back tears. The wave of sensation washed over me again and again, and I felt lost on an ocean, uncertain if what I was feeling was love or a colossal sense of loss.

Five o'clock found us up to our eye sockets in Tampa rush-hour traffic. Five-thirty put us in St. Petersburg at the USGS. At six P.M., I was sitting by the pool at Nancy Wallace's with a long-necked beer in one hand and a handful of corn chips in the other. I turned to Tom. "So. What went wrong when you went to have cocoa with your friend?"

Tom took a long pull on his own beer and stared into space. "Cocoa is a town."

"Oh. So then, you visited a friend there?"

Tom said nothing for perhaps half a minute, then, "No. Our friend was not there."

I had my beer halfway to my lips and stopped. "Are we talking about Jack?"

Tom said nothing.

I slammed my beer down on the teak end table to my right and jumped to my feet. "Send me a telegraph when you're ready to talk, Tom," I said, and, with long, angry strides, headed for the house.

"Wait," he said. He sounded sad.

I turned back toward him, fists balled. "Make it good, Tom."

"I was looking for something Jack told me about."

"What?"

"Something . . . pretty dangerous."

"*What?*"

He stared at the floor.

My willingness to wait and trust Tom had vanished. Seething mad, I sassed, "Is it bigger than a bread box?"

Tom gave me a dirty look, but the anger in it quickly faded.

Suddenly, I realized that Tom's silence on the return trip had come not from his usual introspection, but from intense preoccupation. I forced myself to exhale. "Let's not play twenty questions, Tom. Jack's overdue. Time to give."

He sat leaning forward in the low chair, his head hanging, holding the cold bottle to his forehead as if to relieve a fever. His lips writhed like he was fighting off tears. For the first time in my acquaintance with him, he seemed inadequate and rather pitiful.

I said, "You gave him forty-eight hours. That deadline passed three hours ago. So why are you just sitting there?"

"I couldn't find it," he said.

"Find what?"

"On his map. It wasn't there. I couldn't even see a damned mark in the sand!" He stood up abruptly. He began to pace. "Hell, it wasn't much of a map. What was I thinking? I can't believe this! I let him go without first making him take me there and show me where the damned thing is!"

A surge of fear began to work its way up my spine. What thing? "Tom, show me the map, okay? I'm a geologist, remember? I have special training in reading such things."

He pulled a folded piece of paper out of his breast pocket, stared at it a while.

I took it from his hand. I unfolded it. There, in Jack's narrow handwriting slanting here and there as if applied from varying angles, all capital letters, was a jumble of notes quickly drawn, with just a few lines to indicate geographic features. Notations identified a few structures and geographical locations, like COCOA, ATLANTIC AVENUE, HOLIDAY INN, and STORM SWASH. Tom was correct, it was a pathetically crude map, but it had feeling to it, a sense of intent and geometry that drew me inward. I searched for an indication of orientation, and found a quickly scrawled N next to an arrow pointing toward the top of the page. I unfolded a bent corner, and found a little scribble shaped like the space shuttle. Suddenly, I knew that two of the lines marked the intercoastal waterway and a third the Atlantic shore, and that the kink in the shoreline to the east of the little shuttle must be Cape Canaveral itself. And, next to a rough box drawn in what must be the sand, a notation that turned my bowels to ice: SAM-7 BURIED HERE.

My arms sagged to my side. SAM stood for "Surface to Air Missile," with which one solitary man could shoot down an aircraft, even a shuttle. And a SAM-7 was not one of ours.

– 18 –

Lucy sat at her desk watching the digital clock pulse the seconds, willing the time to pass more quickly. On her desk lay the proposal from the man at the USGS, asking her help with a project on desert dust. With a dull ache, she realized that she had failed to follow up on it, just as many things seemed to be slipping from her of late.

She began her mantra again. *In just thirty-six hours,* she told herself, *I will climb into a T-38 and fly to the Cape. All my worry has been just foolishness. At the Cape I will be on protected territory. He can't make good his threats. He's only trying to scare me. On the Cape I will be completely safe. There is no reason to fear. The target is my mind, not the shuttle. He can't do anything to me, and I have no obligation to tell the others, because it's all just a mind game, and I am holding the ace.*

Suddenly, she felt the hair stand up at the back of her neck. She whirled around in her seat and jumped uncontrollably. Somehow, Len Schwartz had managed to come in the door without being heard and had placed himself directly behind her. His hand hovered in the air, fingers only inches from her. He had been about to touch her. His face was tight with an expression of worry and perplexity. She said, "Why did you come in so quietly? You . . . scared me."

Len withdrew his hand and continued to watch her. "At

least you know that what you are feeling is fear," he said. Then he reached out again and cradled her cheek in his hand, a gentle caress, rubbing her cheekbone with his thumb. "Get some sleep tonight. We've got a long way to go in the very near future." Then, just as quietly, he turned and left the room.

Lucy hung her head to hide the hot tears of agony that slid down her face.

– 19 –

I told Tom, "It will be dark by the time we get there, unless we have Faye fly us."

Tom's face was so flushed with emotion that veins stood out in his forehead. He made a fist of his hand and pressed it to his lips. "I can't involve her in this," he said. "I shouldn't involve *you*."

"But I *am* involved! And you said yourself that you were going to go after Jack if he didn't bring the thing in—this *thing*, Tom; this *antiaircraft missile!* You gave him forty-eight hours. I heard you. So what are we waiting for?"

"Okay. Okay, we'll go. But we're driving. You and me. Faye stays here." I had never seen him in such a state of agitation. He couldn't meet my eyes.

Regardless of what he had said, Tom seemed rooted to the spot, so I got moving instead. I raced to my room and got a jacket and the flashlight I always carry in my luggage. It seemed a flimsy bit of equipment considering what we were looking for, but it was something to grab. I kicked off the sandals I'd been wearing and put on a pair of socks and my running shoes, and rolled a change of clothes up in one of the pink-and-turquoise towels from the guest bathroom.

Then I glanced out the window down toward the pool. Tom had not moved. I ran back downstairs and out past Tom to the guesthouse, and got Faye to open the door.

Apparently just waking up from a nap, she stretched and yawned and started to say something, but I cut her off. "Faye, give me Tom's field gear, quick."

Her face crumpled. "No," she whimpered. "No, you aren't really going out on a job, are you?"

"You packed the gear. You knew this could happen."

"I only packed it because I knew he would insist on coming with us, and if I didn't pack it, he'd hold us up while he diddled around packing it himself. I had no intention that he should actually *use* the damned stuff!"

I said, "I'm sorry, Faye. And trust me, I had no idea. When Jack took off like that, I thought it was some standard operating procedure. But this is—"

"No, don't tell me. I don't want to know. My imagination is vivid enough as it is. Playing cops and robbers was all very fun and exciting before I got pregnant, but you two are on your own this time. I have a baby to gestate. I am staying here! I am going to work on my tan and get fat as a house and have this baby, whether she gets to have a daddy or not!" With that, she burst into tears.

I reached out to put a hand on her arm, but she turned and dug out Tom's kit, handed me the keys to the car we had used that day, and told me to get lost.

Suddenly feeling a little panic of my own, I said, "I've never seen him lock up like this before. He's just standing there doing nothing."

Faye jammed her fingers in her ears. "I do not want to *hear* about it!"

I grabbed one of her arms and tugged it loose. "No, you have to listen. I need your help. Tom went looking for something today and couldn't find it, and instead of coming to get me, he just drove back here and dove into that beer like the world had ended. Something's very wrong, Faye, and it's going to take both Tom and me to make it right, and maybe a whole lot of other people, too. You know him better than I do, at least the deep Tom. Is there anyone else he trusts as much as . . ." I had been about to say, "As much as Jack." But Jack had failed him. Was that why Tom had turned to stone? Or was he afraid that he was failing Jack?

Well, he can trust me, I decided, *and whatever it is that Jack did or did not do or did wrong, I am not yet done with him, and I am going to find him. I'll give him help if he needs it, and if he does not, I will whup his sorry ass for messing with the two people he claims to be closest to!*

Faye's eyes had gone vacant, but the tears still slid down her cheeks. "You think he quit the FBI because of me and the baby, and he did. But there's more to it, Em. He . . . well, you know the score. There are people in the Bureau who are just plain incompetent, and it was driving him nuts. Some of them were so bad that they weren't just screwing up; they were actually a danger to those around them. Hell, they're a danger to us all. They knew about 9/11, or had clues, but they blew it off and now thousands of people are dead."

"There's not a professional alive who never screws up," I said. "I can't count the mistakes I've made as a geologist. And the best physicians are only right eighty-five percent of the time."

Faye's lips tightened with anger. "You're talking about honest mistakes, or learning the hard way. I'm talking about incompetence. And I'm talking about the guys who *fuck* each other because they damn well feel like it, or to climb ahead, or because they're goddamned working for some-body *else!*"

"You mean a foreign interest? Wouldn't the CIA get those guys?"

"You are so naïve, Em. Tom wasn't kidding about the opportunists out there. The people who take advantage of any system. There are people in there who'll sell them-selves to the highest bidder. Or they suck up to some damned shit-heel politician who thinks their personal agenda is more important than the public welfare. It was driving Tom crazy."

"*Now* you tell me," I said.

Faye stared at the floor. "Go ahead," she said. "Go be one of the boys."

That cut deep. Between my teeth, I said, "You make the baby, Faye. I've got another job to do."

I grabbed Tom by the arm and hauled him out to the Mercedes and loaded our gear. "Who's driving, you or me?" I asked him.

Tom's eyes clicked into focus. "I am," he said.

I gave him a pat on the shoulder, and said, "Good man. Let's go find this thing."

We drove the entire way in silence, Tom still lost in the thoughts and worries that had whittled him down to someone who could accomplish little else than drive a car.

It was dark when we got back to the Atlantic shore, dark and blowing hard. From the Beeline, Tom turned south on Highway 520 to the city of Cocoa. From there we crossed an elevated causeway over the intercoastal waterway onto Merritt Island, and then another that led over another waterway to the outer island and the town of Cocoa Beach. At the junction of Highway A-1-A, locally called Atlantic Avenue, we turned north. Cocoa Beach was a strange place, a mishmash of beach and business with a lot of restaurants and motels jutting starkly from the sand. As the Holiday Inn came into sight, I spied huge docks in the distance, up toward the Cape. PORT CANAVERAL, signs read. Something hazy nudged my memory. Hadn't this been the place where Calvin Wheat's cruise liner was due to dock sometime soon?

We parked the car in front of the motel and walked several blocks eastward down to the beach. There, Tom took me to his best guess of where the buried "item" should be. He pointed at the map. "I can't interpret these five lines accurately," he said. "I thought they had to be streets dead-ending by the beach. But our X that marks the spot should be right between the third and fourth. I'm thinking they must be these streets, but that doesn't narrow things much."

Wind lashed the palm trees, and sand moved in plumes around our ankles. I saw Tom's predicament: The map did not match the scene. Was Jack trying to throw us off? Had I gone to bed with a liar? I said, "Even if we were sure we were in the right spot, this wind would have reworked the sand," I said. "It would cover the obvious signs of digging and reburial unless the job was really sloppy in the first place."

Tom stared bleakly up the beach. Clouds rolled past the moon, and the sound of the surf rushed at the sand a hundred feet or more to our right. "Hell, I couldn't find a damned thing by daylight, and now it's dark as pitch," he said bitterly.

I was tempted to say something like, *This isn't like you, Tom*, but held my criticism. Getting mad at Tom was not going to help us find this dreaded item, or Jack. I said, "You think the thing is going to be used against the space shuttle."

He nodded.

"Well, then we have time. The launch isn't for a couple of days."

"Correct, but whoever buried the damned thing might be watching even now. You get it?"

"So it wasn't Jack."

Tom rounded on me. "Are you insane? Jack wouldn't do that!"

I wanted to say *I'm beginning to have my doubts*, but I decided to keep that notion to myself. Tom was clearly at the end of his rope where it came to whom he could trust. Paranoia was making him all but catatonic. If he locked up on me entirely, then he, Jack, and I were nowhere, and the monstrous thing we were looking for might find its target. "Then who did bury the thing?"

Tom shook his head. "I don't know."

This time I was pretty sure he was telling me the truth. I said, "Let's go back to the motel. There was a restaurant there. We can get something to eat and maybe get some other maps from the office, see if we can make a correlation from this one to one that was more formally drawn. I'm sure we'll find some clues that will help," I said, half lying even to myself.

Tom followed me back through the gate and along the wooden walkway that led to the motel. At the front desk, I asked for a map of the immediate environs. The pimply young man behind the desk asked, "Just this motel, or do you want a map that shows all of our hotels in central Florida?"

A little light blinked on in my head. "Both, please." I took what he handed to me and hustled Tom into the restaurant, where I commandeered a table and laid out all three maps. For the moment ignoring Jack's scribbles and the map of this motel only, I turned to the map of all Holiday Inns in central Florida. To my immense relief, I saw something that answered a question I had not even known to ask. There were in fact two Holiday Inns in Cocoa Beach; the one we were at, and another a few miles farther south. I stabbed my index finger at it. "How about this, Tom? We're at the Holiday Inn Express. Could he have meant Holiday Inn Cocoa Beach Resort?"

Tom stared at the map. "Shit," he said. He grabbed for it.

"No," I said. "We'll drive down there, but we both need to eat first—keep our blood sugar up so we can hope to think straight—and you need to tell me more about what's going on. And before you tell me you're not going to tell me, think it through carefully: If you continue to keep me in the dark, you'll endanger the project. We just don't have time to screw around."

A waitress came to take our orders. I said, "We'll each have a cheeseburger and a cup of coffee, and if you can get that inside of ten minutes, I'll double your tip."

She smiled and took off like a seared bat.

Tom leaned his elbows on the table and raked his fingers through his short stubble of hair. "Jack got a call. Someone he knows had reason to believe that someone was going to try to take a shot at the next shuttle launch. Just imagine how that would be. Another Christa McAuliffe."

"You're talking about terrorism."

"Not really."

"How can shooting a space shuttle be anything but an act of terrorism, Tom? Isn't that like being a little bit pregnant?"

"It's a matter of who takes the shot, and why."

"I disagree."

"There's more to it."

"I'm all ears."

Tom bared his teeth in exasperation. "What if it doesn't involve people from another country? Then what do you call it?"

"I still call it terrorism. I call anything designed to scare the shit out of me exactly that, a big fat mind fuck called terrorism."

"I've taught you well, I see, but—"

" 'Terrorism is the foul art of relieving us of our sense of safety,' you always tell me."

"Yes. But what if it's aimed at just one individual? What do you call it then?"

"You think plinking a space shuttle is taking a shot at only one individual? You think maybe no one else would notice?"

"Of course others would notice, but if the *intention* was directed at only one, and the crime is being perpetrated by only one person, then what?"

"Isn't that still terrorism?"

"No, we call it stalking."

"What, some wacko's got a fixation on some astronaut?"

Tom nodded. "Wackos seem to have a particular taste for prominent people. But, no, it doesn't have to be the astronaut that's the real target."

"Oh, you mean like what's-his-name Hinckley shooting President Reagan in order to impress an actress," I said. "So it can be done for the visibility, a sort of 'Look how much attention I can get.' "

"Exactly. Then the game's called 'showing the world how powerful you are.' "

"It still sounds like terrorism to me. It's still extortion of control over others. As you say, stealing their sense of safety."

Tom pressed the tips of his fingers to his forehead. "There's a difference between the act of an organization and the act of one individual."

I said, "Now you're splitting hairs between terrorism and terrorism à la carte. You've got to *hope* this is the act of just one individual, so if you find him, you've ended the problem."

Tom's fingers turned white at the knuckles. "Right . . . but it also makes the job of searching for the enemy different. If you're looking for an organization, there are all sorts of trails that cross and cross again and lead you right to the source of the stink, but an individual is a solo act, much tougher to catch."

The waitress brought our burgers. When she was out of earshot, I said, "But how'd an individual get hold of a SAM-7? Surely that narrows the search."

"You would think."

"How much does something like that cost?"

"Hundreds of thousands. A million, with a rocket."

"Shit! That's one wealthy stalker!"

"Keep your voice down."

"Right. But doesn't this tell us something about this guy?"

"At first Jack didn't think the guy could make good his threat. But he didn't know who he worked for. He has access to equipment. Think drugs, Em. Think people who want to be able to shoot a Coast Guard plane out of the sky if they want to."

"But Tom, people like that wouldn't be taking a shot at the shuttle."

"I agree. But they do hire some very crazy people to run errands for them, and it seems that one of those nasty little errand-boys has become fixated on an astronaut. So he stole an antiaircraft missile from his boss. But first we have to *find* the damned thing."

Now the reasons for Tom's anger at Jack were becoming clear: Jack had found evidence of an *intended* crime and had chosen to leave it in place so that he could catch the monster at his mania. "Well," I said. "We'll find it then. Won't we?"

Tom did not answer.

The second Holiday Inn in Cocoa Beach, Florida, was a splashy tourist resort replete with fantasy swimming pools and whirlpool spas. We parked the Mercedes in the back parking lot as if we were checking into a room, went down a wooden walkway, and found ourselves on the beach, again just a couple hundred feet from the Atlantic Ocean. The wind was fierce, whipping my hair around my face. For the first time since I had arrived in Florida, I was chilled.

Greater hope that we were in the right place had made us more cautious, and we put on the front that we were a courting couple looking for a place to neck. We twined our arms and leaned into each other, smiling and making little giggling sounds. I sauntered along in Tom's embrace, fighting down a sense of near panic. *What if I'm wrong?* my brain kept asking me. *We could be wasting time. Tom can't read that map, and maybe I can't either.* But instead of giving in to panic, I let the anxiety speak to me, letting it guide me. Threaded into this crosscurrent of love and fear, I mentally reviewed the inscriptions on Jack's map and whispered, " 'Upper swash.' That would mean the highest point on the beach the waves reach." I gave Tom a little hug around the waist, a faint armor against the risk he was taking.

Tom squeezed me back.

We walked out across the sand, its looseness slowing our progress. The beach was much as it had been farther north, a long pale sweep of quartz sand catching the scudding moonlight. I squeezed my eyes shut and opened them again, willing them to adjust to see more in the low light.

Forty or fifty feet off the boardwalk, we came to a line of broken seashells and wrack left by the passing hurricane, and my anxiety peaked as I thought of Jack out in the wind that would have driven waves that far up the beach. *"Mira, aquí està.* Upper swash line. Now we turn left. *Izquierda. Vamanos en la playa."*

Feeling my suppressed excitement, Tom gave me an encouraging hug. It was making me slightly giddy to be so close to him. With that distraction, I almost missed the next clues. As we left the beachfront building that marked the territory of the Holiday Inn, we passed into the one stretch I could see where a solid wall of foliage came right down to the beach. Here suddenly were cabbage palms and sea grapes, just as Scott Thomas had shown me; the correct and native vegetation for this area. And right there sticking out of the jungle were five boardwalks, pointing east like fingers, like the five lines on Jack's map. "This is it," I whispered.

"Are you sure?"

"Yes. I'm as sure as I can be, in the dark. I have a flashlight in my pocket, but I don't want to turn it on."

"Keep moving. Don't stop on top of it."

"Right."

"How do you know?" he whispered hungrily.

Now that I had found the spot, I felt like I was standing on a hot griddle. I forced my body to continue the sensuous show of a woman caught in the nectar of the moment. As we shambled along, painfully doing our burlesque of courting tourists, I contemplated his question. How *did* I know? Call it a matter of geologist's intuition, something in the gut, a flash of recognition. It was a compass of the mind, a little needle that knew how to find true north.

But there was another part to this reckoning process, a part that came before the needle swung, a feeling that was a compass of another sort, and that feeling was anxiety, plain and simple. It is the curse of the intuitive mind to grapple with ambiguity: incomplete data, crudely sketched maps, hunches, a sense of pattern that wants just a few more variations before the theme is clear. To embrace the rigors of ambiguity, one must be willing to suffer the anxiety such dissonance and fragmentation spawns. When I was first beginning as a geologist, I had misunderstood that feeling. I had thought it meant I was on the wrong trail. But as the sequence of anxiety and recognition came again and again, experience increasing with layer upon layer of observation, I had come to recognize that the intensity of the anxiety increased until the exact, exquisite moment when knowing came, and vanished into the ecstasy of the *aha*!

But how did I know *this* time? I thought of Scott Thomas, and his subtle reading of the landscape. "I know because Jack took the trouble to mark a significant feature of the beach geometry, and relative to that geometry, these proportions are right. The upper swash. This is where the storm waves reach. See? And there are your 'streets': one, two, three, four, five. They fit perfectly, and make the scale correct. Jack did a damned good job. So this," I kicked the sand where the line of wrack and shells were totally absent, "is a break in the pattern. And the slope of the beach changes ever so slightly. There's a slight hump, as if the sand was replaced over an additional volume. It's not much, but just enough that I can see it even in this little light. In that way," I said, now realizing why I knew what I knew, "he felt the map to be complete. He marked the Holiday Inn, its wooden walkway, the upper swash line, and these five boardwalks coming out of the palm trees; nothing else was necessary. The scale is much tighter, see? In fact, the lines marking the Atlantic and the Banana River, even the shuttle at the Cape were gratuitous, and not to scale."

"Good eye, Em." For the first time that day, Tom sounded truly happy. He gave me a hug borne of delight.

"And it makes sense," I said, still whispering. "It's above the saturated part of the beach, so what's buried here is less likely to corrode. And if you think about it, Jack would look at a beach this way."

"Why?"

"Because he grew up here. He likes sports. He's really good at them. He would have been a surfer. And here there is surf." I pointed out to sea. The breakers were coming in like white panthers, the cresting foam glowing in the light from the moon, which had for the moment broken free of the clouds.

"That's some big surf," Tom said. "I'd hate to see what it takes to come all the way up the beach."

"The storm surge from the hurricane?" I conjectured. "That's why the damned wrack is here. I'll bet with all these motels there's so much foot traffic here that if we'd waited a few more days, we'd have seen nothing. But screw it. How are we going to get the damned thing out?"

"For that," Tom said, "we are in fact going to need some help. We'll need shovels, muscle, and some cover, in case we're being watched."

"Where are we going to find that at this hour?"

"That's the question I was just asking myself." As we had begun to discuss the logistics of the extraction, we had unconsciously gravitated apart, and now Tom put an arm around me and reeled me in close, again playing the lover. "Come on, let's get out of here."

He led me back down the beach. My back crawled with the sensation that someone was watching us. I wanted to get away. I wanted to run back home to the Rockies where I could get my bearings, where I knew my way around, and where there were mountains and valleys I could hide in. After what seemed ages, we finally reached the car and got in. Settling in the leather seat, I said, "So what are we going to do?"

"We have time, but not much. The launch has been re-scheduled."

"It takes a while to roll it back out. Then they have to refuel it. And the wind is still blowing."

"It's been tailing off all day. I think the winds are passing."

"You could try one more time to reach Jack. Maybe he has the guy under surveillance."

At the mention of Jack's name, Tom lapsed into another of his long silences. Then he said, "Em, how well do you really know Jack?"

Something in the tone of Tom's voice put me on red alert. And it made all the other little doubts that had been piling up in my mind about Jack—about his sudden disappearance, and a hundred little dots of peculiarity that had been trying to connect themselves to that one point—began to tumble down on me, and I felt the need to defend myself. I wanted to say, "How dare you! I've *slept* with him! I've made *love* with him! I do not do that casually!" but instead, I said, rather stiffly, "Why do you ask?"

Tom stared out through the windshield for a while, as if the conversation he had started had wandered from his mind. I had time to wonder if I had imagined it. Then he spoke again, his voice like lead. "I mean how much do you really *know* about Jack?"

"What does it matter? We've been through—"

Tom cut across my words. "Yes, Jack knows how to be there for you. I got it. But what do you *know* about Jack?"

"I . . ."

"How old is Jack?"

"Oh . . . I always figured a couple, three . . . maybe four years older than I am. That would make him forty."

Tom's face was hard as rock. "When's his birthday?"

"His . . . birthday?"

"He was born, wasn't he? Then he has a birthday."

"I . . . I don't know. I haven't known him a full year. That means it's sometime in the next few months."

"It was last week."

"*What?*" I pulled away from him.

"The day you first loved each other. It was his birthday present to himself."

I balled my fists up against my eyes. "How dare you! How dare you know that and not me!"

Tom caught me by the shoulders again, but now he spoke with a voice full of tenderness. "*I* know it because I had his personnel file. I'm just trying to illustrate a point.

There's just a whole lot you don't know about Jack Sampler."

I began to shake. A little whimpering voice came out of my throat. "Are you going to tell me?"

"No," he whispered. "There are things that none of us know, things even Jack doesn't know about himself."

"That doesn't make sense."

"It's time you met his mother. If anyone can explain Jack, it's her." He brushed my cheek with the back on one hand, then started the car.

His heart pounded with fear and anticipation as he watched the specialist stand up from his desk, stretch, and wander off to find dinner. Here it was, his chance to get onto the computer and find out when the shuttle launch had been rescheduled. The days of outwaiting the high winds and waves had ended, and his plan could once more go forward. Time to make the bitch Lucy pay him back for everything she had done to him. All the nights of lost sleep. The insult of spurning him burned in his gut like a hot iron.

He looked both ways. No one coming, no one to see what he was doing. What fools they were that they thought he did not know about their setup. They thought him stupid; well, that was handy to let them think so, and he did nothing to change their impression of him. They came and went from the airstrip with the shadow of night, just as he came and went on the boat that they had so foolishly given him to use. He was the pale face they kept around to run errands to the mainland, while the big black Bahamians handled the unwitting slobs from Middle America whose lolling visits made the operation seem legitimate.

He swept down on the machine, hacked into the system, got his information. Lucy would launch at dawn in three days. Three days. Three days! Perhaps it was time to take the boat now, before his swarthy employers had any chance to block his transit. He would have to lay low, wait near the motel, but he had waited before. . . .

He moved quickly, backing away from the machine, out of the room, out of the building so cleverly decorated to look like a quaint Bahamian beach shack. Little did the pigs from Ohio know what was kept in here, or in any of the others along this row. He hurried away through the trees, and was almost to the dock when he heard his name called. Mispronounced, as usual.

"Yeah?" he answered, sliding seamlessly into his stupid dolt act.

"You are needed at the command center. Move!"

His stomach tightened. "Yes, well, I was about to run some errands across at the mainland. Will I be going soon?" he said, hoping he had shown the correct mixture of initiative and obsequiousness.

"No. This boat is needed. You will stay on this island until it returns."

"How long will that be?" he inquired anxiously.

"At least until day after tomorrow," the man said. "And then you must hurry, we will have many errands for you then."

Don't worry, he thought. *I will fly like the devil himself. For I have an errand of my own.*

– 21 –

It was past eleven when we reached Orlando, later still when we pulled into the driveway in front of a modest bungalow-style house that was nestled among graceful shade trees and curving lines of flowers that danced pale and fragrant in the cooling, humid air and the light of the street lamps. The moon was lost behind the clouds and the brighter lights of the city sprawl.

Tom had used his cell phone to call ahead, so a welcoming light was on at the end of the house closest to the carport. A tall, gray-haired woman answered to our knock. "Tom!" she said, her face lighting with a smile. "It's so lovely to see you!"

"I wish it were under better circumstances, Leah."

She tipped her head to one side, eyes alert. "What's happened?" Her voice was soft, but the question carried a note of command. She was Tom's senior by ten or fifteen years and, while her demeanor was gentle and open, it was clear that she was accustomed to being heard and obeyed.

Tom said, "Let's go inside. Please."

"Yes, come ahead. I want you in and the mosquitoes out. But first, who's your friend?"

Tom turned toward me, and a shadow of sadness swept across his eyes. "This is Em Hansen, a colleague."

So I am not being introduced as Jack's girlfriend. I smiled and offered Leah a hand to be shaken. I found hers dry and cool, the bones narrow and surprisingly delicate for such a tall woman. Falling back on my prep school manners, I said, "I'm so pleased to meet you."

"Welcome, Em. Please, both of you come in."

Inside the house, I found what appeared to be the peaceful sanctuary of a calm woman. The furniture and décor were dated but comfortable and well kept, and the effect was one of spaciousness and organization. The dining table, side tables, and coffee table all held neat piles of letters and papers, some bundled with rubber bands or paper clips. There were note pads and pencils close at hand at each location, suggesting that Leah was a woman accustomed to making notes, or that perhaps she was old enough that her memory was no longer entirely sharp. My eyes wandered to the walls, which were decorated with framed lithographs of birds by various artists, and, over the mantle, framed photographs of Jack.

Jack as a boy, smiling in a baseball cap and uniform.

Jack as a teenager, smiling from under a mortarboard.

Jack as a young man, smiling with his arm around a petite and beautiful young woman with dark hair and high cheekbones.

I had to stop myself from going directly to them to study the face of my beloved in the many stages of his growth. And who was the young woman? The picture had to be at least fifteen years old, perhaps twenty. I pulled my eyes away from that photograph, checked the next. Jack in uniform. It was white. Did that mean Navy?

"That's my son, Jack," Leah said, her voice rich with pride. "Or perhaps you know him, if you work with Tom."

I was trying to figure out how to answer that oblique question when Tom spoke for me. "I'm not with the Bureau anymore, Leah. I'm in private consulting. Security. Em is an independent, too. She's a geologist with a knack for forensic work."

Leah studied me. "A geologist. Good for you, dear. But, Tom, you're no longer with the Bureau? Why?"

I in turn answered for him. "He's going to be a father. He married my friend Faye, and it won't be long. Tom, does this mean you've been keeping this happy detail to yourself?"

Tom stiffened at my chiding, and I immediately felt like a rat. I should have let him tell her what he wanted when he wanted to tell it. But why hadn't Jack told his mother the news? After all, he'd been at the wedding. And why hadn't he told her about me? I added this to my growing list of increasingly worrisome questions about Jack.

Leah said, "Oh, how lovely! Tell me about Faye, Tom."

Tom said, "Leah, I'm sorry. I'd tell you all about her, but I'm afraid this is not a social visit. As I mentioned on the phone we're on a job. And we're here because we need your help."

"Of course, Tom. Anything you need." Leah was an interesting study. Her light delivery of words suggested that she was your ordinary suburban housewife who was being politely congenial, but she watched Tom intently, and now held her head with the alert stiffness of one who has spent years making eye contact with snakes.

"Thanks. We need to borrow some equipment, and . . . we need to locate a friend of Jack's named Brad. Jack told me once that he lives nearby. He was in the Navy, and—"

"He lives right next door." She gestured to the house just beyond the carport. "He and Jack have been friends since boyhood. Brad grew up there, and bought the house from his parents when they moved into a retirement home."

"Great. Can I use your phone to call him, please?"

"Why, Tom, it's late. Brad has several small children. I'm sure—" She stopped in midsentence, staring at Tom. "What is going on?" she demanded sharply, all surface layers of polite conviviality stripped away.

Tom said, "I need to talk to him *now,* Leah."

In his usual fashion, Tom was trying to leave Leah out of the loop. But Leah was not a lady who was easily left in the dark. So why come to her at all? Why not just find

Brad in the phone book, or knock on doors until he found him?

Leah picked up the phone, dialed it, and handed it to Tom, a fierce look of disapproval fixed tightly on her face. The phone was cordless, so Tom carried it into the kitchen and pulled the door shut. That left me alone with Jack's mother, two women staring at each other with plenty to say but no way to get started. Or, at least, *I* didn't have a clue. Leah again surprised me. She said, "Tell me how well you know Jack."

I blushed.

She slowly nodded, an abstracted smile floating on her lips. "That's nice, dear."

The blush deepened.

Out of precise politeness, she shifted her gaze to her fingers and started to pick at her cuticles. "Jack is a boy who keeps his secrets," she said. "But you are the type of young woman he would be very proud to know, and I hope that he would eventually bring you home to meet his dear mama."

I closed my eyes. Swallowed. Her words had been stated with calm formality, but in fact they were astonishingly intimate. In this brief, unguarded instant of knowing her, I saw that she was the kind of mother I had longed to have, but could not have imagined: candid, kind, affirming, in charge of her intelligence. A wave of feeling swept over me, as intense in its own way as my hunger for Jack, and I was afraid that if I did not run away quickly, I would drown in it.

Easily reading my emotions, she said, "Jack would not love a woman who was incapable of caring deeply. But please tell me why you are here. Something must be very wrong."

I nodded, eyes still closed.

Tom reentered the room, interrupting our conversation. "He's coming," was all he said.

"Where is Jack?" Leah asked.

"I don't know."

"How long has he been gone?" she pressed, not even trying to cover the urgency of her words.

Carefully keeping his voice clear of emotion, he said, "I was hoping you might know. Has he contacted you in the past forty-eight hours?"

"I haven't seen him since Easter. He called a week or more ago to say hello. Why, is he here in Florida?"

"I think so. He was two days ago."

Leah fixed a hard stare on Tom and sharpened her tone. "What in hell's name is going on, Tom? Come on, none of your dissembling. This is Leah you're talking to!"

Tom held up his hands in surrender. "Okay, if you must know, Jack came down here to find someone who was threatening to take a potshot at the space shuttle. And—and you know what that can mean. Jack told me to tell you code red if it got out of control."

Code red? My eyes shot to Leah. Her gaze flew quickly to one of the pictures on the mantel, just a quick glance, but I couldn't tell which one had drawn her attention. I wanted to snatch at her, get the information from her. Which one held significance? Was it the picture of her son with his arm around the lovely young woman? The one who gazed into the camera like she knew something the photographer didn't. . . .

Leah said, "Did he find this person?"

"Yes, but he lost him. What he did find was the fire-power the son of a bitch intends to use, but we need to dig it up without . . . That's why we need Brad. Jack said he'd know what to do. And you know what *you* have to do."

This was unbelievable. Someone had gotten Tom to talk. Or was he hiding something in plain sight? And was Tom really abdicating to this fellow Brad? That seemed equally out of character. Except that I'd had to all but drag him out of Nancy Wallace's house that afternoon. Perhaps all he wanted was to hand over the reigns and get back to Faye. I shook my head to clear it. Everything had suddenly gone peculiar in my world. But I knew one thing: I was not ready to quit until I saw that *thing* under the sand dug up and destroyed.

Leah said, "Who else is in on this?"

"No one that I know of."

I blinked. She hadn't asked, Have you called the police? or, Who would do such a thing? No, she had cut to the center of the matter, and appeared ready to take command. My mind spun with questions. Who was this woman really? What was her background? And what emergencies had she been through with Jack that, instead of cowering or trying to lean on the forceful personality that Tom presented, she asserted herself, commandeered him, and easily pushed him around?

I heard a knock at the door. Leah said, "Would you let him in, Tom?"

The man who came through the door when Tom opened it was about my age. He was a hair shorter than average height, but thickly muscled through the shoulders and chest, like a smaller, dark-haired version of Jack. He nodded to Leah, shook Tom's hand, and then fixed his quick blue eyes on me. "Who's this?"

Leah said, "This is Em Hansen, a colleague of Tom's and a lady friend to our Jack."

Brad's eyes sparkled, and he gave me a fine grin. "Hey, any lady friend of Jack's!" I stood up to shake his hand, but he grabbed me into a hug that nearly knocked the wind out of me. When he just as quickly released me, I staggered, but Brad's attention was already back on Tom, all jest gone from his expression. He said, "I got through to one of the others. He'll be here in ten minutes."

"He's discreet?"

"About what? Tonight never happened."

What is this, some kind of militia? I began to feel the need to back out of the room. Too much was happening too quickly, and with too little explanation.

The conversation quickly took off and left me. Brad was saying, "How deeply buried is it?" and "So you're thinking we should extract it before daylight."

As the questioning evolved, I saw Leah head to a hall closet and return with a small suitcase. It had an old-fashioned leather handle, and the sides were battered. She put it by the door that led out to the carport and said, "You boys dig some food out of the refrigerator. Make some sandwiches and be sure to get some cookies out of the cupboard. There's fresh fruit in the crisper and bottled water on the shelves out by the carport. If I'm gone before you return, Brad can show you where the key is hidden."

Tom said, "I think you can wait until daylight, Leah."

Leah nodded. "That would be better. I'm not as young as I once was. And Lily—" Leah's eyes shifted to me. She turned and started out of the room. As she disappeared back down the hallway, I saw that one corner of her lips was curled in a sad, ironic smile.

I turned to Tom in question. He turned away, letting me know that my answers lay elsewhere.

– 22 –

We were back on the road before midnight and closing in on the Holiday Inn Beachfront Resort back in Cocoa Beach by one A.M. Brad and the man he had phoned, another remarkably fit specimen named Walt, followed a distance behind us in Brad's jet-black, four-wheel-drive vehicle. I could spot it by its high headlights, and, each time a truck passed going the other way, by the row of surfboards mounted on its roof rack. He had put them there to obscure his mission as a pleasure tour.

During the drive, conversation was sporadic at best. Tom fell into one of his silences, and for my part, I had so many questions that they all jammed into one big heap that was buried under the urgency of the moment. So I ate cookies and thought dark thoughts about the fact that people seemed to be keeping me exactly there, in the dark. In fact, the darkness was increasing. By the time we were halfway back to the shore, the clouds had socked in solidly, obliterating the moon.

It was spitting rain when we got to the motel, and I could hear the surf pounding even over the rustling of the palm trees. We parked in the back lot, planning no pretense of being there for any reason other than to dig the damned thing up as quickly as we could and get it the hell out of there.

We got out of the car and waited. As I turned to look for Brad and Walt, I saw that they had arrived and parked some distance away. They got out and skirted the parking lot. They were dressed entirely in black, and I could not even see their faces. They gestured for us to hang back, and then melted into the night.

They were gone several minutes, and then I suddenly heard Brad's voice, very low, so close to my ear that I jumped. "We're clear," he breathed. "Now show us the site. You lead. We'll find you there." I turned, and, even though he was within inches of me, I saw little more than the whites of his eyes, and inches to one side of his head, I saw the muzzle of his gun.

"Fine," I said.

Tom lifted shovels from the trunk of the Mercedes.

The hair stood up on the back of my neck as I turned toward the beach. The choke point posed by the narrow path to the beach was too dangerous, the sight lines too limited. Anyone who wanted to give us trouble could do it too easily there, even though Brad and Walt were nearby. I could not see Walt, but was certain that he saw me. Brad said, "Go the other way around the far end of the motel. There's another path there. Too much light, but there's no boardwalk, so you can be quieter."

I followed his directions, moving through the security lights and down between two lines of boulders. I noticed that the stone was a beautiful coquina. How I wished I were on a simple field trip. I would bend and touch the stone, see if I could flick a shell loose from the nearest one. But such were the actions of a simpler time, when intellectual pursuits could fill a day. Tonight, I was in the land of terrorism.

The dark masses of the palm trees whipped noisily in the wind. We walked quickly to the spot and started digging, setting up trench lines that crossed in the middle of the blank spot on the sand, marking a big *X*, on the theory that we would hit our object on one transit or another.

It turned out to be only two feet down. Tom hit it with his shovel, a hard *tunk* of metal on metal, muffled only by a heavy layer of plastic that was wrapped around it. Once we'd found it, we quickly uncovered it, and as quickly had the hole filled back in. Then we backed away and let our two bits of the night steal out of the shadows, wrap it in black cloth, and disappear it into the thrashing palms.

As we reached the Mercedes, I saw Brad's four-by-four whip out of the lot, turn right, and head up the street.

"Now what?" I asked.

"Now we go back to Orlando and see what we caught," said Tom.

The first moody indigo of dawn found us in Brad's garage sucking down strong coffee. The missile lay at our feet, still wrapped in its shroud of plastic, which was sealed with green tape. It was an ugly thing.

"It's a SAM-7 alright," Brad said. "But here's a puzzle: its effective range is only a few miles. To hit the shuttle, Mr. Bad would have to get it onto the Space Center at least."

"Maybe he's too crazy to know that," Tom said.

"Let's hope," Leah said. "Crazy doesn't mean he's stupid."

Tom asked, "Can you tell where it came from?"

Brad mulled this a moment. "The Russians built them. No, wait; it's one of the newer Chinese ones, like we heard our brethren have found in Afghanistan. I have to tell you, I'm more than a little bit curious how it came to be buried in the beach by the Holiday Inn."

Tom said, "That is exactly what I would like to know."

"Jack could tell us," Leah said, her voice fading. "But right now I care less about where this came from than where my boy has gone."

Tom said, "We'll find him, Leah. When we know where this came from, I think it will tell us where Jack is. I think he followed whoever buried this back to where it came from. It's the only explanation that makes sense."

I could think of another explanation. Jack had gotten in over his head, and he was . . . buried somewhere else. I pushed the idea out of my mind. I had to do something—anything—to keep busy. So I squatted down next to the missile and began to examine it. It was about five feet long. The launcher consisted of little more than two tubes. I gingerly put my hand over one of the tubes to touch some sand that was stuck to the plastic.

"That's the sighting unit," Brad said. "The tracking head has an array of heat-seeking sensors and a microcomputer that adjust the trajectory of the missile to keep the target in the center of the array. The other tube holds the warhead and the rocket. There's a protective cover over the seeker and the warhead that would have to be removed before use. I'm glad we found this thing. Now we've got to figure out where Jack is."

I said, "Perhaps we can work the puzzle backward."

Leah said, "What do you mean, Em?"

"I mean, maybe this thing can tell us where Jack is."

"How?"

"Well, it's got a story to tell. Look at all the sand that's stuck to the outside of the plastic. That's quartz sand from the beach where we dug it up. Sand is highly variable—size, shape, crystal characteristics, accessory minerals, and rock fragments—so it may be possible to 'fingerprint' it with a petrographic microscope or an SEM."

"Which is what?" Tom inquired.

"A scanning electron microscope. Don't worry your head about what that is. Concentrate on the sand. Look *inside* the plastic," I said, poking at the wrapping with a screwdriver. "The sand inside is not quartz. See? Quartz is glassy. This is opaque and off-white."

Tom folded his long legs to crouch next to me. "What does that tell you?"

"Well, it looks like some kind of carbonate."

"Explain."

"Calcium carbonate is the mineral that limestone is made of. The sand stuck to the outside, from Cocoa Beach, is principally quartz." I pointed at one of the larger grains inside the plastic. "That's a bit of shell; see the ridges?

Probably a bit of a *pectin,* a scallop. There is no quartz in here. All these grains are busted bits of shell that have been worn smooth. Except these." I pointed to more spherical bits. "These are oolites, formed in a gentle swash zone where the waves keep rolling things about. There aren't any oolites, or much shell debris at all, outside the plastic. Nothing gentle about Cocoa Beach. And I don't know what this is." I pointed to some pinkish bits that were finer in size. "These are something else entirely, though maybe still carbonate."

Tom was paying strict attention. "So what does this tell us?"

"We can presume that the quartz sand came from Cocoa Beach, because the whole thing was buried in it, coating the outside of the wrapping. But what's inside doesn't match, so it follows that what's inside came from wherever the thing was packed. Furthermore, the packing itself is crudely done—hardly a factory job—so I'm guessing that whoever buried it wrapped it himself, and at some other location where there is a lot of loose sand. See this? Sand only, very little silt or clay. That suggests another beach. So the question becomes, where did the stuff inside come from?"

"Do you think you can figure that out?"

"Quite possibly, with the right help. I'm a generalist, Tom. I know a little about a lot, so I'm good at putting together big pictures. To do this job, I need the help of specialists, people who know a lot about a little. And I have to find the right specialist who has the right finicky little focus." I shook my head. "That could take time."

Brad glanced at his watch. "Almost time for my family to wake up, and for me to get ready to go to work. I'm going to go give my wife and kids a kiss and then call in sick. I'll be right back."

Walt cracked his knuckles. "I'm with you, bro."

Leah said, "I'll start making breakfast. An army travels on its stomach. "Tom, you'd better call Faye before she wakes up and it occurs to her that you should call."

Tom followed Leah out the door.

Suddenly, I was alone with the missile, this instrument brought to this land for the express purpose of shooting our national pride out of the sky. It lay on the cement like a corpse stiff with rigor mortis. I wished fervently that it were in fact a once-living thing that had died, because then that would be the end of it. But machines can be produced in great numbers, and where this one came from, there had to be more. And, while it had been designed and built a long way away, it had been buried like an evil seed in my nation's shore. I stared at it, knowing that such objects had been in my country right along, some built by our people, some by others. The only real difference between today and the day before was the expansion of my own sad knowledge of one human's capacity for brutality toward others.

I shuddered at my own capacity to ignore the abundant clues of such brutality that had surrounded me all my life. While I am not by nature a very trusting person, I could not comprehend such evil, nor, I liked to believe, was I capable of it myself. My blood ran cold at the thought of the kind of mind that *could* unleash such violence. Where did such people come from? And, more central to my current task, where did they hide?

23

Brad intersected me a few minutes later as I was walking across the lawn to Leah's house. He gave me a mischievous grin. "So you're Jack's new lady."

I nodded, even though I was no longer one-hundred-percent sure what I was agreeing to. I decided to deflect him. "Yeah. . . . So Brad, tell me about the mystery moves you and Walt were doing this evening. What kind of special training taught you to do that?"

"That was a little gag we learned as SEALs. So Jack-o didn't tell you about his little pal Bradsky?"

"No."

"I'm so insulted," Brad said, pantomiming his heart being torn out. Then he gave me a knowing wink. "That Jack. He's three years older than I am, and I guess I have always idolized him. We'd spend all day Saturday out on our bicycles, exploring the countryside—this is back when the countryside wasn't so far away from here. We'd be collecting snakes, climbing trees, wading chest-deep through the swamps."

"You waded through *swamps*?"

"Yeah, you just have to know what you're doing. But Jack did. He always knows how to handle himself, that boy. He taught me A to Z about reptiles, birds, plants. Hell, I followed him everywhere, even into the SEALs."

"The SEALs. I take it that's not just a merit badge you got in Cub Scouts."

Brad gave me a sideways look. "No. So Jack's holding out on you big-time! Oooo, not good, Jack. The Navy's Special Ops unit. Stands for 'SEa Air Land.' Jack didn't tell you about all that?"

No, he did not. He has not told me a great many things. I had trouble forcing my voice out. "I knew he'd been in the service, but until I saw the picture on Leah's mantel, I didn't even know which branch."

Brad's smile faded a notch. "Oh. So you're just getting to know each other," he said doubtfully.

Just then, I heard the sound of aircraft approaching low and fast overhead. Brad whipped his head around and quickly spotted them, catching a glimpse through the trees. It was a group of military jets flying in formation, heading east.

Brad grinned as he shaded his eyes to track them as they disappeared toward the rising sun. "Hey, Lucy! We're proud of you, girl!"

"What are you talking about?"

Brad made a big gesture at the passing jets. He was all but dancing. "There they go! Won't be long now."

"Who's 'they'?"

"The astronauts. They always fly in from Houston in those T-38's. Nice little jet trainers. They're wasted on the Air Force, but at least they give them to the astronauts so they can keep their hours up."

"Wait . . . that's the astronauts arriving to go up in the shuttle? They come over Orlando?"

"Yeah. So does the shuttle, when it lands at the Cape. Makes a signature double sonic boom. Sets off the car alarms. But this is the crew of the shuttle arriving, big fanfare. They come in a couple days ahead. I guess that means the orbiter's rolling back out of the assembly building. They rolled it back a week or more ago because of the winds off the hurricane that's been nattering around in the southern Caribbean."

"But that means they're going up."

"That's what I just said. Hey, don't worry. We got that thing out of the beach." Brad squinted at me. "Oh, I get it. You're thinking there might be a second one out there." He gave me a friendly nudge with his elbow. "Don't you think Jack would have told us?"

"What if there's another one he didn't know about?" I didn't want to say what I was thinking, which was, *What if he's the one who put it there?* Even as I thought that thought, I knew it didn't quite make sense, because why hide something and then tell someone where you hid it? *Unless he did hide it, but then decided that he should tell Tom, because Tom's almost like a father figure to him. Maybe he thought better of it when Tom argued with him, and . . . what am I thinking?!*

Now I was certain that I was not making sense. Had my doubts about Jack grown to the point where I suspected him of madness? Of violence?

I wanted desperately to ask Brad questions about Jack, but just then Brad opened the door that led from the carport into Leah's kitchen and ushered me through. Inside, he turned his attention to Tom, who looked entirely out of his element, busy dispensing glasses of orange juice. The moment to pump Brad had passed.

So my lover had been in the Navy SEALs, a macho group if there ever was one. Having grown up in a land-locked state, I knew next to nothing about the Navy, and nothing at all about its special ops unit. I had no use for water beyond drinking it and taking a shower, but it seemed that I'd gotten in bed with a man who knew how to just about live in it. I wondered what other little surprises Jack had in store for me. If and when he showed up again.

I felt Leah watching me. Our eyes met and locked for a while. I wondered if she could tell that I was thinking angry, suspicious thoughts about her son. At that moment, I would have paid any price to know what she was thinking, to know what she knew about him, but I was so far off my emotional balance that I lacked the nerve to ask.

Finally, breaking the silence of our interaction, she said, "Come eat, Em. You must be starving."

Starving. Was that what I had been, to fall in love with a man who had told me so little about himself?

Over a breakfast of scrambled eggs and grits, we made plans.

Brad and Walt would make inquiries regarding the weapon. "We need to find out where it came from. Who bought it? Who laid the plan to use it here?"

"It may have been stolen from whomever bought it," Tom said.

Brad shook his head. "These guys may be crazy, but they're not stupid. They're usually into low-cost options, like using somebody else's equipment. This they would have purchased. They would notice if it went missing."

Tom said, "You keep saying 'they.' Jack thought it was a solo act."

Brad shook his head. "That's some major money there. I'd like to meet the solo terrorist who can afford a SAM-7."

Tom knit his brow in a particular way I had come to know spelled obstinate with a capital *O*. "Jack told me the guy was an errand boy for a hive of drug runners. But I'll call in some favors, see who's active in this area. Find out who's got a beef." It was strange watching Tom try to operate outside his expertise and jurisdiction—not that he had a jurisdiction anymore. It was half a year since he had turned in his badge. To me, he said, "Em, you're in charge of forensic analysis of the geologic materials we found associated with the weapon."

I said, "Okay. There's a protocol to this. I have to extract representative samples of the sand from inside and outside the bag. Then I need to split each sample into two. I'll want someone to witness all this, because we're talking evidence of a crime—lest we forget that we may need to cover our asses somewhere down the line, or need to make this stick if we're trying to get someone jailed—we should make up a chain-of-custody document to carry with the samples. I'll then express one set of samples to the FBI's forensic geology lab in Washington, D.C., for safekeeping. The other set I'll take across to St. Petersburg and pull every string I can to get the provenance of the sand inside the plastic."

"Provenance?" Tom queried.

"It's a fifty-cent geological term that means, 'where it came from and what that means geologically.' "

Tom waved his hand in dismissal. "For once, spare me the intellectual frivolities and just give me an *X* on a map."

Tom had a way of getting imperious when a job made him anxious, and that had a way of making me want to get just as arrogant right back at him. "What it means geologically and where the *X* is are one in the same, Tom. This is war, and war is one big game of geopolitics."

Walt looked at Brad and said, "What's she talking about?"

Brad said, "White girl angry."

Walt grunted.

I said, "Walt, you've been trained to fight. What do you fight over?"

"I fight for justice."

"I said *over*, not *for*."

Tom said, "The slogan used to be, 'Peace, freedom, and the American way.' The current administration changed it to suit the times."

I thought, *Uh-oh, Tom's getting sarcastic. An even worse sign. The master of manipulation is not in control of the situation, and worse yet, it's got him downright scared.*

Brad matched Tom's tone. "As I recall, that change had something to do with jets full of people flying into big buildings full of people. And if you're calling me a patsy, maybe you're right. I joined the Navy to follow someone I admired, and his name is Jack Sampler. But when I had become a soldier—and I mean fully trained as one—I began to see that I had a job to do, and that was to protect people who can't protect themselves."

Tom lost his cool entirely and said, "You're talking about a warrior. A soldier is some poor slob who's been trained to follow orders. Em's right, this is all a game of geopolitics. Those assholes didn't care if we caught Bin Laden, they just wanted to get their grubby hands on Afghanistan so they could run a damned oil pipeline from the Caspian down to the Indian Ocean. They're a bunch of opportunists."

Brad stood up and planted his feet as wide as his shoulders. "Bullshit. The secretary of defense was on our brothers' asses every day to chase that SOB down. Whatever you say, boss. If being worked over by politicians means we get to roust a few terrorists into the bargain, so be it. Tonight, we disarmed a terrorist on our own shores."

Tom stayed in his chair, but his face was getting red. I'd never seen him this worked up before. "Right. We're talking about an antiaircraft missile. Now, how do you suppose that shit head got hold of the thing in the first place? Oh, yeah, it was our brilliant Reagan administration sent about 900 of the goddamned things to the Mujahideen so they could shoot Russian helicopters out of the air, and surprise, a good number of them turned up missing. The problem with arming those jackasses is that we don't seem to have the same ideas about how they're supposed to be used. Imagine that, they shake down Uncle Sam for something to harass the Soviets, and now we're finding them right back here buried two feet under a place where our children are playing. If you don't think that's totally fucked, you're *insane*!"

Brad leaned toward Tom and spoke through his teeth. "Tom, you're a former G-man, and I suppose you think you're different from me, but you guys have violated peoples' civil rights left and right, and as we speak you have big-time problems in the Bureau. My comrades and I are warriors. If we don't care, or we quit and walk away, who is going to do the job? And who is going to keep the powers-that-be honest? I'm just a reservist these days, but some of us are staying in for careers, and those few that reach the top hope to make a difference someday, because just like you, we believe in protecting the Constitution and the freedoms that we still enjoy in this country."

Tom turned his face away. For once, he offered no comeback.

By the time I had collected my samples and rigged a crude chain-of-custody documentation for them, it was seven A.M. I was ready to head straight back to St. Petersburg, but Tom was still off somewhere talking to Brad and Walt, so Leah insisted that I try to get some sleep. But when Leah showed me to her spare room, I was jolted into full wakefulness again as I surmised that I was in Jack's boyhood bedroom.

Feigning fatigue, I closed the door and greedily got to work snooping. Here was a trove of personal treasures collected by the boy who was to become the man. Here were relics that had given meaning to his young life. The shelves were filled with field guides, snakeskins, animal skulls, rocks, game balls, and sports trophies, an eclectic mix that suggested both a loner who liked to explore and a team player who liked to compete. He had books on electronic surveillance, code breaking, and weaponry. There were several volumes on military history, primarily eighteenth- and nineteenth-century naval battles. A corkboard was shingled with jokes cut out of newspapers, wise and witty sayings from Kipling, funny pictures of himself and pals horsing around making faces in four-poses-for-a-dollar booths. On the walls were posters of coral reefs, sailboats, and what the well-dressed medieval soldier is wearing. There was one very sweet photograph of him and Brad, ages approximately nine and twelve, out fishing on a boat in the ocean, not a spec of land in sight. Brad had caught a mackerel, and Jack had an arm around him in congratulations; a couple of good-looking boys out having the times of their young lives. In all, it was a calm, friendly room. Yet something was missing. What could that be?

Certainly it was not Jack that was missing from the

room. The essence of his searching, mischievous character was here just as certainly as he had been with me ten nights earlier, when we had consummated our love. He was here in force, in layers and details I had not imagined existed. And yet there was a blank spot in the chain of information.

I lay down on the bed, but the sensation of Jack's presence was so acute that there was no hope of sleep. My neck was rigid with stress and my eyes would not close. I kept staring at the ceiling, trying to read words I imagined that Jack would have etched there with his eyes.

Suddenly I realized what was missing: Jack's father.

I got off the bed and toured the room, searching for anything that would point toward whoever Mr. Sampler had been. Finding nothing, I headed down the hall past several more pictures of Jack, and into the living room. Jack's face appeared again and again, but he was the only male present. I walked into the kitchen to check for candid snaps on the refrigerator door. Nothing. Worse than nothing, in fact. Just like Jack's room, the rest of the house was beginning to strike me as lost in time, out of sync with the present moment.

I heard a step behind me and turned to see Leah just coming to rest, leaning against the door frame, her arms folded across her chest. "You're not sleeping," she observed.

"No."

She smiled guardedly. "What is it you are trying to discover?"

There was no point in denying that I had been snooping. "I was just trying to glean a younger Tom from the photographs," I said lamely.

"Glean," she said. Her eyes narrowed as she mulled my choice of words.

My stomach shrank to the size of a baseball. "I'm sorry to be skulking around. I'm just realizing that I don't know much about Jack. He doesn't offer many details about himself."

Leah's eyes went to slits, and her lips tightened to a thin, straight line. After a moment she closed her eyes the rest of the way, as if in meditation. When she opened them again, she said simply, "That's probably for the best. The past is just the past, after all."

"But Tom said you were the person to ask."

She shook her head. "Not today." She sighed, then said again, "Not today." She straightened up. "Well then, you'll be on your way I suppose."

"Yeah." My heart was busy joining my stomach in its little nut-sized packet.

"Let me give you my cell phone number. If you discover anything about where Jack is, will you please let me know? We both know we can't trust Tom to do that."

"Certainly."

She wrote the number on a piece of paper and held it out to me, then gave me a very stern look. "You will give this to no one else?"

"If you say not."

"I say not."

"Then I shall simply memorize it."

"That depth of care won't be necessary. I can always change it if necessary. Well, it's time to go." She glanced at the door, an indication of where I was to go.

I passed through it to the carport. Leah followed me, carrying the suitcase. She closed the door behind me and put the case in the trunk of her car. "I hope we meet again, under better circumstances," she said. Then she bent suddenly and gave me a light kiss on my temple, got into her car, and drove away.

24

Tom had the car up above eighty. My brain was cooking with fatigue, but the rate Tom was driving had me wide-awake. "Okay," I said. "Time to fill me in on a few things, Tom."

"Speak."

"Why aren't we just calling the cops, or the FBI, or the CIA, or the fucking armed services?"

"The police wouldn't know how to deal with this. Jack and I *are* the FBI. This is on our shores, so not CIA. And we *are* using the fucking armed services."

"No, Tom, you are retired from the FBI, and Jack is on leave, remember? This missile came from somewhere else, so that makes it a job for CIA. And Brad and Walt are obviously very highly trained, but they are not on active duty."

Tom shook his head. "It's better to keep this tight. If we run a crew of FBI or CIA or big army in there right now, we could lose all the connections."

"What connections?"

"The connection that got that thing into the hands of whoever put it there. This is high-stakes poker we're playing, Em."

"I know that, Tom. But don't you think you're being a little paranoid? Don't you think there's maybe *somebody* out there in your profession who has an ounce of integrity?"

"Yes. But I don't know which ones anymore. They've all started to look and act alike."

I flopped back against the seat. "Then it's a good thing you retired."

"I agree."

"And Jack should, too."

"Same again."

"What are you talking about, Tom?"

"I asked him to go into consulting with me. He is considering it. He figures when you two get more committed, you'll want—"

"*What?*"

Tom glanced sideways at me. "Wait a minute, hasn't he talked to you about this?"

"No!"

"Sorry."

I kicked the dashboard. "You sons of bitches!"

"Watch it there. You don't want to set off the air bag. It could break your leg if—"

"*Fuck* the airbag! And fuck your idea of security!"

"Em, your language is getting—"

"Fuck my language! There's some funny business going on here. Try this: Why did Jack's mother take off like that?"

"She's a smart woman. She knows that whoever buried that thing may have been watching. Might have followed us to her house. And people who do that kind of thing aren't nice people," he said, sarcasm beginning to make his tone crisp. "So she went somewhere else where they won't know to look for her."

"But she had that bag packed and waiting! And it looked like it had been waiting for years!"

Tom did not reply.

I kicked the dashboard again. "So now you're into 'I'm not going to tell you.' You *have* to tell me, Tom! There's too much riding on this! I love Jack, truly I do, but that's the space shuttle we're talking about. Seven people will be on board that thing, and hundreds of millions will be watching. It was *bad* when those jets hit the World Trade Center. Let's not let them knock out the space program, too. It's the thing we still get to feel good about."

"Yes."

"So let's tell NASA. Get them to scrub the launch. They can say it's another malfunction, or the hurricane winds again. Anything. I'm sure they're masters at that kind of bullshit."

Tom was suddenly spitting mad. "Yes, they are. But do you want to tell them? Hey, here's a cell phone. Give them a call. Tell them what you want to tell them. Who do you ask for? And how are you going to get them to believe you?"

"We've got the missile. All we have to do is show it to them."

"And where did you get this missile, Ms. Hansen?"

"In the . . ." I stopped and stared. I couldn't believe what Tom was saying to me. "You're extorting silence from me. You have all the connections it takes. You could stop that launch with one phone call."

"And I will if I deem it necessary. But right now, it is not. We still have time. We have to find Jack and know what he knows. Because for once, my dear Em, you know exactly what I know. We are *both* in the dark."

"Oh my God."

"Right. So let's analyze your samples and find out where our friend has gone."

"But how would he know where it came from?" I asked, for the moment forgetting that I had ever suspected him of having put it there himself. It was simply too difficult to keep both thoughts in my head at once: that Jack was a good man who did the right thing, and that Jack was a psychotic shit head who aimed killing weapons at space shuttles. And why did I even think the latter?

"All he'd have to do is follow the son of a bitch home."

"You're still thinking it's just *one* son of a bitch. That means that you do know something you haven't told me. Jack could be wrong."

Tom gritted his teeth with exasperation. "I have all but put it in neon for you: Jack told me it's just one man."

"But how did he *know* that?"

Tom clenched his teeth. His knuckles grew white. "Because he has a friend going up on that shuttle, and that person knows this man."

Back in St. Petersburg, we drove straight to the USGS and tracked down Miles Guffey. Even as tired and stressed as he was, Tom managed to slow himself down, sink his hands into his pockets, and say, "Hey, thanks again for dinner the other night. That was some stimulating conversation."

Miles looked back and forth between Tom and me, evaluating us over the tops of his reading glasses, no doubt trying to discern the message embedded in the fact that Tom had come with me to his office. "I'm so glad you enjoyed it. Yeah, like I said, I'm real concerned about all that."

"Then you might be interested in helping us figure out which island one of these sand samples came from." He beamed at Miles as if he were an old fraternity brother inviting him to a striptease party. "We've made splits of them to send to the lab in Washington, but we thought you might like to have a shot at them first."

Miles' eyes went wide with interest, but mine went narrow. *So Tom was misdirecting me again. He's known all along that we're looking for an island. So what island would that be?* I looked up at the map of the Caribbean that hung over Miles Guffey's desk. I located Cocoa Beach, then the islands closest to it. *The Bahamas . . .*

Following my gaze to the map, Miles said, "Well, there are only 700 islands and 2,400 uninhabited islets and cays in the Bahamas. This shouldn't be too tough."

In no time at all, Miles had someone expressing my matching samples to Washington, and had a specialist examining my sand sample. Next, Miles turned to the sample from inside the plastic. "What's the provenance?" he asked.

Tom let his eyelids drop and rise again, his quiet signal that I should keep mum on certain details. I said, "Well, both were collected on an Atlantic shore beach. The first is from the coating of sand outside of an article of evidence, but the other came from inside, presumably transported in with the article from somewhere else. The carbonates looked exotic to the beach, especially those little pink things."

Miles gave me one of his sloppy grins. "Oh, so y'all been fishing for square grouper, huh? Right ch'ar, them's forams. We'll call us in a specialist on those." He picked up his phone and punched in four digits. "Hey, get me 'Livia, will ya? No, you tell her it's important. No, this time I am not crying wolf. Aw, shit; tell her I got her some foraminifera from the Bahamas, that'll get her going." He hung up without saying good-bye, and, still grinning, turned to me and said, "Sometimes y' jus' have to know what trough the pig is feeding at." He chuckled. "Olivia Rodríguez did her doctoral dissertation on them little thingies. Makes her heart go all pitter-pat."

Sure enough, in about the time it took for a healthy person to all but sprint from her office to his, Olivia Carmen Rodríguez Garcia arrived at his doorway. Her eyes were little dark holes. "This had better be good."

"Oh, it is. Y'all'll like this one! Looky here!" He had used the time since putting the phone back in its cradle to pour half the sample into a little black cardboard tray and shove it underneath a petrographic microscope. "Just to the right of the *Homotrema,* check out that little turdlike one."

Olivia switched on the light source, bent to the eye pieces, and began to adjust the focus. "Well, yes, that's *Homotrema rubrum,*" she said. "This other one is more interesting. A *Spiroplectammina,* I think. And here's a *Quinqueloculina.* Hmm . . . in order to narrow it from genus to species, I'd need a SEM. Where'd you get this, dear?" She had turned and was looking at me.

I blinked and fed her question back to her. "Well, that's what we're trying to understand. And, um, this man's from the FBI."

She glanced back and forth between Tom and me, but spoke to Miles. "Get Jane over at the University SEM on this. Have her pick the bugs and get them coated. Call me as soon as the sample is prepared."

A scanning electron microscope is capable of enlarging our view of a sample by thousands of diameters. To do this, a loose sample is first "picked," or sorted to select preferred grains. This is done by a person with steady hands who holds a fine brush that is wetted against the tongue then touched gently to the grains of interest. They are thus lifted out of the surrounding materials and stuck with gum paste to a backing. The tiny sample is then coated one molecule thick with gold, then set inside the vacuum chamber of the SEM and pummeled with electrons. The returning electrons "read" the sample, and it can be digitally displayed on a TV screen and enlarged to make a pinhead seem the size of an elephant. The machine can also determine mineralogical makeup of target points of the sample, a kind of mini analytical lab at the snap of a finger, or almost that quick.

Olivia brought another woman along to view the samples. "This is Hannah Jenkins. She is a pelagic specialist, I am benthic."

Tom looked to me for a translation.

I said, "Floating versus bottom dwelling. It makes a difference if you're trying to pinpoint where something came from. A bottom dweller stays put, while a floater can move around with the currents. It could have come from somewhere else. So the benthic is of more use to us as a positive indicator of source, but either way we need to know what we're looking at, so we don't draw the wrong conclusions."

He nodded.

Olivia said, "The combination we're finding here suggests a certain overlap of environments." She opened a thick book called *Carbonate Depositional Environments* to an article about the Bahama banks written by a man named Robert Halley, and showed us a map that illustrated what she was saying. "Benthic forams tell us a few things. The suite we have found here shows an overlap of these areas in which each would have lived. It's not very accurate, really, but it's a best guess."

Miles looked over her shoulder. "The Berry Islands."

Tom asked, "Can you narrow it to a specific island?"

"No," said Olivia. "Foraminifera aren't that specific. I'm not even certain that it's the Berry Islands. But I'd say definitely the Western Bahamas."

Tom nodded. "Excuse me," he said, as he pulled his cell phone from his pocket and left the room to place his call. I tagged along and did my best to listen in as he reported the island group to Brad. As he listened to what Brad had to say in return, I saw Tom smile for the first time in days. As he signed off, he even turned that smile on me. "He's got a line on Jack," he said. "He's on a sailboat, or at least he borrowed one from an old friend. He took it out of a marina in Stuart, a port town a hundred miles or so south of Cocoa Beach. So it looks like he's crossed to the Bahamas ahead of us."

It was two in the afternoon when Tom steered the Mercedes back into the driveway at Nancy Wallace's domain. It was, once again, raining cats and dogs, big splashy drops that hit the gravel like something out of Dr. Seuss. We had been gone less than twenty hours, but it felt like a week. I had been up and going hard since half-past six the morning before, and each time I blinked I was afraid my eyes might stick shut.

A question punched through my fatigue. "Tom, why did Jack call it 'killer dust'? I mean, what are the other associations with the word 'dust'?"

"Look to Miles for that answer."

"Anthrax."

"Yes. In its most lethal, highly developed form, it is a fine dust. The doses that came in those letters were finely ground. Less than you'd find in a packet of sugar."

"But plenty deadly."

Tom said, "You keep a close eye on Miles and Waltrine and let me know anything that occurs to you. And keep after him. I have a feeling he knows more than he wanted to say about that island group."

I heard a sound behind me. The front door of Nancy's house opened, and Faye walked out. Her eyes were puffy from crying. She moved forward at a slow, angry stroll, the motion causing her roundness to sway luxuriously. Tom looked on her with longing, but did not get out of the car. Instead, he opened the window and held out his hand.

"Glad to hear from you," she said icily. She did not take his hand. Instead, she swung her pregnancy toward him, all but stuffing it in his face. *This* is your priority, she was telling him.

Tom dropped his arm to the side of the car. "Sorry, hon. I should have called."

Faye ran a hand through his grizzled hair, grabbed the back of his head, and gave it a nasty yank. "That is *such* an understatement."

I thought, *You didn't call.*

Tom said, "And I'm only here to drop Em with you."

Faye's fingers stiffened into claws. She dug them into the back of his neck.

Tom took her hand from his neck and brought it around to his face. There he spread it between his own, sadly smoothing the tension from it, kissing it gently, stroking each finger separately with his own. He said, "This is where you get out, Em."

"Why?"

"I'm going back and you're staying here."

Faye yanked her hand away. She spun on her heel and stormed into the house and slammed the door.

I said, "You stay. I'll go. I'm the one with the sand samples. I'm the one who can find out which island."

"Get out, Em. Now. Brad can find him."

"Then *let* Brad find him. What do *you* need to go for?"

His voice tightened. "To help Brad and the others. To make goddamned sure you're not right about this guy having friends."

I was ready to kick the dashboard again. Jack was out there playing macho-boy games when I wanted him here and in my bed. He was out there helping someone else, some other *woman* when I needed to be able to dream about a life that had him in it, safe and sound. But I also wanted to be able to dream about tomorrow without dreading it. I felt selfish and infantile, because I knew he was doing something noble, even if I was jealous as hell that it might be for another woman. Because there was a woman astronaut going up on this flight, and it was women who were usually stalked by crazy men. I was willing to bet dollars for doughnuts that the young woman in the photograph in Orlando and the woman astronaut were one and the same.

And I wanted to know if Jack was indeed the friend I thought he was or some kind of monster. My guts writhed, trying to reconcile the tender man who had lain beside me with the gun-toting men in black who had melted in and out of the shadows near Cocoa Beach. These were trained killers who went home at night and cooed at their kids and made love to their women, and when someone called them, they left those kids and those women behind and went and did dangerous things. I said, "You had to help Jack. Now you have to help Brad, whom you only just met. What *is* it with you guys?"

Tom stared at his hands. He spoke very softly. "Men who fight together become brothers in a very deep sense. If one of them is in trouble, there are no questions asked."

I glanced over at the house. Faye had returned to the doorway, and stood with her arms curled in against her body, her fists crammed against her eyes. Even from this distance, I could see that she was trembling with fear.

Tom said, "Get out of the car, Em. I have to go now.

Please. If I stay any longer, I won't be able to do what I have to do."

"Let me go in your place."

"You don't have the training."

Tom started the Mercedes. He gave me an angry push. "Go!"

I opened my door and got out.

Faye's voice rose over the sound of the engine like an injured bird, swooping, begging for him to stay, but Tom was gone.

– 25 –

I sat by Nancy's pool in the strange inside-out room defined by screening, my head back, eyes to the sky, watching the little chameleons run around upside down between me and the afternoon clouds, which were building again into big woolly black things. "They think they know which island group the thing came from," I told Faye, "but not which island of the group."

Faye lay flat on a chaise lounge, shaking with tears. "I keep telling you, I don't want to hear about it."

"I understand that. But I need to talk about it."

"*You* need to talk about it. *I* have to figure out how to raise a child without a husband."

"Tom will be fine," I said, not at all sure I believed it myself. I was in fact beyond worry over the whole thing. I was so scared that I was flattened against the deck chair as if something extremely heavy lay against my chest. The great weight even pushed my head back, training my eyes on the sky, the province of the strange African dust. And yet if asked, I could not have named exactly what it was that so frightened me.

"Okay, damn you," she said through her tears. "Say it."

"There's something very wrong."

"No shit."

"I mean something beyond all this. Something about Jack. A piece of the puzzle missing."

Faye was silent except for a steady sniffling.

"I'm sorry, Faye. This is the last thing you need right now, but it feels critically important."

Fay took in a long, shuddering breath. "Fix the problem in time," she suggested, wiping her nose with the back of her hand. "Maybe that will help."

"The thing is . . ." The thing was what? "It's like I'm digging, going down layer after layer, but I can't find the trapdoor that keeps the dark things hidden. There's something about Jack down there, something he's not telling me. It's all locked up, and I can't reach it."

"Something from before you." She turned her head and looked at me. She was a portrait of grief, and yet she was rallying for me, turning her excellent mind to the game of helping Em one more time, fighting her despair by taking action.

I loved her so much right then that I began to cry myself. I said, "I've never really known much about him. No facts, really. Now I've seen where he grew up, but still there were huge holes in the picture. It's like whatever he's not telling me isn't even really there."

"Describe the holes."

"The holes. There were pictures all over that house but . . . not a single photograph of his father. Where's his father?"

"Dead, maybe? Your father's dead. These things . . . happen."

"Yeah, but if he was only dead, there would be pictures. There are pictures of my dad all over the place at the ranch."

"Maybe his parents are divorced. A bad divorce, and his mother doesn't want to be reminded of it."

"There's more. His mother had a bag all packed, and it looked really old, like she'd had it ready for a long time. What does that tell you?"

"She likes to travel?"

"Now you're being flip. This is serious."

Faye picked up a leaf that had fallen onto the pool deck

and used it to touch my hand. "You know Jack is abnormally attached to Tom. He's like a big brother to him, or more so. It's like Tom's a father figure."

"Yes . . ." Fatherhood seemed woven all through this puzzle.

Faye rolled onto her back and stared up at the chameleons. "And there's something in their relationship that goes beyond that. You know and I know that Tom's kind of a paranoiac. He's more than careful whom he tells much of anything, and there's almost no one he'll rely on. Except Jack."

"I know. He keeps saying, 'I'd trust him with my life.' Where's *that* at?"

"Well, on the face of it, he trusts him that much. Em, don't normal people have friends they can rely on?"

"Don't ask me about normal. I'm the beat-up cowgirl from Wyoming with the deceased father and drowned brother and the alcoholic mother who kicked me out. I'm the unemployed geologist who keeps getting mixed up in crimes that nobody pays me to solve. I'm the thirty-five-year-old single woman who's infatuated with an FBI agent who ran off tilting at some other woman's windmills the morning after she fucked him for the first time."

"Don't say it that way. He loves you. You made love together."

Tears at last began to roll down my cheeks, hot and thick. "And I want to do it again. But I don't know where he is. And he doesn't tell me things, not anything about himself, not really."

"He tells you that he loves you. Can't you believe that?"

"But then he leaves a map showing where he buried a fucking Chinese surface-to-air missile."

Faye sat up abruptly. "He *what*? Em, did I hear you say that? You think *Jack* put that thing there?"

I slapped my hands over my mouth as if eels were coming out of it. I wanted to run and scream, beat the words into the earth where they couldn't hurt me. "I didn't mean it! I just—he's trained in the art of killing, Faye! I'm sup-posed to trust him?"

"Yes, Em. I always used to think that police dogs must be terribly vicious. Then someone explained to me that they're actually very calm and big-hearted, because you need a really stable animal for that training. You have to be able to teach them to attack, yes, but also to let go the instant you command it. I think it's the same with these warrior men."

"Jack's not a German Shepherd."

"You're scared out of your wits that Jack's not as good and stable and trustworthy as you hope he is. Well, let me tell you, Em, you don't ever get to know somebody until you open yourself up to them and do it the hard way, just like the rest of us poor fools. You think I knew Tom when I married him? Bullshit. You think I know him now? Every woman gets to know her man the same way, by living with him. That's when you get to see inside the shell, sweetie, not before. Up until then it's all chocolates and roses, and that's all very nice, but it's crap. You only get to know if they're good for it by putting it to the test."

"Alright!" I yelled. "Alright! I put it to the test. I slept with him. I opened my body and my soul to him, and it was beautiful, and it scared me silly, and he ran away! Where's *that* at?"

"I don't think he ran away. I heard him that morning, talking to Tom. He was in anguish. He was afraid you'd leave him, but this was something he had to do. He felt he had no choice. He had some kind of promise to a friend, Em. I think that argues well for him."

"*What* friend?"

"We don't know. I don't think Tom even knows. Or maybe he does and he can't say."

"This brotherhood thing! I just don't get it!"

"They have a bond. I think you want something like that for yourself. But you're not built that way."

"What kind of paranoiacs can't call the police when there's a crime going down?"

"These guys are paranoid, Em, you're quite right, but for good reason. There are things out there they deal with every day that scare them shitless. Call it posttraumatic stress if you must, but they band together, and bond, and they do their guy thing, and this is what it looks like. I don't like it either. If Tom was here right now, I'd be kicking him in the nuts, I'm so angry. Hell, I wanted to be the millennial woman whose man built a new alliance with her. I didn't want to get married. I wanted every day to be a new day, no strings. And then I got pregnant, and all the old tribal stuff came home to roost. Now the baby has the priority, and I'm just the vehicle for it, and Tom's gone off to slay the dragon that he feels is threatening it. God help me, Em, I didn't ask for *any* of this!"

I said, "Where was Jack's dad?"

"Maybe she had him out of wedlock. Got knocked up. These things *happen,*" Faye said, looking down at her own belly. "Or maybe she's gay, and had a turkey-baster job. It's nobody's business, Em."

"She's as heterosexual as you or I. She's middle-of-the-road white bread Americana at heart. And she's keeping a secret."

"And Em, the great sleuth, can smell a secret," she said sarcastically.

"I don't know this pattern. It's a new one. I just know there's a pattern to it. It's staring me in the face, and I can't figure it out."

Faye closed her eyes and sighed. "Describe what you see."

"I see . . . a man who has a strong—no, overweening—sense of loyalty and secrecy. And he's the man with a thousand faces, an actor. Those two parts of him fly at each other. Where'd he learn to morph like that? And he's forty years old and didn't tell me it was his birthday. And he's never been married, or if he has, he's sure covered it well. No kids, or does he have a love child stuffed away somewhere?"

Faye stuck out a hand. "Hold it. Stop. You're really

around the bend here. And you said a moment ago that you thought he put that thing in the sand himself. And you're calling Tom paranoid?"

I pulled my shoulders up around me, my skin beginning to crawl. "I don't know. It's a feeling. Jack's loyal all right, but it's as if . . . he molds easily. Parts of him are like putty."

Faye laughed derisively. "So you're saying that you think he might be some kind of double agent maybe, who doesn't have control over what he's doing?"

"No . . . that's not it."

"You think he's evil."

"No!"

"Make up your mind. You think he's capable of bringing a weapon onto American soil that can bringing down a space shuttle."

"No, I don't think he'd do that. Not the Jack I know. But the Jack who was here two days ago was not the Jack I know."

"Ah. Now we're getting down to it."

"What in hell's name had him so upset, Faye? He wouldn't even respond to me, and then he grabbed me so roughly it scared me. It *hurt*. Since then, I've had to think through everything I know about him, and I've realized that it's a pretty short list of facts."

"Do you think he's capable of firing a rocket at a space shuttle, or not?"

I was pulled up with my knees under my chin now, like a little girl. "I don't think so. But *someone* put it there."

Faye leaned toward me and stroked my hair. "Yes, someone put it there. Someone pretty crazy. But I don't think Jack's crazy. Do you?"

I could not answer her question.

I borrowed a Mercedes and drove back over to the USGS. At the desk, I asked for Miles Guffey. I was going on raw instinct now, homing in on the path—any path—that might yield information.

"He's gone on a trip," said the receptionist.

"Oh. Well, how about Waltrine Sweet?"

"Left with him."

"Oh. Is Dr. Rodríguez in?"

"She went home. It's her daughter's birthday. She told me to tell you you should drop by if you wanted to." She handed me a slip of paper with an address and a little map.

Olivia Rodríguez Garcia was making rice fritters stuffed with cheese (*granitos*) and a sort of fried coconut dough (*arepas de coco*) for her ten-year-old daughter and half a dozen of her girlfriends. The girls laughed and cooed over the crunchy treats, licking the oil from their fingers, threatening to rub it on each other's party clothes.

Olivia offered me some. "Try. You've got to love them," she said, pursing her dark lips into a rosebud of culinary ecstasy.

I bit into a rice fritter. My teeth broke through the crust and into the hidden cheese. My mouth watered. I suddenly realized I had not had lunch.

"Good, hmm?"

"Good."

She fixed her dark eyes on me. "So, Miles and Waltrine have gone on a little trip, eh?"

There was something in her tone I didn't like. If I'd had hackles on the back of my neck, they would have stood up. "Yes. Is that why you invited me to your daughter's party?"

"Try *unas arepas*. Some people like them with honey. Miles has taken an unexpected leave. Sorry. This must be an inconvenience for you." She raised her eyebrows and shoulders, as if to say, *What can you expect?*

"Do you know where he went? Or how long he will be gone?"

"I have a suspicion he is going somewhere on his boat. That sample you brought him seemed to excite him." She shrugged her shoulders. "I am not privy to his plans. This is how it is with him. He is not a team player. I have a center to run. Our projections for the coming year are due tomorrow, and he has given me nothing."

I stared at her, wondering if I was looking at someone stirring up trouble, or just a very, very frustrated administrator trying to deal with a very, very loose cannon. "I think I'll drive over to his house and see if he's left yet," I said, and excused myself.

Olivia Rodríguez Garcia did not say good-bye. She was too busy staring out the window, no doubt wondering how to spin this one at USGS headquarters.

Three P.M. found me at Miles Guffey's house, racing up the driveway to avoid the afternoon downpour but getting soaked to the skin anyway. My hair instantly lay plastered to my forehead. Both the bad and the good news was that I couldn't park closer to the door because both Waltrine Sweet's and Miles Guffey's cars were there ahead of me.

Gaining the entryway, I pressed the doorbell. Nobody answered. Deciding that my so-called colleagues must be around back somewhere where they couldn't hear the bell, and that they were damned well going to receive me whether they wanted to or not, I dashed around the side of the house, trying to stay underneath the eaves. For my trouble, I got further soaked as rainwater sluiced off the roof, along the palm fronds, and down my collar.

I was thwarted in my circumnavigation of the house by a tall wrought-iron fence, but from the gate I could see Miles and Waltrine out by the dock, loading gear onto the boat. *Strange time for a boat ride*, I decided. Pamela's pet schnauzer cocked an ear inquisitively my way and began to yap ferociously. Miles looked up from his task, smiled uncertainly, then came and opened the gate. "C'mon, hurry!" he said, as if I were in a mood to dawdle. "It's raining puddles!"

We sprinted to the dock and jumped in underneath the

cover of the upper decking. Miles led me around to the back of the saloon and in through a set of double doors and handed me a towel.

"Hi," I said miscellaneously.

"What brings y'all to the *Dingo*?" Miles asked.

"The what?"

"This little pile of pleasure be the trawler *Sea Dingo*. My wife's parents gave it to us. They're Aussies that made their money selling Land Rovers, so this is the *Sea Dingo*, get it? I guess you'd a' had to been there. I get y'all a drink?"

"No thanks," I said. "I won't be staying long."

Waltrine was stuffing junk food into the lockers, somewhat crushing a king-sized bag of Nacho Cheesier Doritos in the process. She moved on to cramming a chest freezer full of steaks. It looked like they were packing for a long voyage.

The *Sea Dingo* was a cabin cruiser, at least forty feet long, plenty beamy, had a full galley with freezer, fridge, microwave, sinks, range, and ovens, and down a half-flight of stairs I could see a tight hallway leading off to two bunk rooms and two separate bathrooms, or should I say, "heads." Up a half-flight of steps, I saw the wheel and an array of radios, radar, and sonar equipment. Catching me ogling the layout, Miles said, "There's even a washer and dryer. Central air. Pretty cushy, huh."

"Where are you off to?" I inquired, taking the direct approach.

Miles stretched ever so casually. "Oh, just a little pleasure cruise, eh, Waltrine?"

"Sure, boss." She bent back to her stowage. She was now cramming fresh greens and salsa into the refrigeration unit.

I said, "I'm going to be blunt. I came down here to maybe work on your project and now you're taking off somewhere. Funny thing is you didn't mention to me earlier today that you had plans to go anywhere. So I gotta ask:

Does this have anything to do with those sediment samples I brought in this morning?"

Miles looked at Waltrine and Waltrine looked at Miles. "Not so far as I know," he said. "You know sumpin' I don't, Waltrine?"

"No, boss."

Yeah, and Mickey Mouse is ambassador to Portugal. "Well, then, where you off to?"

Miles gave me one of his goofy grins. "Oh, just going gunk-holin' is all." He broke into a cackling laugh. "Y'all can get on with Olivia Rodríguez about the project, get y'se'f set up with some nice samples to run. We'll be back in a week or so, I imagine."

"Or not." Waltrine spoke with her head inside the refrigerator. "We didn't get no funding, so we figgered to just go piss up a rope," she said.

Miles' laughter ripped up into near-hysteric giggles. "They's called 'lines' on a boat, darlin'. Go piss up a *line*. And the maps is charts, rhymes with farts." He took a sip of his drink.

I studied the two of them. Their spirits were somewhere between high and dangerously giddy, and at the same time, weirdly somber. Here they were, the two remaining principal investigators of a project in which the third principal investigator had been last seen flying over the rail of a cruise liner at the urging of someone with muscle. *Uh-huh, this was just a little old pleasure cruise alright.* I said, "Well, it sure is a nice boat. Mind if I look around?"

"Help y'se'f," Miles replied.

I stepped upstairs into the pilothouse. The place was a mess of loose charts and equipment, with electrical lines snaking all over the place. Miles Guffey was, plain and simply, such a slob that if there was something in there that was going to tell me anything about the purpose or destination of this voyage, it could be staring me in the face and I would likely miss it. But, being a geologist, and thereby by birthright a map junkie, my eye was drawn to the chart desk. There, on top of a disarrayed stack of books, the remains of a rather ancient-looking ham sandwich and a hand puppet designed to look like a giant cockroach, sat a book of charts that was open to a familiar-looking bit of geography. I stepped up closer. Sure enough, it was the Berry Islands. I turned and walked back down the steps. I had seen all I needed to see.

Back at Nancy's, I found Faye in the guesthouse, packing her bags.

"Are you going somewhere?" I asked.

"*We* are going to the Everglades," she said. "Just as we planned. I am not going to wait here for Tom. He has my cell number, and he can phone me if he condescends to do so."

"You look tired, Faye, and God knows I am. Can't this wait until tomorrow?"

"No." She handed me a sealed envelope. "This is for you. Tom said to give it to you only if things went completely wrong, but I figure this qualifies."

I turned the envelope over and read the address. It was my name, written in Jack's handwriting.

It had stopped raining for the moment, so I moved outside onto the pool deck to share the moment with the chameleons and the dripping palms. I settled into a bench, oblivious to its wetness, and tore open the envelope. It contained a folded piece of lined paper and a second envelope. I unfolded the single sheet of paper and began to read.

It was dated two days before, the day I had found him so distraught and disheveled in the guesthouse. "My darling Em," it began.

I'm sorry I have to take off like this again without getting a chance to say hello, not to mention goodbye. But Tom says you're seeing some man at the USGS about dust. I'm truly sorry how things went. I had such plans for us, such hopes. But if you're reading this, things didn't go well for me. I have an important request. Would you please go down to the Everglades, to the address below, and look for a woman named Winifred Egret. She's looking after someone for me. Everything's taken care of financially, and this someone is in good hands, but I wanted you to meet her one day, because she's essential to me and so are you. I hope it's no imposition. Give Winifred and her people the enclosed letter, and she'll know it's okay to let you in. I love you, Em, more than you could possibly know. You're the one I was always looking for, rest assured of that. There have been others along the path, but you were the destination. How ironic that dust should get in the way of our building our common ground together.

It was signed, simply, "Jack," and gave an address that was more like a set of directions. It started out, "Alligator Alley (I-75) to Route 833, turn north." The inner envelope was sealed. On it he had written, "Winifred Egret."

I sat for quite a while, trying to take in this one additional fragment of the man I had fallen in love with. Like everything else I had learned about him in recent days, it was incomplete, something thrown together in a hurry instead of being taken slowly and allowed to mature unhindered. But I was beginning to suspect such romantic, glancing communications were the key to Jack Sampler, and that his was a life strung between long-range wishes and the exigencies of the moment.

At length, I got up and walked back to the guesthouse, back to Faye. I moved slowly, as though through a long and drugged sleep. "Okay," I told her. "I guess we're going to the Everglades."

– 26 –

As Faye drove us south over the high vault of the Skyway Bridge, crossing Tampa Bay from the southern tip of the St. Petersburg peninsula, I found myself scanning the wide expanse of glinting water, casting idly about for the *Sea Dingo*. I couldn't see it. I had been in Florida less than four days, but the place was so flat that already anything that raised me up and wasn't an elevator got my attention. From the acrobatic center of the span, built high enough to accommodate the largest of ships in full sail, boats as small as *Sea Dingo* appeared like tiny toys, indistinguishable from one another. The landward sky was a symphony of clouds, layer upon layer of shapes and sizes, but the scene was lost on me, except to note, quite clinically, that the sky over the Gulf of Mexico was surprisingly clear. *That gives Miles clear passage,* I decided.

I no longer cared where Miles Guffey was going. My world was shattered. His cruise seemed to be happening somewhere else, in a separate reality. I did not speak until hours later, when we swept south of Fort Myers, and Faye started asking what I wanted for dinner.

"Nothing," I said.

"We're a pair."

"Mm." My mind was on Faye's cell phone, which was riding on a charging jack on the dashboard to keep it topped up. Reception had been excellent so far, absolute flatness being a virtue with such things. But Tom had not called. I had tried him a couple of times, but had gotten no answer.

Faye said, "I'm going to head on down the Tamiami Trail to Everglade City. There are some little bed-and-breakfast inns there, and we can see if the stone crab is in season. Tomorrow we'll rent a canoe and paddle out into the Ten Thousand Islands. They're mangrove shoals. Some are shell middens built up by the Indians that used to live here. Caloosas, I think. Or whoever was here before the Seminoles. Then the next day, we can drive down to Flamingo and look across at the keys. And then—"

"What's out there in the dark?" I asked.

"Swamp," said Faye. "A thousand themes and variations on wild plants growing right out of water. It's beautiful, once you get to know it, and get over how dangerous it is for a human. If you walked out there, you'd be panther meat, if the mosquitoes didn't drain your blood first, and the first nick you get is an infection that could kill you. A person gets disoriented in the tangle of vegetation. When the lightning sets it on fire, it burns with a rage, because the white man has drained the swamp enough to expose the peat. And yet the white man in all his wisdom has bladed roads all through this darkness and sold it to every sap up there in snow country that has a dream of easy living. Go figure."

"So there's a bunch of snowbirds out there? Why don't we see their lights?"

"They never moved there. There's no way to live there, not really, not unless the damned developers get a whole lot more aggressive. No, there's nothing there but the damned roads. So, on to Everglades City."

Darkness. It was whispering to me, calling me into its heart. I said, "Jack's letter said something about Alligator Alley. That's part of this Interstate highway, right?" I opened a map and put my finger on it. "Yeah. Right here. It crosses the Everglades north of the . . . what is this . . . Tamiami Trail. I want to go there."

"Oh, so you're going to share Jack's letter with me, then?"

"He wants me to go look someone up for him."

"Who?"

"Winifred somebody."

Faye tossed her hands in the air, something she could easily do on such long, straight stretches of road. "Sure, sure. Why not? Get to know the locals; that always works for me. What the fuck. Alligator Alley it is."

After another twenty minutes, the road curved eastward. You notice these things when you're in a place that's so flat that the roads don't even have to dodge the slightest hills. The edge of the road lay in pitch-dark shadow.

Faye said, "We don't want to go into that ditch."

"What ditch?"

"Down here, there's always a ditch beside the road. And we don't want to go into it."

"I'll bite. Why not?"

"Because there are alligators in it."

"Oh. Good. Now you tell me."

"Down here ditch means water, and water means alligators. They go together like gin and tonic and a little bitty twist of lime, which I would be guzzling right now if I was not carrying an underage passenger." She patted her tummy. "Just you and me, kid."

"Tom's going to be fine, Faye. He's a big boy. He knows how to look after himself."

"Screw Tom. More important, Em, where are we going to stay tonight?"

"I don't know. Some motel, right?"

"There are no motels here. Not out here in the middle. Alligator Alley goes straight east to Fort Lauderdale, but there's nothing but swamp in between."

"Nothing?"

"Well, there are alligators."

"Always it's alligators."

"But no poodles."

"No poodles?"

"The alligators make canapés out of them."

"Charming."

"Pick their reptilian teeth with the shin bones."

"Faye . . ."

"Where was this place Jack wanted you to go?"

I opened the letter. "We turn north on 833."

"Find it on the map."

I did. "It looks like it leads north toward a place called Clewiston. But then, why would he have us come all this way south first? We could have saved time by going east from Fort Myers on Route 80."

"There's nothing else in between?"

"Just swamp. And a couple roads. Wait, here's a place called Devil's Garden. That sounds charming. But still, it's closer to Route 80."

"What did you say the person's name was?"

"Winifred Egret. Must be some kind of hippie that made herself a new name."

Faye's eyes widened. "Egret is a Seminole name. Take the wheel a second," Faye said. "Give me that map." She took it and turned on the overhead map light. "Holy shit!" she said. "There is too something else in there. Your Jack is directing us to the Big Cypress Indian Reservation."

We drove onward for a little over an hour, during which time we saw only dark sky, dark highway, and a solid, dark curtain of foliage to either side of it. Finally, we cut north on Route 833. I still could not see a damned thing to either side of the road except vegetative darkness and the cloudy night sky crowding low overhead. Faye drove onward until she came to a crossing with a smaller road. She pulled over, unsure of where we were. "Is this our turn?" she inquired.

No one was in sight. The crossroads was marked only by a couple of sign boards and a building that announced itself as the Ah-Tah-Thi-Ki Museum. The structure was large and architecturally refined, not what I would have expected to find that far from any sign of a metropolitan area. I stared at it as if it had just landed from space. The lights were out.

The car idled.

I pressed the button to lower the window on my side. The night was reasonably cool, no more than seventy degrees. A pungent scent of decaying leaves slid in on the humid air. I heard an animal call, deep and aggressive. I hoped it was a frog. A mosquito whined.

Faye said, "Well, what do you think, *compañera*?"

"I *think* this is the turn. . . ."

"Not good enough. It's dark and I'm tired." Faye nodded at one of the signs. "Billie Swamp Safari, two point four miles, give or take a stop to kick a stray reptile off the tarmac. I've heard of that place. We can stay at a chickee."

"What's a chickee?"

"Thatched hut. Seminole house. Open air, plenty of mosquitoes this time of year."

"Oh. Great."

"You didn't want to go to Everglade City. But hey, we're a coupla crackers in a Mercedes out for a lark. We'll just roll in and catch some winks and phone what's-her-name in the morning."

"He didn't give a phone number." If we had been in Wyoming, being out in the middle of nowhere would have seemed normal. I would have suggested we just pull off the road out of sight and sleep in the car. But here there were strange noises, and more darkness than I was quite used to dealing with.

"Well, you wanted an adventure. We're sure Alice-down-the-rabbit-hole this time."

Faye put the car into gear and turned left. We drove our two-point-how-many miles through more darkness. Eventually we came to a great, big sign that read BILLIE SWAMP SAFARI and had a painting of a man in patchwork Seminole attire pointing to our right. We turned that direction and drove down an even narrower road that gave way quickly to gravel. It was pitch dark, and if Faye had told me then that this was all her idea of a joke, that we were actually

on a disused trail going nowhere, I would have believed
her. Suddenly we burst into a clearing where there were
cars parked along a row of thatched huts, and big signs
galore indicating that this was the place. One said GIFT
SHOP. This hut was closed, but there were lights behind it,
so we parked the car and got out. We could hear two things:
mosquitoes, and human voices beyond the huts, so we
headed double-time down a pathway between two huts and
found ourselves in front of a restaurant called the Swamp
Water Café.

"What the hey," said Faye. "Let's see if we can get us
a bite of key lime pie or something."

"Always eating," I said, for something to say.

"Eating for two," she replied, ducking quickly inside before the whining mosquitoes picked her up and carried her
away.

Inside, we found a setup that looked very much like any
other wayside restaurant of the Formica tabletop variety. A
young, very blond woman cheerily asked us how she could
help us, and Faye said we'd like pie and a place to stay for
the night.

"Okay," she said. "Anything to drink with that?"

I was feeling kind of frowsy, so I said, "Coffee, please.
Milk for my friend. She's eating for two."

The waitress smiled. "When you due?"

Faye lowered herself into a chair. "About two months."

"Last little trip beforehand?"

"You got it."

"Well, y'all kick back and let us do the cookin'. Your
order will be right up."

That all seemed very positive and homey, so I began to
relax a notch.

The waitress made a beeline to a middle-aged man in
khakis who was sitting at another table drinking something
hot, spoke to him a moment, then disappeared into the
kitchen. The man picked up his cup and wandered over
toward us, taking his time. "Hello," he said, crinkling a
sleepy smile up around his blue eyes. "My name's Bill. I

hear you ladies want a place to stay tonight."

"That's right," said Faye. "I hear you have chickees to rent."

"That's right. You have a reservation?"

Faye shook her head.

My heart sank. I began to wish I had taken Faye's suggestion of a nice, cozy bed-and-breakfast in Everglade City.

Bill did not look perturbed. "How long you expecting to stay?"

"Just overnight," I said quickly.

"No problem then. We're pretty well booked up on the weekends, but we can certainly accommodate you tonight. Do you want the nighttime package?"

"Sure," said Faye.

I glanced at her. She gave me a quick smile and a shrug of her shoulders. She wanted an adventure, and she was going to find it come hell or high water, the latter of which was only too easy to locate in a swamp.

"Okay," said Bill. "You ladies enjoy your pie, and I'll get you your Seminole storyteller." He got up and wandered out of the café. The door was just closing as the waitress brought our pies and drinks.

It was about then that I began to notice something funny about the Swamp Water Café: None of the people working there were Indians. I asked the waitress, "Are we really on the Seminole reservation?"

"Yeah."

"Well then, where are . . ." I trailed off, embarrassed at my brashness.

"All the Indians?" she inquired.

"Yeah."

She pulled up a chair and sat down. "Oh, they don't work here."

"Oh, so they're over in the gift shop?"

"No, not really."

"The office?"

"Sometimes."

"Oh."

She laughed. "Folks are always confused by this. Thing is, the Indians don't have to work. They get a couple thousand apiece every month from the casinos. So why work?"

"Why indeed."

Faye asked, "What do they do?"

The waitress made a "who knows?" gesture. "Drink. Drive fast cars. Naw, I'm exaggerating. They just live their lives like the rest of us. They run the tribe, do their cultural things, but why wait tables or make beds if they don't have to? They're good employers, pay well."

The door crashed open and another blue-eyed man in khakis came in, but this one was younger than the first and swaggered shamelessly as he moved toward us. "Hi, ladies," he said, helping himself to the fourth chair at the table. "I'm Black Hawk. I'll be your storyteller tonight."

I about gagged on my pie.

Faye leaned onto her elbows and grinned serenely. "Fly me, big fellah."

Black Hawk looked somewhat disconcerted, but he recovered quickly. "Okay, well, I'm a friend of the Seminole. I went away and did my service for my country and now I'm back. Seminoles are very private people. But they trust me, and have told me a few of their stories." He bunched up his arms and leaned onto the table, his big, well-muscled shoulders heaving up like summits on a mountain range. I guess we were supposed to be impressed. "Okay. Well, so what do you know about Seminole storytelling?"

"Nothing," Faye said. "We got lost out there on Alligator Alley and we thought we'd drop in for some pie."

Black Hawk glanced at the door as if planning his escape.

I felt like escaping myself. Since getting in the car that afternoon, life had felt like it was slowing down, everything grinding to a crunch even as we sped along the highway, as if the scale of our surroundings dwarfed the passage of time. My muscles felt like they were moving in thick glue. I said, "Don't mind her. We were just out looking for a man who got thrown off a cruise ship, and we took a wrong turn at St. Petersburg."

Black Hawk glanced back and forth between us. He wrinkled his brow importantly. "I just got out of the marines, myself. We ride on Navy ships. We don't have all that cushy life the cruise ships have. I don't trust them anyway. They're all registered in Panama or Libya, and where do they get all that money? They buy whole islands out there in the Bahamas and take all those tourists out there and run them ashore and turn them on little spits until they're brown. Here in the Everglades we have natural history. We have gators and lots of birds, other animals. Raccoon. Possum. I grew up nearby, been coming out here since I was in high school."

I said, "Tell me that again about the cruise ships."

"The part about the Libyan registration?"

"Yes . . . but also the part about the private islands."

"Oh, they have these private islands. Cays, we call them. There's thousands of islands in the Bahamian banks, and these guys buy up whole little islands so they can run their cruise ships in there, and the paying passengers think it's all a big deal."

"And you could hide all kinds of operations in that sort of place."

Black Hawk looked at me out of the corner of one eye, like a cow who's certain it's about to get hit with a prod. "Hey, I don't know what you're into, but . . ."

Just then a third man in khakis came into the restaurant and hurried up to the table. This one was short and swarthy. "I'm Gator," he said. "Your swamp-buggy tour is ready and waiting for you. Come on, Black Hawk, give the ladies a break. You'll make them late with all your nonsense." He gave us a merry wink and waved us toward the door.

"Are you a Seminole?" Faye asked.

I was ready to kick her. Maybe I should have.

Gator said, "No, I'm Cuban."

"*Oye,*" I said.

"Sí," he said, giving me a look of appraisal. "This way, please."

We were met at the door by the first man, Bill. "Let me show them where they'll be sleeping," he told Gator, "Then they're all yours."

Bill led us out past a low wall that enclosed a shallow pool. Inside, I saw some long, dark shapes. "What are those?" I asked.

"Alligators," said Gator. "I ought to know." He held out his arms, twisting them this way and that under the fluorescent light that illuminated the pool, showing us some nasty scars. "This one's from the first time I got bit, before I knew better than to yank it free. This is the second. See? Just bite holes here. No rips. Healed lots faster."

Bill said, "Quit scarin' them, Gator."

I found myself hustling along to keep up with Bill. The path grew darker and darker, the light from the distant spotlights near the restaurant a waning memory. Our only light now came from an electric lantern Bill was carrying. A couple hundred yards down the path, with the unseen mosquitoes zeroing in on us in a symphony of whines, he pulled briskly up by one in a string of huts about ten feet on a side. Like all the other huts, it had a steep-pitched roof thatched with densely packed palm fronds. These smaller huts had undressed log frames enclosed by some sort of siding. Bill set the lantern down and quickly opened a combination padlock and showed us in. I was quickly getting the idea that when there were mosquitoes about, folks didn't tarry much.

Inside the hut, we found two primitive cots made up with army blankets and a drapery of mosquito netting. Bill showed us how to light a kerosene lantern that rested on a low, rough-cut table. The light danced drowsily about the space, faintly illuminating the inside of the thatching. Outside, I could hear the odd twittering of night birds and some deep, more guttural animal calls, a kind of booming. Inside, I could hear mosquitoes. One landed, stung. I slapped it.

Bill said, "I hope you don't mind that this chickee is haunted."

Faye said, "All the comforts of home."

"You ladies have any insect repellant with you?" Gator asked.

Faye laughed ironically.

Gator produced a tube and passed it to her. She passed it to me.

I said, "Faye's being very particular about her pregnancy."

"It's natural stuff," Gator said encouragingly.

Faye mashed a mosquito on her arm and swung out her hand to retrieve the repellant all in one motion. "Forgot about this little detail," she muttered, swatting her other arm, then her neck. "Welcome to the Everglades, Em."

I was so tired I wanted to just fall over onto a bed and sleep, but Faye wanted to experience the full night package, whatever that was. So swamp buggying we did go.

The buggy turned out to be a giant platform with rows of benches and four balloon tires on each side. Gator helped Faye up onto a loading dock from which she could climb the last steps up onto the thing. We settled ourselves in the second bench and Gator fired up the engine. On the only other occupied bench were yet another man in khakis and the waitress from the café, all cuddled up as if they were parked in a convertible above the city lights. Gator said, "This here's Emilio, and you already met Glenda."

Faye said, "You all have a sort of military air to you around here."

I looked at her. I couldn't tell if she was joking about the khakis, or if she was serious. Fatigue seemed to press me into the seat.

Emilio said, "We all been in the marines. Bill was in the marines, so he knows he's got good men if he hires one of us. Right, Glenda?" He gave her a macho one-armed squeeze and a kiss to her forehead. She tittered.

The big buggy rocked and swayed as Gator maneuvered it about the parking lot and headed out into the darkness, breaking the relative tranquility of the night with the rumble of the engine and the sweeping play of the headlights. The guy who was now bussing the waitress sat up and switched on a spotlight and began to pan it across the darkness; it picked out a high-wire fence and a big automatic gate that was just opening. I saw water and the dense crush of vegetation. We splashed into the water and continued, the buggy rolling ponderously and the spotlight dodging this way and that.

"There's one," said the waitress.

The man with the spotlight riveted it on a small deer. The thing looked attentive, but not concerned. It chewed. We stared.

"What is it?" I asked, ready to totally swoon over the rare Everglades deer, or whatever it was.

"Fallow deer, from India," Emilio said.

Gator turned off the headlights and Emilio switched off the spotlight and handed Faye what looked like a strange-looking pair of binoculars. She put them to my eyes and gasped. "Night-vision goggles," she said. "This is wonderful! Oh, my God! It's . . . fantastic!"

It was a long time before I could get the goggles away from her, but when I put them to my own eyes, I popped into a world of electric-green wraiths. The goggles gathered light like a fiend, and anything that reflected any light was intensified. A deer lifted its head and looked at me, a tracery of monochromatic green. It shifted and walked away, its silent movement stolen from the darkness by the miracle of technology. The stars were bright, and the atmosphere all around was charged with false lights that looked like fireflies. It intensified my growing suspicion that I was dreaming this whole experience.

We drove on with the headlights off, wallowing over the irregular bottom of the swamp, which at this location proved to be a lacework of stagnant streams winding through stands of palms and cypress. In the next five minutes we snagged ten massive spiders and their webs from as many overhanging trees, listened to the waitress scream, and saw five different species of deer exotic to North America, each a different pattern of electric green in the night-vision goggles. "What's the gig with the exotic deer?" I whispered to Faye.

Faye snorted. "I offered you a nice B-and-B in Everglades City. A canoe ride. A land of sunshine. But no, we follow your nose into the darkness. Into something downright strange."

"Chief Billie wanted a wild game park," Gator informed us. "He went down to Texas and went shooting on a friend's game park, and thought it would be nice to have one here, too. Except the tourists complained. So now instead of shooting, he has us take people out for swamp tours. In the daytime, you'll get your fan-boat ride and a reptile show, too."

Faye said, "Bring on them alligators."

I wondered why life had thrown me into a swamp full of lunatics while my lover was off chasing terrorists.

"So what brings you ladies down our way?" Gator asked.

"The spirit of adventure," Faye said sweetly.

I said, "I'm looking for someone named Winifred Egret."

Gator stamped on the brakes. The buggy jolted to a stop. He turned around. "Well, why didn't you say so?" he asked. "But she doesn't take visitors."

Faye grabbed the goggles back.

Shit. I leaned back in the seat and stared at the few fuzzy stars that had managed to send their light through the humid air.

"Em has a letter of introduction," said Faye.

The other guy picked up a two-way radio and spoke into it. "Hey Rolfe, Miz Egret to home in her chickee?"

I heard an unintelligible crackling in return.

The man with the radio made a gesture to Gator. "Let's get moving again before the skeeters suck my last pint of blood, okay?"

Gator put the machinery back in gear, and we lurched

forward. "Aw heck," he said. "I was looking forward to telling you ladies some Seminole stories. You can't get nothing good from Black Hawk there, he don't know anything, he just wants you to think he's real buff. He takes steroids. Wears three T-shirts under that khaki. And did anyone tell you that chickee you rented is haunted?"

The radio crackled into life again. I could make out, "Say who's coming."

The man with the radio said, "She's got a letter."

"Who from?"

Faye said, "Jack Sampler."

The man with the radio relayed the name.

I wasn't liking this. I grabbed the goggles back from Faye and stared through them, trying to convince myself I was somewhere other than where I was. I was dead tired, pissed off, and jangled from the strong coffee and sugar in the pie. I wanted to be in a bed, no matter how rustic. I wanted to roll over in it and find Jack there. I wanted to go home to Utah, or Wyoming, or wherever it was I was from. I wanted to be on a high Rocky Mountain lake at dusk with a fly rod in my hands listening to Townsend's solitaires singing, not slopping around on a tourist buggy swatting mosquitoes in an unfamiliar terrain I could not see.

The radio said, "Okay. Take 'em on in."

Gator cranked a hard left and headed into the trees.

– 27 –

We exited through a back gate from the game preserve. Beyond it lay a grove of orange trees and a dirt road, and on that road a Jeep was waiting. At the wheel of that Jeep was Leah Sampler.

I stood there staring at her for quite some time, mosquitoes be damned.

"Hello," she said, managing to make it sound as if we'd just bumped into each other at the market. "Who's your friend?"

I couldn't find it in myself to take things that coolly. I said, "There are a few things you'll have to explain to me."

"I imagine so. But get in, will you? The insects are getting bad."

Faye slipped Gator and Emilio each a tip. I think she slipped a little cake to the waitress, too, even though she'd already looked after her at a handsome rate back in the Swamp Water Café. We both climbed into the Jeep and buckled up. It was an open model, the late descendant of the World War II item, all nicely done up with a roll bar and big tires for the swamp, and she got it rolling at a good clip very quickly.

"So where are we going?" I asked.

"To see Winifred Egret," she replied. She managed to leave sarcasm out of her tone. I give her credit for that.

"And you obviously know Winifred Egret," I said.

"Very well. It shouldn't be too great a stretch that I, as Jack's mother, should know her, too. In fact, I introduced Jack to Winifred."

"Oh." Now I felt kind of stupid. "It was just a shock is all."

"No, a shock is a shock. You're entitled."

"So then you probably know whomever it is he wanted me to meet. His note said I should look Winifred up to meet someone else who was important to him."

"Yes," she said, to herself as much as to me.

Somewhere in there, Faye introduced herself to Leah, because I had not, and Leah said, "Ah, Tom's wife. I'm so delighted to meet you." We rumbled along the road in the dark with the motion of the Jeep blowing the insects off of us. After a while we turned off the dry land that bordered the citrus groves and headed back into the swamp. Leah gave a scant travelogue. "The higher, drier parts of the Everglades are called hammocks," she said. "Win's hammock is a bit remote. I daresay the directions Jack gave you would have taken you as far as her daughter's house, and she would have screened you to see if you should be allowed to go farther."

"Is there some reason things are secret here?" I asked pointedly.

"No. And yes. The Florida Seminole are the only American Indian tribe never conquered by the white man. They are very private people. But being able to win at war does not mean you can win as a culture. As a sovereign nation, the Seminole tribe has been giving way steadily to the pressures of white so-called civilization. The Seminole are falling faster from slot machines and alcohol than from bullets."

"Someone back at the café said each member of the tribe gets X thousand a month just for being alive."

"That's true. The tribe shares and shares alike, the pie gets split evenly, every man, woman, and child. Some blow the money on whatever our consumer society can serve up. Other, more traditional Seminoles like Winifred Egret pre-

fer to bank the money and live farther from such influences."

We splashed down through a narrow ford between two
hammocks and rolled up onto the other side. We had turned
enough times now that I had pretty much lost my sense of
which way we were heading. That's a hard thing for a geologist to admit, but it was totally dark under the spreading
canopy of the swamp. I tried to identify the trees that tangled around us, but everything was new and alien to me.

Presently we pulled up in front of a small cluster of
chickees that were standing on slightly higher land. Some
were closed in. One was wide open, little more than just
four tree trunks with the bark removed, supporting a
thatched roof. A fire burned on the bare earth beneath it.
An elderly woman sat by the fire. As I stepped down out
of the Jeep and approached her, I saw that she was wearing
the traditional dress of the Seminole woman, a long skirt
and blouse made up of horizontal bands of delicate patchwork. She said, "You're Jack's friend Em, hm?"

"Yes," I answered.

"Welcome. He came to visit a couple months ago. Told
me about you."

He told you but not his mother, I noted. I took out Jack's
note and handed it to her.

"I can't read," she said. "I'm almost blind. Funny Jack,
he knows that. That's for the others. I don't get so confused
by people."

I put the note away and waited.

Winifred Egret turned her ancient face toward Leah.
"Take her inside and tell her what she wants to know. The
pregnant one can stay with me a while. I like babies."

Inside the chickee to the left, Leah offered me something
to drink, which I refused. I was too tired to observe the
social graces. We both sat down on low chairs carved out
of stumps and looked at each other over the soft light of
the kerosene lantern that hung from a wire hook above our
heads. There was little else in the hut but two simple cots
and Leah's ancient suitcase.

Leah's brows and nose threw deep shadows over the rest of her face. "You're wondering why I'm here," she suggested.

"I'm wondering why *I'm* here," I parried.

She took in a deep breath, let it out. "I used to bring Jack here when he was little," she said shyly.

It was my turn to sigh. "I'm sure that's just a tiny little bit of a very big story," I said. "We probably don't have much time. Why don't I just ask a few questions."

"Okay."

"Are you hiding here?"

"Yes."

"Because of what Jack's doing?"

She shook her head. "I hide whenever things get . . . like this."

"Ah. Who did Jack want me to meet here? Was it Winifred?"

"No."

I turned my palms up, as if to ask, *Then who?*

"I think you'd better ask some other questions first."

I felt a deep fatigue settling about me, weighing me down into the hard-packed earth beneath my feet. "Alright, then. Who is Jack's father, and where is he?"

Leah's eyes closed. She became very still. It was a long time before she spoke, but when she did, her voice was faint, and yet hard as ice. "He was someone I barely knew. He . . . we . . . I became pregnant with Jack. He . . . Jack's father was away when I found out, and I thought it better that he . . . stay away."

"He was unkind to you?"

Leah drew her breath in sharply, an expression of deep emotional pain. "He was not a well person. He came back later—when Jack was three—and he realized that Jack was his. That he was the father. I was very young. I let him see Jack. He'd take him places. I thought it would be okay, or good, even. I didn't *know*." The last word twisted in agony.

"Know what?" I asked, keeping my voice as soft as possible.

Her eyes were still closed, and yet in the light of the lantern, I could see tears sliding down her cheeks. "He . . . hurt Jack. Not physically," she said hastily. "There were never any marks . . ."

My mind raced, filling in voids in the mystery of Jack Sampler. "The abuse was emotional?"

"Yes." The word was a gasp.

"I'm so sorry."

Leah's words suddenly came in a flood. "He would put him in a closet and leave him there, tell him he would only let him out if he played the game correctly. Then he put him in a deep, damp hole in the ground, in the dark. You get it? He was torturing him. Methodically. He was—"

"This was sexual?"

"No, it was worse than that. This was ritualized abuse. He was training Jack, training him to be just like him. He was . . . teaching him to lie, to split off, to become a . . . a . . ."

"I'm not sure what you're saying, Leah. Was his father a—what did his father do? For a living."

"He said he was in sales. God knows what he was selling," she said, her voice suddenly stronger, anger breaking through the pain. "Do you understand what I'm saying? There is a network of people out there, and they are sick. Terribly, terribly sick. They train little children to be like them. They t-torture them until they learn to dissociate, to split their personalities into two, or three, or however many. And they give them nasty little jobs to do. They train them to become activated by a tap on the shoulder, or a phrase. Then they go and do whatever it is that's asked of them."

"Jack is a *multiple personality*?" I could not keep the shock from my voice.

Leah's eyes shot open. "No! I caught it before that. No, he learned to split, but not into fragments. Haven't you noticed? He's a wonderful actor, our Jack." She was speaking now with a fury, her hands wringing each other like battling dogs.

"Leah," I said. "You must have been terrified."

Her eyes focused on me for the first time since we came into the hut. "Yes. I was."

"You ran."

"Yes."

"You got Jack away from him before his personality collapsed."

"Yes."

"You raised him well, Leah. He's a fine man. I love that fine man you raised, all by yourself, from an infant."

She lowered her gaze.

I said, "This man terrified you."

Her voice came as a wraith. "Oh, yes. The threats were . . . when I told him to leave us alone, it started in earnest. He'd follow me through the town, always watching me. People would say it was because he loved me, or because a man needed to be with his son. He could be very charming, you see, and people believed him. Didn't believe me. People want their world to make sense." She drew in a ragged breath. "They told me I should marry him and do right for the child. But I said no. He—"

"You went to the police."

"Oh, God yes, everybody always asks me that!"

"I'm sorry, I'm trying to understand—"

"The chief of police was his cousin. Do you get it? He was probably another . . . I told him to go away or I would. He told me he'd get the government to take Jack away from me."

"You mean the courts."

"I mean the *government*. That's who he worked for, don't you see?

"No, wait—"

"Our precious United States government! They—"

"No, wait, this is insane! I've heard of ritual abuse, but it's Satan worshipers, crazy religious cults that—"

"Some of them are in cults, but not all. But the government is right in there harvesting a crop of smashed-up personalities to put to their dirty little purposes! Jack's father was a p-professional k-k-killer."

"No! He made that up to scare you, he—"

"How I wish that were true! He took us in the car one night and *showed* us!"

"So you ran away."

"We left town and I changed our names, and we moved all over the place, looking for a town where we could live. Finally, we came here. Worked in Everglade City for a while. It has a long tradition of being a way station for people who have escaped from somewhere else. I got to know Winifred when her granddaughter . . . ran away once, and I helped. So we settled here in Florida. Moved to Orlando when Jack was twelve."

"Sampler's not your name?"

"No. It's my grandmother's maiden name. When Jack came of age, I figured he had a right to his birth name, but he'd learned to answer to Jack, so . . ."

"You never married."

She shook her head. "I didn't trust myself."

"And you always worried that the man might come back, so you kept a bag packed, ready to leave at any moment."

"I heard finally that he had died—or been killed—but I had no way of knowing how deep it all went. Maybe they'd come for Jack at some time. I had to be on the ready. I learned how to drive so I wouldn't be followed. And no one comes to this hammock without Winifred's knowledge, or the whole tribe's, for that matter."

My stomach was tight as a fist. "You did a great job with Jack. He's an honorable, faithful man. . . ." Words began to evaporate in my mouth. Did I truly know this about Jack? I had trusted him originally because Tom Latimer trusted him, and until ten days ago, Jack had never wavered from Tom's model of trustworthiness, so I had assumed . . . what?

As I sat there, hearing this horrible tale, bits of my world began to get up and float, like dust on the air. If there were people out there who would put small children into damp holes in the ground to force them into mental illness, then were any of us truly safe?

I thought again of the terrible instrument of destruction I had found buried in the sand a scant twenty-four hours before, and wondered: *Did Jack go off to track that monster, or is he the monster himself? What frail membrane lies between the two?*

Leah was speaking rapidly. "I took him to specialists, had him cared for as best I could. There was no one then who knew what to do. Nowadays at least I could take him to some kind of deprogrammer, or a specialist in posttraumatic stress. They're getting better every day at dealing with these things. They know now that the nervous system holds a charge from trauma, a deep nervous energy that gets locked into our very fibers. It's there in case we get a chance to run away. Lower animals know how to switch it off when the danger's passed, but we have the cerebral cortex—the highest part of the human brain—and it can override that protocol. So the trauma hangs in us like a bomb. That's the stress, all locked in there, banging around. . . . Jack did amazingly well. I think it was because he always took a part in helping us escape. They say that's essential, that the victim take part in saving himself."

I couldn't believe what she was saying—didn't want to—and yet the connections were finally forming. Jack, the child of trauma, had been raised by a desperate, stoic, *intelligent* woman. She had moved heaven and earth to get him safe and keep him there. . . .

Leah's words had run to a halt. She made both of her hands into fists for a moment, squeezed them, and then released them, flicking the fingers as if they held drops of water. "So now you know."

"There's more. Isn't there?"

"What has Jack told you, Em?"

"He left a note saying I should come here if things didn't go well for him."

Very forcibly, she said. "We don't know yet what's happened, or will happen. Jack will be alright."

I said, "This must be torture for you. I love him, and I've known him only half a year. He's your child. You've worked so hard to raise him to be a whole man, and here he's gone and done something terribly dangerous."

"He's always done dangerous things."

I thought about that. The swamps he walked through with Brad. The Navy SEALs. Working for the FBI. "He seems okay with working for the government," I said stupidly.

Leah's laugh was derisive. "Some say he's looking for a father, and a family. He had some good officers above him in the Navy. And Tom's been good to him. Not all men are shits. He has a strong will to protect people, to do the honorable thing. I suppose he's still compensating for what happened to him."

"What do you do for a living, Leah?"

"I'm a psychiatric nurse," she said, her voice heavy with irony.

As much to myself as to her I said, "I think Jack has a good spirit. I think he would have led an adventuresome life regardless of what happened to him when he was three years old." Having spoken the words, I grabbed hold of them for dear life.

Leah focused on me, her lips twisted in abstract amusement. "I can see why he loves you," she said.

– 28 –

Leah took Faye and me back to the chickee we had rented
at the Swamp Safari, and we slept there that night, deeply
exhausted and oblivious to the whining of mosquitoes outside the netting that draped over our cots. In the morning,
the overhanging thatch and shuttered sides of the chickee
kept us unaware of the daylight until Faye's bladder moved
her toward the bathroom. When she opened the door, we
awakened to a world of sunshine so bright and cheerful that
I was certain we had dreamt the entire experience of the
deep swamp, the elderly Seminole woman, and the unexpected and gut-wrenching meeting with Leah Sampler.
Surely her part of it had been exactly that, a bad dream.

It was barely ten in the morning but already sweltering
hot, at least eighty-five degrees and ninety-nine percent humidity, even inside the deep shade of the chickee with the
shutters open to catch the nonexistent breeze. Faye returned
and handed me a bottle of water and an orange. "Eat,
drink," she said. "I want to go for a walk."

I combed my hair and pulled it back into a ponytail to
get it off the furnace of my neck. My hair had curled wildly
in the humidity, spinning into corkscrews at the cowlicks
along my hairline. I sat on the edge of my cot and peeled
the orange and ate it, wondering if this meant I was truly
in Florida. Because that was where oranges were grown,
right? My mind was a muddle. I could no longer recall how

many days it had been since we left Utah, or since Jack had left me sitting just like this, at the edge of a bed. I realized with sadness that I no longer felt the wave of sensuosity pull at me at the thought of him. I decided that, even with this fairly heavy night's sleep, I was still too tired, and certainly too disoriented, to feel much of anything.

I got dressed, and we went outside to greet the day and get a first good look at where in blazes we were.

It was a crush of green. Faye led me away from the Safari headquarters toward a path that led into the vegetation. As we walked along the row of chickees, I realized that they were all built on stilts right over shallow water. The water was dark with tannic acid. Everything around us was a passionate crowding of green in every imaginable tint and shape and texture.

We turned off the path onto a boardwalk that led over the water and into the deep, hushed shade of the swamp itself. Here, all was a dappled green as spots of light filtered down through the canopy of lush vegetation. Green grew on green as epiphytic plants—bromeliads and orchids—sprouted off trees, and ferns lavished their fronds to the humid air. Even the water was green, covered to every last inch with dots of tiny floating ferns. A heron picked through the shallows, making her way with measured, careful steps. Songbirds twittered. Frogs charrummed.

The world of the swamp was complete, entire, and compelling, our narrow path of wood a jealous glimpse of its depth and power.

"There," whispered Faye. She was pointing at what looked at first to me like a stretch of tire tread cast off a tractor-trailer rig, except that it was floating in the water and dotted with clusters of fern plucked up from the water's surface. I slowly realized that the tread had eyes, and, a foot or more closer to me, a pair of nostrils. It blinked, its dark reptilian eyelids clapping side-to-side instead of toward me. "Alligator," she sighed. "Isn't she beautiful?"

Beautiful? I was not certain what word I would have

chosen to describe this dark, reptilian presence, but she did possess the splendor of being integral to her surroundings, floating there serene and unhurried; here, I was the ugly intruder. It was my kind who had brought the wallowing swamp buggies and the roaring fan boats and the lust to drain her homeland to a pathetic, dying vestige of itself.

She and I observed each other for long minutes. She was there for the duration; I, for just a blink in time, a sojourner passing through. With respect, I turned and left her to her domain.

Breaking back into the bright light at the end of the boardwalk, I felt suddenly exposed, my soft hide prey to the harshness of the sun. We walked along the gravel path back toward the cluster of chickees around the café.

As we approached this outpost of human civilization, our buggy driver from the evening before converged from another path. He was carrying a gunny sack with something heavy in it. "Morning, ladies, you sleep okay with all those ghosts?" He pulled out a key and unlocked the door to the nearest hut, which was about three times the size of our chickee.

"I slept like a log," I said. "Those deep croaking sounds were like a lullaby."

Gator grinned. "Alligators," he said. "They're so sweet and cuddly."

"Pays to advertise," Faye commented.

"*Verdad*. Would you like to see our little museum?"

I said, "What do you have to show us?"

"Something very special," he said. "Come on in and meet my friends."

Inside, the air was cold, almost like stepping into a walk-in refrigerator. Gator flicked on an overhead light and a second switch that turned on an array of lights in glass-fronted terrariums, and suddenly I was in the presence of an array of snakes and lizards, each coiled or reclining in its own private world. CORN SNAKE, read the sign over a spectacular orange serpent. INDIGO SNAKE, read the one over a creature scaled in a deep, glossy blue. Their beauty was beginning to grow on me.

Gator stepped past a small set of bleacher seats and over a low barrier. Opening another set of locks, he reached down into a wooden cage and set down his burlap sack. He closed that cage and opened another. "Come over here, Em," he said. "Sit down. Close your eyes and hold out your hands."

With misgivings, I did as he asked. The small hairs began to stand up on the back of my neck. Then something very cool and dry touched my skin. It was an odd texture, leathery yet soft. It was heavy and rounded. It felt . . . nice.

I opened my eyes. I was holding a small black alligator, less than three feet long. A very torpid one, thanks to a low body temperature produced by the extreme air-conditioning. She was barely moving her claws, as if slowly swimming in her sleep.

"Thank you," I whispered, more to the alligator than to the man.

From the reptile display, Faye and I moved on to the café and ordered a big, midday breakfast of eggs and bacon and grits and toast. I put ice in my coffee and swilled it down, still trying to convince myself that I was awake and not dreaming. We ate out on the deck on the far side of the café, watching the airboat drivers load up stacks of tourists from Miami and whang them around the near parts of the swamp. Scrub jays took off and landed on the wire fence that enclosed the exotic deer. I thought about Jack, and his mother.

By my second cup of coffee, it occurred to me that I had left Winifred Egret's camp without meeting the special person Jack had wanted me to meet. Leah had never answered my first questions. How had she managed that? I pondered the delicacy of her evasions, realizing that in the process of telling me the frightening tale of Jack's father, all other questions had dropped from my consciousness.

Had she played this trump card to steer me around an even darker secret?

I looked out across the tapestry of vegetation and water, letting the hypnosis of its deep, feminine wiles slow my thoughts and motions even further. There seemed to be a halo of light over the Everglades, an insubstantial yet powerful energy, like connective waves of heat. The scene was lush and ecstatic and yet wounded, a woman in pain, just like Leah. Like Faye. Like me. Florida was a land of sex, but its sexuality was vulnerable, a target of rape in the eyes of all who wished to dominate it.

Jack had come to manhood here. In the passion of its fecundity, he had learned to love and honor all things feminine. At last, I began to understand the man I had come to love.

As I was munching down on my last strip of bacon, Gator hove into view with a cup of coffee of his own.

Faye said, "Have a seat, Gator-man."

"Thank you," he said. Settling in to my right, he went after the sugar packets, draining about three into his java and giving it a good stir.

Glenda wandered over and sat down across from me with coffee and a bowl of grits, humming cheerfully. "You have a nice visit with your people last night?" she inquired.

Faye said, "Yes, thank you. You and what's-his-name enjoy yourselves?"

Glenda laughed amiably. "Emilio? Oh yeah, once we got away from them spiders. I hate spiders. Yeah, Emilio's fun, but we's just pals. Y'know. You work out here, y'all get to know each other."

Faye said, "You know Winifred Egret then?" She didn't even try to make the question sound casual. She tapped her fingers on the table restlessly. She hadn't said much since waking up, and seemed even more irascible and out of sorts than even a summer pregnancy, a night in the swamps, and a renegade husband might explain.

Glenda said, "Well, not like we's family or nothin', but yeah, you get to sort of know what's going on."

I said, "So who lives out there with her?"

Gator said, "Miz Egret?"

"Yeah. She's not all alone out there, is she?"

Glenda replied, "Oh, no. There's always someone looks after her. She can't but hardly see, y'know, so's they can't leave her all alone, though if anyone could handle it, it would be her. She's got her great-granddaughter Lily there most of the time, although she needs lookin' after, too, but then there's others in the family as comes by."

Faye said, "Oh, so she's got a great-granddaughter there. How old is she?"

"Well into her teens. Older maybe, but you wouldn't know it. She's funny in the brain."

"How sad. What happened? Was she injured?"

"No, born that way. They say her brain didn't form right. She can't think as good as other folks."

Gator said, "The way I hear it, the frontal lobes of her brain never formed. The part we use for reason." He pointed at his own forehead. "They say the reptiles have a primitive brain that reacts to situations mechanically, the mammals have a second one stacked on top of it that gives it emotions, and we humans have also an upper brain, which gives us the capacity to reason. But sometimes we reason our way right into trouble. Evolution. You tell me who's smartest."

Faye glanced at her belly like she was sorry she'd asked.

Oblivious to Faye's sudden discomfort, Glenda continued. " 'Course the tribe's got a place for Lily, and what with the money each member gets from the gambling, she's looked after. And her dad sends money just in case. They give her little jobs to do so she don't feel left out."

With that comment, Faye looked like she was about to burst into tears, so I changed the subject, hoping to get some answers into the bargain for the questions Leah had steered me around asking. Such as, why did Leah come here? And whom did Jack want me to meet? I said, "You guys know if a man named Jack Sampler ever visits out there? Big guy, kind of burly, and blond?"

"Oh, sure, Jack. Yeah, he comes down here all the time." Glenda looked at me kind of funny. "He's the one that sent you down here, right?"

"Right."

She tipped her head at me, puzzling with something. "Then don't you know?" she asked.

"Know what?"

"He's Lily's father."

A bomb detonated deep in my heart. Shreds of reality flew every which way. I opened my mouth, tried to repeat the words, test them, see if they might come down out of the sky where they seemed to be floating, like so much dust on the wind. "He's—"

Faye's cell phone rang. She dug the thing out of her pocket, switched it on, talked to it, listened to it. Said, "No! Damn it, speak to *me*! Where are you? Are you alright?" Tears began to spring from her eyes. She handed the phone to me.

I put it to my ear. Heard Tom's voice. It crackled with the weak connection. It seemed to belong in the clouds, with the dust and the disclosure that my lover had a child. Tom said, "Em? You get anything out of Miles Guffey?"

At first the words made no sense to me. My ears rang like hollow pipes. All sounds around me were far away.

"Em?"

I took a deep breath. "Why didn't he tell me, Tom?"

"Who? Tell you what?"

"Jack. Tell me about Lily."

Tom went into one of his silences. Then he said, "It's a painful topic, Em. Especially now. Where are you?"

"In the Everglades. At the Big Cypress Reservation."

"Leah's there?"

"She was last night."

"I'm surprised they let you through. Leah will have tightened security by now."

"Security? What is this need of security, Tom?"

Tom availed himself of a deep breath. "Lily is a secondary target. We still don't know where the stalker is."

"So the primary target is Lucy. Jack's old girlfriend. Ms. Egret's granddaughter. The astronaut is a Seminole."

"One-quarter. Leah told you?"

"No. She didn't have to. I'm a goddamned detective, remember?"

"Em, Jack is a good man. He looks after his friends. But you can be damned certain that Lily is the reason he's got his ass on the line right now. I'm sorry, Em, but we have to change the subject before my cell battery runs out. Miles Guffey, Em. Did you get anything out of him?"

Answering Tom's question suddenly seemed like a life raft, a job to do, something to hang onto. "I think he's on his way to the Bahamas," I said.

"What?"

"I went to his house yesterday afternoon, and he was packing the boat for a long trip—at least six bags of junkfood's worth—and he tried to tell me it was a pleasure cruise. Total bullshit. He had the charts for the Bahamas all over his chart desk. The chart for the Berry Islands was on the top of the stack."

"Do you know which island?"

"No."

"Damn. Can you get it out of him? I don't care what you use—pliers, crowbar—just get a location out of him, will you?"

"I would if I could, but as I said, Faye and I are in the Everglades. Why, do you think there's a connection between his trip and yours?"

"I don't know. But when I show a man evidence, and he suddenly gets an idea to leave town, I have to wonder. What's his phone number?"

"I imagine he left already. He might have a cell phone on board. And there were all sorts of marine radios."

"What's the name of his boat?"

"The *Sea Dingo*. It's a big cabin cruiser, maybe forty feet."

"When'd he leave St. Petersburg?"

"I don't know. Yesterday, I'd guess. Six P.M. earliest. Maybe he waited until daylight to start."

Tom said, "Well, goddamn it, figure it out!"

"How?"

"Use your head. I'll be monitoring this phone." His voice trailed off like he was about to hang up.

"Wait! Any word on Jack? Where are you guys?"

Tom said nothing for a moment, but the connection stayed open. I could hear noise in the background. Heavy engine sounds. I could also hear the gears in Tom's brain grinding as he tried to decide what he was going to tell me. All he said was, "You stay with Faye."

I said, "I have to know how to reach you if you go out of cell coverage."

He said, "We're forming up on a boat. Jack took one from here. He's turned off his cell phone, and we haven't been able to raise the boat on the radio. We have to assume he's maintaining silence."

"Where are you? What's the name of the town?"

Tom paused a moment, then, "Ask Faye her grand-mother's maiden name. And her favorite mammal since she got knocked up—that's the marina. If you can figure out how to get hold of Miles Guffey, get it out of him where he's going and call me immediately. If there's anything he can tell us, it can save precious time. We could be out here for weeks trying to figure out what island, and if it's not in that chain, it's even worse. Otherwise our only hope is to get hold of someone who's seen Jack's boat, and we have to do that without tipping anyone off that there's anything unusual about the fact that he's out there in it."

"I understand."

"I'm getting off now," he said. The line went blank.

"Where is he?" Faye asked.

"White boy speak in code. He says to ask your grand-mother's maiden name and your favorite mammal."

Faye grabbed the phone and put it to her ear. Swore when she realized that Tom had hung up. "White boy in major shit! I—I have two grandmothers. Okay, one is Stewart and the other's Schiller. The manatee."

I retrieved the telephone from Faye and dialed information for Miles Guffey's wife, Pamela. When I reached her, I asked if she could tell me how to reach her husband. "I just tried to call him on the cell," she said. "He's got the damned thing switched off. But he told me not to expect to hear from him for at least a week." I took down the number and tried it myself. No luck.

I turned to Glenda and Gator. "Has anyone else come looking for Lily lately?"

Glenda said, "Yeah, about three weeks ago. Big guy, blond. Looked kind of like Jack, come to think of it."

"You tell him where she was?"

"Oh, hell no. We all told him she'd been sent away."

"Good."

I stared up into the sky for a while. It was well past noon. *Endeavor* was due to launch at dawn two mornings following. So forty hours, give or take. That surely was not time enough to search 700 islands and 2,400 cays. I thought about Lucy, a woman geologist whom I had never met, who would soon climb aboard a rocket, and I thought about Lily, her afflicted daughter. And I thought about Jack, who had made a promise to protect them. "Give me the keys to the car," I said.

I went out and got the Florida map atlas Nancy kept in it, brought it back to the table, and turned to the index map on the back cover. "Gator," I said, "you do any boating?"

"*Soy Cubano,*" he snickered. "Don't we all get here on boats?"

"If you were going by boat from St. Petersburg to the Bahamas, how would you go?" I traced my finger down the Gulf coast to the southern end of the peninsula. There I ran into a sting of islands, the Florida Keys, which swept westward like a bent tail. "Would you go down around the islands here, or would you cut in closer to land?" *As in, somewhere where you'll stop at a dock for lunch, and a certain cowgirl from Wyoming can chase you down,* I was thinking.

"I'd go through here," he said, tracing his short index finger west to east about forty miles north of where we were. "The Okeechobee waterway. It's a system of canals. You go in here at Fort Myers. See? There's a river here, the Caloosahatchee. It's been dredged so you can get boats through it, otherwise it would be too shallow in places. The Caloosahatchee comes out of Lake Okeechobee." Here he stabbed his index finger at a big, round lake, the largest in a string of lakes that ran down the axis of the state. "The dredged waterway goes up the Caloosahatchee and into the lake here at Moore Haven, follows a channel just inside the flood-control levee for oh, ten or fifteen miles to Clewiston, then you go through the middle of the lake and come out the other side into the St. Lucie canal. That puts you out in Stuart." He traced his finger along the blue line for the canal and out to the Atlantic Ocean.

"Where did you say?"

"Stuart."

I looked at Faye.

She looked at me.

"Yo' gramma," I said. I peered at the map. There it was, as big as life. "They got a Manatee Marina there?"

"Sure," said Gator. "My brother, he kept a boat there for a while. They stack 'em up there like they're in mailboxes."

I couldn't quite envision that, but my mind was running the trip backward, rewinding, trying to figure out where along all those miles of waterway Miles Guffey and the *Sea Dingo* would be by now. "How fast does a boat travel?" I asked.

"What do you mean?"

"Well, if some friends of mine took off from St. Petersburg yesterday afternoon, say, and were coming through the canal, where would they be by now?"

Gator looked at me like I was making a funny joke with him. "Ah, depends on the boat," he said.

I closed my eyes and thought, *Well, duh*. "Okay, a big, squarely built cabin cruiser. Say, forty feet long. Really wide."

"Well, that still covers some area. But if you mean not at all modern or streamlined, like a trawler," he said.

"A trawler! That was it."

"Then usually about eight knots."

"Knots. What's that in miles per hour?"

"Add ten percent. But you may as well subtract it again, because there are tides and currents, and going through the waterway you have to stop a lot to wait for the bridges to open."

Ah! Bridges! Places where boats stop!

I turned to Faye. "Tom told me to find Miles's boat and get some information from him. Something he needs for what he's doing."

Faye's eyes turned dark with anger. "I will not aid or abet this any further," she said tersely.

"But he can't find Jack unless—"

Faye lurched up from the table and gave me a look that could have peeled paint. She said, "If you want to play cops and robbers with the little boys, Em, go the fuck ahead. I am going back to my little grass hut and gestate a baby!" She stormed away and slammed the door behind her.

I stared at the map.

I felt Gator's eyes on me. He was studying me, his scarred arms laid out on the table in front of him so he could lean on them. "This has to do with my man Jack Sampler?"

I wasn't sure what to say. But it was beginning to occur to me that this man Gator was smarter than I had first bothered to presume.

He tipped his head and looked at me kindly, as if to say, *It's okay*. His great, dark eyes were soft, searching. He said, "Jack is a man I owe. Enough said?"

There wasn't much to say, except yes or no. It seemed that lots of people owed Jack. He had grown up watching his mother suffer. Had it made a martyr of him, or a maniac?

Gator patted my hand. "You need to find that boat? I got a couple reptile shows to do this afternoon then one swamp tour, but I'm off duty after that. The Caloosahatchee's not far. I can get you there."

I trained my eyes on the index map. I picked up a paper napkin and held it to the bar scale. Jabbed my thumbnail into the folded edge of the soft paper to mark the beginning and end of a map inch. Thirty-five miles. Shifted the napkin along the bar to add a second thirty-five, and a third. Having thus marked off one hundred and five miles, I slid the napkin over to the shoreline of the Gulf of Mexico where it swept south from Tampa Bay to the mouth of the Caloosahatchee. "About a hundred miles," I said. "Divide by eight. Twelve hours?"

"It's easier than that. Let me show you." Gator tapped his finger on a spot on the map index about twenty miles upriver. "Map 105," he said. He opened the atlas to that page. "How tall's your friend's boat? Like, twenty feet?"

"I'd say. The cabin is all above the waterline, and there's a deck above that with a big canopy over it and radar and antennas and all like that."

"A flying bridge. Call it twenty-five feet with the radar and radio masts folded down. These first bridges are high." He pointed at five places where highways crossed the mouth of the river at Fort Myers and Cape Coral. "Any boat small enough to navigate the channel can go under them. But here,"—he indicated the point where a highway marked "31" crossed the river—"See? The river narrows here. The spans are shorter, lower. This is Wilson Pigott Bridge. First low clearance. I think that one's a lift bridge."

"So what are you saying? He'd have to slow down there while they open the bridge?"

He smiled. "No, he'd have to stop. They don't open the bridges after nine in the evening, and they stay closed until six A.M. So it doesn't matter how fast he was going, even at twenty knots he wouldn't make it this far before nine last evening. Most guys with a brain tuck in behind a barrier island at dusk and wait until daybreak. Some of the waters back there are only a couple feet deep. See these channels? You got to run through one of these mouths between the islands, and at certain tides it's a rip. The channels are marked, but not all that good. I've been through there with my brother in full daylight, hanging on the depth sounder, and we still lost it and run aground on a dredging pile. The channels are narrow, and it's too easy to miss a marker." He traced the route Guffey's boat would have to navigate inside the barrier islands, a spattering of obstacles large and small. "And not only is it real shallow in here if you get outside where it's dredged, but there are other boats anchored here and there, swinging on their anchor lines, and just 'cause they're out there don't mean they know what they're doing. Some fools pay out a lot of scope, run aground when the tide turns. You go through there on slack tide in the dark, you don't even know which way they're lying, and you can get tangled in an instant. I wouldn't risk my boat like that if I had one."

"Guffey's real proud of his boat."

"Like I say." He tapped his finger back on Wilson Pigott Bridge. "But even if he did keep running in the dark, he couldn't get past this point until this morning at six."

I took hold of his wrist and turned it to read his watch. It was almost noon. "So he could have been running six hours by now. Where would he be?"

"My guess is he's still out on the Gulf. If he got off last night like you say, he would have run down the coast until he ran out of daylight, or got tired, and then gunk-holed in behind a barrier island for the night. But I'll go you one better. Come on." He led me out of the café, down several paths, and into an office, where we found Bill sitting behind a desk reading a magazine. Gator got out a phone book and looked something up in the government pages, then dialed the phone. "*Oye*, Gus? Hey, my man, this is Eduardo Batista, your man from Miami. *¡Recuerdas!* Hey, yeah, long time. *¿Como su esposa? ¿Sus hijos? Oye,* I'm calling with

a favor to ask. Who me? Yeah. Yeah. I'm trying to track
a boat for a friend here. Yeah, it's her husband, she hasn't
heard from him. Kind of worried. She wants to know if
he's gone through the first lock there. Okay." He turned to
me. "What's the name of the boat?"

"Sea Dingo," I said.

"Trawler *Sea Dingo.* Eastbound. Yeah. You sure? Okay.
Good man. I thank you." He hung up the phone. To me,
he said, "That was my friend Gus at Wilson Pigott." He
grinned. "That's why I know the name of the bridge. He
said *Sea Dingo* hasn't gotten there yet, but he knows where
he is. Heard him cussing someone out on the marine radio
about half an hour ago, they all been having a good
chuckle."

"What's going on?"

"Something about a Sea Ray kicking up a wake. They're
these go-fast boats; people who drive them got no manners,
all a bunch of new money. Some woman's on *Sea Dingo*'s
radio down by Cape Coral telling them to go home and
stuff their BMW's up their butts."

"Sounds like Waltrine." For the first time in two days I
found myself truly smiling. "Maybe Guffey's letting her
drive while he catches some Z's."

"Yeah, he'd be tired. That means he ran most of the
night, came all the way down in open water, then turned
in maybe south of Sanibel Island here, where there's a
lighthouse and all like that. But anyway, he's a couple
hours downriver of the Franklin Lock, which is the first
place you'd be able to catch him."

"He's got to go through locks?"

Gator grinned at my naïveté. "Yeah. The lake is higher
than the ocean, so the boat traffic has to go up through
three locks to get there. Slows him way down, especially
if there's traffic." He opened the atlas again and tapped
each lock and each place a highway crossed the river. "Lift
bridge. Swing. At LaBelle here, another lift bridge, then
here's the Ortona Locks. From there, you can see the river
runs real straight; it's been channelized. Leads you right

through to Moore Haven. One last swing bridge—the railroad, those are really low, maybe five feet—and then one more lock to get you into the lake."

"And all of them close again this evening at nine?"

"That's the story. He's down there by Cape Coral now, ain't no way he's going to make Okeechobee in time to get all the way through by nine, and he won't want to be out there in the dark, either." Now he grinned at me, very satisfied with his analysis.

I smiled and nodded to him. "So he'll have to tie up somewhere for the night."

"Yeah. That's your best bet. The lock tenders are Army Corps of Engineers. They don't let anyone get on or off while they're going through there."

"I'd like to get to him as soon as possible."

Gator looked at his watch. "I'll be off at seven. See you then. Until then, I think your friend needs you." He gave me a tender smile.

Faye was in the chickee, lying facedown on the cot, which is hard to do when you're that pregnant. She had swiped my pillow and placed it to one side of her belly to support it.

"Any way I can talk you into touring the canals of the Caloosahatchee?" I asked.

"No."

"You'd think you were aiding and abetting."

"Mind reader." Her voice was thick. She'd been crying again.

"The way I see it, he's already committed, so he needs help, not . . ." I trailed off, uncertain which was correct, action or inaction.

Faye said nothing. She kept her back to me.

I said, "Listen, maybe this is a bunch of boys playing white knight, but *somebody's* got to do it."

"Why Tom?"

"So his child can grow up safe?"

"Being born is not safe. Living is not safe."

I sat down on the edge of her cot and began to massage her back. "I'm so sorry, Faye."

The tears began to flow again. "I had so hoped he and I could make it work."

"It's not over."

She put her hand on the great roundness of her belly.

I asked, "Is he kicking?"

"She."

"You know it's a girl?"

"It had better be. No fucking war games."

I sighed. "Girls can join the army now, and the FBI. . . ."

Faye cried a long time, softly keening, rocking herself and her unborn child. I smoothed her clothes, stroked her sweaty back through the cloth. At length, she said hoarsely, "When you see Tom, send him home."

I put a hand on her shoulder and squeezed. "I will," I whispered.

– 29 –

"The surface of Lake Okeechobee isn't much higher than the ocean," Gator informed me, as we bounded along in his little Toyota sedan over a rough two-lane blacktop. The road ran straight as a die between cane fields that stretched as far as I could see in either direction. We were traveling north of the Big Cypress Reservation, heading for the Caloosahatchee River. It was early evening, and the thunderheads had built up high and wide and fuzzy, ready to pelt us as soon as we were foolish enough to drive under one of them. And yet I felt an urgency to get after them, as if they could draw me closer to Miles Guffey's boat, and his boat could bring me to Jack.

Eduardo "Gator" Batista continued his educational travelogue. "Right now Okeechobee's surface is maybe twelve feet above sea level. There's a levee built around it, because one time it flooded and killed about 3,000 people. You know, the Everglades are all water, really, just a little land in there to confuse the folks up north with more money than sense, make them think this is farmland, or a good place to build a retirement house. When you add a whole lot more water all at once—in a hurricane say—well, there's nowhere to go to get away from it."

"So that's why they built the canals? To drain the swamp? Aren't there bad jokes about that?"

"Yeah. They came and built all these canals and drainage ditches. It drained, alright, and the first thing that happened was all that peat began to catch fire with the lightning." He shook his head. "Some people think nature's something they've got to tame, like a wild animal. Me, I like my animals wild."

I ran my gaze over the scars on his arms. "Especially your alligators."

Gator opened his mouth to show me his teeth and made a claw with one hand.

"Yeah."

"How . . . exactly did you get those bites?" I asked.

He grinned. "Oh those? I used to work at an alligator farm. Took me a while to learn how to handle them."

"Farm? They really do farm alligators?"

"Yeah. All you eat is the tail, that's where the meat is. They make key chains out of the claws." He shook his head. Laughed. "Tourists."

I shook my head, too. Florida seemed one big clash of man and nature, or man's nature versus nature's compulsion to exist, with all the certainty of water running downhill and taxes being due on April 15. "So do you think I can catch him at the Ortona Lock?"

"He's past there by now. I've had my friends tracking him all afternoon." He gave me his grin. "Not much to do here in the Everglades, so they're only too glad to assist. *Sea Dingo* called for the lift bridge at La Belle *como cinco y medio*. Five-thirty. He's averaging less than seven knots. Don't worry, he won't get to Moore Haven before the bridge-and-lock there closes for the night."

Gator slowed to avoid skidding off the road during a series of sharp right angles. We caught up with a rainstorm. Everything went wet as the little windshield wipers struggled with a sheet of liquid. I held on for dear life.

The streets were shining with water when we reached Moore Haven. Gator drove straight to the town docks. An osprey settled onto a phone pole a hundred yards away and glared at me. No sign of *Sea Dingo*. "Not here yet," he announced. "What I tell you?"

"You're sure he hasn't gone on through to the lake?"

Gator shrugged. Put the car in reverse, executed a smuggler's turn, and headed over toward the swing bridge that carried the railroad across the canal. Clearance was only about five feet. No way *Sea Dingo* was going to crawl under that. The bridge manager was in his pilot box, so Gator got out and talked to him. The man shook his head and climbed out, headed down the road on foot. Gator returned to the car. "He says she's not come through yet. He's got a couple trains coming, so he's done for the night, not going to open it again until the morning." He looked at his watch. "*Ocho y media.* You got it made. Let's go get some dinner." His smile positively twinkled.

"Okay."

"*¡Splendido!*"

Gator took me to a little café with searing blue paint. Inside, my nostrils were greeted by the savory aroma of Caribbean cookery. "Let me guess," I said. "Black beans and yellow rice."

Gator gave me an appreciative nod. "Wait 'til you taste her *plátanos.*"

Dinner was just the sort of wonderful meal you can find only in a wayside café where the cook looks like somebody's mama. She fussed over Gator—called him 'Uardo— and was reasonably solicitous over me, even though she was clearly trying to promote Gator's obvious interest in a shy young lass with doe eyes and skin as rosy as a ripe plum who watched him expectantly from behind the counter.

When we were done, and barely able to move for the largess of Mama's cooking, we paid our bill—or should I say Gator paid; he would not hear of my even contributing to the tip, so gallant was he as he shamelessly ogled the daughter—and headed back to the dock. Sure enough, there was *Sea Dingo*, all tied up and shipshape, the only boat in sight. It was past ten o'clock. The osprey had gone to bed, and had been replaced by a nighthawk. The scene was illuminated by streetlights. Things looked very, very quiet.

I walked along the dock until I was next to the place where the rail was folded back to make it easy to get aboard. I called out, "Permission to come aboard, skipper?"

I got no answer. No light came on in the cabin. No one stirred. The only sound was the steady hum of an air-conditioning unit somewhere deep in the boat.

A small pickup truck drove by in the street, spraying something from a fogger mounted in its bed. That explained the lack of mosquitoes.

I turned and looked at Gator. He shrugged eloquently.

I stepped aboard. Walked around to the back door of the main cabin and knocked. "Miles?" I called out. "Waltrine?"

No answer.

Gator still waited on the dock. "Gone to dinner, you think?"

"Must be."

"We could come back later."

"No. Knowing Miles, they probably found a bar. But they could come back any time, and I don't want to chance losing them. I need to wait." I looked at him with apology in my eyes. "Are you in a hurry to get back?"

Gator stepped aboard. The boat shifted ever so slightly with his weight. "You can't just sit out here." He checked every door and window large enough to let me through. All locked up tight. "How many people you say were on this boat?"

"Two."

"*Oye,* this thing'll sleep six easy. Plenty of room for you."

"Sleep?" It hadn't occurred to me that I might be staying the night.

"Let's try this," he said, and headed up the ladder to the flying bridge.

I peered up after him. Heard rustling, a satisfied, *"Bueno."* He reappeared at the top of the ladder and waved me up.

I clambered up the ladder moving gingerly past an array of fishhooks and rods that were mounted behind it. On the upper deck, I saw what he had gone looking for: a rubber skiff lashed to the roof. It had its own outboard motor, all neatly tucked up, the whole works covered with a tarp.

"Little Zodiac," he said. "You can get in under the cover here like a good stowaway. Us Cubans know how to do this, eh? I tuck you right in. I'm going back to Mama's and get some dessert, know what I mean? You go ahead and stay here, and I'll come get you in the morning, okay?"

"But what if I fall asleep?"

"Then you can talk to him in the morning. The engines will wake you up. He'll run them for a while before he gets going, you'll have time."

There was merit in Gator's plan. Miles might arrive back half plastered. That in turn might be good or bad; it could loosen him up, or it might make him craftier, if his performance at dinner with Tom was any indication. Waltrine I did not want to see drunk under any circumstances.

I had not reckoned on finding the boat but not its crew. My plan had been to have a brief talk with Miles, extort the needed information from him, phone it to Tom, and go back to Faye.

Faye. When you see Tom, send him home, she had told me. She had seen it before I had: I would see Tom, because I was staying with the boat. "You get a message to Faye tonight?" I asked. "I don't want her worrying about me, too."

"Of course. You got a passport?"

"No. Why?"

"Boats going through to Stuart are usually going to the Bahamas. If you go there you'd better stay out of sight of customs."

"Oh." *In for a penny, in for a pound*, I decided, and climbed underneath the tarp.

The engines rumbled me awake while it was still half dark out. I clambered out of the Zodiac, discovering to my dismay that my legs were staying asleep longer than the rest of my body. I had slept folded up in such a cramped position to fit in between the seat and the front roll that I was amazed to find that I had slept heavily enough to miss the return of the skipper and his first mate. Now I could hear them talking. I looked to where the voices were coming from, and spotted open portholes between the flying bridge and the pilothouse below.

"Yeah, he just called," Miles was saying.

"Where is he now?" Waltrine asked in response.

"He made it to Freeport. We'll be in Stuart by five, with any luck. Get fuel, that's six, be across to Memory Rock before daybreak tomorrow. Be at West End early afternoon. He'll be at the Old Bahama Bay. Pick him up after we clear customs, and we'll be at our destination by tomorrow midnight or, at worst, the next morning."

"He have any trouble?"

"Well, course he did. You ever try traveling with nothing but a tail tux that's spent a night in salt water? No passport? No money? People aren't so quick to help ya."

"What are you talking no money? I wired him a couple thousand," Waltrine said.

So Calvin Wheat's alive. I leaned closer to the porthole.

Miles said, "Cast off, will you? I want to be first in line for that swing bridge when she opens."

I heard a door open. I shrank back toward the Zodiac to stay out of sight. Crouched. My mind raced. *He's in Freeport, that's in the Bahamas. Why, why are Miles and Waltrine going to meet him without telling anyone? And why didn't they tell anyone that Calvin's alive? Are they still going for publicity?*

Against whom?

The guy who threw Calvin overboard, or . . .

No, it would be bigger than that. He was on a cruise ship, collecting dust samples. He was just short of proving not only Miles Guffey's theory, but also an accessory theory of his own: that someone is messing with anthrax out there. Someone who might sell it to the wrong people.

Then what's the connection between being thrown off the ship and the guy with the anthrax? Or was he in fact thrown off the ship? There's something that still does not make sense here.... My mind tumbled down the road of alternative interpretations, through various combinations and explanations of available data. What was the connection between Guffey's departure and the sand found inside the wrapping of the SAM-7? Was there a connection? Calvin Wheat was alive, which made sense, because Miles and Waltrine had gotten over seeming convincingly upset about his disappearance almost as soon as it occurred. Did that mean that he had not in fact gone overboard? Because if he had been thrown overboard, how had he survived? And how had Miles and Waltrine known of his survival so soon? In fact, how had they known of his disappearance? Had they invented the whole story to draw attention to the project? Were they now heading out to the Bahamas to quietly retrieve their missing man, or to stir up some other kind of trouble?

He came to Freeport with no money, and nothing to his name but a tail tux that had spent some time in sea water. That sounded like he had in fact become separated from a cruise ship the hard way. *Brad said that such falls were survivable, given extraordinary luck or special training....*

It struck me all at once. *They aren't going for publicity; they're going for revenge.*

The boat swung away from the dock, snapping my thoughts back to my present situation. I hunkered down, my head on a swivel, looking for Gator. I wasn't sure how he could help me, or even if I needed help. Everything was happening faster than it was supposed to, too fast for me to follow. I was on a boat with two people who were either doing something very wrong, or who were doing something very naïve, and I wasn't sure which was worse. I couldn't decide whether to jump off, climb back under the tarp and continue eavesdropping, or climb down the ladder and say, "Howdy do, where's the toilet?"

I glanced over the side and suddenly realized a certain

fact: I was on a boat, and boats meant water. My stomach lurched at the thought of jumping into it, of being immersed in it. Besides, it looked oddly dark, black as coffee, almost. Was it tannic acid or pollution?

I heard a car approaching the dock. Gator. I turned and saw him get out of the car. He stood stiffly alert, feet apart, his eyes wide with concern as he scanned the boat for my location. I caught his eye. I wanted to give him a gesture to indicate my situation and what I wanted him to do, but I wasn't sure what either of those was. I considered making a throat-cutting gesture to indicate that he shouldn't say anything, but he might take that wrong and think I was in trouble. Maybe I was. So I waved bye-bye instead, no doubt looking like the scared idiot I was.

It was quickly getting light out. I could see down through the porthole to a clock on the chart desk. It was five 'til six. *Sea Dingo* came to idle a few hundred feet from the railroad bridge. Still uncertain what to do, I lay down on my belly so that I could move up closer to the portholes without being seen. I waited. Five minutes crawled past. Ten. I told myself, *We'll be through the bridge in a few minutes, then into the lock. It looks like I can climb ashore there. Yes, that's what I should do.*

I heard Miles key the microphone on his radio, say, "Moore Haven Lock, this is the trawler *Sea Dingo*. We're waiting west of the railroad bridge. Will it be opening soon?"

"Thank you, *Sea Dingo*. I'm sure he'll be along in a moment."

The microphone clicked back into its holder. "Fuck," said Miles Guffey.

"What's keeping him?" said Waltrine.

"Fuck if I know. Whyn't you gimme some coffee, wouldja?"

Waltrine yawned. "Sure, boss; send the black girl for the coffee."

"Oh, go fuckerself, Waltrine," Miles said conversationally.

"I do regularly. Black or white?"

"The fucking?" he inquired.

"The coffee, asshole."

Now Miles yawned. "Man, we are testy this morning."

"You started it."

The day was only minutes old, and it was already going to hell. *Coffee,* I thought. *That would be nice. A bathroom would be even nicer.*

Give up, I told myself.

Easy for you to say. Here I am in the chase scene of my own damned stupid home movie, and it's moving at a snail's pace. Probably the worst danger I am in is dying of a burst bladder.

"Oh, good," Miles said. "You found the guava Danishes. You warm them up in the microwave?"

I wanted to growl, but my stomach got there ahead of me. *I am going to die a miserable, embarrassing death soaked in my own piss on the roof of a boat that belongs to a mad scientist who is eating guava Danishes that smell so good I um drooling,* I informed myself.

Waltrine said, "No, I didn't use no microwave, I just breathed fire on them. It's in my job description. And I am *gonna* be breathing fire if this sonnabitch don't get this show movin'! Fuckin' Cal gonna be an old man by the time we get there!"

Ah! That confirms it! They are off to pick up Calvin Wheat. So: Was the missing man routine a ruse, or did it really happen?

Miles clicked the mike again. "Moore Haven, this is *Sea Dingo*. Any update on that bridge opening?"

"*Sea Dingo,* sorry about that. He's got a train coming through in ten or fifteen minutes. He'll open after that."

I looked back toward the dock. Gator was still waiting by his car. He had produced a pair of binoculars, and was watching. They looked big and expensive. I wondered how a man who wrestled farm alligators, chauffeured swamp buggies for a living, and drove an old, beat-up Toyota could own such equipment. *And night-vision goggles,* I remembered. *They have to cost a grand or so. Did I miss something here?*

Suddenly, the ludicrousness of the entire situation moved me to action. *How bad can it be?* I decided. *This is just a couple of my scientific colleagues down there playing games. I'll go on down and present myself. If it's a bad deal, I'll ask to be put off at the lock, tell them there's a witness right back there on the dock, watching.*

But then another thought occurred to me: *What if they're armed? I don't want to surprise them. . . .*

But right then, Waltrine spotted me. "Holy shit!" she bellowed. "Miles! There's somebody on the upper deck!"

I whipped my head around. She had come up the ladder behind me. I about peed my pants. So much for the macho stowaway act.

Miles Guffey's eyes appeared close up to one of the portholes. "Well, well, well, if it ain't our little private eye come to join us," he said jovially. "Nice t'see ya. How d'ya take your coffee?"

30

Lucy opened her private notebook and prepared to write in it. She sat on the edge of her bed in the house NASA kept at the Cape for departing shuttle crews. The clock was ticking down. *Endeavor* was almost done with its crawl back out to launch pad B. Tomorrow they would begin the long process that would bring them to final readiness. At dawn on the following morning, they would lift up into the sky.

She sighed. If she did not hear from Jack by midnight, she knew what she must do. She must tell Mission Control of the threat.

But between that time and now was a whole day, and he might still call. . . .

As was her custom, she turned to the back of the notebook, a fine, leather-bound journal in which she wrote only a few sentences at the beginning of each day, and pulled out a photograph. The picture was eighteen years old, and soft from handling. She smiled pensively into the little face depicted there, a newborn infant staring out into the world. Tiny Lily, born in Switzerland during her first summer out of college, quick while nobody was watching. Her deepest secret, almost perfectly kept.

As always, her heart wobbled a moment, tumbling through the irresolvable uncertainty that this moment always touched. Could she have learned to care for her? Could a life as mother and wife have filled her? Was it sane or acceptable that she had given her to her great-grandmother's people to raise? Would she ever find the strength to visit her, now that her dream of space was almost realized?

And why, of all insane things to do, had she told *him* that Lily existed?

She ran the tip of one finger along the edge of the photograph. Sighed. Put it away. Began to write. *Dearest Lily, Daddy promised to keep you safe. Mommy is going to space very soon. She'll bring you home the brightest star. . . .*

Calvin Wheat stood on the dock in Freeport, just down from the Old Bahama Bay Hotel. This was the West End, the customs dock where Miles Guffey and Waltrine Sweet had agreed to meet him.

It was early morning but already stifling hot. No breeze. Perspiration beaded on his forehead and ran down his temples, leaving streaks in his spiky hair. The aches from the impact of falling three stories from the bow of that cruise ship intensified if he stood still too long, so he paced, now and again swinging his arms to fight the odd numbness that settled often in the small finger of his left hand. He must have jammed his neck pretty badly. He'd hit the water at modified attention, toes pointed, as he had been taught in the Navy, but he had hit hard. It had been too difficult to gage the descent. At least he was alive. Alive, and still walking. Hell, as long as he could move, he would take his revenge. Yes, by God, he would!

There was one single thing that he required in order to wreak that revenge, and he knew now exactly where to find it.

Twenty-four hours to launch. In half that time, he must slip out with the fast boat again, hurry west to Stuart, where he would hide it in the marina, then take his car up the coast to Cocoa Beach and dig up his special tool. *Bang, bang,* make an angel out of Lucy!

Except that he was being watched. He was certain of it now. The instrument he had found stuck up inside the hull of the fast boat was tiny, but he knew a tracking device when he saw one. Lucky that he had found it before his employers did.

The man in the sailboat had been anchored off the next cay too long now—three days—and he never left, not even to take a swim or walk on the island he was pretending to visit. And the stupid fucker had screwed up. The setting sun had glinted off his spotting scope. Stupid fucker. Stupid. Did he have any idea what firepower existed on this island? Did he think he could give chase in that puny sailboat, for shit's sake?

He had surreptitiously monitored the marine-radio scanner the men from the east had brought to the island, and had never heard a peep out of the man in the boat. But someone had tried to reach him.

He imagined that he would go over there and shoot the bastard, just as he had spun a thousand fantasies that he could face a man in combat, or in the smallest argument. . . .

His employers were watching the man in the boat as well. They were staying shy of his end of the island, and covered their heads with foolish fishing caps when they went out, as if that could disguise their ethnicity.

He itched to be moving. Perhaps he could slip out from the dock on the far side of the island, and that fucker wouldn't see him go. But no, he must wait. Wait, wait, wait.

Itch, itch, itch.

Wait, the men were coming toward him. They were bringing him something. He didn't like to talk to them, didn't trust them. Knew they laughed at him behind his back. Blond devil, they called him. "Hey blond devil, here's a gun," they were saying. "We have an errand for you. See that man in that sailboat over there . . ."

31

The center of Lake Okeechobee is like no other place I've been on Earth.

The colors are wrong. The water reflects the sky a disconcerted gray instead of blue, and it it's so full of tannic acid that it curls off the bow like Coca-Cola, complete with the foam. The sky itself is a confusion of vague tints all smeared into each other.

The surface is wrong. The horizon is lost, and the water does not appear flat; instead, implausibly thick with humidity, the boundary between lake and sky seems to curve upward like an inverted bell jar except with no clear edges, just a blur of moisture fading from more to less distinct. The sides thus hemmed in by humidity, the zenith seems unreasonably high.

And yet the lake is beautiful, reaching up from its own depths of strangeness to captivate the heart and break it all in one overwhelmingly soft and lonely moment.

The air itself is so humid that my body was soon slick clear down my torso, but the motion of the boat through the air kept the experience from being cloying. Perspiration poured down between my breasts and from under my arms in rivulets.

I stood up on the flying bridge, doing just that: flying. I had decided, after a decent cup of coffee, followed by eggs, bacon, and three glasses of water, that life on a boat could be good. Waltrine lent me shorts and a tank top, and I kicked off my shoes and went barefoot. With my hair pulled back in an elastic band, I felt at one with the elements.

Clouds built steadily all around us, fiercest in the west, cumulus rising by seven-thirty and thunderheads appearing by nine; they were dark as gunmetal by ten and growing wider, which meant they were coming straight for us.

The boat plowed steadily through the dark water, creating a constant kissing sound where the bow wake slapped itself falling. We moved on autopilot, chugging relentlessly from marker to marker, now passing small islands formed of dredging spoils and populated by troops of white pelicans crammed in next to cormorants.

I had been on the lake less than two hours, but already the rest of the universe seemed far away. The train that had finally come through at quarter to seven was hauling twenty or more gondola cars full of crushed limestone. Miles Guffey had watched it broodingly. I had thought at first that he was merely annoyed at being kept waiting, but then he opened a drawer and pulled out a newspaper story from the *Washington Post* that reported where that limestone was coming from and why, and where it was going to: It seemed that real-estate developers had bought themselves a huge loophole in the law, thwarting the professed federal plan to "replumb" the Everglades from a ghostly relic back into a thriving ecosystem. Using a mining law dodge, they were excavating vast quantities of the underlying limestone between Miami and Lake Okeechobee, digging down into the ground water, which created both rubble to sell as concrete aggregate and lakes around which to build expensive houses. Guffey was pissed because not only were the aquifers within the limestone thus forever crossed and the vitality of the ecosystem further ruined, but the rock was being sold for seven cents on the dollar. I sighed. It seemed that Florida was indeed a land of extremes: extreme beauty, extreme fragility, and extreme greed.

Once finally through the bridge, we had headed into the

lock, cut through the flood-control levee. The concrete
walls of the lock had loomed above our heads. Genteel men
in uniforms had handed us lines and informed us that we'd
be coming up about a foot. Doors had closed behind us,
and others cracked open ahead of us, letting in a surge of
water that sent us sloshing back like we were in a huge
bathtub. After a minute or two, the forward doors had
opened further, and we were handed into the canal that ran
along the west shore of the lake. It was bordered by a ghost
forest of dead trees that evoked the fierce but inanimate
ceramic army found buried in China. The bases of their
bleached trunks were lined with the lush greenery and bird
life that I was coming to know as essence of swamp. Alligators floated somnolently about us like semisubmerged
logs, and anhingas slid in and out of the water. The canal
hugged the inside of the levee, whose unnatural uniformity
and steep bank surprised the eye in this land of subtlety.

Miles had greeted my presence on his boat with equa-
nimity. He had not seemed dismayed, or even particularly
surprised. He had given me breakfast as if I were just some
customer dropping by his café, and began to tell me stories
of his life in Florida and in the profession. I had settled in
surprisingly quickly, rationalizing that I should wait half an
hour or so to work my way into his confidence before asking the question Tom wanted him to answer. A cell phone
awaited me, plugged into a charger to the right of the
wheel. I would ask to borrow it, citing that I needed to
reassure Faye. I would take it out of earshot and make my
call.

But a half hour stretched quickly into an hour, an hour
into two, and somewhere in there, I realized that he had
unplugged the cell phone and hidden it. Where? Clearly,
he had read my intentions. A game of cat and mouse had
begun.

I played my end of the game with small talk. "In the
Rocky Mountains, there's a small pool of water in the center of a wide valley," I told Miles. "It's called San Luis

Lake. Indian myth says it's the navel of the Earth, that man first climbed up from the underworld through it."

Miles returned tit for tat. He chuckled at my story, tapped the key on the autopilot with one deft finger to correct his course by one degree, and leaned back again in his captain's seat. "I'd believe that easily about this place," he said. "I heard it said once that in the beginning, the sky loved the ocean, and she gave him children in the form of clouds. Then the sky grew fickle, and he tried to love the Earth, but she did not know how to receive him, and lay barren. Even so, the ocean became jealous, and sent her children to rain down upon the Earth and sting it with their lightning bolts. But she was foiled, because in raining on the Earth, she made her rival fertile."

"Is that a Seminole myth?"

"Nope. I just made it up. Everything's about sex here in Florida." He laughed his mischievous laugh, then flared his eyes at me, grinned even more widely, and said, "I love it on this boat. It almost makes me forget how pissed I am."

I took this as some sort of opening. "Who are you pissed at?"

Miles giggled raucously and made a wide circle with one hand. "Everybody. I'm pissed at the Survey, of course. They should be funding this damned project. But more than that, I'm pissed at the whole profession. Things seem to be decaying, going into a state of bureaucracy that's so far from our original raison d'être that I'm about to scream. It's all just paperwork now, and justifying our positions. I'm past sixty-five, you know; I was about to retire in plain old disgust when this project developed, kind of caught my interest. I decided, out of sheer cussedness, that I was going to jam it in their faces."

I knew that in part I was hearing the trumpeting of a mired bull elk, but I spoke to the kinder side of that equation. "You're an idea man, Miles. That's a dying breed."

"God, I hope not. I'm too young to die." He sobered abruptly, and gave me a dark, impenetrable look. "That's part of it, I suppose. Kids aren't taught to think anymore.

They're taught to fill out forms. Little answer for each slot. Everything's digital. Hell, it's an analog world out here. Look at it! It's a continuum of interlocking, blended qualities, not discrete little quantities. Where's the lake stop and the sky start? I mean really. We've been taught to think that things have edges, but they don't. It's all one planet. Explain that to some bureaucrat with a time card to punch. The damned paperpushers want prepackaged, predetermined results, everything in its separate little slot. I'm not kidding you! When I propose a project I'm supposed to fill out a computerized form that asks what the results of my investigation will be. Well, that don't work in a world where half the data are missing and another quarter are hiding where we don't know where to look for 'em. How're we supposed to get the broad view on things if we think inside of preset slots to fill in? How're we supposed to quantify ambiguity?"

I understood what he was saying. His was a world of observation and inspiration, of integration, of simplicity and originality of thought. I had stumbled across genius more than once in my life, and it was always thus, the ability to stand back far enough to see what was simple and obvious in a field of information that seemed chaotic and inchoate to everyone else.

I moved to the chart desk and began to pick idly through the messy stack of books and charts. "Where are we going?" I asked, wondering where in hell that cell phone had gone.

Miles laughed, a quick grunt. "I ain't telling *you*. Y'all's getting' off at Stuart."

I closed my eyes. So that was it, he wasn't upset by my presence because he saw it as merely an odd ornament in the background of life's occurrences, something with which to amuse himself along the way. He was en route to mess with destiny, and I had fallen fanglessly into his world for a moment, a blink of time.

With this insight came an electrifying realization: I had

observed him observing me. The student had just surpassed the teacher. I knew something he did not.

Or perhaps, with our differing angles of observation, he saw one field of data and I saw another, and the two fields overlapped. Yes, that was it, because he understood the dust business from a height and breadth of vantage I could only guess at; he saw time and space as only four of perhaps ten dimensions that turned in concert; I saw perhaps five or six, if you counted one or two modifying processes that affected the march of time through space or space through time. And here we hung together, immersed in a time and space both fluid and sticky, caught like two flies in the amber of a vast ecosystem that was both lushly sensuous and dying. In that moment, I perceived the slowing of time always ascribed to the South; it was not a lassitude, but rather a surrender to the march of events, whatever the pace. Miles had cursed the bridge man for making him wait unnecessarily, but once moving at maximum speed, eight knots was what there was available and therefore plenty.

So the puzzle took on a new character. It was a matter of divining the overlap between two fields, mine and Miles's.

As the far shore of the lake began to resolve itself from a smudge to a blur, Waltrine brought another round of iced teas up to the pilothouse, and I said, "Tell me more about the connection you made with the astronaut who's about to go up on the shuttle."

"Lucy?" Miles asked. "Why, she's a friend of your Molly Chang's, that's how I got to know her. You knew Molly wanted to be an astronaut."

Oh my God, yes. . . . I had forgotten that. Our conversation seemed long ago, almost in another lifetime. Knowing that the astronauts were human beings who had friends pricked at my conscience. I had gotten this far by thinking of them as mere cultural icons, so much Spam in a jumpsuit. But now one astronaut in particular was entirely too real to me.

Miles said, "No, I've never met her. We put a proposal across her desk to get her involved in the program. You can see the headlines: ASTRONAUT TRACKS KILLER DUST CLOUD FROM SPACE." He panned a hand across an imagined page of newsprint.

"I suppose that would help publicize your cause," I said dryly.

"*Our* cause," he said, smiling, giving me a wink. His attention wandered. He stared out at the shoreline, which had now sharpened from a blur to a line, something drawn with a blunt chalk on a sidewalk. "I was on this lake when *Challenger* exploded," he said. His gaze shifted to the north, toward Cape Canaveral. "You could see it right out there, clear as anything. It was cold that morning, real cold, and I was listening to the countdown on the radio and thinking, they're going to go up in this weather? And they did, and that was that."

I said, "You could see it this far away?"

"Sure. It was cold, so it was clear, and there's no mountains in the way nor nothing. You can see a long way. We're not much more than a hundred miles from the Cape here. But hell, if conditions are right, you can see them lift off from most anywhere in the state, clear as a bell."

Waltrine snorted. "This state is *so* flat."

Her sardonic humor clanged against my skull. This time, I did not find her wisecracking funny in the least. Like the rest of America, my brain had become imprinted by the image of Christa McAulliffe and her ill-fated fellow crewmembers being blasted from the sky by a leaking O-ring, the scene ground into my memory by an overzealous news media. And, inextricably part of a nation in grief and trauma, I still reeled from the image of jet aircraft crashing into tall buildings in New York City, forever expunging from our hearts our naïve sense of safety.

And I knew something Miles and Waltrine did not. In my mind's eye, the great wall of sky had once again filled with a disaster that yet could unfold if I did not help Tom find the right island.

"Tell me where you're going," I demanded.

Miles laughed unkindly. To Waltrine, he said jokingly, "Lock her in the hold."

"It's important."

Miles did not even bother to make eye contact with me as he replied. "You want to swim home from there, or do you prefer being put off in Stuart, where you can at least rent a car?"

We came out the far side of Lake Okeechobee through locks that stood open at both ends, but the railroad bridge just beyond it was down, and we had to stop and wait for it to be lifted.

"Lake's down two feet," Miles informed me. "No need to drop us into the canal, we're already at the same level. Okay, here comes the train. Damn, another load of limestone."

I peered ahead through the front windows of the pilothouse, watching the gondola cars rumble by. When they passed, the section of track over the river began to rise as counterweights descended to either side. Like every other object sticking more than five feet above the surrounding terrain in Florida, it had cell-phone antennae on it, a nasty reminder that I wasn't doing my job.

Miles noted my interest in the bridge. He said, "Even with that clearance, some sailboats can't get their masts under. So there's a guy makes his money coming out here with a couple plastic barrels he'll tie to your mast, and he pumps water into them so's the boat heels over enough they can squeeze it under."

Waltrine muttered, "Here in Florida, everybody's got a scam."

I could see no signs of civilization other than the lock and the railroad bridge. Everything else was a solid bank of green jungle down both sides of the canal that now stretched east of us.

"Welcome to the St. Lucie canal," Miles said. "This vegetation is just a thin wall. "There's orange groves beyond. Used to be like that all the way through to the coast, but there's a network of canals and drainage ditches that run all through here like a grid. There's the outlet for one of them," he said, pointing to shallower canals that spilled out into the St. Lucie from either side.

The canal and side ditches were cut into limestone, and in no way resembled a natural river system. The side ditches came in at right angles and dropped over concrete ramps, and the St. Lucie was a constant width, its squared-off banks cut into the rock giving the edge of the waterway the appearance of a curb. The contrast between rampant nature and man's slice through it was extreme.

The boat chugged onward, kicking up its coffee-colored wake. "And not all of this remaining fringe of swamp vegetation is native, not by far," Miles intoned. "That's Brazilian pepper tree there, a real scourge. Brought in back in the 1930s as an ornamental. Now it's all over the place, and you can't get rid of it for love or money. Birds drop the seeds all over the place. Crowds out the natives like you wouldn't believe. That's Australian pine. Same kind of problem. Sucks up water. It's a mess." He sighed.

I gazed at him as he sat there expounding on unnaturalness, ensconced in his air-conditioned trawler, sucking down drinks that clinked with ice from the chest freezer in the galley, and I thought, *None of us is quite in sync with anything anymore. Or more accurately, not one of us is entirely in synch with everything.* I felt sad and discouraged, and wondered if I was catching Miles Guffey's malaise. He was not only a bull elk caught in the mire, he was an aging elk forced to watch the world proceed into a future he did not wish to inhabit. His was the disease of aging sages everywhere, who look out on the unconsciousness of younger generations and call it madness.

Our run down the St. Lucie canal took on a sense of

stateliness. I got to hanging out at the stern studying the symmetry of the wake that rolled out behind us like static wrinkles. Because all things were constant—the width of the canal, our speed through the water, the angle and amplitude of the waves—the wake was in a constant state of breaking against the curb of the canal. I stared at it in wonder and resignation, surprised and yet resigned to find another layer of Florida just as synthetic and hypnotic as the land of Mickey Mouse.

The largest of the thunderheads grew steadily toward us. At length, the downpour started, great splooshing drops that bounced and rolled on the waves like glassine pebbles before giving up their clarity and merging into the darkness of the waters of the canal.

I told myself that I was trying to figure out how to extort the information Tom needed from Miles, but the fight was quickly spilling out of me. I wondered if it was in anybody's best interest to do as Tom had bidden me. Certainly if I gave him the information he sought, he would be in more danger than if I didn't. Jack had found the damned missile, and we had dug it up, so the shuttle launch was no longer at risk. Or so I hoped. And Tom would stop the launch if he deemed it necessary. Jack was out there somewhere in the Bahamas gunk-holing about in his borrowed sailboat, and at a rate of 700 islands and 2,400 islets, he'd be at it for quite some time, just as clueless as Brad and Tom. I tried to tell myself that they were just a pack of overenthusiastic puppies and that they'd all come yipping on home when they got hungry enough.

The only problem was that, just like Jack and Tom, I wanted to know where the man who had buried that hideous weapon in my soil had gone, and I wanted him gone for good.

So where was he?

Jack seemed to think he had gone offshore. Why? Because he had the profile of a drugrunner, and drugrunners in these parts zipped about in fast boats or small planes, meaning they were going to another jurisdiction that was not far away.

The sediments inside the plastic case suggested the weapon had received its crude packaging in the Bahamas, but perhaps even that was wrong. If it was correct, one might suppose he was somewhere in one of the groups of islands closer to the Florida peninsula, but that might not be so. Fast boats went as fast as fast cars, and the distances were not great.

My mind wandered. There was also the question of Calvin Wheat. How had he gotten to Freeport in a wet tuxedo? Why had he kept his miraculous survival a secret? And precisely what mission had brought him across the Caribbean, and Miles and Waltrine across the state?

I could not unravel even one of those knots.

So I stared at the wake. From the back of the boat. Watching where we had been instead of where we were going. And in so doing, figured it all out.

– 32 –

I had been trying to figure out where a terrorist would go from Florida if he were trying to hide. Instead, by watching the wake leave the boat, I turned the logic around and considered the evidence from the other end of the chain: If I were a terrorist trying to run an operation just off the Florida coast, where would I put it so that I could hide it in plain sight?

The answer was damned simple when I lined up *all* the evidence: not just Jack's, but also Calvin Wheat's. I mentally checked and crosschecking my idea to see if it held together, starting with what I knew of Calvin Wheat.

The good Dr. Wheat had embarked on a cruise and had been thrown overboard. (It made less and less sense that he might have jumped; speaking for myself, if I were going to jump off a ship with the idea of swimming ashore, I'd have worn something other than a tuxedo). Wheat was a microbiologist who had a gripe with another microbiologist who had a known expertise with weapons-grade anthrax. That anthrax-wielding microbiologist had last been seen heading offshore, supposedly to the Bahamas. The two men had been scheduled to meet at the conference on Barbados, but only one had arrived.

Next, I considered Jack Sampler's behavior.

Jack had gone to Florida to help Lucy prevent a madman from threatening the space shuttle. Jack had gone incommunicado for several days, and then had come to Tom with the location of an illicit weapon designed to take down aircraft. Believing this à la carte terrorist to be acting alone, Jack preferred likewise to go it alone than call in a posse. Presumably Lucy disliked publicity.

What the two lines of evidence had in common were a) weapons, b) terrorism, and c) the Bahamas. So next I considered the Bahamas.

The Bahamas had a long history of looking the other way regarding pirates and smugglers of all stripes; so, who would get excited if the owner of a sunny little islet happened to import a few moderate-sized weapons? And who would notice a small laboratory in which someone was culturing a drum or two of anthrax? I realized that Tom and Jack did not fully understand the enmity between Calvin Wheat and Ben Farnswroth, or Chip Hiller for that matter. It was also common knowledge that cruise lines purchased whole small islands in the Bahamas to provide a "private" taste of paradise to their customers. Such settings commonly had paramilitary "guards" looking over them. And, one might suppose, a well-stocked islet might also have a tiny clinic, just right for culturing germs. Such an operation would be a magnet for men who do not fit in normal society: psychopaths of every variety.

Tom and Jack wanted to believe that the stalker was working for drugrunners. I saw the potential for a terrorist cell. The FBI had certainly guessed wrong before.

Putting the whole picture together, I had one very pissed-off microbiologist on his way to settle a score with a competitor who might very likely have gone to work for terrorists, and my boyfriend trying to find a psychopath he believed to be a solo act. It didn't take a genius to figure out that both might be working out of the same island, and that the thing they would have in common would be a terrorist cell that was larger and better organized than either of them. Calvin Wheat had gotten a free ride on the wrong cruise line, perhaps by a design of which he was not aware. His old nemesis had discovered that he was aboard, or even engineered it, and had made sure he would not make it to the the conference, let alone the private islet. A group hiding surface-to-air missiles and an anthrax lab on its island might not notice if one of their errand boys took off with one of their boats and one of their missiles to settle an old score. Miles Guffey and crew did not know the magnitude of the terrorist cell. Jack did not know for whom his miscellaneous psychopath was working.

But Tom had figured out that there might be a connection and had sent me to find Miles and shake him down for his destination. Somehow, I had to get that information to Tom. And for Faye's sake, I had to talk him into sending someone else to help Jack.

And all that meant I had to figure out how to get off the boat and phone Tom. But the damned boat was in the middle of a canal, and even if I could get my brain around the idea of jumping off a perfectly dry boat into that much water. I had only to remind myself that that water was full of large, carnivorous reptiles that had not been refrigerated into lethargy.

For the past ten or fifteen minutes, we had been passing houses. Houses meant telephones. I looked hungrily at their private docks, and wished a rowboat would cut loose and bump against the side of the *Sea Dingo,* but no such incredible luck came my way. I briefly contemplated pulling the inflatable off the roof and lowering it over the side, but I figured I'd get about twenty seconds and a hernia into that project before Miles or Waltrine caught me at it. So it was time to simply insist.

I hurried up to the pilothouse. Miles and Waltrine were halfway through a large bag of Doritos, munching away. "Listen," I said. "I've got to make a call. Really, it's critically important."

"Say why," Miles drawled.

The words jammed in my throat. If Jack and Tom felt they couldn't tell their official colleagues, I surely couldn't tell Miles Guffey.

"Not going to tell me? Aw . . ." He turned back toward the wheel.

"You're going out to the Bahamas," I said. "Calvin Wheat knows a man out there who's synthesizing weapons-grade anthrax. You've got to tell me which cay."

"This is personal. You're getting off in Stuart."

"I don't know what in hell's name you plan to do there, but let me tell you, he has friends."

"I assume he does," said Miles.

"Just what do you think you can accomplish? Go out in a blaze of glory? I've got friends who can help you. Shit, Miles, you've—" I looked up ahead. We were approaching a lock.

He picked up the microphone on the radio jack and said, "St. Lucie lock, this is the trawler *Sea Dingo,* coming to you from the west."

A voice came back through the speaker. "*Sea Dingo,* come ahead and tie up on your starboard side."

Miles said, "Did you notice you can smell the dust already, down at the coast? I was just hearin' that on the radio here. We'll be there in just a couple hours. In fact, I was thinking we'd be able to smell it already here, but not quite. Just wait until we get to the sea. The air will be hazy with it where the thunderstorms haven't cleaned it yet."

I was only halfway listening. I was examining the wall of the lock. It appeared to have iron bars at intervals. Surely I could climb them, if not the rope the man was lowering for us to tie up the boat. Or I could just yell that I was being held against my will and demand to be taken off the boat. This last seemed the most expedient, but I might lose precious time explaining myself to the Army Corps of Engineers. I stepped outside the pilothouse and headed back to the stern to gage my options.

Sea Dingo pulled in against the cement wall of the lock. Thinking I was being helpful, the man in uniform at the top of the wall lowered me a thick line. "Don't tie up," he warned politely, giving me a fatherly smile. "I'm going to lower you twelve feet."

"Sir," I said, "can you get me off this boat?"

"Not while you're in the locks, dear. Y'all can tie up down below if you like."

I took hold of the line and leaned on it. It was very rough, yet slightly slick; I didn't think I could climb it. The iron bars were out of reach. I looked up at the man, caught his eye again. He seemed kind and fatherly. "The captain here won't let me off the boat," I said, letting my lower lip quiver. It didn't take any playacting.

The man nodded, then disappeared from sight.

Behind us, the massive doors swung shut. Ahead of us, massive doors cracked open. Through the crack between them, I could see a drop-off. The boat lurched. I held on to the line.

Minutes passed. The boat slowly sank lower and lower in the lock. Had the man heard me? Had he understood? Would he do anything to help?

The doors opened wider. A weird salad of floating plants rushed downhill toward us. The boat dropped more rapidly.

I heard a voice over the loudspeaker in the pilothouse. "*Sea Dingo,* proceed to dock on your starboard side immediately outside the lock."

He did it! I almost danced a jig. Now I had to hope that Miles would do as the man had said.

Sea Dingo eased away from the cement wall. It headed out of the lock, but slowly.

Waltrine appeared at the doors to the saloon. She held out a cell phone. "Go ahead," she said. "Make your fucking call. But you're cutting us in."

"Tom," I said into the cell phone. "It's me, Em." I resisted an urge to shout over the noise that came through the connection. I tried to analyze it. *Engines,* I decided. *And wind. He's on a boat, too.*

I cupped my hands around the mouthpiece. "Tom, I'm on Miles Guffey's boat,"

I turned and walked to the far end of the upper deck, where I could speak without being heard through the portholes and watch the ladder from the lower deck as well.

"Make it quick," Tom growled.

I bared my teeth at the phone in frustration. "I've got your information."

"I no longer need it."

I almost threw the damned phone into the canal. "You've found Jack!"

"Yes."

Controlling my frustration with great difficulty, I said, "I've also figured out the big picture. There's a part you don't know."

For a moment he said nothing, then, "Speak."

I said, "You and Miles need to talk."

"What's that supposed to mean?"

"Calvin Wheat is alive and waiting for Miles and Waltrine at Freeport. They won't tell me where they're going, but I think it's the same place you're headed. So you've got a trio of scientist-vigilantes heading your way. Not good, huh?"

Tom swore, then said, "This isn't amateur night we're headed into. What the fuck do they think they're doing?"

"Their bioterrorist and your 'friend' have something in common."

"Explain."

"This line is secure?"

"My end. I'll have to risk yours."

I said, "What I said back in Tampa."

Tom said, "You mean that we're dealing with more than one man." He paused. Then, with annoyance mixed with something else—fear?—he said, "It seems that you were correct in your assumptions."

"You've found the man?"

"No. Yes. We . . . we found Jack."

My heart lurched as a jolt of adrenaline rushed through my body. "Is he okay?"

"Yeah, he's just ducky. Son-of-a-bitching cowboy. He's had the bastard staked out, didn't dare use his phone or radio. Brad ran out there in a fast boat, found him anchored. . . . I can't tell you all this, their surveillance is too good. We're on our way to . . . help him. You keep your vigilantes the hell out of here."

Jack's seen the stalker crawl into his nest of terrorists.

"No, Tom. You need these vigilantes, or at least you need Calvin Wheat. There's something you don't know."

"Cut to the chase, Em."

"They have weapons-grade anthrax on that island."

Tom let out every curse he knew.

I said, "Wheat knows how to handle it, or how to destroy it. And just as important, he will know how to locate the stockpile. Tom, you can't go running in there and chance setting off an explosion that will release it. I don't care if you think you're immunized; you'll be the first to die. I want you alive so I can kick your ass for doubting me. And so Faye doesn't kick mine. And so you don't let that much anthrax loose on the rest of creation."

"Are you sure about this?"

"Yes, or as sure as I get, Tom."

Tom muttered something that sounded like, "Fucking geologist weasels on every fucking point."

"Okay, you want more? The ship Calvin Wheat was on was called the *Caribbean Queen*. Tap into your computer. I'll bet you get an itinerary that puts in at a small cay in the Berry Islands."

Tom said, "Just a minute." Away from the receiver he said, "Brad, give me that phone cord. I've got to go online." I heard him clicking keys.

About then, a weird tight sensation crawled up my spine, and I whirled around just in time to see Miles Guffey's face appear above the deck of the flying bridge as he climbed straight up from the wheelhouse. He took a seat at the second set of controls and swung it around so he could look at me. He seemed oddly satisfied.

I said, "Pretty spry."

"For an old man?" he inquired. "I ain't dead yet."

I stared into Miles's smile. To the phone I said, "I'm going to guess that Miles knows that cruise line's schedule, too, and that boat is due at that island day after tomorrow. I'm going to guess also that he thinks he can walk on in there under the cover of all those tourists."

Miles said, "I do love a smart woman."

Into the phone I said, "Miles is confirming this." Trying to sound flippant, I asked Miles, "Aren't you a little concerned that they might have guards on this island? You never know. . . . They might be armed. Even with an island full of shark bait they might not take kindly to another boat making a landing."

Miles replied, "Who said anything about motoring up to the beach? It's amazing what you can do with scuba. Just pop up behind the dunes and shuck off your gear, and you're just another yayhoo from Kansas walking along the sand. 'Oops! I just stubbed my toe. Can you take me to the clinic? I need a Band-Aid.' The clinic would be where Farnsworth's got the setup."

To Tom I said, "You catching this?"

"What's your location?"

"We're a couple hours' run west of Stuart. Probably twenty-four hours from where you are. But Calvin Wheat is in Freeport. Sorry, Tom, but you're going to have to cut Miles in on this."

"Goddamn it. You put that crazy son of a bitch on the phone."

Faye was waiting for me at Manatee Marina. "They left before he even called me," she said, as we watched the dock attendant pull out the fueling lines and start to pump diesel aboard the *Sea Dingo*. "I missed them." She looked toward the east. Tears began to roll down her cheeks.

"I'm sorry, Faye. They were already well offshore when I got the call through to him."

She did not make eye contact. "I know," she said. "He phoned me with instructions. Come on, I've got the plane over at Whitman Field. It's just a few minutes away."

"You've got the plane? How'd you get up to St. Petersburg and back so quickly?"

"I drove up this morning," she said. "I had a feeling."

"So what are the instructions?"

"Tom told me to take you to see a man about a Zodiac."

Quoting the master, I said, "What's that supposed to mean?"

"You tell me."

"Are we going east?"

"Yes, that much I know."

"We don't have our passports," I said. "In fact, I don't have one at all."

"Don't worry. I was able to make certain arrangements." Stalking away ahead of me, she grumbled, "When I set up in flying, I meant to run a delivery service. I never meant to be smuggling geologists into the Bahamas."

• • •

Freeport was an array of hotels and whitewashed houses throwing evening shadows. Faye taxied the twin up to the general aviation building. A man was waiting there, holding a gallon jug. He stood casually in his shorts and luau shirt, staring at us through dark aviator's sunglasses. He was young and fit and looked like he was on his way to a stadium to cuss and scream and root for his favorite team.

I opened the door to the plane. "Dr. Wheat, I presume?"

He did not smile. "Yeah. That's me."

"You got any luggage?" Faye asked.

He laughed without smiling. "Just this gallon of Clorox and a ziplock bag for my little treasure hunt. I hope your friends brought their masks."

I said, "Well then, climb in. We have a ways to go yet."

The sun was dipping low toward the ocean through dust-reddened air when Faye's twin-engine Piper touched down at the airstrip. As we rolled to a stop between a white sand beach and a row of palm trees, she popped open her window. I could smell the salt kicked into the air from the surf, but also the throat-constricting odor of dust.

As the three of us climbed out of the plane, a man came out of a small building and walked briskly toward the plane. He was dark as pitch and was wearing white trousers and a splashy shirt. "Ms. Carter?" he inquired in a brisk British accent.

"That's me," Faye said. "And you are?"

"Hesperos, at your service." He grinned broadly. "Your cousin Edward said to show you all courtesies."

I looked at Faye. "You have a cousin out here?"

She shrugged her shoulders wearily. "Okay, so he's really an old boyfriend. It was the best I could do on short notice, given the coordinates Tom gave me."

The man turned to me. "You are Ms. Hansen?"

"Yes."

"Mr. Latimer has sent a boat for Dr. Wheat. He asks

you to proceed through the trees here to the dock on the harbor side of the island. A man named Philemon is there awaiting you."

"Did Mr. Latimer give you any instructions?"

"Just what I've said." He smiled. "I understand from my friend Philemon that you will all soon visit a not-too-distant cay with the purpose of cleaning up a rather filthy mess." He bowed deeply. "I am so delighted to hear."

I said, "*I* am going to this place?"

He bowed again. "Philemon is very reliable; all the local gentry use him when they . . . have an errand that requires discretion and . . . security."

Faye said, "Please, Em. Go. Make sure the reliable Philemon does not engage the wrong targets." Her head sagged forward with fatigue. She was pale, and her lips had gone thin.

I put the back of my hand to her forehead. She was sweating. "Are you okay, Faye?"

"I've been getting very tired these last couple of days. And a little bit achy." She put her hand against her belly, low down, as if fighting menstrual cramps.

It was at that moment that I finally noticed that the great bulge of her belly was riding lower than it had been the day before. The baby was no longer sitting high like a rising balloon, but instead was on its way to where gravity would take it. I'd seen it many times back in rural Wyoming: In the last weeks before a child was born, it dropped down into its mother's pelvis, bringing its weight to bear on the cervix. But it was too soon! "Oh, Faye! Why didn't you tell me? No, I can't leave you, I—"

Calvin Wheat put an arm around Faye to support her. She winced with pain. She said, "No! You go! Go help Tom and bring him home!"

"Hesperos," I said, "do you have another pilot here who can fly this thing?"

He grinned broadly. "I am her cousin's pilot. Allow me to take her in his Lear jet."

"She needs to get to a fully equipped hospital. You can

have her in Miami or Fort Lauderdale in less than an hour. Hurry, please!"

"Of course," he said.

I turned to Faye. "I never intended you should go back alone. I was just along for the ride, to make sure Calvin got on the plane, I—maybe I should come with you. If this progresses . . ."

Faye closed her eyes. "Get lost! You want to be my hero? You can do more good here."

I said, "I'm not sure what I'm supposed to do."

Faye said, "If nothing else, you can go and watch, and tell me what truly happens."

Faye's statement stunned me. I did not fully understand it, but it hit a deep chord. The call to duty arose in me then, and I was ready. "You go. And when you get there, you relax and wait. You hear me?"

"Git," she said, teeth clenched.

With Calvin Wheat behind me, I followed a path through sand so white it seemed to glow. The dock jutted out from a cliff of petrified dunes into shallow water.

The man waiting there was bigger and darker than Hesperos, and he looked mean.

The boat . . . was not big. There was hardly much more to it than the raft in which I had spent the night on *Sea Dingo*. A low bolster of inflatable tubing ran across the bow and along both sides, projecting as two points at the stern, one to either side of a pair of beefy outboard motors. Below the tubing, the craft rode on a hard fiberglass bottom that cut into the water with a vee.

I heard the engines on the Lear jet start up. With a jolt I realized that I knew next to nothing about what I was getting myself into, except that it involved greater exposure to my least-favorite medium than I could possibly contemplate. It had been less than twenty-four hours since I had stood trembling at the idea of boarding a big boat in a narrow canal, and now here I was getting on a small one sitting low to water that continued to the far side of the Earth.

It occurred to me that I might still have time to make it back to the airstrip before they took off if I ran at full speed.

I hesitated. A little voice inside me squealed, *What am I doing here?*

The wave of feeling that on land had seemed a thing of pleasure here became a sodden pull on my stomach. I felt nauseated. I asked myself why I was doing this. For Jack, who dropped everything and ran off? At that moment, I could not remember what had gotten me started on the road that had brought me here.

Jack was a face I had not seen lately.

But Faye . . .

Faye is my friend of the heart, and she is in travail and needs me to get on this boat.

I forced my legs to carry me along as if attached to a different brain. *We are going,* I told them. *We are on an island in a foreign country without a passport, we are going to climb into an open skiff with a total stranger and . . .*

And what, go to war?

Somewhere in the past days, a cog had completely slipped. The scene in front of me was not making sense. My legs tightened. I felt like I was swimming in molasses. The dock thrummed under my heavy footfalls, and I had a hard time making eye contact with the man in the boat.

Calvin Wheat jogged up behind me. He said, "Nice boat! Permission to come aboard, skipper?"

The big man in the boat nodded with debonair pride.

I did my best to make a bad thing worse by saying, "We're taking a *raft*?"

The man in the boat glared at me. "I was told only one passenger."

The Lear jet burst over the line of palm trees and took off like an arrow toward the west. I followed it with my eyes. It seemed to be taking civilization with it, leaving me out here in a darkening world. "No," I said, trying to sound confident. "I was told to go with you."

"Well, then," he said, "It is not a raft, my dear; a rigid inflatable boat. Observe: Eighteen feet of lovely Zodiac marine architecture with twin two hundred-horsepower Evinrudes. Gray, so m'lady can travel unseen on the night sea. Depth sounder, GPS, roll bar—"

"*Roll* bar?"

Calvin said, "It's gorgeous. Man, would I like one of these for scuba."

Focusing on my affront rather than Calvin's compliments, Philemon glared at me anew. "We are not going to what you Yanks call an ice-cream social. Fish finder—"

"*Fish* finder?" I said.

"We may need to watch for your friends. I understand they are pinnipeds?"

"Pinnipeds?"

"SEALs, my ignorant darling. Will you step on board, please?"

I said, "You're Philemon?"

He tightened his lips and showed me the whites of his eyes all the way around the irises. "Yes . . . and you are whom?"

"Em Hansen."

"Well then, m'lady Em, this is your royal barge. Step aboard, *please!*"

I did as he said.

Philemon was dressed head to toe in black. He handed Calvin Wheat a similar set of clothes, and told him to put them on.

Calvin hurriedly climbed into them, and wound up having to roll up the sleeves and pant legs quite a bit. He accepted a dark hood, but put it into his pocket. He then stepped aboard the boat and helped himself to a life preserver. Clearly, Calvin Wheat was no stranger to boats.

I asked, "You've been to sea before? I mean, other than on that cruise ship?"

Calvin Wheat looked up at me as he adjusted his buoyancy vest. "I did my time in the Navy. That's how I survived that fall. I was lucky enough to go through a school where they dropped us out of helicopters going twenty knots. You hit it right, you just bounce over the water." For the first time since I'd met him, he smiled, but it was not a nice smile.

Philemon said, "Good man."

"How'd you get ashore?" I asked.

"Just born lucky," Calvin said. "I was treading water only half an hour when a sailboat came by. I'd been just trying to figure out how to inflate my pants and use them as a floatation device."

Philemon said, "Lucky is the thing to be. I am glad to have you on my boat. Now, as for you. . . ." He turned to me. "Put this on. A bit big, but better a too-large BC than no BC," he said, handing me another buoyancy vest. Then he shook his head. "You glow like the full moon." He opened a locker under a seat in the boat and pulled out a dark poncho. "Tie it around the middle with this bungee. Not in style, but it will have to do. Now, here are the rules: You sit in the bow and hold on tight to the lifelines. I need your weight as far forward as you can get it. Yes, like that." He stepped back behind a console that held a steering wheel and an instrument array and sat down in a long saddle behind the wheel, which looked like it had been lifted from a large motorcycle, and started the engine. Calvin uncleated the lines that held us to the dock and then took a seat in the stern. Philemon's face suddenly split with a devilish grin. "And we go!" he said, thrusting forward the throttle.

The boat all but stood on its stern. It took off like a bullet. With a sickening drop, it slapped back onto the water, having raised and dropped me eight or ten feet in as many seconds.

The wind and water rushed at my face as the boat charged over the chop. I felt dizzy with the rush. "Philemon!" I hollered, uncertain he could hear me over the roar of the engines. "What's the plan?"

"Your friends have gone ahead, and they have invited us to join their party. Very kind of them. I love a good party!"

"I hardly think this a festive occasion!" I shouted.

"Oh no? You think it's nice that bad boys come to my islands and do naughty things? Nonsense!"

"Philemon, do you have any idea what you're getting into here? I mean this could get quite violent."

He howled with mirth and goosed the throttle farther open. "Emily! You are talking to a former member of Her Majesty's Royal Marines! Special Boat Service at your command!"

Calvin Wheat said, "Special Boat! Cool!"

I said a silent prayer that whatever Special Boat Service was included the proper handling of a speeding whatever the hell he'd said this was. "So you're a former military guy."

Philemon said, "Since my 'retirement' you might call me by another name . . . a consultant!" He roared with laughter. "I do jobs that require discretion; for a price, but this one I do for the brotherhood. My American friends want help cleansing filth from my waters? Philemon is their man!"

The brotherhood. There it was again, a sense of belonging that stretched around the globe, so close at hand and yet a thing beyond an insurmountable gulf. I changed the subject. "Are we far from the island?"

"Thirty miles. Not far. The cay you wish to visit is privately owned, just like Sir Edward's," he said.

Sir *Edward's? Leave it to Faye. . . .*

"Will this boat get us there and back?" I shouted, glad that the noise of the engines covered the panicked squeak that was finding its way into my voice. "I mean, it doesn't seem very large!"

Philemon threw back his head and cackled. "Special Boat Service! Our motto: 'Not By Strength, By Guile!' But this boat has muscles. Observe!" He pressed the throttle even farther. The boat skipped like a stone over the tips of the waves.

"Calvin," I said, "what's the plastic bag for?"

Calvin Wheat grinned, his white teeth going pink in the

dying sunset. "After I douse the germs with bleach, I'm going to liberate the lab journal," he said. "I figure I can still make it to Barbados and give my talk. Imagine the look on Chip Hiller's face when I slap that thing onto the opaque projector and show the whole goddamned profession where he's been getting his funding and what he's been doing to get it! Revenge doesn't get any sweeter than that!"

I fell silent and endured the slamming ride. The poncho whipped, and the air whisked around me full of salt spray, buffeting my hair into my face in great tangling locks. I held on tight to the lines and tried not to think of where I was or what I was doing. It was getting dark. I wondered idly if it would be worse or better when I couldn't see what was going on around me. "What are we going to do when we get there?" I asked.

"We? *I* am going to take Dr. Wheat ashore. Then, because you have been kind enough to join us, *I* am going to join the party. *You* are going to drive this boat," he said, working his lips about his grin. "In your American bank robbery films, you are the gun moll, the getaway."

I decided that I must have heard him wrong. I turned and faced forward. Ate spray.

Ten minutes passed, twenty, during which time Philemon opened gear bags and showed Calvin Wheat how to handle an apparatus called a rebreather. It was apparently like a scuba arrangement, except that it had only a very small tank and created minimal bubbles. He set him up with a mask and fins. Apparently, they intended to approach the island without being seen.

As it grew dark enough that I could no longer discern all the features on Philemon's face, he said, "It is time for your lesson."

"Lesson?"

"You have a way of repeating things." He cut the throttle suddenly to an idle. "Come here. I am going to teach you to pilot this boat."

"Me?"

Calvin Wheat laughed.

Philemon said, "You. What are you, nothing else than ballast?"

"But I—"

"It seems your friend Mr. Latimer has greater faith in you than you have in yourself. He says he's seen you ride a horse at a gallop. This is nothing after that. Come. You sit here in front of me." He slid back and indicated that I should sit in the saddle in front of him.

Gingerly, I moved back, slowly taking in the surprising stability of the boat. I lowered myself into position.

He smelled of spices I could not discern, and rich ale. He grasped my right hand up into his and placed it on the throttle. My left hand he put on the wheel. "There," he said. "Throttle in, and we go!"

The boat shot steep into the air, almost jumping onto its tail. I screamed, certain it would flip. It charged, leaped forward, and lowered itself into the wild skimming motion, at a steeper angle for the lack of my weight in the bow.

"There," said Philemon. "We are planing. This switch here controls the angle of the props. You set it here if we are in very shallow water. Near the island, this will be a problem. You understand?"

"I . . . think so." In fact, I understood only one thing. I was out in the middle of a darkening ocean. Worse yet, I was there with a very big, very strong man who spoke to me like I was an idiot. What else was I going to say but yes?

"Good. Now, give it a turn!" He cranked the wheel hard to the left. The boat roared to the left, leaning, leaning, kicking up, slapping the waves. He cranked it to the right. It looped around and did as he bade it. "Now you do it, m'lady Emily." He pulled the throttle back to an idle and let go of the controls. The boat came to an abrupt halt.

I gripped the wheel. Pushed the throttle. The boat leaped wildly, roared into life, kicked up its bow, and bounced rhythmically over the waves. After a moment, the motion began to remind me of galloping a horse. I began to relax.

I turned to the left, then to the right, feeling the rhythm shift with our angle to the wind and the waves.

"Ah, you are finding it," said Philemon.

He gave me two more minutes' practice then asked, "Where are we?"

I looked all around us and instantly the pleasure of the moment fell into a dungeon of anxiety. All I saw was a darkening soup of sea and sky. Low clouds were scudding in. My body contracted with an emotion I did not dare admit even to myself.

Philemon read my fear. "GPS, right here," he said. He tapped the instrument. "Our position. This line is the path we have taken. Tap this button to find your way home. Miracles of modernity. You will be fine."

"Are you telling me you won't be going back with me?"

"I am teaching you that you are not lost. You may not know where anything else is, but you will know where you are."

I smiled in spite of myself. He was thinking like a geologist. "Thank you, Philemon. When and how do we communicate with the others?"

"They are traveling under radio silence. Wait for a light signal. Three flashes, then two. When you see that signal, follow it in slowly, with the engines quiet, like this." He demonstrated.

Calvin Wheat said, "Shit, that's quiet."

Philemon said, "Keep your voices down, please. As you approach the cay, watch the fish finder. We will come up beneath you. Our friends approached the island from the other side. If things do not go well, it is possible I will leave the cay with your friends in their boat, in which case they will radio to you when they are clear and you may leave. Here, use this ear bud to listen, just like your fools in the airports with their cellular telephones. Follow the GPS back to Sir Edward's, and we will meet you there."

"What if it goes the other way around, and they all need to come with you?"

Philemon put a hand on my shoulder. "Lady Emily, if

this radio goes live before we're off that cay, all hell has broken loose, and you run this boat up onto the beach if you have to. You hear me?"

"Yes."

He gestured up ahead. "There," he said. "That's our cay. We approach from downwind. Dr. Wheat, are you ready? Very good. Lady Emily, tell me what your men look like. I have only spoken with your Mr. Latimer on the telephone."

I described Tom, Brad, the taciturn Walt. "They have two more I haven't met."

"That will have to do," he said. "Very good." He stood up and took off his shirt and pants, revealing a layer of neoprene that fit like a cutoff pair of overalls. He quickly put on an equipment belt and loaded a large knife and two handguns, and attached a gear bag to it by a rope.

"How do you keep your pistols dry?" I asked.

"These weapons are designed to fire wet. We just open the bolt a tad to allow the water to flow from the barrel." Philemon allowed himself a low chuckle. "Otherwise the weapon goes kapoohey!"

He produced a huge set of fins and put them on his feet, put a diving mask on his face, set its snorkel and his rebreather in position, and gave me a nod. He checked to make certain Calvin Wheat's gear was secured to his belt. Then he glided to a stop, engines off.

The cay owned by the cruise line was a long shadow to the east of us, barely discernable from the sleeping sky and ocean that held it in their embrace. Around it I could see several other small points of land and small dots with lights, presumably boats. The closest lay to the south, just off the next islet. Was that Jack? None of them were moving. "Can other boats see us?" I asked. Beyond the pale illumination of the screen, all was dark as pitch. I wondered what kind of boat Tom and the others were in. I wondered if they had rendezvoused with Jack. I tried not to wonder if Jack was even still alive.

Philemon said, "I think not. The larger yachts will have

radar, but we are small. Besides, we were never here. This night never happened. You understand?"

"Yes."

Calvin nodded. "When I get to Barbados, I'll tell them I saw the lab journal floating by...."

Philemon smiled. "That which floats may be all that's left of this cay come daybreak. Ah, speaking of day..." He opened another locker under the saddle and produced a set of night-vision goggles that made the ones I had seen in the Everglades look like dime-store reading glasses. He rigged them on his head, changing its smooth, sculptural shape into something alien, inhuman. As the last light faded, he scanned the island. "Lady Emily," he said. "Things get too bright on the island, you put these on. The intensifiers are designed to cut out to avoid overloading."

I put the bud from the radio into my ear. It let out a small, thin static. Philemon set the speaker so that he and Calvin Wheat could listen, too.

It was so dark now that I could barely see my hand in front of my face. I heard Philemon in the stern. He whistled softly, barely a sigh escaping between his lips. Suddenly, the sound of the static shifted slightly, and Philemon went on the alert. "There," he said. "Our signal. Dr. Wheat, after you." And without saying good-bye, the two of them rolled over the side and slipped into the dark, shifting waters.

I was all alone in the boat, in the dark, surrounded by water.

Waves slapped at the hull. I tried to imagine the sound came from some other source; a cow slapping her tail at flies, perhaps, or my mother pouring Kool-Aid out of a jug at a family picnic. The thought made me feel my loneliness.

Time scraped past. I sat in the bottom of the boat watching for the next signal, feeling clammy, trying not to notice the slight swell that constantly reminded me that I was in a boat in the middle of the ocean. I let my mind wander off to one side of my head, ignoring the deep and abiding sense of panic all that water raised in me.

A half hour passed, perhaps an hour.

Suddenly, a flash turned my eyelids red. I sat up, opened my eyes, and turned to the east, toward the island, toward the source of the light, just in time to feel the concussion of the explosion thump my chest.

My body shook with adrenaline. I was terrified and angry all at once, and had nowhere to go with it. Bright shards of light peppered the night, followed by the reports of small arms. In between the flashes, I could see nothing but splotches in my vision. I watched for the signal, but saw chaos instead.

The shaking in my arms and legs became violent. I told myself that I must be cold. My body cramped from head to foot, and I was terrified that I was about to pee or vomit or both. I heard a boat rev its engines near the island. I reached for Philemon's night-vision goggles and put them on, turning my universe once again into a tracery of black and electric green.

Then I saw it: a long boat shaped like an arrow, taking off like a shot to the west.

The radio coughed into life. I heard Tom's voice: "Em! Come!"

I slapped the throttle, and the boat stood almost on end. Crashing back into the water, it took off like a bolt of lightning toward the island.

Time telescoped. The flashes grew closer and closer, weirdly ghostlike through the goggles. The delay between flash and report shortened, merged. Sound rocketed across space. I began to wonder what would happen if a stray bullet caught me, or the boat, or—

I could now discern a vague line where water turned more solid, but knew that distances appeared different in the dark. I had to be traveling at fifty or sixty miles per hour. Would I hit the shore? Worse yet, would I strike it in the right place?

The radio crackled. I said, "Tom?"

"To your right! Your right!"

Now I could see men running down the beach, all the same electric-green color. Which were friends? Which foes? My stomach lurched, but a crazed chemistry in my blood took over. I spun the wheel and yanked back on the throttle, skidding the boat. I fought to think thoughts other than those that crashed about my mind, fought to go completely blank except for the tiny point on which I must focus. I became that point.

Another large flash briefly overwhelmed the goggles, and then I could see men splashing into the water. I counted one, two, three . . . one man dragging another. That made four. They disappeared beneath the surface. Where was Jack? Not a one of them had his shape, his magnificent size, nor Philemon's.

I spun the inflatable ninety degrees, giving them the side, and shut the throttle. The boat careened to a stop. I could see no one. Where had they gone? Had I overshot them in the compressed depth perception of the dark? I glanced at the fish finder, saw nothing.

Then suddenly a hand rose from the darkness and slapped the far side of the boat. Realizing that they had dived underneath to use it as cover, I lunged to the far gunwale and grabbed at the arm. It was slick with neoprene. A face appeared, distorted behind a diving mask, weirdly glowing with electric-green light. Had I connected with the right people? Was this one of mine, or was it the dreaded other? A finned leg rose over the side, landed in the boat. The man heaved himself up, rolled aboard, flopped onto his back, gasping. "Thanks, Em," he said. I recognized Brad's voice.

More men rolled aboard, each helping the next. I saw Walt flop into the hold and lie panting, his face black with camouflage. Brad got another by the arm and pulled. A fourth. Fifth—

Philemon burst over the side of the boat, kicked off his fins, and jumped into the saddle, all in one sinuous motion. Without ceremony, he tugged the night-vision goggles from my head.

Where was Jack? And was Tom one of those who lay

gasping at my feet? I groped in the dark, touching faces, arms, hands. Nothing felt familiar.

I saw Jack running down the beach then, half dragging another man. I watched them scatter into the water, saw Jack heave himself like a plank onto the roiling fluid. I lost him, now glimpsed him again, my vision a flurry of black dots from the flashes. Philemon whipped the boat around and caught Jack on the fly, plucking him from the water with one arm as if he were little more than an inflated tube himself. A half second later, he snagged the final man, then opened the throttle full and swung this way and that, making a crazy line through the water, harder to hit. We tore away from the island, heading full tilt for the next.

Jack rolled to his knees. "Give me a weapon!" he shouted. Suddenly seeing me, he roared, "Get down!"

Philemon grabbed my poncho and threw me to the floor. "Your friends," he said, "they like a loud party." His sarcasm was soft-edged, sad. "This is what war is like," he said, his voice barely audible over the roar of the engines. "Your American war movies make you think soldiers can see what they are doing in the night, but that is not right. At night, war is blind chaos. Then there is an explosion and it blinds you. Someone can come right up to you and you don't see him until he is close enough to snatch your face from your head."

Craning my neck from the awkward position into which Philemon had thrust me, I saw another boat coming after us. It was larger, moving faster, closing quickly, a string of flashes coming off its bow.

Jack pulled something off his shirt, yanked a pin, hurled it at the pursuing craft. Walt raised a weapon, fired. The following boat suddenly bucked, humped with flame. The wall of noise hit me like a hammer, boxing my ears, rattling my teeth.

Now we are safe, I told myself.

Suddenly, Philemon slumped to the side, his hand lazily drawing the boat into a slew as his body crumpled. His warm bulk rolled against me.

"Philemon's been hit!" I cried. I struggled to support his head. With one hand, I felt for a pulse, but found sticky ooze instead.

Jack jumped to the controls. In the pale haze cast by the fire that now engulfed most trees on the island, I could see that he wore a strange gadgetry across his eyes. He looked strange to me, half man, half machine.

My skin crawled with fear. I rolled Philemon onto his side, putting the wound high, and felt for a pulse. I found one, fast but steady, and his stomach still moved with a rapid breath.

Brad shouted, "Where'd your target get to?"

Jack roared back, "He headed west. I've got him with the goggles. There! No need for speed. I holed his gas tank. He'll be stalling any moment now."

"There he is!" someone yelled.

"He's mine!" Walt hollered.

"No, *mine!*" Jack insisted.

One lone form stood out against the sleek contours of the boat. The man ducked.

Jack cut the engines and let the Zodiac drift. The night was suddenly silent except for the soft murmur of the waves.

I heard a voice call out across the waters. "I only worked there!" the man on the far boat shrieked, his voice cracking with hysteria. "I didn't know! Please, don't hurt me!"

"Keep back," Brad said. "I saw him pack an Uzi onto that thing. Nasty little alley sweeper. Wait, check this out." He flipped a switch, turning on a spotlight on a long wire, and aimed it toward the other boat.

"Don't worry," Jack said. He raised a rifle to his shoulder. Aimed. Fired. Again. Again. Again. The bullets flew from the muzzle like angry bees. His body heaved with the recoil. Suddenly, between the concussions of the shots, I heard a screech like a wild animal caught in a trap. The man slipped to the deck, a stark pale shape in the spotlight.

Jack grinned. "Got him!" he whispered.

There was a cracking sound and a dull explosion.

"Shit!" Brad howled. "Fucker got the port tubing! He was just playing dead, Jack!"

"We'll see how dead we can get him," Jack hissed. He opened the throttle and slewed wildly toward the boat, whipping it to the left at the last moment so that the right side bounced against his opponent's craft. The man rolled back onto his haunches, still holding his gun. I feared that he was readying himself to fire, but instead he cowered back as if unarmed. He was husky and blond, and his eyes were wide with fear. In a split second's recognition that etched itself in my mind, I realized that he looked like . . . Jack.

Jack leaped aboard the boat and kicked the gun from the man's arms. He grabbed the man by his head, wrapped it in his arms, and gave it a sickening twist. As bone cracked, Jack roared, "That's for Lily, you shit-eating bastard!"

The last look on the man's face as life drained from him was one of pouting self-pity, his lower lip extended like a child's.

I fell to the bottom of Philemon's boat in horror, my bearings completely lost, my eyes squeezed shut to erase the last look of that dying man. I tumbled up against something firm like a human but as unresponsive as a slaughtered calf. Even in the darkness, in all the chaos of the moment, I knew that I was embracing a corpse. Believing it to be Philemon, I wrapped my arms around it, holding on as if it were my own life that had escaped it. I ran a hand upward, thinking to touch Philemon's rich hair, but what I found was thin and stubbly. I opened my eyes and looked, only to find that my hand rested in hair that shone silver in the wan light of the GPS. I stared into eyes that stared unseeing into the great beyond.

Tom.

– 34 –

On the television screen in the hotel suite, space shuttle *Endeavor* loomed like a vague sentinel through the haze. The clock ticked down. A voiceover track announced the progress of the countdown. *T minus one minute and counting.* . . .

Jack shifted from the place where he had been waiting patiently in the shadows. "Let's step outside, Em. The sky is clear and still dark. We'll be able to see it lift off."

"No. I don't want to leave Faye."

Nancy spoke from her vigil at the other side of the bed, "She's sleeping, Em. The doctors in the emergency room said she just needs to stay down and rest to hold onto that baby. You'll wake her with all your fretting. I'll stay with her."

Forty seconds . . .

I touched Faye's hand, listened to her breathe. Sometime in the next few hours she would awaken, and ask me how Tom had fared, and I would have to tell her that I had failed her. That the whole world had failed her, unable to come to peace.

Jack pulled me gently toward the balcony adjacent to the room.

Outside, it was clear and cool, the sea breeze ruffling at the palms. The lights of Fort Lauderdale were slowly dulling as the first tinges of dawn crept into the eastern sky.

Through the open door, I could hear the sonorous voice pronounce the final countdown, that calm recitation of descending numbers, so familiar and yet still stunning after all these years: *Ten . . . nine . . . eight . . .*

My heart pounded. All my life our hungering for weightless space had been a scene inside the box called television. But now, in spite of the shock and horror of the long night at sea, pounding relentlessly over the waves as my friend and teacher grew stiff and cold beside me, my heart lifted. I was witnessing the dream, one American among millions filled with pride.

Seven . . . six . . . five . . . four . . .

Tears filled my eyes. Faye, trying to hang onto the tiny life that dwelt within her. War is the tearing of families. War is good-byes left unsaid. I wanted to rise up like *Endeavor* until I found a vantage high enough from which to embrace, all at once, both the brightness of my hopes and the dark ambiguities of human existence.

Three . . . two . . . one . . .

Through the open door, I watched the monitor display the close-up of the ignition beneath the rockets. Streams of sparks spewed out into the blast of fuel. It set off a noise like a string of firecrackers, the reports too reminiscent of recent experience for comfort. I cringed.

Jack tightened his grip around my shoulders.

I tensed, uncertain how I felt about being enfolded in an embrace that had so recently extinguished a life.

Jack read my feelings. He turned to the north and wrapped his strong arms around himself as the shuttle lifted off, a bright streak of intense light and vapor now appearing above the row of buildings and palm trees that formed the horizon, now accelerating, rising, rising, flying up through a cloud that turned incandescent. The craft climbed the hill toward the stars, escaping the bonds of Earth—

"She did it," Jack said with satisfaction. "I'll be damned."

AUTHOR'S NOTE

I did not set out to write a book about terrorism. In fact, we have the mischievous genius of Gene Shinn to blame—or thank—for this book getting written.

I've noticed that geniuses have a few traits in common: First, their minds are agile enough to spot the simple pattern to puzzles that seem overwhelmingly complex to the rest of us. Second, they often take a complex course through life, for the simple reason that they find the pathways most of us follow too narrow, constraining, or just plain uninteresting. Third, they're so far out ahead that we don't even know that they're leading us. Which, fourth, makes them impossible to manage. This is all true of Gene. He's one of those wild children of the sciences who got so far out in front of us all with his research that the status quo finally got embarrassed and presented him with an honorary doctorate.

If required, I would deny that Miles Guffey was patterned after Gene, but I shall hereby state (with applause) that the hypothesis Miles expounds in this book is in fact Gene's. Gene and microbiologists Dale Griffin and Chris Kellogg and marine ecologist Ginger Garrison, along with a host of colleagues, are the real people who are investigating the impact of African dust on coral reefs and human health. They are doing so on a pathetic shoestring budget for the U.S. Geological Survey in St. Petersburg, Florida.

In the 1950s, Gene was majoring in zoology while on a music scholarship at the University of Miami, and spearfishing on Caribbean reefs to feed his young family, when he began studying and photographing corals. By the mid-1960s, Gene was running a field station in Qatar, where he studied Persian Gulf coral reefs from a dhow. In the early 1970s, he opened a field station for the USGS in south Florida, where he observed the slow death of coral reefs. No one knew why the corals were dying. Gene put together his and various other peoples' observations and conjured the idea that what was killing the reefs was disease-laden dust blowing off Africa. He said, "It's so widespread it must be something in the air."

What Gene had was an idea. It wasn't even a hypothesis, let alone a theory. To move from an idea to a hypothesis, you need hard data, and to get data, you need funding. So Gene applied for funding. The USGS provided some funds to investigate the past record of dust in sediment and corals, but no funds to determine if the recent death of corals was caused by dust. He acknowledges that they pay his salary and only rein him in occasionally.

Gene widened his search to other government agencies. Each had a different reason for refusing him. As the list of refusals grew, so did Gene's irritation. The ocean was not only a place of beauty and recreation for him, it was inspiration and dinner, and it did not seem reasonable that humanity should ignore its well-being.

Gene finally obtained enough funding from a new public health program in NASA to pay the salary of a new Ph.D., microbiologist Dale Griffin, who has to date identified over 130 live pathogens in samples of African dust. Gene's idea was now a hypothesis. At the time of this writing, Gene is still struggling for sufficient funding to fully test this hypothesis.

Gene first described the project to me in 1999. He asserted that the dust represents a bioterrorist threat. He reported that tons of anthrax manufactured during the Cold War cannot be accounted for. He was convinced that no security agency had considered the threat posed by the clandestine entrainment of such pathogens into intercontinental dust clouds.

I did not want to write about terrorism, but an important project having trouble getting funding did interest me. What worried (worries) me was (is) the growing trend of scientific research being increasingly predicated and directed by vested interests and the politicians who cater to them. When big money directs research, big money influences, and even dictates, findings. We live in the age of bean counters, people who confuse the bottom line with the moral line. Corporate culture is quickly becoming human culture, to our peril as a species.

I set out weaving a story about the funding of scientific research. Gene kept pushing the terrorist angle. I systematically resisted the idea until September 11, 2001. On that day, unthinkable terrorism came to America. In the weeks that followed the September 11 attacks, deadly weapons-grade anthrax began appearing in envelopes mailed to journalists and U.S. Senators. The first death occurred in Florida.

Confronting the shock of these attacks has been difficult for all of us. Living with the subject of terrorism to the depth it takes to write a book about it seemed beyond me. This is because I have been a victim of the "little" terrorism that is commonly called stalking.

Lucy's experiences were based on mine, with an important difference: While Lucy kept her silence and was able to call in a white knight, I fought through police and judicial channels. While Lucy was able to realize her goals, I suffered the loss of my home, my community, and my livelihood. It seems that in our culture, it is easier to tell the target to duck and cover than to deal effectively with the attacker. And if that target is female, she is, in one way or another, blamed for being targeted.

During my efforts to hang on to what I could of my life, I discovered that three of the six women who worked in my office had suffered similar experiences, but none of them had prevailed. One woman had married a policeman in hopes of gaining security against her former husband, but the harassment and fear for her safety continued. Another suffered stalking at the hands of the policeman who had been her husband. With the glassy eyes of the traumatized, she described the night he tied her to a chair and repeatedly placed a bullet in his service revolver, spun the chamber, put the muzzle to her head, and pulled the trigger. When she later tried to escape, he used the police network to track her down.

Stalking is too vague a term. The crime is the extortion of power, and the weapon is terror. Women suffer terrorization at the hands of men who feel a sick need to control them. Women are beaten, raped, and harassed until their lives are reduced to bare survival, and sometimes they are indeed killed. If they use lethal force in self-defense, they are held to the standard of whether a *man* would have found self-defense necessary, and so are routinely jailed.

Victims of stalking are not usually weak women; ironically, sick men typically select strong women as the targets of their manias, just as terrorists attack strong nations. What stalkers and terrorists have in common, aside from sick minds, is cowardice. They are opportunistic. They exploit the vulnerable. They attack strength, not power.

We don't condone terrorism from outside our country. Why, then, are women vulnerable to torment when it comes from within? The answer to this question runs as deep as all the other notions and rationalizations that suggest women are somehow less valuable than men. Why does the public hear so little about this astonishingly common problem? Because the stigma that is pushed on women who have been abused is so debilitating that we learn to keep our mouths shut. We are blamed for being caught "in the open." If raped, we are considered "damaged goods." This tells us that we are commodities, not fully empowered citizens, thus demoralizing its victims by the twin burdens of vulnerability to terror and shame for being victimized. The discounting and blaming of women sends its tendrils outward, eventually affecting every soul in human culture. We are one world.

As with all my sisters who've shared this experience, healing from this loss has become a central feature of my life. While I bear the cost of resurrecting myself, the man who stalked me persists in our society like an opportunistic virus, draining our cultural vitality one victim at a time, exploiting our ignorance and attitudes and the consequent inadequacies of our judicial and protective systems. I draw a crude parallel between those who stalk women in America and the terrorists who engineered the September 11 attacks. Both take advantage of our vulnerability as an open society. The engineers of the September 11 attacks thrive on their own systems of tribal obligation, international finance, and the unresolved rage that discounts our culture, just as stalkers within our culture exploit systems that discount the feminine *half* of its population. At the root of both situations—terrorism large and small—is the abuse and subjugation of women.

Marginalized women raise nasty sons, and thus the sickness is perpetuated.

So writing about the big terrorism—terrorism between whole peoples, ideologies, or nations—is a double-edged sword for me. It is horrifying in and of itself. It is also salt in an old wound, because when the "little" terrorism happened to me, no one sent troops to avenge me, and no one beefed up security measures around me. As an American in post-September 11 culture, I mourn the loss of our sense of safety even as I acknowledge that it never truly existed. Madness is as old as mankind. We must not only treat the disease, but also strengthen our societal organism so that it no longer gets sick.

The act of healing, while demanding everything of me, has given me in return a life more filled with meaning. And while I at first feared that experience had stolen my innocence (a confusion borne of that societal conditioning that teaches that the victim is damaged goods), I was to discover that what I had lost was, in fact, ignorance, and that deeper knowledge helps me to release the pain and anger of trauma, and brings a deeper capacity to give and receive love.

There remains the question of vengeance.

Given who I am (a woman living in a culture still based on men's rights and values) and what I believe (that we are an evolving species with much to learn about our capacity for violence and the causes of it), I am still glad that I took the measures I did to avoid a lethal confrontation. But had he succeeded in cornering me before I was able to escape, I would have willingly used lethal force to stop the attack. And had I the mandate to do it, I would have sought him out and brought him to justice for his atrocities. But justice should not be confused with vengeance. Justice is ending the cause of suffering. The desire for vengeance is an urge felt by those who must heal.

Healing occurs one heart at a time, but one heart can inspire a multitude.

What of the "big" terrorism? Through writing this book, I have learned that there is a connection between African dust and terrorism: That which blights a people brings out the beast of rage and the opportunism that dines on it. We must open our eyes to opportunism at every level. We must empower all. Education is the key.

We live in a time of tall challenges, in which we have increased our numbers beyond the carrying capacity of the planet. We live on the cusp of globalization of our economies, in which some profit beyond imagination while others sink into servitude. And we live in a time of great hope and discovery, in which humans enjoy unparalleled freedoms, up to and including escaping the planet that spawned us.

So much is up in the air, just like the dust that blows off Africa.

With great love and respect, I thank you for reading.

Sarah Andrews

September 11, 2002

**Keep Reading for an Exciting Excerpt
from Sarah Andrews's Latest Mystery:**

EARTH COLORS

**Available in Hardcover
from St. Martin's/Minotaur!**

As I walked down Sheridan Avenue, I was feeling a mixture of nostalgia and dread. The nostalgia was there because I had spent the embryonic beginnings of my career in geology in the oilfields nearby. The dread was there because of the reasons I had returned.

The air was cold and dry, and the great backdrop of Rattlesnake Mountain loomed like a frozen wave on the western horizon. It was late March, too early for campers and the skiers didn't come this way, so the wide streets of Cody, Wyoming, were dotted only by a smattering of local pickup trucks. The crush of summer tourism would not begin until May, when the snowplows opened the east entrance to Yellowstone National Park.

I shifted the backpack child carrier, redistributing the weight of the baby girl who was riding in it. "This town was named for Buffalo Bill Cody," I said, as I continued along the sidewalk, trying to dispel the unpleasant mixture of feelings by chatting with the baby in the habit I had developed when I carried her along on my walks. "Buffalo Bill was a scout who became the first and last of the great Indian Show hucksters. He made a lot of money and built that hotel over there, and named it after his daughter." We were passing The Irma, a classic Victorian-Western confection that fronted proudly on Sheridan Avenue, the main drag through town. "But when he died, he was flat-busted broke, and the story goes that his widow sold his corpse to pay the bills; true or not, his burial shrine down in Denver is something of a tourist trap. Imagine living your life as best you can only to have your grave become a roadside attraction. But of course, the Buffalo Bill Historical Center was named after him, and if he hadn't already been dead, he could have certainly held his head up over that."

The baby gurgled conversationally as she bobbed along behind my shoulders.

"I'm going to take you to just one of the five museums housed in the Center," I told her. "The Whitney Museum of Western Art. It's time we started on your cultural education. You just stick with Auntie Emmy. I'll start you out with some cool cowboys and Indians stuff, like Charlie Russell or my all-time favorite, Frederick Remington."

Of course I didn't expect a seven-month-old baby to know a Remington from a Pokémon card. My real reason for taking her to the art museum was so that her mother could take a much-needed nap. Her mother was my dear pal Faye Carter Latimer, although Faye didn't use the Latimer part, out of rage. The baby was Sloane Renee Latimer, the most cheerful half-orphan you've ever met. At least, once we got her past the colic she was cheerful. The colic was dreadful. When Sloane Renee screamed, the world stunk.

I truly hoped that Faye was getting some sleep, because it had been a long drive up from Salt Lake City, and the purpose of her visit was worrying her even worse than it was me. She was supposed to meet with a potential client. I should have been fairly relaxed. I was just along to fill in the cracks between single motherhood and her career. I could kick back and indulge in visiting my favorite museum in the whole world.

My anxieties stemmed from a variety of stimuli, not least of all was the fight I had just had with Faye. I had left her staring at the wall in our room at the Pawnee Hotel. The Pawnee is a good old girl of a hotel, but many rungs below what Faye was used to on the great ladder of hostelries.

It had been one of our small but deadly fights.

"Why didn't you book us a room at The Irma?" she had inquired, keeping her voice neutral.

"This was cheaper," I had replied, trying to sound matter-of-fact.

She had come back quick and harsh: "Is this some kind of a joke, or are you trying to tell me you think it's time I began to live within my diminished means?"

She had given me the opening I had longed for, but I had diverted. "I'll just take a walk while you get some rest," I had said. "You'll want to be fresh for your meeting."

"Fine," she said, making it sound like it wasn't. "I'm not sure I can sleep in a place like this, but we'll see if fatigue can prevail where my silver spoon dumped me off."

I scrutinized her words as I continued down Sheridan Avenue, now passing various shops that sold Western-wear and Indian trinkets made in China. It had been the most direct communication we had had since before the baby was born, and I tried to tell myself that her efforts to get her business might therefore be a good thing. Perhaps the fresh stress of trying to function in the outside world would pry her out of the brooding silence she had dwelt in since her husband's death.

Further down the street, I noticed that I was doing some brooding of my own. It began to hit me that I was at least as tired as Faye. After all, we had gotten up at four and had been on the road since six, and I had done most of the driving. I cast a longing glance at a saddlery, wondering if I'd ever own a horse again. *When I inherit the ranch, the first thing I'll do is buy another horse,* I told myself, but the thought brought its usual sadnesses. Life was marching by, and the viability of ranching continued to spiral downward. In the next block, I sniffed at the heady scent of cinnamon rolls that spilled from a café, and wondered if I'd ever have a disposable income again, so I could indulge in the little goodies that somehow make life seem more secure.

"Do you smell that, Sloane?" I asked the baby. "Just as soon as you grow more teeth, we'll try some. You're going to *love* cinnamon rolls." I stopped, realizing that I had not had lunch. I knew that I should turn around and make myself a peanut butter and jelly sandwich from my stash of ingredients in Faye's car, but instead I followed my nose into the café, saying, "But as your mother always says, there's no better time than the present."

The rolls were fresh and sweet, without being cloyingly so, and rich in the spicy liquor that so delightfully oozes from the swirls of that pastry. I shared my prize frugally with the baby, giving her tiny bites and making mine last too, then dawdled over a cup of coffee, relieved at the way the sugar and caffeine revived me. But no matter how slowly I savored the treat, it was too soon gone, and someone else was waiting for the table, so I got up and prepared to leave.

I was just putting on my mittens to push the door open and leave when I about collided with a man who was just coming in from outside. He had his collar turned up against the cold and his head tucked down, so I didn't see his face at first, but something about him was instantly familiar: the thickset torso, the wild brush of hair, the humble clothing designed for manual labor. Recognition registered somewhere deep in my gut before it even hit my brain, and when he looked up, ready to dodge me, his eyes widened as he recognized me, too. It was Frank Barnes, my old oilfield boyfriend. I had not seen him since I had moved on to a better job in Denver. How many years had it been?

I started to step back, unsure of my welcome, but he grinned, so I did, too. "Frank! How are you?" His hair had gone silvery gray. How old was he now? Fifty?

He clasped my shoulders with his thick, rough hands and stared happily into my eyes, then his gaze slid sideways. As he took in the little creature that was riding papoose on my back, his mouth sagged open in happiness.

"Em! You've got a . . . a baby!" His eyes shot next to my left hand, upon which I had already placed a mitten.

My stomach tightened. "She's . . . I'm babysitting for a friend." Immediately I wished I had lied and claimed her as mine, because Frank had left me for—*No, I left him*, I asserted to myself—*or more precisely, I left town to take that job, and while I was gone, he—but I suppose I was never really going to come back . . .*

We were being jostled now by other people who were trying to come into the restaurant, so Frank let go of my shoulders and stepped to one side, but his eyes stayed locked on Sloane Renee Latimer. His face had spread into a delighted grin. "She's beautiful," he said, offering her a callused finger to grab. He leaned his big face close to hers and said, "You certainly is. Yes, you certainly is." The baby was totally enthralled by his big, grizzled smile. Her eyes had gone round, and she was giving him her best drop-dead-gorgeous dimpled grin.

"Yes, she has me wrapped around her littlest finger. This one, right here." I was relieved for the distraction. It gave me a moment to pick my wits up off the floor. Frank had passed on into the ranks of the Married People, and I was still Single, something of which I was not proud. I was beginning to wince, now that I was almost thirty-nine, when the headlines of supermarket tabloids trumpeted statistics about women who did not marry by thirty, or thirty-five.

Too quickly, Frank's gaze shifted back to me. "You're just leaving. Can you stay? I was just going to grab some . . ."

"Ah, sure."

Beaming with delight, he led me back toward one of the tables and helped me off with the backpack. He set it down expertly, flipping the bail out to steady it. He held out his hands and she gurgled. He offered me a quick *may I?* glance and then undid her shoulder harness and lifted her from the backpack.

She made a sound of glee. Holding her in one arm, he unzipped his jacket with the other hand, spread wide the layers of goose down, and nestled her inside against his flannel shirt. Sloane laid her little heady right down against his neck and patted his chest with one tiny hand. I tried not to sigh audibly as the memory engulfed me of how secure I had always felt there.

The woman behind the counter boomed, "Hey there, Frank! Who's your buddy?"

"Pretty little thing, huh? She's with my old friend Emmy here." He carried the baby over to the counter but lifted one finger away from his two-handed cuddle to indicate my presence. To Sloane, he said, "What you having, little one? Some nice salami and Swiss? Cup of coffee? Hm?"

The woman behind the counter laughed. "Your usual."

"Yeah."

She reached out and tickled the baby by one ear. "That'll be up in just a few. I'll call ya."

Frank brought Sloane back to the table and sat down. The two of them seemed lost in a lovefest, he kissing and caressing, she settling down and looking drowsy for the first time all day. "What brings you to town?" he asked, his lips lost in the soft down of her hair.

"I'm just babysitting while the baby's mother takes care of some business here in Cody."

"What kind of business does she do?"

"Oh, she's a pilot, and she uses her airplane to transport things that need special or discrete handling. She calls her business, 'Special Deliveries.'"

Frank raised an eyebrow.

I laughed. "It's nothing too complicated, really. She's got a potential client here—some old guy who's a family friend or something—who's here for some special meeting at the art museum. Bunch of specialists in for some reason. The one Faye's meeting has some artwork that the museum wants to include in an exhibit. Collectors can be fussy about who handles their treasure, and how it gets where it's going. Insurance and such. So the idea is that she'll meet with the guy and the curator, and they'll see if they can work things out." I smiled, thinking of the early days I knew Faye. "The fact is that she doesn't really have a business. It used to be that her biggest problem in life was figuring out how to use her trust fund to dispel boredom. She bought a hot twin-engine plane and got to tooting around with expensive stuff, like jewels. Growing up with the trust fund set, I guess she knew a lot of people who needed things moved on the quiet. It was a good day when it covered her expenses."

"But then she became a mother."

"Right. Then she got pregnant, and decided that she truly loved the man and wanted to do it by the book, so she married him. Unfortunately, her trust fund turned into a pumpkin the instant she got hitched." I shook my head. "And like you, I don't know how well her flying service is going to mix with motherhood. I picked up a pilot's license myself along the way—"

"Really?" he said, obviously impressed.

I was glad I had at least slipped that success into the discussion. "It's nothing as fancy as Faye has; just the basic single-engine VFR rating—but it taught me that you've got to stay sharp and concentrate or you shouldn't be at the controls. Well, the baby doesn't seem to need as much sleep as most babies, and when she does konk out, Faye often lies awake."

"Sleep deprivation," Frank mumbled. "Worry." He grunted empathetically. "Well, Em, you always did get yourself involved in interesting things."

I smiled uncomfortably. Yes, Frank knew that I traveled in strange circles, going places and hanging out with people he was unlikely to meet. He had all but never left northwest Wyoming, except to go to Vietnam. Now he was married, and had a son. How old would that child be now? "How's your wife?" I asked, unerringly coming up with a sure way to jam a wedge into the conversation.

Frank turned and looked at me squarely, the pleasure in his eyes suddenly extinguished. "She drinks," he said bluntly. "I'm just in town to attend an Al-Anon meeting."

I made a quick study of my boots. "I'm sorry to hear."

"Yeah. Well." Suddenly he laughed, like wasn't life

crazy? "Hey, that's what I get for foolin' around. Ya knock the lady up before you know her, and ya take home what ya catch."

I gave him an embarrassed grimace. "Tell me about your son."

Frank glanced away. "He's fine," he said too quickly. "Growing gangbusters. Great kid." His voice caught. "A couple challenges. School stuff. But what did he expect, with me for his dad?" Fighting his way out of his emotional logjam, he said, "How long you be in town?"

"Just until tomorrow, I think."

"You gotta meet him."

"I'd like that."

Now his gaze once again dropped to my left hand, from which I had removed the mitten. "You married?" he asked, trying to make it sound like an idle question.

"No."

"Seeing someone?"

I met his eyes. This was a new Frank, a more blunt and inquiring Frank, not the reclusive soul I had known and had somehow left so long ago. But the turbulence was still there, and the pain, now mixed with new agonies, and the joy his son had brought him. Had all this blown the re-straints off his personality? "Yes, I'm seeing someone," I said, steeling myself for his reaction. "He's overseas. The Middle East. Military reservist who got called up with this current fracas. You know the pace."

Frank gave me a compassionate stare.

I couldn't stand his caring. "I'm doing great, Frank. I've been working on my Master's in geology at the University of Utah. I've almost got the coursework done."

His face brightened. "That's great, Emmy."

"Thanks. I've been living at Faye's so I can help with the baby while I go to school." Realizing that this sounded pretty shiftless for a person my age, I added, "The baby's dad was killed, and . . . I figured she needed a friend."

"Killed?"

I closed my eyes. This wasn't going well. Each time I

tried to divert the focus of the conversation away from my-self, I managed to open another door into a room I did not want to enter. "Tom was an FBI agent," I said, picking the version of the truth that was easiest to say, and easiest to understand. "He was killed in the line of duty." This wasn't precisely accurate: It avoided certain facts, such as that with the baby coming, Tom had left the Bureau so that he wouldn't have to take on risky projects. That there was "just one more job" that he felt he had to do. That I was with him when he died.

When I opened my eyes, Frank was staring at the baby, his face raw with emotion. He gave Sloane Renee a squeeze, as if she was a life ring cast off a boat in a storm. Kissed her hair. Nuzzled his nose against her scalp. She began to fuss. "Oh, there, there," he whispered. "There, there. I'm just old Frank. I don't bite."

The woman at the counter called his name, and he handed me the baby while he got his sandwich. Back at the table, he ate quickly, taking in huge bites without tasting his food. The coffee he bolted after adding three little tubs of cream. As he slurped it down, he asked, "Where you staying?"

"We're just down at the Pawnee."

He nodded. His kind of place, cheap, comfortable, and unpretentious. "I'll walk you there."

I said, "Actually, we're on our way to the museums."

"My truck's parked halfway down."

We loaded up and left the café. I toted the backpack over one shoulder and he carried baby Sloane. A block down the sidewalk, Frank asked, "So your friend has an airplane?"

"Yes, a twin-engine turboprop job, goes like spit. But it's just been sitting in a tie-down in Florida, and she wants to bring it home to Utah. She worries about corrosion from the sea air. So if ol' Mr. Krehbeil has the bucks, I guess she'll be doing some flying again. Or maybe I hope he says no, and she gets reasonable and sells the plane."

Frank stopped dead in the middle of the sidewalk. "Who'd you say her client is?"

I spun around and slapped my hands over my face in embarrassment. I couldn't believe I had spilled the client's name. What was I thinking, that just because Frank never left Wyoming he wasn't part of the world? "Oh, nobody," I said lamely. "Just some old geezer who needs some paintings moved."

The look on Frank's face was scaring me. "You said, 'Krehbeil.' It's not a common name."

"Yeah . . . but you didn't hear that. She's supposed to be real discreet about this stuff, you know? *Tell* me you don't know him! Oh hell, Frank, I thought he was from back east somewhere. It never occurred to me that he might be from here, and that she might be taking the artwork somewhere else!"

Frank's face tightened further. "If he's any relation to the Krehbeils I'm thinking . . . well, you don't want to get mixed up with that bunch, Em."

"No, wait! I'm sure he's from somewhere back east. The contact was some guy Faye knew in college, and this is his dad or something."

He shook his head. "You know there's a lot of fancy people from the East who come out here for the summer, especially that artsy set. The Krehbeils got a hobby ranch outside of town here, up beyond the reservoir."

I winced, realizing how thoroughly I had stepped in it. "Old money?" I asked, knowing the answer.

"Yeah, if you mean the guys who have it didn't make it. Miz Krehbeil was in her eighties, and the place goes back a generation or two."

"What do you mean, *was* in her eighties?"

Frank looked both ways and lowered his voice before he said, "She died a few months ago."

I didn't understand his clandestine behavior.

"That's not unusual for someone in her eighties, is it?"

Frank had begun to hunch his shoulders like he always did when he was half mad and half worried. "No, but there's rumors that everything wasn't quite right."

"It must be a different Krehbeil."

Frank hugged the baby more tightly with one hand and reached out the other to cup my elbow. "Em, this isn't good. I know you. You wind up right in the middle of every fight that's going down. It's an instinct of yours."

Sloane had picked up on the tones of our voices and was beginning to fuss. I reached out and took her into my arms, shaking my head vehemently. "No way, Frank. I was a headstrong little twit when I worked around here, but I've grown up a lot, I swear it. Hey, this little baby here has taught me a lot about being responsible and covering my butt. It's Faye that's out chasing trouble this time, not me. And the job won't go through anyway. Even if the old guy does want her to do it, he won't pay enough to cover the avgas it would take to fly the plane, let alone what it would take to make the plane legal to fly. It has to go through its annual airworthiness check, and there are always expensive repairs, and Faye's annual FAA flight review to fly commercially is overdue. She's kidding herself. She doesn't even have a current medical clearance. Hasn't flown since she was seven months pregnant."

Frank's scowl deepened. "She was flying an airplane at seven months?"

"That's another part of why your pal here was a preemie." On cue, the baby broke into a full bawling cry. We had arrived at his truck as we began to argue, and had stopped walking. "I'd better keep moving, rock her to sleep," I said.

"Here . . . I'll bounce her," he said.

"Just put her in the backpack, please." I didn't like to be hard on Frank, but it really bothered me when Sloane got tweaked, and I wanted to be alone with my inadequacy. In the months since Sloane Renee had been born, I had held her for hours every day, trying to walk off her colic, trying to get her to sleep so Faye could, too. And since the introduction of solid foods, I had given her at least half of the feedings. I knew her every mood and every dimple, knew what made her smile and what made her cry, or knew these things as well as anyone did, but that did not make her mine, and she at times like this, she let me know it. "I'm sorry. I think just walking quietly is the best thing, with as few distractions as possible."

"Then I'll stop by later," he told me, and to Sloane he said, "You're a lucky baby. Auntie Emmy's a very good mom." He gave me a look of longing. He turned. He started to walk away, but turned back. "I . . . I'm not sure I've made it clear about the Krehbeils. There's really been some talk, Em."

"See you," I said, a bit more forcibly than was necessary. I turned also, and headed resolutely toward the museums. I felt like a prize also-ran. Here was a fine man who was wonderful with children, and I had left him.

One block farther along, I heard him call to me again. I spun around to hear what he was saying. A passing truck swallowed his words, but they sounded like, "Take care." A common enough phrase, and yet the look on his face said that it was less a wish than a warning.